A Very Big House in the Country

Claire Sandy

PAN BOOKS

First published in 2015 by Pan Books
an imprint of Pan Macmillan
20 New Wharf Road, London N1 9RR
Associated companies throughout the world
www.panmacmillan.com

ISBN 978-1-4472-7625-8

Pan Macmillan does not have any control over,
or any responsibility for, any author or third party websites
referred to in or on this book.

1 3 5 7 9 8 6 4 2

A CIP catalogue record for this book is available from the British Library.

Typeset by Palimpsest Book Production Limited, Falkirk, Stirlingshire
Printed and bound by CPI Group (UK) Ltd, Croydon, CR0 4YY

Visit www.panmacmillan.com to read more about all our books
and to buy them. You will also find features, author interviews and
news of any author events, and you can sign up for e-newsletters
so that you're always first to hear about our new releases.

This book is for Stephen and Emily Carlile,
my favourite newlyweds

DAY 1
Tuesday, 11th August

Dear All Next Door

Thanks for feeding the cat and the gerbils and the fish. The fish might die. They do that a lot in our house. My number's on the fridge in case of emergency, but unless the house gets sucked into a black hole, please don't call – WE NEED THIS HOLIDAY!

Evie & Mike & Scarlett & Dan & Mabel xxx

Nothing looks as good in real life as it does in the brochure.

Evie was more than old enough to know this simple fact of life, but as the family Ford Focus nudged its way westwards out of London, she found herself hoping for an exception in the case of their rented holiday home.

Rashly, the brochure in her lap promised 'Paradise'. Evie flicked though the glossy pages as the car slowed beside a derelict kebab shop. The colour photography dwelt in porny detail on a long straight drive edged with topiary balls, leading the eye to a grand slab of Georgian architecture the colour of a warm biscuit. Maybe Wellcome Manor would be as good as it looked. Maybe it really would be a kind of paradise.

'How much further?' whined Scarlett from the back seat.

'Ages yet, darling.' Evie kept her tone light. She'd vowed to stay in Lovely Mummy mode for this much-anticipated fortnight. 'And do leave it more than three minutes before you ask again.' Then again, maybe she'd be in Sleep-Deprived, Packing-Like-a-Madwoman-Since-6 a.m. Mummy mode. 'It'll be worth it when we get there, I promise.'

'It's just some boring house,' said Scarlett, who, at seventeen, was an expert in what was boring and what was not. 'It's *old*.'

'So am I,' murmured Evie. She'd aged ten years on this car journey and they hadn't even reached the M3.

As the scenery morphed from grimy brick to quicksilver motorway, the front seats had to warn the back seats more than once to simmer down or they'd 'turn this car round *right now*'. Patch barked tunelessly from junction 4 to Stonehenge; Dan made little Mabel cry by shouting 'Bottom' in a variety of accents; Scarlett's outrage at being ripped from the bosom of her friends was almost visible, like a mangy fur stole around her shoulders.

'What!' Mike was exasperated by Dan's request. 'Why didn't you go before we left?'

'I did,' said Dan.

'You'll just have to cross your legs and hang on,' said Mike.

'I want to go too,' said Mabel, whispering into Patch's fur, 'Go *where?*'

As Scarlett shepherded her brother and sister behind a hedge on the hard shoulder, Mike asked Evie, 'Did you pack Mrs Misterson II?'

'Of *course*.' They had a brief communal flashback to that family day out when the original Mrs Misterson – a grubby baby doll, felt-tipped all over and half-bald – had gone missing; Mabel had screamed her way around Wookey Hole. 'As you'd know,' Evie continued in the same urgent undertone, 'if you'd been there to help pack. Like you promised.'

'Yeah, well . . .' Mike sniffed and sighed and fiddled with the satnav.

By the time he had finally come home from work, the cases were packed, the fridge was cleared, the dog was on his lead, the windows had been checked (twice), water bottles had been filled, Kindles had been charged, medication for every minor medical eventuality had been lined up, healthy snacks had been chopped up and stashed in ziplock bags, and the younger children were so ready they'd had time to become un-ready again, dropping juice on their clean gear and reading new comics bought for the journey. Evie had even remembered to set the house lights on timers, to hoodwink any burglar crazy enough to imagine the Herreras had anything worth stealing. For mums, the family holiday is more stressful than a business trip.

'You said you'd just do an hour in the office and then—'

'I know, I know.' Mike chopped the air with his hand. 'I got involved. It's hard not to.'

Evie glared at him, aware that if the glaree doesn't look at the glarer, the glare is more or less void. From the hard shoulder came the sound of a small girl falling in her own wee. 'Mike, give in and look at me. I'm not wasting this brilliant glare.'

When he laughed, Evie found his hand on the steering wheel and squeezed it. 'Come on, love. Get your holiday-head on,' she said. 'After all, your legs are already on vacation.'

'Don't diss the shorts,' warned Mike as their children clambered back into the car.

'What is there to diss,' asked Evie innocently, 'in ten-year-old yellow nylon shorts that are fraying at the crotch?'

'Crotch!' shouted Dan.

'I'm missing the party of the year for this,' said Scarlett when they stopped for coffee at a Little Chef.

'You'll live, Scarlett,' said Evie, looking around, yearning for her husband to hove into view with a loaded tray. She needed caffeine, and she needed it *now*. Preferably intravenously.

'You're ruining my life,' said Scarlett.

'Yeah, sorry about that.' Evie knew there was no point in arguing. 'If it's any consolation, I'm planning on ruining Dan's and Mabel's as well.'

'I don't mind, Mummy,' said Mabel generously.

'You're too kind, Mabes.'

Mike appeared, tray aloft. 'Hang on!' he yelped, as greedy hands grabbed at his wares. With great ceremony he handed Mabel a milkshake.

'I asked for banana!' spat Mabel, with an abrupt change of tone. 'This is strawberry!'

'But you love strawberries,' said Mike.

'She used to,' corrected Evie, sighing and standing to return the rejected shake. 'Before Dan told her that—'

'Strawberries come out of pigs' BOTTOMS!' yelled Dan. He was happy, so very happy, to have the opportunity to shout 'Bottoms' in a public place.

'Shush, Dan,' said Mike sternly. 'Evie, sit down. Mabel will just have to make the best of it.'

They locked eyes for a moment, a silent tussle in their stare. Evie's eyes were saying, *Let it go just this once, so we arrive without bloodshed and tears and milkshake in everybody's hair.* Mike's eyes, just as eloquent, and with the same fetching bags beneath them, said, *We spoil these kids rotten and I've been driving for two hours, and when I was Mabel's age I took what I was bloody well given.*

'Actually,' said Mabel, 'I *do* like strawberries.'

As a breed, Border collies are highly intelligent; Patch had missed that memo. He couldn't herd sheep, or fetch help, but, boy, could he fall off things and into things (plus a nice sideline in getting his head stuck in other things), so it was inevitable that he would slip his lead and race off across the scrubby wasteground behind the Little Chef, ignoring the shouts of his name (Evie wasn't convinced Patch *knew* his name) as he dodged Mike's increasingly frantic lunges.

'Dad, don't hurt him!' shouted Scarlett, as Mike's face thudded into the dirt once again.

'That jumper's dry-clean only!' yelled Evie, as another rugby tackle failed.

'This is like crap bullfighting,' said Scarlett.

'She said "crap",' said Mabel.

'This creature,' said Mike, dumping the wriggling Patch

on the back seat, 'is going straight to the dogs' home when this holiday's over.'

Nobody took that seriously. Everybody knew Mike loved the dog with the same fierce possessiveness that he felt about the others stuffed in the airless car with him. Evie glanced at him as he put the car into gear. He was a looker, her bloke, even with that scowl on his face. A day or two of country air, and the scowl would be history – that was the theory. Mike did a serious job and he took it seriously; duty often claimed him on weekends and evenings. Half of her resented the intrusion, while the other half envied his sense of purpose.

'How many green bottles,' asked Dan, 'were we up to?'

'Not sure,' said Mike. 'But I lost the will to live at thirty-eight.'

'Daddy's joking,' said Evie.

'Daddy isn't,' said Mike.

There was grit in his super-short dark hair and a smear of mud across his not-exactly-big-but-definitely-*there* nose. Evie experienced a small jolt of happy achievement at bagging such a healthy specimen all for her very own. It was a feeling that still sneaked up on her, even after twenty years. Admittedly, it snuck up less than it used to, and it died a death completely as her eyes strayed below his waistline; lustful pride couldn't win against Mike's yellow shorts.

The kids had arranged themselves in height order on the back seat. *Here are some we made earlier,* she thought.

Nobody knew where Dan's Titian hair came from, but Scarlett had Evie's wiggy, wayward, mucky blonde mop.

Scarlett's eyes were like Evie's in design – slanted, sea-coloured, either judgemental or indulgent, depending on mood/point in menstrual cycle – although they gazed out through kohl flicks that Cleopatra might deem a little much. Dan was lean, like his dad, whereas Scarlett was 'robust' (the official term) like her mother.

And Mabel, their last-born – an emphatic full stop to their brood – had her father's brunette looks and clever, searching, occasionally inscrutable eyes. *Those freckles across her nose, however*, thought Evie proprietorially, *are down to me.*

She frowned. 'Dan, what happened to your face?' Clean enough to eat your dinner off when he left the house, her son now looked like a miner coming off-shift.

'Dunno.' Dan shrugged. Trivialities such as basic hygiene meant little to him; he was a busy person, with things to break and people to dismay. 'Why didn't you invite somebody my age, Mum? I've got no one to play with.'

'There's a worldwide shortage of ten-year-old boys, haven't you heard? I'm sure your big sister will let you hang out with her.'

'Yeah, right,' said Scarlett, laughing for the first time since London. 'It'd be my *pleasure* to hang out with somebody who picks his nose and keeps it for later.'

Spotting her opening, Mabel was there in a flash, heart-shaped face shining. 'I'll play with you, Dan,' she said in the tiny, throaty, sugary voice that could make her sound like a very small, very camp man.

'Who knows a good joke?' Mike was being hearty, like a dad in a cereal ad.

Evie quailed. She'd heard all the kids' jokes. *Please God, if you're there and still talking to me,* she begged, *don't let Mabel tell her chicken-crossing-the-road joke.*

'Why,' shouted Mabel, 'did the chicken . . . ? No, hang on. I mean, when did the chicken . . . ? On the road, see, there's this chicken and . . .'

'I want to die,' said Scarlett.

'We're almost there,' said Evie. 'We're almost at paradise.'

'Why now?' wailed Evie. 'Why do we have to get lost at the eleventh hour?' Somewhere in this sunny snarl of overgrown lanes, Wellcome Manor awaited them, but the satnav kept directing them down the same rutted road. 'I hate the satnav,' she said vehemently as the car bumped and jolted. 'She's always had it in for me. The bitch is trying to come between me and my cream tea.'

'What's a cream tea?' asked Dan, as Scarlett said, 'That's the fourth time we've passed that stupid tree.'

'A cream tea is a colossal waste of money, Son,' said Mike, squinting at the map on his knees.

'A cream tea is one of Western civilization's greatest achievements,' said Evie. 'There are scones, there is cream, there is jam. There are doilies. There is a pot of tea. There are no mugs.' She stabbed the air, violently anti-mug. 'There are dainty teacups and silver spoons.' She closed her eyes, in a swoon. 'And, best of all, there's no washing up.'

'Worst of all,' said Mike, 'you pay fifty quid to have a

cucumber sarnie, and all sane people know that cucumber isn't a proper filling. Plus,' he rattled on, as Evie opened her mouth to disagree, 'scones are stupid and teapots are poncey and finger-sandwiches sound downright rude.'

'Finger-sandwiches . . .' said Mabel thoughtfully from the back seat.

'No, darling,' said Evie, knowing where this was going, 'they're not sandwiches filled with fingers.' She turned back to Mike. 'I don't care what you say, husband o' mine, I'm having my cream tea if it kills me.' She'd been looking forward to scones from the moment they'd plumped for Devon as their holiday destination. 'So just you—'

'I think,' interrupted Mike, 'we're here.'

Everybody fell silent as the car turned through an open pair of high ironwork gates that spelled out 'Wellcome Manor' in ornately curling capitals. The car scrunched over gravel – such an *expensive* sound – and the drive that Evie had perved over in the brochure unfurled in front of them.

Wellcome Manor ignored the rules; it was *better* in real life.

Pillars on either side of the broad front door crumbled photogenically. Wisteria crawled across rows of tall sash windows. Hundreds of summers had baked the house, so that it seemed to exude a healing warmth as it towered against a backdrop of sky so blue it was surely Photoshopped.

It was a magnificent house, but as the car slowed to a stop, it seemed to Evie a friendly house, sitting back and smiling in the sunshine.

'This *is* paradise,' she murmured.

Already out of the car, with her arms folded, Scarlett said, 'See? Old.'

'I love it I love it I love it!' Mabel was easier to please. (Except if you gave her carrots; *never* offer Mabel a carrot.)

Half-swallowed by the car boot, Mike shouted, 'Take a bag, everyone!' with the air of a man expecting to be ignored.

'Yoo-hoo!' The venerable old front door opened and a couple waved from the wide step. The woman held a baby in her arms, and a boy approximately the size of Mabel jumped up and down at her side. Mabel tore off at the sight of him, and Dan followed, dragging Patch on his lead, unaware that the dog was only partway through a complex toilet event.

The Ling-Littles had arrived before them. 'Welcome to Wellcome!' Clive's voice boomed.

'Thank you kindly, good sir!' called Evie, as Mike's head sank lower into the boot.

'Lord of the manor,' he muttered. 'As if he owns the place.'

'Be nice!' Evie was wasting her breath. Mike and Clive were oil and water, their only common ground being their wives' firm friendship.

Laden with bags, she lurched over the gravel like a drunk. She could tell their holiday home had impressed Mike; she could read his thoughts by the set of his shoulders or the jut of his chin. Prising him away from London had entailed blackmail, ultimatums and a shooting-from-the-hip late-night conversation ending with, 'We need some quality time. There are *things to discuss*.'

'These aren't gardens,' said Mike. 'They're grounds. I feel like a servant carrying m'lady's bags.'

Wellcome Manor grew as they approached it. It was a house of distinct personality, sure of itself. Arches carved in the dark yew hedging offered tantalizing glimpses of secret views beyond, and they could just see the roofs of outbuildings huddled around the back of the house.

Scarlett thawed a little as she took in the stone lions at the foot of the steps and heard the splash of a Border collie running into water. 'There's a pool?' she said, all her hauteur dissolving.

'Round one to us,' said Evie, but she'd lost Mike to Shen's welcoming embrace. Evie kissed Clive politely, wrinkling her nose at the smell of his cigar. He was a bear of a man, short-necked, massive-shouldered, always dressed in City-boy uniform.

And then Shen was upon her, gabbling, dragging, kissing, commanding Clive to take the bags, and foisting her six-month-old daughter into Evie's arms. 'Fang wants her godmother.'

'And her godmother wants *her*! Hello, you.' Evie loved her god-daughter for many reasons: her sunny nature; her dimpled knees; her faultless fat face, which blended, beautifully, her father's English ruddiness and her mother's Chinese elegance. She also loved her for being called Fang – 'It was my grandmother's name!' Shen had snapped defensively when the vicar giggled at the font.

'Just look at this entrance hall.' Shen's accent and rapid speech still held a trace of her ancestry. '*Look* at it!' she ordered, as if Evie wasn't looking hard enough.

'Bloody *hell*,' said Mike, gazing about him. This was a

compliment; he said it like that whenever Evie felt energetic enough to break out her suspenders.

Double-height, the hall was painted the colour of a dove's underbelly. Doorways topped with plasterwork cornices offered up further rooms, each as sumptuous and delicious as this one. All the painted surfaces were perfect; all the furniture, both antique and quirkily modern, gleamed. There were no signs of wear and tear, no evidence of the argy-bargy of everyday life. They'd stepped into a magazine shoot, where the only smell was the aroma of cut flowers, and the light was flattering.

'This is just the beginning. Through there's the sitting room. *One* of them.' Alight with happiness, Shen was at her best around costly things, which might explain why she got twitchy in Evie's kitchen. 'And through there's the cinema room . . .' She paused to allow that to sink in.

'A cinema room!' Evie clapped. 'You'll be telling me there's a mezzanine next.'

'There's TWO!' shrieked Shen, her teardrop black eyes creasing to nothing with the sheer joy of such la-di-da trappings. She took Evie by the arm, peremptory and despotic despite Evie's eight-inch/eleven-year head-start. 'You'll *die* when you see the bedrooms.'

As the women rushed up the stairs, skittish at the prospect of Fired Earth tiling and distressed floorboards, Mike turned to offer a full and manly hello to Clive, complete with mandatory talk of route taken and traffic encountered, but was silenced by Clive's hand, held imperiously up in the air.

'Clive Little,' Clive was saying into his phone, cigar still clenched between his teeth. 'How did the meeting go?' He made a comically apologetic face at Mike who mouthed, '*S'OK.*'

Sauntering off, Mike put his head around the kitchen door. Not particularly interested in kitchens, he could see that it was easily splendid enough to hospitalize his wife.

'Dad, there's a trampoline!' Dan skidded in, his Converses squeaking on the black-and-white chequered floor, flushed cheeks competing with his hair's glorious Titian (Evie's adjective; Mike knew his son was a ginge). 'And one of those big outside bath-things that Mum likes!'

'A hot tub?' said Mike to his son's receding back. Mabel ran in, hand-in-hand with the little boy who'd greeted them at the door; Miles and Mabel had been born a day apart in the same hospital, and it was this happy accident that had first bonded their mothers. The two children were great friends; she was so good at climbing trees and farting to order that Miles overlooked her being a girl.

'Dad Dad Dad, can we get in the pool, can we – yes?'

'Yes. Hang on. NO!' Mike looked to Clive for backup as the pair sped out again. 'Don't get in on your own!'

'Bollocks!' Clive was saying into his phone. 'We turn that place into flats and whack 'em out by the end of the year.' He made a winding-up motion to Mike.

Take as long as you like, thought Mike. Listening to Clive was a crash course in the immoral nuts and bolts of big business. Fat cats like Clive had driven the last house-price crash, creating heartache for millions and unpaid overtime for Mike.

Last year Mike's housing trust had been able to fund

two assistants. Now that they were down to one, taking work home was inevitable for the Senior Neighbourhood Services Manager. Mike agreed with Evie when she said that he took on too much, that it wasn't good for him (by which she also meant, he knew, for *them*), but what could he do? Leave vulnerable people out in the cold? Literally.

He recalled the family who'd kept him late in the office. With one eye on the clock, he'd listened to the familiar story of job loss, mortgage arrears, foreclosure and sleeping on friends' floors until they ran out of friends. With Evie and the kids waiting, he'd had to pass them over to his assistant, but Mike couldn't shake the memory of their faces.

The private sector was better-paid; Mike could make much more money working for the likes of Clive. But he wouldn't make a *difference*. He wouldn't be able to help the bewildered people thrown about like flotsam after a shipwreck.

Two weeks, thought Mike. Two *long* weeks with a man whose conscience had been neatly excised before Mike was even born.

He tuned out the braying phone call and felt the mile-long velvet sofas calling to him. *Thank God,* he thought, *my wife digs up such amazing bargains.*

A floor above, taking in the four-poster's linen hangings and the cream curtains that pooled on the floor and the soaring cross-timbered ceiling, Evie thought, *Thank God my husband is so amazingly gullible.* How could a grown man with a Masters degree believe that the amount they'd spent could rent a house of this calibre? 'A bath in the room!' she squealed at Fang, as Shen Riverdanced in the dressing room, all the better to demonstrate its size. '*In* the room!'

When Evie had told Mike the cost, he'd paled, as if somebody had walked over his grave. After some *How much?*-ing, he'd caved in, little knowing that Clive was contributing three times that amount. They owed their holiday to Clive.

A snuffling noise came from the arctic-white duvet that trembled on the bed like a displaced cloud. 'Prunella?' queried Evie and moved nearer, to see Shen's diminutive dog.

'Fnnfh,' said Prunella by way of hello, as if she had a head-cold. Evie wondered about the sadists who'd first bred pugs: *Hey, guys! There's a gap in the market for a dog with a crumpled face that breathes like an asthmatic sex pest!*

'Down, Prunella,' said Evie. 'Off my bed. Bad dog!'

Prunella, resembling a cashmere pig dipped in soot, looked disgruntled as she righted herself from her slutty, legs-akimbo pose.

'Stay, Prunella!' Shen was out of the dressing room in a flash; her high heels never impeded her speed. She could run, jump and kick ass in platforms that would break Evie's ankles if she stood up in them. 'Good dog!' Shen pulled herself up to her full height, slender shoulders back, breasts (a Christmas present from Clive) jutting out. 'That's *my* bed, and Pru's welcome on it.'

Prunella lay back among the bedclothes, emanating doggy *whatev*s.

'And there was me, assuming we'd toss a coin for the *best room in the house*.'

'Finders, keepers.' With a deft movement, Shen twisted her fall of razor-edged black hair into a chignon and secured it with a clip magicked from thin air. It took Evie an age to produce even a wobbly topknot with her own streaked-to-buggery haystack; she'd never be envious of her friend's wealth, but Shen's hair left her green from head to toe. 'I'd better bagsy the second-best room, before Lady Muck arrives with her brood.' Evie dreaded the third family's arrival so much she couldn't use their real names.

'Oh, yeah, about that . . .' Shen had grown super-offhand. 'Françoise isn't coming.'

Evie gawped. 'When did this happen?' She was delighted, but confused. And then she was suspicious. 'Sh-en?' she encouraged. 'Is there something you want to share with the class?'

'She just couldn't come, for some reason.' Shen was nuzzling Prunella in a frankly unhygienic manner.

'For some reason like you had a massive row with her?'

'A small disagreement.'

'Knew it!'

Like Shen, Françoise was a key member of the Uber-mums, a school-gate clique identifiable by 'done' hair and handbags that cost the same as Evie's parents' first house. These massive accessories were brandished like shields, and their size served to accentuate the sparrow dimensions of the Ubers' starved bodies.

Uber-kiddiwinks were ferried to St Agatha's Primary and their infinite tutors in enormous four-wheel drives, as if traversing a hostile Outback rather than terraced streets; Uber-husbands, both current and ex, were 'big in the City'.

Françoise had a lover, a timeshare and a face so packed with Botox that she needed forty-eight hours' written notice to simper. Like all the Ubers, she was openly baffled by Shen's friendship with Evie: the stylish ex-model and the tousled middle-aged mum. When Shen smuggled Evie into Uber coffee mornings, where the catty gossip was devoured but the Danish pastries shunned, Evie felt Françoise look her up and down, stirring her skinny latte, wondering, *How did that civilian get in?*

'What was the row about this time?' Evie sat on the bed, eager to hear.

'She had this crazy idea that I'd poached her daughter's French tutor.'

'*Et,*' said Evie, faltering as she dredged up her GCSE French, '*il est vrai?*'

'A little *vrai,*' conceded Shen. 'But you know Miles is gifted at languages. All's fair in love and tutors.'

All Ubers believed their perfectly ordinary and nice children to be gifted. The vain, domineering Françoise's row with the argumentative Shen was inevitable; sooner or later *everybody* fell out with Shen.

Except Evie.

Despite Shen and Evie's many differences – their ages (twenty-nine/forty), their attitudes to grooming (non-stop/ annual leg wax prior to wedding-anniversary sex), their child-rearing styles (Tiger Mother/Meh Mother) – theirs was a natural, fluid friendship, fuelled by jokes and jibes, but underpinned by intimacy and the certainty that they had each other's backs.

Prunella rolled off the bed and click-clacked after them, as Shen led the way to the second-best bedroom. In Evie's arms, Fang regarded her in that serious way some babies have. 'Are you the prettiest little thing? Are you? *Are you?*' A thought struck her. An unwelcome thought. 'What are we doing about Françoise's share, Shen? I can't pay the extra – Mike will flip, we just don't have it.'

'I know, I know.' Shen waved her hands. 'Don't panic. I invited another family. It'll be great.'

Something about the way she said it made Evie wilt. 'Oh God, Shen, who's coming?'

Instead of replying, Shen pushed at a door. 'Ta-da!' she said.

'Ta-da *indeed*.' Evie stepped into the second-best bedroom, a tone-poem of greys and faint pinks and knocked-back blues. A chandelier dangled above the vast bed, stacked with more pillows than Evie had ever owned. 'Me like.' She tried not to drool. 'Me want.'

'Then move your stuff in pronto and stake your claim, before the Browns arrive.'

'The Browns? What, Paula and what's-his-name?'

'Jon, yes.' Shen was brisk, all the better to get it over with. 'And lovely Tillie, who we've never met, but who's Scarlett's age apparently; and little Amber, who's in Miles's and Mabel's class. Yes, them.' She opened the door to the en-suite, but Evie was wise to her and refused to be distracted . . . *Hang on. Ooh, A free-standing bath!* Evie shook herself. 'Shen, the Browns are . . .' She didn't like the word that sprang to her lips, and was instantly ashamed of it.

'Weird?' Shen was more forthright. 'Yup. But the Browns were the only ones available at the last minute. Probably because they're weird,' she ended, with a shrug.

'I wouldn't say they're weird, exactly—' began Evie.

'Although they *are* weird,' Shen cut in.

'Yes, all right, can we stop saying "weird"? Paula makes me feel bad. She's so nervous and . . .'

'She jumps if you say hello.'

'Yeah, and she tries to escape if you chat.'

'And her clothes . . .' Shen was unable to understand women who stepped out of their front doors less than catwalk-ready.

'She makes me feel guilty,' said Evie, realizing it properly for the first time. 'As if I should make more of an effort with her.'

'Then I'm giving you a chance to do just that!'

'If you fell off a tower block,' said Evie, jiggling Fang, 'you'd land in a vat of champagne jelly. I'm not letting you off the hook just like that.'

'Yes, you are.' Shen smiled.

'Yes, I suppose I am. As usual. Come on.' She reluctantly tore herself away from the second-best bedroom. 'Let's get stuck into paradise.'

The kitchen ticked boxes Evie didn't know existed. It was high, it was wide, and the back wall was a bank of folding glass, which opened up, concertina-style, to the Portland stone of the terrace, and the emerald-neon of the lawns beyond.

Rows of copper pans hung in strict size order above the range. The handmade cupboards, slightly oversized, so as to make even a full-figured (ahem) woman like Evie feel dainty, were painted an elusive colour somewhere between grey and green and blue. Evie stroked the ice-white worktops the way she'd stroked parts of Mike, back in their early days.

The vacuum-packed hot dogs and frozen chips that came out of Evie's plastic bags sullied the style of the room a little. Shamefacedly she opened the pantry door and jumped, to find a young woman in there. 'Elizabetta! Hi, or . . . um . . . *ciao*.'

'*Ciao*.' Shen's Italian nanny had the body of a chorus girl and the demeanour of a nun. 'May I?' She took the hot dogs reverently and put them on a shelf.

'I didn't realize you were coming.' Evidently Shen and Clive's notion of quality family time was a little different from Evie and Mike's.

Not quite dusk, the blues and purples and whites of the flower beds had begun to melt. With the candles in the outsize lanterns lit unobtrusively by Elizabetta, the terrace felt like the place to be.

'The view,' said Mike simply, settling himself into a metal-and-mesh garden chair that bore little relation to the white plastic monstrosities that squatted in their own yard. 'When,' he turned to Evie, 'did people start naming their kids after Victorian servants? We've got a Mabel, and a Tillie arrives tomorrow. Sounds like the cast list of *Downton*.'

'We almost called Dan "Edward", remember? Just as *Downton*-esque, in its way.' Edward was Evie's favourite uncle; she recalled how they couldn't name any of the kids after Mike's family, and felt a sudden jab of compassion.

'Right,' said Clive, emerging from the French windows and rubbing his hands together. 'Din-dins?'

An excited babble broke out. It seemed that all of them, from the oldest to the teeniest, was *starving*.

'Seriously,' said Mabel seriously, 'I might die if I don't eat right now.'

'As it's the first night, I vote for . . .' Evie anticipated the acclaim that her inspiration would receive, '. . . a takeaway!'

Jubilation broke out. Mabel and Miles hugged each other. Scarlett broke off from texting to cheer. Clive said, 'Bravo!'

Shen clapped her hands and said, 'No need! Elizabetta will prepare dinner.'

Elizabetta looked as if this was news to her. Not particularly good news.

'It'll be,' Shen promised, aglow, 'highly nutritious, organic, balanced and vegetarian!'

Mike groaned as each adjective hammered a nail into the coffin of his KFC.

Evie smothered the children's complaints. She'd let Shen win this round; there was plenty of time to stray from the path of righteousness. She ruffled Mike's hair as she stood and followed Elizabetta into the kitchen.

'Can I help?'

'Of course not.' The voice was that of Shen, who crossed to the wine rack in the fridge and tugged out a bottle of champagne as if birthing a glass baby. 'She doesn't need any help.'

'Elizabetta?' Evie double-checked.

'You go sit.' Elizabetta moved about purposefully. The sundress she wore, its nautical stripes clean on her strong, brown limbs, was one Evie recognized from Shen's wardrobe. Regal with her employee, Shen was also generous. *Perhaps*, thought Evie, *it makes up for moments such as these*.

She looked closer at the girl's closed, mutinous face.

And perhaps it didn't.

The embers of the day.

Out on the terrace, as the others lazily discussed the weather – 'Amazing summer we're having', 'Apparently the hottest this century', and so on – Evie watched her daughter amble around and remembered the days when she herself would happily have worn shorts that short.

Scarlett, bent over her phone, surfed from trend to trend, cherry-picking styles and details, but was always, irrepressibly, herself. Her hair, naturally lively (a term Evie preferred to the more truthful 'messy'), was usually growing out of some terrible experiment; at present, Easter's fringe was in her eyes. She seemed to be in a lipgloss phase; her mouth was jammy as she smiled to herself over some txtspk message from 'home'.

The teenager had been mourning 'home' all evening. 'I wonder what they're doing at home now,' she'd mused at intervals.

'Who cares?' had been Dan's take on it, easily won over by the treehouse and the ping-pong table.

'I wish my mates were here.' When Scarlett said this for the fifth time, Evie pointed out that a possible mate would arrive tomorrow. 'Tillie's your age.'

'I'm not a toddler,' Scarlett groused. 'You can't put us together and say, *Play nicely.*'

'Make her feel welcome. The Browns are new to the area, remember.'

'Why're you always on my case?'

'Because I went through a forty-three-hour labour and ruined my boobs for you. That, madam, is *why*. Give Tillie a chance.'

'Like you gave her mum a chance? You think she's a nutter.'

Evie hoped that she hadn't used that word. She sat up, remembered something. 'Hang on,' she said to Mike. 'Don't we have two other children?'

'They're in bed,' said Shen. 'Elizabetta took them up half an hour ago.'

'But,' said Evie, confused, 'I didn't hear any screaming or death-threats.'

'Elizabetta knows her stuff,' said Shen. She was smug, as if she'd made Elizabetta, rather than just hired her.

'Oh.' Evie felt strangely redundant. No cooking. No

putting children to bed. She could learn to like feeling redundant.

'Poker, anyone?' Clive slapped down a pack of cards, the diamond on his pinkie glinting.

Reaching out to deal, Evie said, 'But not for money, obviously.'

'Of course we play for money.' Clive seemed shocked. 'Or what's the point?'

'Oh, I don't think . . .' began Evie, knowing how Mike felt about wasting cash.

'I'm in,' said Mike, taking out his wallet.

The men and Shen were evenly matched, whereas Evie played poker like an escaped chimp. She was soon out, and a whole three pounds down, so she sat back and watched, as the champagne bubbles worked their glorious dark magic on her.

Clive's poker face was a jolly one, whether he had a good hand or a dreadful one.

Despite being a few glasses ahead of the others, Shen played to win, her wits as sharp as her cheekbones as she held Prunella on her lap, kissing her extravagantly.

'I make it a rule,' said Mike, fanning out his cards, 'never to kiss anything that licks its own bottom.'

'When'd you get so picky?' Evie leaned back, noting his ace.

He swatted her leg. Mike didn't know his own strength; that was a sexy thought. He winked at Evie.

I love you. The thought came clear and cool, like the champagne she was drinking like tap water. Did Mike know she loved him? They said it, of course, but perhaps over the course of a marriage the phrase lost its currency. When they'd first started dating, Evie had often thought it – *I love you, Mike Herrera* – at random moments. Halfway through a shared bag of chips. In a cinema queue. In the millisecond before he saw her, as he waited outside the Tube.

'I do believe,' said Clive, with the muddy diction that his omnipresent cigar produced, 'I've won.' He laid down his cards.

'Again?' Mike's voice went girlishly high.

'Your Daddy-waddy won again!' said Shen to Prunella, who didn't care.

'All yours.' Mike pushed the pile of coins in the middle of the table towards Clive.

'Put it back in the pot.' Clive pushed it back.

'It's yours,' said Mike. 'Take it.'

Maybe, hoped Evie, *Clive didn't hear the edge to Mike's voice.*

'It's only a game, mate.'

He'd heard it.

'A game you won,' said Mike. 'Fair's fair. *Mate.*'

Clive regarded him thoughtfully, then took the money, smiling to himself as if he'd overheard a joke the others couldn't catch.

'I'm bowing out,' said Mike. 'Too rich for my blood.'

'Just you and me, then, Wifey.' Clive regarded Shen across the table. 'This should be a walkover.'

'Careful, Clive.' Shen pursed her bee-stung lips. 'Don't get on the wrong side of me.'

'I know, I know,' said Clive, dealing showily. He went on, as if airing a famous quote, 'You're a great wife, but you'd make an even greater ex-wife.'

Evie knew that Shen often taunted Clive with that phrase, lampooning his inability to stay wed. His specialist subject on *Mastermind* would be alimony. Evie had needed a spreadsheet to get her head around the timeline: with three marriages and six children, Clive was a one-man population explosion.

'By the time my lawyer had finished with you,' said Shen, 'you'd be living in a studio flat, with just the one spare pair of tighty-whities.'

'Shush,' said Evie. 'She doesn't mean it, Clive.'

'Oh yes, she does!' roared Clive.

'That reminds me,' said Evie, eager to change the subject; Mike had no patience with the Ling-Little exhibitionistic spats. 'Isn't your son arriving tomorrow, Clive?' Evie reached for the unusual name, the champagne rendering her brain slippy and unreliable. 'Zac, isn't it?'

'Zane.' Clive sighed it out.

'Can't wait to meet him.'

'Let's see if you still feel that way when you've actually met him,' said Shen.

'Have I got this right?' Evie closed her eyes and drew a diagram in the air. 'He's your . . . fifth child, and your second-oldest son, yeah?'

'Congratulations.' Clive looked at her hard. 'And for the top prize – which wife is he from?'

As if, thought Evie, *Zane was a calf and his mother a prize heifer.* 'Um, ooh, second?'

'Well done.' He blew out his cheeks. 'First smell of trouble and the boy goes home.'

Draining her glass, Shen said, 'I'm pooped.'

'Must be all that cooking you didn't do, darling,' said Clive. 'And all those cases you didn't carry.'

'He's so funny,' deadpanned Shen.

All of them sleepy, but too comfortable to move, they sat outside in the balmy night until Evie stretched, saying, 'That's me done', as a church bell – clear as, well, a *bell* – tolled the late hour. She heaved herself out of the chair and kissed the top of Mike's head. 'See you up there, yeah?'

Savouring the house's peace, she anticipated the joy of her panelled bathroom and its insanely fluffy towels as she padded through the house. With the colours toned down, and the air still, Wellcome Manor felt like a good place, a safe place. Paradise, though? That was a big ask.

The phone in her pocket cheeped needily: **Have you told him yet? Are you mine, all mine? xxxx**

Every paradise, thought Evie, stilled on the turning of the stair, *has its serpent.*

DAY 2
Wednesday, 12th August

Hi!
   Please rescue me. Surrounded by oaps & kids. House
OK. Stupid girl coming later – already can't stand her.
Tell me all about the big party. (Actually don't!)
                                    Scarlett xxxxxxxxxxxxx

Usually first out of bed, the one shouting, 'Don't make me come up those stairs!' and sorting PE gear while excavating mould from sliced white, Evie luxuriated in having the palatial bed to herself.

A happy X-shape, she stretched out her arms and legs, gazing at the rectangle of blue framed in her window. There was no laundry to fold, no packed lunches to cobble together from a dejected Mini Babybel and some elderly ham. Nobody disturbed her haven of high-thread-count Egyptian cotton and the countless small pillows that had bemused Mike. 'But why so many?' he'd asked, almost in tears.

She felt fresh and clean and virginal.

This was the perfect opportunity to send a text without Mike's knowledge.

Some women, she supposed, would feel racy; Evie felt grubby as she rewrote the lines a couple of times before feeling able to send it. The tone had to be right. She mustn't sound as if she was having second thoughts, but she must make the point that she'd agreed to tell Mike *after* the holiday.

'What's that?' Evie, yawning, peered into the tumbler of vivid green slosh that Mike held.

Mike opened his mouth, but Shen's voice came out – or seemed to – as she spoke for him. 'It's a kale smoothie. Packed with nutrients and highly delicious.'

'Is it?' Evie asked Mike, as she opened one of the fridges and searched for calorific contraband. 'Delicious, I mean.'

'Tastes like very old knickers might, if somebody boiled them.' Mike put down the drink. 'Sorry, Shen.'

'I told you, Mike, my conscience won't let me make you a *fry-up*.' Shen curled her lip as if he'd mooted sodomy for breakfast. 'I won't do that to your body.'

'My body won't mind,' said Mike. 'Honest.'

'I never fry. Besides, I'm on the 5:2 diet.'

Her arms full of white bread, bacon, chocolate spread and butter, Evie said, 'We're not on any diet, so . . .' She slammed a copper frying pan onto the hob; cooking with these beauties would amount to a workout. She appraised Shen suspiciously. 'Is this one of your fast days?' Stuff got thrown on fast days, and the little woman had good aim.

'Nope, but my body is a temple, and nothing like *that*,' Shen gestured witheringly at the slagheap of deliciousness on the marble, 'ever enters it.'

'My body,' said Mike, lustily unscrewing the Nutella, 'is one of those old-fashioned pubs.'

'I'm bored,' said Dan, sticking a grotty finger in the Nutella.

'The Browns will be here soon,' said Evie, using the jaunty tone that never worked when she used it to say, *It's tidy-your-bedroom day,* or *I know! Why not start your school project on the Nazis?*

'The kids are girls. One's Scarlett's age and one's Mabel's, so it's all right for them, as usual.'

'It's not.' Scarlett snatched the Nutella; it had a short life-expectancy around the Herreras. 'I've never met this Tillie before. And Mabel says the little one's a wuss.'

'I want smiles,' said Evie sternly. 'I want everybody to get along.'

'We'll be nice, Mum, don't worry.' Scarlett kissed her mother and Evie forced herself not to touch the warm spot on her cheek. It had been a while since Scarlett had spontaneously kissed her like that.

As bacon sputtered its lovely song, Evie broke with tradition and made a cup of green tea, instead of her usual extra-strong builder's with two sugars. It seemed appropriate. The glass doors were folded back and, as the cliché says, it brought the garden indoors. It also brought Elizabetta indoors, slipping in from the dazzling terrace like a nymph, brown feet bare, her bikini three concise triangles of gold. *Does she realize*, thought Evie, *that she's at the peak of her loveliness?* That old quote was right; youth *is* wasted on the young.

'Is Fang sleeping?' Shen asked Elizabetta as the girl bent into the fridge.

'Yes, madam.' Elizabetta foraged, her voice muffled by row upon row of worthily dull food items. 'She is awake all night, so I let her rest. I go check on her now.'

It was too much to ask of a man to ignore a proffered bottom wearing just a gold scrap. Evie caught Mike's eye and he jumped. 'I wasn't,' he spluttered.

'S'OK,' she whispered as the nanny made for the stairs. 'I stared too.'

'But I didn't . . .' He gave up. 'She's distracting,' he admitted.

'As long as it stays up here.' Evie tapped his forehead. 'And doesn't travel down here.' She merely gestured at his shorts, figuring that direct contact with your husband's equipment in a shared kitchen would be bad taste.

'I'm too tired even to fantasize,' laughed Mike.

'Tired?' Shen was scornful. 'How come everybody's tired these days? Nobody complained of being tired before washing machines and cars and . . . and . . .' She looked around her. '*Blenders*. Machines to do all the work, yet we compete over who's the most tired. I've done an hour in the gym over in the stable, but you don't hear me moaning.'

It was news to Evie that there was a gym in the stable, and it wasn't the sort of news she liked. A big cake in the stable, yes. Or Ryan Gosling whimpering her name. Gym? Not so much.

'But you, dear girl,' said Evie, sandwiching rashers between doorsteps of bread, 'are twenty-nine, and we,' she gestured to her husband with her sarnie, 'are forty and forty-one. Those extra years wear you out, I tell you.'

'Especially,' said Mike, his mouth full, 'if you don't have a nanny.'

But we do have a nanny, Evie almost said. *ME.*

On his first cigar of the day, Clive sat outside, shaking out the newspaper, whose headline roared: *UK TO SWELTER IN HEATWAVE*. He, too, was in appalling shorts; perhaps they were contagious. The cut was classier than Mike's, but the pattern was vomity, and the legs that stuck out of them weren't half as nice as the tanned, athletic pins of Evie's husband.

Hovering and making conversation, Evie said, 'Looking forward to the Browns arriving?'

'Nope.' Clive didn't take his eyes from the newsprint. 'Don't know the people.' Not one for small talk, he ignored topics that didn't interest him. 'Besides, somebody else is on his way.' Clive raised his voice to call, 'Shen! What time is Zane the Boy Wonder expected?', his attention still half-claimed by the paper.

'Any minute now.' Shen was playing peek-a-boo with Fang, who stared pityingly at such foolishness, her eyes two round dark Os. 'His mum said to expect him for breakfast.'

'Mum,' said Scarlett, emerging into the sunshine with a cereal bowl, 'that breakfast bar is bigger than our dining table at home.'

'I know.' Evie smiled, wondering at the unbreakable bond between teenagers and cereal bowls.

'And the bedroom,' said Scarlett, chubby shoulders already blushing in her strappy top after half a day of holiday sunshine, 'is, like, as big as the ground floor at home.'

'We get it,' said Mike, intent on his iPad. 'Our home is a dump compared to this palace.' He looked up. 'D'you know how many people slept on pavements last night? They woke up cold and hungry, feeling lucky if they weren't assaulted. All day they'll worry about where they'll end up tonight. Ask them if they'd like our centrally heated, carpeted family home.'

Mulishly looking down at her food, Scarlett opened her mouth, shut it abruptly and stomped down the terrace steps, taking her Shreddies with her.

'Seriously?'

Evie recoiled from the venom of Mike's, 'Yes, Evelyn, *seriously.*'

Her full name only appeared at times of great stress; she'd been 'Evelyn' when her finger had slipped and she'd bid £8,000 for a vintage saucer on eBay. Evie wondered what was on Mike's mind, to turn him so shitty so early in the day.

'Life's hard,' said Mike.

'And then you die,' laughed Clive.

'The sooner they learn,' Mike wasn't laughing, 'the better.'

Evie refused to see the world as an assault course of sharp edges and hidden trapdoors; she was grateful that their three youngsters had a home that was warm, both literally and metaphorically.

'Car!' shrieked Dan, tearing around the side of the

house in Speedos and wellies. 'Car! Car! Car!' He sounded as if he'd never seen one before.

'The Browns,' chorused Evie and Shen. Evie kept her tone light, but Shen made no bones about how she felt. As they traipsed through the house to the front door, she said, her lowered eyebrows two elegant brushstrokes, 'Paula'll be a bag of nerves. As usual. And Jon will look as if he'd rather be somewhere else. As usual.'

'Let's make the best of it.' Evie couldn't resist adding piously, 'It was you who invited them.'

'Beggars can't be choosers,' said Shen, as they stood on the front step and watched the newcomers decant themselves from a low-nosed BMW, which trailed its own bespoke fog of gloom. 'Like we said, there's something weird about that family.'

'I've changed my mind,' said Evie, watching Paula and Jon Brown peer up at the massed windows of Wellcome Manor, shoulders set as if facing a firing squad. 'There's something *sad* about that family.'

A cricket set had been unearthed; another noise competed with the poetic sounds of leather and willow.

Not that Paula's voice was loud. It was, in fact, as mousy as her appearance, but it droned on and on, persistent and fretful.

'Sorry. I shouldn't let things get to me. I'm sorry, but . . .' and she was off again, taking the mug handed to her by Evie, but not raising it to her lips.

'It'll be fine.' Shen was airy, surreptitiously crossing her eyes at Evie, who ignored her; no need to disfigure their stay in this harmonious house with an us-against-them vibe.

'I'm not complaining about your driving, Jon, honestly I'm not, but you do like going fast, and I did say, around about Bracknell, that you should slow down a little bit, and you said you would, but . . .'

If Paula went missing, Evie could give the police only the sketchiest of descriptions. *Medium height, medium weight, nothing-y hair, nervous expression.* Sensing that Paula was close to tears, Evie put her hand on the woman's arm.

'It *will* be fine,' she repeated, more soothingly than Shen's brush-off. 'I've had one of those on-the-spot fines before and they're a pain, but all you do is present your licence at a police station and—'

'That's just it!' Paula turned to her husband, who was leaning, arms crossed, head down, against one of the fridges. (A cream Smeg, Evie noted, slightly ashamed at the obsession with fixtures and fittings that Wellcome Manor had sparked.) 'Please don't go to the police station, Jon. Please.'

The other adults were confounded by such high emotion about a mundane matter. Scarlett, wandering in barefoot, caught the mood and gawped at the tableau.

'For God's sake.' Jon's voice was educated, low. Straightening up, he spoke in the gritted-teeth undertone that was compulsory for private tiffs carried out in public. 'It's a legal requirement, Paula. The nearest police station is a few miles away, and I'm off to get it over and done with.'

And he was gone, all wiry, blond six-foot-two of him, with no farewell.

'Oh, well,' said Paula, smiling grimly, her head wobbling. 'Oh . . .' she hesitated, while everybody looked at her, '. . . well,' she repeated.

'Let me show you around.' Evie broke the spell, taking Paula's arm. 'You missed the welcome hamper.' She smiled. 'Moët, foie gras and quails' eggs, but not one packet of Monster Munch.'

The woman smiled vaguely, allowing herself to be shepherded out. 'Girls . . . ?' She looked behind her, and little bespectacled Amber, a paper-doll version of an eight-year-old, much smaller than her classmates Mabel and Miles and somehow more flimsy, rushed to enfold herself in her mother's skirts.

Tillie, older, taller, stayed in position against the pantry door, recreating her father's pose. She was a grave-faced girl, with Jon's fine bones and intelligent air, but her clothes suggested a freedom of thought and opinion. She'd bound up her hair in a wispy floral scarf, and the striped dress cinched at the waist with a man's belt betrayed a love of foraging in charity shops. The skinny calves ending in Doc Martens made Evie smile; she'd worn them herself, about a million years ago.

With an infinitesimal nod, Evie communicated with her own older daughter. Understanding, but not liking, the coded suggestion to 'play nicely', Scarlett said, carefully bored, 'Tillie, isn't it? Wanna see the pool?'

'OK.' Tillie followed her out.

'Don't get in!' shouted Paula.

'Amber,' said Mabel confidingly, as if letting her in on a secret, 'there's a treehouse!'

'Really!' Amber's pale face lit from within. 'But . . .' She looked at her mum. 'I'm not allowed to climb treeth.'

Butting in, Shen said, 'It's low, Paula. They'll be fine.'

'Yes,' said Paula. She was smiling in the way that women smile when sending menfolk off to war: brave, despite the hideous dangers. 'Off you trot, darling.'

'No,' said Amber. 'I'll stay with you.'

'*See?*' hissed Shen as the subdued group moved on. 'Weird.'

Wellcome Manor worked its magic. Even Paula wasn't immune to the cheering properties of silk and sisal and wet rooms.

'This room,' said Shen, looking round appraisingly at the painted floorboards and immense sleigh bed, 'will do nicely for you and Jon.'

'It's far too nice!' Paula was so aghast at the luxury that Evie felt ashamed for nabbing the second-best room with such haste. 'We'll take an attic room.'

'They're for the kids!' snorted Shen.

'I sleep in the pink one,' said Mabel, fresh freckles already crowding her nose.

'The girly one,' said Miles.

'The girls can share,' said Evie brightly.

'Yay!' Mabel applauded.

'No!' Amber's sobbing was sudden, noisy, violent.

'Darling,' began Paula, folding over her like a closing umbrella.

Whispering hotly in Evie's ear, Mabel said, 'She's always crying. I don't want to share with her.'

Damn. Where was Mike when there was tricky parenting to be done? He was always around for food fights. 'You're sharing,' she said firmly.

Evie might have brought a serpent to paradise, but her husband had brought something far worse: a metaphorical Redcoat's uniform.

'This,' he said, waving a guide book to the local area, 'is full of things to do in the vicinity.'

'What's a vinissitee?' Mabel loved mangling new words.

'The area round about,' said Tillie.

'My big sister,' said Amber, in her hushed squeak, 'knows all the words in all the books.'

'So does . . .' Mabel tailed off. 'No. My big sister doesn't. But she knows how to disable the parental locks on her computer.'

'*That* you pronounce perfectly,' said Scarlett.

'I don't fancy a vinissitee,' said Mabel.

Earlier, among the crumpled sheets, Evie had prophesied that Mike would have trouble peeling the children away from the manifold delights of Wellcome Manor. The pool had been discovered not only to be whimsical (a brick-edged circle in the grass, alongside a cottagey pool-house), but also relatively safe (no deep end).

'I want,' said Dan, 'to do somersaults on the trampoline.'

'May as well order the taxi to A&E now,' said Evie, resisting the urge to comb the ginger – no, *Titian* – fright-wig on her son's head.

'Were trampolines,' asked Mabel, 'invented by tramps?'

From the terrace Clive snorted in amusement.

A mobile phone by the sink bleeped and Evie jumped a foot in the air, even though it wasn't her phone. Shen peered over and read the message. 'Zane. Won't be here until lunchtime, apparently.'

'The cheese museum,' said Mike, soldiering on, 'is open today.' With a kids' TV-presenter level of enthusiasm, he added, 'They let you make your own feta!'

'I hate feta,' said Mabel, that throaty voice surprising everyone, as it often did.

'Who is feta?' asked Amber.

'I think,' said Evie diplomatically, 'that's a no to the cheese museum.' *What child*, she thought, *would say 'yes'?*

'Hmm. Really?' As a parent, Mike should have been aware of the average child's innate lack of curiosity about cheese. 'OK, then, how about a nice arboretum?'

Evie rather enjoyed the children's faces. She shared a satisfying, don't-let-Mike-see-us-smirking smirk with Shen.

'I don't know what that word you said is.' Even Mabel wouldn't tackle 'arboretum' this early in the day. 'But it sounds boring.'

He persevered. 'An arboretum is a tree – um – place,'

explained Mike. 'A lovely place full of trees, where you learn about trees.'

'You make a compelling case,' said Evie.

'It sounds even more boring than when I didn't know what it was.' Mabel had the finality of a hanging judge.

Amber looked tearfully at Paula. 'Do I have to go to a tree place, Mummy?'

Dan was forthright. 'Trees suck.'

The dogs made a sudden clamour in the hall, Patch's berserk yammering loud above the bass-line of Prunella's springy jumps against the front door.

Clutching her throat, Paula jerked Amber towards her. 'Who's that?' she squeaked.

It was Jon, and from the way he ploughed through Patch and Prunella's extravagant welcome, he wasn't a dog person.

'You were quick!' said Clive.

'What kept you?' said Paula. 'Can I get you something?' She was on her feet. 'You must be thirsty. A coffee?'

'I'm fine,' said Jon.

'Perhaps a nice—'

'I said I'm fine.' Jon sat and looked at the stone floor just long enough to make everybody – possibly even the thick-skinned Patch – feel uncomfortable, before saying, 'The village is rather quaint', as if he'd been rehearsing that for a while outside the door.

Paula didn't seem to have heard this conversational gambit. 'Or a croissant? There's some—'

'Not hungry,' said Jon. A touch late, he tacked on 'darling'.

'I could do you a nice omelette.'

Jon made no reply, looking at his wife as if she was talking a foreign language.

'I'd love an omelette, Mum,' said Tillie.

Good girl, thought Evie approvingly. Tillie had saved her mother from an awkwardness that her father either didn't notice or didn't care about.

Clive said, 'Mike here is looking for takers for the cheese museum.'

'Sounds great!' said Jon.

'You're both mad,' said Clive. 'Buzzing off to museums. I work far too hard all year round to do anything but lie in the sun on my hols.' He put on some sunglasses that probably cost more than all the sunglasses the Herreras had ever owned, put together.

'Yeah, well,' said Mike, hyper-casual, 'you old blokes deserve your rest. No point trying to keep up.'

Clive's eyes were invisible behind his shades, but Evie noticed his tummy shrink as he pulled in his gut.

The pool was a magnet, drawing all the Wellcome Manor iron filings to it. Clive stretched out, magnificent tum already a fetching shade of flamingo, as Scarlett swam lazy lengths in a frilly two-piece beneath a sun that blazed in a most un-English manner.

On a modishly industrial sun-lounger Paula neither lay down nor sat up; she'd invented a whole new awkward position of her own. Evie felt naked in her utilitarian navy cossie next to Paula, still in shapeless skirt and shapeless blouse, feet still in sensible courts.

'Where's Amber?' asked Paula, with an anxiety that suggested they were living under siege, rather than in a luxury holiday rental.

'We sold her to a passing circus,' said Shen. At Paula's horror-struck look, she relented and said, 'Oh, Paula, it's been *years* since I sold a child to a circus. She's playing pong-ping.'

'Ping-pong,' corrected Clive sleepily, popping his panama hat over his face. 'And don't tease Paula, darling. She's not at home to Mrs Sarcasm.'

'No, no, I don't mind. I just . . . I . . .' Paula dribbled to a halt and shifted slightly, so that she looked even more awkward and uncomfortable than before. She clearly hadn't been at school the day they covered How to Enjoy Your Hols.

Evie gave herself up to the sun's relentless seduction and shut her eyes. Two minutes later she was shaken awake by many small hands.

'It was amazing!'

'Table tennis rocks!'

'Patch ate a ball!'

'Did you,' asked Evie, rising up and squinting, feeling the toxic itch of sunburn across her chest, 'give Amber a go?' The recessive little girl might struggle to hold her own against Miles and the raucous brother/sister combo.

'She won!' shrieked Mabel.

'Lovely. Stand back a bit, though, eh?' said Evie; one day they'd get the child's volume control sorted out, but for now Mabel whispered in crowds and made like a megaphone in church.

'She beat Dan,' said Miles. 'Really beat him. Really, really.'

'Well done, Amber,' said Evie, charmed by the flush on the girl's pinched face, which transformed it from anaemic to bonny. Paula's attempt to create a morbid mini-me wasn't quite working; Amber was as full of pep as the other kids.

Like a baby newsreader, Fang had a gaze that was level and steady as she let Elizabetta wipe her dimpled hands. They were alone in the kitchen.

'Let's get your pretty little hands clean,' said Elizabetta. She patted the baby's nose with the wet wipe. 'And that naughty nose!'

Fang laughed. A lot. She found noses hilarious. As she laughed and laughed and laughed, her nanny ran water over the dishes in the sink.

'I *love* to wash the plates!' said Elizabetta in that wide-eyed, over-enunciating manner that people use around a baby. 'I don't want to lie by the pool! I don't want to walk about in the expensive bikinis! I don't even want to sleep. I really, really enjoy being up all night with you, because Madame Shen is too lazy to get out of bed and hold you.'

Fang's head jerked around at a sudden, sharp buzz.

'Somebody left their phone,' Elizabetta said to the baby.

'They have a message. It is private, Fang.' She reached up to a shelf, found a phone among the plates and beakers and read the screen. 'Listen to this, Fang.' In her heavy accent, Elizabetta read out the message: **'I refuse to be your dirty little secret any more xxxx.'**

Padding past the pool, Scarlett held her iPhone so close to her face that it was almost up her nose.

'Give that here,' said Evie, from her deckchair.

'Give what where?'

'The phone. Give.'

'What?' Scarlett looked confused, then amused, then horrified. 'You're not serious, Mother.'

'Hand it over. It's only a phone. You're not in *Sophie's Choice*.'

'Think about what you're doing, Mum.' Scarlett gathered her resources to fight this terrible injustice. 'This isn't a phone. It's my *life*.'

It might have struck Evie as funny, but instead it struck her as sad that her daughter could genuinely believe her life could be compressed into a SIM card. 'Give.' She held out her hand.

'My friends . . .' Scarlett held out the phone; she knew her mother's face as well as she knew her own. One was *ancient*, of course, but the raw material was the same, and Scarlett knew by her expression that Evie wouldn't back down.

'There's a friend over *there*.' Evie gestured to a distant

bench beneath a willow, where Tillie sat, the book in her hands every bit as inevitable as Scarlett's phone, her retro ruched swimsuit and men's shoes the polar opposite of Paula's bland camouflage. 'If you can be bothered to make the effort.'

'God, Mum, you go on as if you know everything.'

If Mike were around, that 'tude wouldn't go unpunished, but Evie remembered the hormone hurricane-years better than he did and was consequently more forgiving. 'You'll thank me for all my nagging one day.' *When you've learned that the resources in your head are far superior to the whirling party on your phone.*

'Not today, though, Mum.' Scarlett's self-righteous stomp was spoiled by her flip-flops.

'Wait for me.' Dan sped after her, Patch at his heels with a Müller Light tub stuck to one ear, reminding Evie of how a family break without the dog had felt unthinkable; now that they'd arrived, Patch was a hairy liability, bound to break something costly, or to poo in something antique.

In less than half a minute Dan was back; evidently there'd been a sisterly request along the lines of *Bog off.*

'Never mind, honeybun.' Evie ruffled her son's hair, relieved that he still allowed such sappy behaviour, and shaded her eyes with her hand as she watched Scarlett, her outline dappled in the haze, nonchalantly approach Tillie beneath the tree. With equal nonchalance Tillie got up, and the two disappeared through an arch in the hedging.

'Want to stretch your legs, Shen?' called Evie across the azure pool.

'Sure.' Shen rose with one fluid movement, nothing like the carthorse-in-labour struggles of Evie escaping from her low seat. 'Let's find that grotto.'

'Count me out,' said Clive, flopped onto his back.

'Nobody asked you.' Shen put her arm through Evie's, leaning in, confidingly. 'Zane texted again. He won't make it for lunch. Says to expect him at dinner time.' She pulled a face. Even grimacing, she was pretty. 'He's going to ruin the holiday. I feel it in my bones.'

'Give him a chance.' Evie had heard the odd bulletin about Zane's exploits. 'How does his mum cope with him?'

'We don't really speak. And, no, I didn't have a row with her. She can't forgive me for being younger than her.'

'I assume you mean she can't forgive you for shamelessly nicking her husband.'

'If you leave diamonds lying on the carpet, don't complain if somebody takes them home.' Shen spotted Elizabetta gently bumping Fang's buggy down the terrace steps and summoned her with a wave. 'Did you know she's married a toy boy?'

'I also know the age difference between them is half the difference in your marriage.' Mrs Clive #2 was a Pakistani beauty, whose allure had only deepened as she entered her fifties. What's more, the woman had been gracious and welcoming to the upstart model who'd waltzed off with her husband, via an accidental pregnancy. 'You Clive-wives could all be friends. You have a lot in common.'

'Correction: we have *nothing* in common,' said Shen, taking Fang and kissing the top of her downy head. 'They lost Clive. I intend to hang on to him.'

'They probably felt the same,' said Evie. 'What does a grotto look like?'

'We'll know it when we see it,' said Shen, as the polite lawn gave way to Wellcome Manor's version of a wilderness. As wildernesses go, it was tidy, the wild flowers and grasses startled to have been let in. 'My marriage is different. Clive's got it right this time.'

'So he should, after all that practice.' Evie easily dodged Shen's swipe. 'How is it different?' Marriage was on her mind. Good ones. Bad ones. Shaky ones. Her own.

'We do more together, as a family – you know?'

'Like what?'

There was a pause. 'We went to Harrods last week.'

'If we leave out shopping, what do you do together?'

'We're here, aren't we?' Shen's temper, never particularly elastic, began to twang. 'Clive and I are for keeps.'

'So you trust him?' Evie wondered if his first two wives had trusted Clive.

'I let him have his secrets,' she said. It was a statement. It didn't invite comment.

Evie had to comment, however. 'Not sure I could manage that with Mike.'

'No,' said Shen, archly. 'You two have no secrets then?'

'Fair enough.' Evie bowed her head, as if Shen had cuffed her. Shen knew all – thanks to a long night of Pringles, house-red and empathy, just before they'd come away.

'Listen, Evie, all women – even past-it ex-wives – are a threat. I maintain a scorched-earth policy with all women.' She reconsidered. 'Obviously not with you,' she said kindly. 'Clive would never fancy you.'

'From anybody else,' said Evie, 'that could sound rude.'

'I was going to add,' said Shen, 'that – besides – I love you, you fool.'

As they delved deeper into the manor's grounds, Shen turned that last admission over in her mind. It was true; it was also unlikely. She travelled lightly, never getting too attached. Not a navel-gazer, she left the self-analysis to others, preferring to drive a tank through her life, rolling over obstacles and never looking behind her. But Evie *was* necessary to her.

I trust her, Shen thought. Evie had saved Shen from the Ubers, who, frankly, were the most tedious ragbag of stapled-together old bats that Shen had ever encountered; their polite titters over coffee didn't compare with the belly laughs she and Evie shared.

And I love her. Shen thought it again, for the sheer joy of experiencing the feeling. *Even though*, she thought, *Evie's hair's a shocking mess. And I'd happily burn every garment she owns – cut-off denims, seriously? And nobody has to look their age nowadays, yet she won't let me pay for Botox. And obviously she's too good for Mike, although that's no reflection on him; all women are too good for their husbands.*

'I think the grotto's just a myth,' said Evie. 'Shall we give up?'

'I never give up,' said Shen. 'Let's make a strategic retreat.'

After lunch, Evie went to the summerhouse, a product of the gingerbread-house school of architecture, with a thatch and a low front door. The sounds of her extended holiday 'family' were distant here, just the occasional faint scream of an eight-year-old or the irritated yap of a twenty-nine-year-old. Setting her laptop on a rustic table, Evie yanked her mind round to her work.

Or Mum's 'work', as the Herreras called it; the inverted commas were audible.

Distracted for a while by the cottagey interior – the computer looked all wrong, as if Hansel and Gretel were about to LoL at YouTube – Evie applied herself.

Her deadline loomed. And the title bothered her: *Love Finds a Way*. *Too slushy*, she thought. *Not sexy enough*.

Because sex was the name of the game, in Evie's line of business – the post-*Fifty Shades of Grey*, raunchy online publishing business. At the beginning, when she'd gingerly written her first sex scene, face aflame, legs knotted with embarrassment, she had entertained daydreams of fame and wealth.

After publication of *His Masterly Touch*, the first novella under her pen name of Lucinda Lash, the daydreams were downsized, but she still looked forward to a long-haul holiday, with one of those butler people bringing her cocktails by a private plunge-pool.

Reality struck. By her eighth title – *Don't Be Gentle* – Evie knew to expect pin-money from her 'work'. Even she was doing the inverted-commas thing now, but writing had saved her life. That was really how it felt.

When she and Mike had met, it was Evie who had the

career. No inverted commas. Possibly a capital letter. She was a young gun in advertising, a junior copywriter who relished the sitting up late, drinking stinking coffee and throwing ideas off the walls/her colleagues' heads.

Mike had wondered how she found satisfaction in such a shallow industry, but then he also wondered how she could spend an hour in the bath or cry at Pixar films. (*They're computer graphics*, he'd say; *you're an unfeeling monster*, she'd sob.) Scarlett's arrival, unplanned but as welcome as if she was a *lorryload* of cream teas, had thrown a spanner in the works of Evie's career, but she'd intended to work twice as hard to catch up, after her maternity leave.

Then the doctors had talked of 'issues'. Evie loathed that word, such a catch-all. In Scarlett's case – teeny, tiny, brand-new Scarlett's case – the word meant uncertainties about her eyes. There were problems with their development; Evie had remained calm while they coolly discussed operating. All had panned out happily, but a year, then two, then three had passed and Evie was still at home. Happy to be there, of course, and over the moon that Scarlet's eyes were healthy, but the glorious career had stuttered to a halt.

Two more babies, two more anchors. Beautiful anchors, yes. Beloved, longed for and cherished, but – like all anchors – they were heavy. That specific part of Evie that could only be expressed by creating something was locked away. Until she bashed out that first story.

Scribbling out the tale, her characters springing to lusty life, had felt like a new beginning, right at the tail end of the worst year of her life – the worst year of her husband's life. It had given her back a corner of the world that was hers, and hers alone.

This was her last book; Lucinda Lash was about to hang up her thigh-high boots. There are only so many ways to say 'willy', and soon Evie wouldn't need to make unlikeable blokes do things with the tip of a whip to mute, soppy girls.

She'd left her current characters, Clay and Roxana, mid-bonk. They were a lively pair, much given to sudden unbuttonings. Roxana's breasts were cheerful creatures, always 'bobbing' or 'bouncing', while Clay's untidy parts stiffened helpfully if Roxana so much as coughed. She caught up with them on the hood of a Jaguar convertible:

Clay thrusts again and again as she screams his name, her nails digging painfully into the solid muscle of his back.

A noise outside the gingerbread house made her look up, one hand instinctively slamming her laptop shut. This knee-jerk feeling, close to shame, was horrible: she lived in fear that Mabel or Dan would happen upon one of her characters' proud members.

A rustling from the nearby patch of high grasses was insistent enough to coax Evie from her seat. 'Hello?' she said uncertainly, approaching the greenery.

The noise continued, turning to grunts. Parting the grass, Evie let out a shocked 'Oh!', then an appalled 'Eew!' Maybe the dogs had been reading her books; Patch had exuberantly mounted a placid Prunella, who seemed oblivious to the

undignified kerfuffle at her rear end. 'Off! Out! Stop it!'
Evie, glanced, paranoid, back to the distant house. 'Patch,
for God's sake!'

Disengaging, Patch slinked away. Prunella trotted after
him. No hard feelings apparently.

Thank God, thought Evie, *that Pru's been 'done'*. She'd
have to flee the country if Patch made Shen a grandmother
to a litter of non-pedigree, very stupid puppies.

Holidays are about surviving the gaps between one meal
and another. Evie was as fixated on her dinner as a convict,
or an OAP in a care-home. The others evidently felt the
same; the question 'What's for dinner?' had begun the
moment lunch was tidied away.

The list of dos and don'ts was long. Amber couldn't bear
food of different colours touching; Mabel's antipathy to
carrots was well documented; Clive had the high standards
of a man who eats out a lot; Scarlett didn't know what
carbs were, but believed them to be poisonous; Dan needed
baked beans daily or he pined; and Mike didn't believe
dinner was dinner unless it incorporated meat and two veg.

As for Evie, she put her foot down and said, 'Elizabetta
isn't cooking tonight.' A noodle was a fine thing, and tofu
was a noble beast, but neither of them was welcome at
the table that evening.

A genteel battle began. 'Fish,' said Shen, tying a starched
apron neatly around her middle. 'Steamed fish in a herb
broth.'

'Lasagne,' countered Evie. 'With garlic bread.' She noted, with some degree of *grrr*, how right Shen looked in this top-of-the-range kitchen, whereas she herself, worn out from three straight hours of fictional nookie, looked like the tramp who invented the trampoline. 'Plus optional dough balls.'

'Over my dead body,' said Shen sweetly.

'Fine by me.' Evie crossed her arms.

'Can I help?' Paula had entered the room without a sound, and both women jumped at her question.

'Actually,' said Shen, 'yes, you can. You decide. Disgusting, artery-clogging lasagne or delicious, heavenly fish?'

'Lasagne,' said Paula, with rare conviction.

'Ree-sult.' Evie tried to high-five herself: it wasn't pretty, and the others pretended not to notice.

As Shen and Evie set to, opening packets, marshalling pans, switching on the oven, Paula moved to the doors and looked out. 'I'm sure you'll think I'm mad, but . . .'

'But what?' asked Evie, wondering why Shen was always standing in front of the drawer that she needed to open. 'Shen, why are you using bottled water to wash the salad, you wasteful trollop?'

Paula pulled her shapeless cardigan about her, the only cardigan in service in the south of England on this blistering day. 'I saw somebody.'

'I use bottled water because I don't trust taps,' said Shen. 'How d'you mean *somebody*, Paula?' She prodded Evie. 'Why are you boiling water for the pasta sheets in a pot? There's a spout there that gives boiling water.'

'I saw a figure. Out there.' Paula lifted a wavering finger to point. 'Watching,' she added.

'Who's watching us?' Mabel popped up from nowhere, Mrs Misterson II grasped to her chest.

'Nobody, darling,' said Shen, sharpening a knife.

'A man,' said Paula. 'In the bushes.'

Shen and Evie shared an exasperated look. Apparently Paula had read some unusual child-psychology books.

'A man in the bushes!' Miles popped up too. Were there perhaps underground tunnels in the kitchen?

'Paula's joking, sweetie,' said Evie.

'If only I were,' said Paula.

'It's probably a giant killer-fox!' Miles put that out there.

'Nothing,' said Evie firmly, 'is in the bushes, girls and boys.'

'In films it's always quite a dangerous murderer,' said Dan, full of hope, as Amber shrank.

'Or . . .' Mabel pondered, 'a mutant chicken! With ladies' legs!'

'Paula made a mistake,' said Shen, firmly. 'There are no murderers at Wellcome Manor, kids.'

'Yes, I'm always wrong,' said Paula, continuing to gaze out, like a neurotic guard dog.

Noting that Shen chopped tomatoes oddly (that is, not the way she herself would chop them), Evie approached the boiling-water spout with care, as if it might bite. 'Lay the table, if you like, Paula,' she said.

'OK.' Paula opened a drawer, closed it, opened another. 'Um, which table? This one in the kitchen? Or the one in the orangery? Or the one in the drawing room? Or the one—'

'The outside one,' Shen barged in, evidently unable to bear an inventory of every table in the many-tabled house.

'Shall I use a tablecloth? Where are they?' Paula looked about her, lips compressed. 'Wine glasses? Or . . .'

'You know what?' Shen swiped up some cutlery. 'I'll do it.'

The terrace table was laid in the blink of an eye. Evie added a jam jar of foliage. 'It looks so inviting,' she said, wrapping her arms around herself. It was seductive, this picture-perfect 'lifestyle' living.

The béchamel sauce cooperated. Evie stirred, enjoying the meditative nature of the chore.

'Did you use semi-skimmed?' Shen was as sharp as an SS officer.

'Nope.' Evie smiled. 'Full . . .' she luxuriated in the words, '. . . fat.'

The children floated in and out, the stuffing knocked out of them by the heat of the day and the sheer amount of running about they'd done. 'I'm starving,' repeated Dan, over and over.

'A third of the world,' Tillie said, hoisting herself up to sit on the worktop, 'goes to bed hungry every night.'

'Are they,' asked Mabel, 'on the 5:2 diet?'

In a high chair, Fang kicked her butterball legs convulsively as she was fed, a spoonful at a time, by her nanny.

Scarlett was admiring Elizabetta's latest bikini. The girl seemed to have a limitless supply of tiny fabric triangles. 'Come and have a swim with us later,' she said, conversationally. 'It'd be nice to have a girl to hang out with.'

Evie, inwardly bemoaning her daughter's clumsiness,

saw Tillie's head droop, just for a second, before it bobbed up again, her face carefully non-committal. Perhaps the two weren't destined to bond, after all.

'Thank you, but . . .' Elizabetta's answer was steam-rollered by Shen.

'Elizabetta's working, not on holiday, darling.'

'Oh.' Scarlett pulled a face over at Tillie, who was look-ing at her book and didn't notice. 'Sorry. I guess.' Then she jumped. 'Christ, Mum, that lasagne is massive.'

'Will it be enough, though?' Staggering to the range with the bath-sized dish, Evie counted heads. 'With Zane, there'll be . . . um . . . fourteen of us.' It was like being a Walton. A really posh Walton.

Shen didn't answer; she was lost in watching Fang eat. Eyebrows up. Eyebrows down. Sudden hiccup.

Drawn in, Evie was mesmerized too, standing – tea towel limp in her hand – as Fang kicked and jiggled.

'Getting broody?' asked Paula.

'God, no!' Evie snapped out of it. 'I've done my time down the baby-mines, thank you very much.'

'Gee, thanks, Mum.' Scarlett was touring the kitchen on the lookout for stray titbits; she liked to help herself to a 'starter'. 'Were we that bad?'

'No, you were . . .' Evie time-travelled for a moment, and Scarlett was one-third of her current height, with a dandelion head of hair. 'You were wonderful,' she said wistfully.

'Eh?' Scarlett moved off, allergic to her mother's emotions, but not quite able to quench a small smile.

The grand front door slammed, and feet sounded in the hallway.

'Is this,' murmured Scarlett, doing her utmost to sound detached, 'the famous Zane?'

'No, it's your famous father,' said Evie, raising her voice to ask, 'How was the cheese museum?'

The rhetorical nature of the question was lost on Mike. He told her how the cheese museum was; he told her at such length that he and Jon were still sharing dairy factoids as Shen's shout of 'Come and get it!' sounded through the house and grounds, and the families converged on the long table on the terrace.

'Shouldn't we wait for Zane?' In Evie's worldview, food = love; she hated to think of a boy turning up to the debris of dinner, knowing that he'd been left out.

'No,' said Clive. 'If he can't be here on time, he doesn't get to eat.'

'He may have been held up,' said Paula.

'If there's any holding up being done,' said Clive, laying a napkin across his lap, 'you can bet your bottom dollar it's my son doing it.'

'I'll save him some.' Conscience salved, Evie persuaded the lasagne out of the oven.

Chattering and pushing, the smaller ones beat the bigger ones to it. Tillie and Scarlett were at opposite ends of the table, until a jerk of Evie's head sent Scarlett to the other girl's side. Paula held out a chair for Jon, who only broke off from cheese-based banter to refuse the cold gin and tonic she held out.

'I've got malnu-thingy,' said Miles earnestly. His hair,

usually as sleek and black as a surfacing seal's, stood on end.

'Me too,' said Evie.

'They let us stir some whey!' Mike's excitement was such that Evie pitied him.

'Thank God,' said Scarlett to Tillie, 'we didn't go with them.'

Knives and forks were snatched up, and Evie was just about to plunge a serving spoon into the lasagne when Clive stood and tapped a glass.

'Not *grace*,' said the godless Mabel.

'A toast,' said Clive, raising his glass. Ruddy-faced from a full day's sod-all, he raised a beefy arm. 'To the ladies. And their cooking prowess. And of course,' he clinked Evie's glass, 'their beauty.' He winked at her. 'Blue suits you,' he went on.

'Does it?' Evie looked down at her Primark top, snatched up en route to the children's swimwear section. Silently she congratulated the two rectangles of cheap jersey for holding their own against Shen's oyster-coloured silk camisole.

'This looks amazing.' Mike held out his plate. 'Evie bashes out top-quality stodge.'

'Why, thank you, kind sir.' Evie privately preferred Clive's compliment. As if there was a lock on that section of his brain, Mike was unable to comment positively on her physical appearance. When she agonized over what to wear on one of their rare nights out, taking pains with her headstrong hair and following a YouTube tutorial on Smoky Eyes, before presenting herself to Mike with a part-trepidatious/part-satisfied 'Well?', he would reply, 'You look fine' or 'You look all right' or, on one memorable evening, 'Right, let's go, or we'll never get there.'

She held an unctuous scoop over Paula's plate, which was swiftly snatched away.

'Not for me,' said Paula piously. 'I hate lasagne.'

'But you said . . .' Evie hastily redirected the serving spoon to another plate.

Shen spat out a mouthful of Viognier. 'Why the f . . . lip did you tell us to make it then?' Never backward about being forward, she treated Paula to one of her full-on boggles.

'Look at Mummy's silly face,' said Miles, slipping a tomato to Prunella.

'Because Jon loves lasagne.' Paula had half-stood. 'I'll make some toast or something . . .' She was being vague.

Shen was not. 'Oh, sit down, for God's sake. I'll warm some soup for you.' Off she stomped on her high heels, illustrating perfectly the idiosyncratic mix of bad temper and generosity that Evie couldn't help liking.

There was an awkward pause, punctured by Prunella coughing up a tomato, at some length, beneath the table.

A pattern was emerging. Just as they had last night, everybody congregated on the terrace after dinner had been cleared away.

Scarlett prowled with her returned iPhone held high,

then held low, chasing reception, as if the phone led the girl, rather than the other way round.

The Browns segregated themselves from the cheerful card game at the table, preferring the loungers just outside the lanterns' campfire glow.

Out in the black void of the garden, the children ambushed each other. 'It's carnage,' said Evie, studying her cards and wondering once again why Lady Luck never sat on her lap, or even mouthed 'hello' across the room. 'Why aren't they tired?'

'It's Paula's talk of something in the bushes,' said Shen. 'They're all fired up.'

'Later, though, there'll be nightmares.'

'Yeah, thanks, Paula.' Mike slept nearest the door and would be the recipient of a small knee in the groin when Mabel crept into their bed.

'How old do you think she is?' Guessing people's ages was one of Shen's favourite pastimes. She loved collecting humans who were older than her.

'If by "she" you mean Paula, keep your voice down,' said Evie primly. 'They're feet away.'

'Older than Jon, for sure,' said Clive.

'Unless he's one of those infuriating Richard Madeley types,' suggested Evie, getting drawn in despite her misgivings, 'who looks thirty-seven all his life.'

'I'll find out,' promised Shen, the bit now between her veneered teeth. Bending over to refill Evie's glass, she said, 'They're not very *physical* with each other, are they?'

'They wouldn't, for example,' said Clive, 'do *this*.' He slapped Shen's appley buttocks with a resounding thwack and pulled her onto his lap, ignoring her half-serious screams of annoyance.

They were striking together: one so dainty, the other such a bull. Evie wondered how she and Mike seemed to the outside world. Together for twenty years, and first loves (unless you counted a couple of false starts), were they now parents first and lovers second? Or were they barely lovers at all? The hand-holding had slipped in recent years.

Reaching for his hand, Evie was cheered when Mike put her fingers to his mouth and kissed them, his smile shunting dimples into each weathered cheek.

He leaned in and Evie bent towards him, anticipating a sweet nothing.

'Go easy on the champers love,' said Mike. 'If Clive expects us to reciprocate, that stuff's a hundred quid a bottle.'

Knowing the price of everything was a vibe-killer. Evie dropped Mike's fingers and he picked up a booklet. She realized something. 'Where's Zane? It's getting late.'

'I haven't had a text for hours.' Shen didn't seem concerned.

'That door is getting locked, if he's not here by the time we go to bed,' said Clive.

'You don't mean that.' Evie said it hopefully.

'He does,' said Shen, poking Mike. She was big on poking and prodding and general manhandling. 'Your go.'

'Sorry. Sorry.' Mike threw down any old card.

'What's that you're reading?'

'A manual the owners compiled about the house.' He squinted at the page, held it nearer to the candles. 'There's a gnome-reserve nearby.'

'Be still, my beating heart,' said Clive.

Ignoring him, Mike said, 'Oh, and listen to this: "Enjoy Wellcome Manor's beautiful grounds right through the night, with the sophisticated outdoor lighting system."'

'Maybe Paula will feel better with the lights on. Scarlett!' called Evie, ploughing past the inevitable tut. 'Put down your phone for a millisecond and see if you can find the switch for the outdoor lights.'

'Where?' Scarlett seemed bemused, as if light switches were obscure exotica that she couldn't be expected to know about.

'Just *look*.' Mike was irked.

'God-*duh*.' Scarlett stamped off, her face red. 'Is this it?' she shouted from within the house. 'Or this?' The kitchen lights flashed on and off. The hall lit up, then died. 'Or this?' The orangery became floodlit, then dark.

'Just leave it.' Shen took pity on Scarlett and the girl sloped back, telling the terrace at large, 'I'm going up.'

'Before Mabel?' Mike smiled, in a transparent attempt to repair father/daughter relations.

'Yeah, well, there's nothing to do here, Daddy dearest.' Scarlett readily accepted the olive branch. 'Tillie?' She waited until the girl's head went up reluctantly. 'I'll take the bed near the window, yeah?'

'Whatever.' Tillie went back to her book.

Scarlett shot her mother a look that clearly said: *See?*

Watching Tillie curled up as tight as a shell, Evie conceded that she didn't make it easy for Scarlett. The girl had the same aloof air as her dad, intensified by the Brown clannishness. 'I'm out.' Laying down her comically poor hand of cards, she leaned against her husband. 'Somewhere out there,' she murmured, 'our kids are running riot.' She hoped against hope that he'd offer to round them up; in marital tit-for-tat, it was only fair, as she'd cooked dinner.

'I hope next door remembers to water the plants,' said Mike.

'Mmm.' Evie couldn't give a single hoot about the spindly geraniums huddled on their patio at home. 'How can you even think about our so-called garden, with all these grounds to romp in?'

'It's not "so-called".' Mike looked hurt, as if he'd personally laid their balding lawn and personally positioned every weed just so. 'I miss it.'

Now wasn't the time to tell him about the dead rat behind the shed.

Their terraced house, a jerry-built extension bulging from it like a boil, was too small for the Herreras. Should a seventeen-year-old girl have to share her bedroom with an eight-year-old? *No*, was Scarlett's adamant view, and Evie agreed. They had no option, however.

The garden was a work-in-progress (and always would be). In the kitchen, tester pots of paint queued patiently, awaiting the mythical refit. The sagging sofa was almost replaced each sales season. Even the brightly coloured oilcloth on the dining table – venue for dinners, potato-print sessions, guinea-pig lying-in-states and impromptu quickie sex – needed replacing.

It was crazy to miss such squalor, but Evie realized, with a pang, that she did. A bit. Crazier still, in that case, to be plotting her escape from it.

A mind-reader, Shen leaned over the table to hiss, 'Have you told him yet?'

Evie shook her head, eyes flashing a warning to be more discreet as, with perfect timing, her phone spasmed in her pocket.

Mike reached for it. 'I'll read it to you.'

'No!' Evie clamped her hand over her pocket. 'It'll be nothing.' She turned away to scan the message: **Sorry. But I'm IMPATIENT! xxx.**

'Probably from your lover,' joked Mike.

'If only!' Evie switched off her phone, hating how glibly she lied and how trustingly Mike swallowed it.

The night sprawled, as they do on holiday, time stretching and bending. Evenings back home flew by in a whirlwind of homework, catching half of *EastEnders*, and small rows about who used the last of the hot water. Here, there was time for cards, for wine and for various games of musical chairs.

Shen moved to sit beside Mike. Evie perched on the end of Tillie's sun-lounger. Paula hovered, stood, sat down again. Jon stayed resolutely where he was. When Clive wandered over to a bench, placed as if by design just out of the lanterns' reach and shaded by a bower of something scented, Evie followed him. He had to scoot up to make room.

'Am I disturbing you?'

'Not a bit.' Clive was never knowingly under-charming

– one of the reasons Evie tended to keep her distance. She distrusted such easy manners.

'I wanted to apologize.' She set off without knowing where she might land. Suddenly her planned speech was both gauche and – gulp! – *insulting*. 'For Mike, I mean. His crass remark. Earlier.'

'I don't get it.' Clive's bushy brows knotted together. He seemed amused, as he often did, like a man who's overheard a joke.

'He said . . . oh, something like . . .' stammered Evie. 'He said you're too old to dash about on holiday,' she said finally, kicking herself for dragging up what he'd already forgotten.

'Oh, that.' Another pulling-in of his considerable belly undermined Clive's shrug.

'It was hurtful. And not true. Obviously not true.'

'Hurtful maybe, but correct.' Clive shrugged. 'I is what I is. And I is fifty-five years old.'

'Hardly at death's door!'

'But older than you. I could be your father.'

'Now you're flattering me. And besides, I'm sure my mother would have mentioned it.'

Clive guffawed.

Relaxing, Evie leaned back, drawing nearer to Clive. 'Mike would kill me, if he knew I was apologizing for him.'

'Don't worry,' said Clive. His voice was soft now, softer than she would have imagined that such a gruff, hearty, confident voice could sink to. 'I'm very good at secrets.'

'I didn't mean it was a secret.' Evie was sensitive to that word, these days. 'I just meant—'

Clive was doomed never to know what she meant. A terrible commotion began in the distance: loud bangs and shouts as if a riot had broken out in their tranquil retreat.

'Jon!' Paula went rigid at the revving noises and the inexplicable clang of some huge structure collapsing. Within a second Jon was at her side, arm around her, as if they'd been expecting just such a calamity.

'What the hell?' Mike led the charge through the house, adults and children and dogs careering over the black-and-white tiles of the hall to fling open the front door.

'We're being ram-raided!' shouted Scarlett, hurtling down the stairs in jim-jams and novelty slippers.

The gates at the end of the long, straight drive were laid out flat on the ground.

'Mum!' Tillie waded through the bodies to her mother. 'It's just some idiots, Mum.'

Evie held onto Mike's arm, holding him back, feeling how much he wanted to tear forward. 'Can somebody call the police?' she pleaded. A giant vehicle, its headlights blinding, was trundling over the eight-foot gates that Evie had so admired the day before, as if they were kindling.

'Hang on.' Clive went to the head of the steps and stood between two giant stone urns. Mike, shrugging Evie off, stood by him; Evie knew her husband was brave, but more than that, he was loath to let Clive take charge. 'Listen.' Clive cupped a hand around his ears.

'It's kids,' said Mike, relieved, angry and boiling with the need to do something.

Shouts and screams competed with the monstrous noise of enormous wheels. It was more drunken-escapade than killing-spree.

'Who are they?' Evie wondered aloud. 'Neighbourhood yobs?' She'd never used the word 'yobs' before; it felt very great-auntish.

'No,' said Clive, taking the steps slowly and plodding towards the mess of mangled ironwork and giant tyres. 'It's a London yob.' Flip-flops flip-flopping angrily, he yelled, 'ZANE! Turn that engine off, you damn fool!'

More screams and splutters. Then the engine died. The lights went out. And the holidaymakers, so terrified only moments ago, hurried up the drive to see Zane atop a massive tractor, its front wheels resting on the bespoke ironwork.

At the wheel of the tractor was a young blonde girl in bra, tutu and wellies. And there were other females – all similarly under-dressed, all brandishing tequila bottles, all singing a Rihanna song.

'So that's Zane,' said Scarlett. Evie knew that tone; Scarlett was impressed by the man-child who'd made such an absurd and expensive entrance.

'I don't understand,' gibbered Paula, clutching Amber to her as if they were about to be kidnapped. 'Who is he?'

'My stepson,' said Shen, hands on hips.

Dan crawled across the tangle of the flattened gates. 'This is AWESOME,' he proclaimed.

'Aw, innee sweet?' said one of the girls. There was, Evie noted, quite a lot of vomit in her hair extensions.

'Oh dear,' said Zane. 'We seem to have damaged this attractive gate.'

As his harem whooped at this bon mot, two things were obvious about the boy. One, he was the sort of drunk only achieved by conscientious day-long application to the full range of WKDs and Breezers. Two, he was off-the-scale handsome. Like a prince from a tale in the *Arabian Nights*, Zane had a strong nose, jutting lips and a long, sensual neck. His hair was as black as the night around them, his eyes equally dark, but with a glint. 'Oh, and hi, Dad.'

Clive jammed his hands into his pockets, then turned back up the drive without a word, only the vapour-trail of his cigar proof that he'd been there at all.

Unimpressed by good looks or toothy smiles, Mabel yelled, 'Put a top on!' at the tutu girl. She was, at eight years old, an accomplished prig.

Miles wasn't. 'No, don't – I like your boobies!' he told the girl, who nodded graciously at the compliment.

Glaring at Zane, Shen said, 'You've brought shame on your father.' From Evie, this would have sounded comic, but from Shen it sounded ominous.

'Lighten up, Stepmummy.' Zane threw an arm around the nearest girl.

Pulling off her heels to clamber over the wreckage, Shen screamed, 'Get down from there!' When Zane didn't move, she set about him with a shoe and the boy put up his arms to defend himself.

The girls in the tractor, of course, loved it; in their state, everything up to and including a nuclear strike was hilarious.

'Get off him, you mad old cow!'

Oooh, thought Evie. *Bad move*. Telling Shen what to do was never wise; calling her a 'cow' was unacceptable; calling her 'old' was lighting the blue touchpaper and retiring.

'Hey, you! Slut-face!' shouted Shen. 'You don't get to talk!' She pointed with such vehemence that the girl slammed the tractor into reverse.

'No,' yelled Mike, joining Shen on the wreckage. 'Turn off the engine, love. Come back and get it tomorrow.'

'My dad,' said the girl slowly, tutu wilting as the ramifications hit home, 'is going to kill me.'

'Good,' said Shen. 'If he needs any help, tell him I'm available.' She fixed her evil eye on Zane, hypnotizing him out of his seat. 'You. In the house. Now.'

As the party, keeping its distance from Zane as if he was radioactive, returned to the house, Evie glanced back to see Mike helping the girls down from the tractor. He'd be consoling and advising them to go straight home and 'fess up, she knew. This confrontation was chicken-feed, compared to what he dealt with at work. As usual, he was on the side of the underdog. Mike's heart bled for the whole world.

On the terrace, the serenity of earlier was replaced by a courtroom scene, with the accused slumped on an ornate garden chair.

'I'm so wasted,' slurred Zane.

Seeing him close up, as she brought him iced water from a miraculous tap in the fridge door, Evie revised her original opinion. *You're not drunk at all.* The tractor had been a set piece for the adults' benefit, as was this scene. Zane sat carefully arranged, the image of the bad boy caught in the act, one long leg stretched out in rolled-up chinos that revealed bare brown ankles. One fine-boned hand lay across his brow.

Pacing up and down, up and down, Clive had switched to whisky.

'You could have killed someone,' said Tillie, more wonderingly than accusatory.

'Yeah – myself hopefully,' said Zane.

'Oh, *please*,' laughed Tillie, going inside.

The girl's handle on Zane impressed Evie. For Scarlett, staring at him through her fringe, his handsomeness was all, but Tillie's attitude hinted at greater maturity. 'Dan!' She appealed to her son to stop recreating the night's events, with his scooter as the tractor, Patch as the passengers and his little sister as the gate. 'Enough, sweetie.'

All the while Shen circled Zane, Prunella in her arms, telling him what he was: a fool, a disgrace, a hooligan. She interspersed this with possible punishments. These ranged from the mundane ('no allowance for a month!') to the ambitious ('I will lock you in your room until 2020!'). She hammered him, like a tent peg, but he never even looked up.

'Cheeky little sod,' said Mike, rather enjoying the spectacle. He stood up, put a hand on Shen's shoulder. 'It's late. Why don't we pick this up in the morning, when young fella-me-lad's sobered up?'

'No!' said Shen. 'I want to shout at him all night. I want him to be sorry.'

'He's sorry.' Mike addressed Zane, making the boy lift his head for the first time since he'd entered the house. 'Aren't you?'

'Yeah,' said Zane, as if he'd taken a course in How to Annoy Parents with Simply the Tone of your Voice. 'Sure.'

'See?' Mike smiled. 'He's dying of sheer sorriness.' Bending to her ear, he said, 'Shen, let him sleep, and then go for the jugular tomorrow.'

Shen wavered on her heels. Her shoulders lowered. She was tired too. 'OK,' she said grudgingly. 'But he can't go to bed without some food in him.' She thrust Prunella into Zane's surprised arms. 'Here. Take her for a trot around the gardens. Make yourself useful for once. I'll rustle you up some noodles.'

'Well,' said Evie, standing up. 'He knows how to make an entrance.'

The noise Clive made was like a laugh. 'Hope he knows how to make an exit. He's on the first train home tomorrow.'

'Aw, come on,' began Mike, but got no further.

'He's staying,' said Shen. 'There's no way I'm sending him back to his mother so that she can say I can't deal with a teenage boy.' She stalked to the kitchen, where she banged a wok onto a burner and turned the flames high enough to burn a witch.

Climbing the stairs, Evie plodded in step with her husband, both of them sleepy from the sun and the wine and the drama.

'First-world problems . . .' said Mike in a sardonic undertone as they reached their door. 'When I compare what went on tonight with the stuff I see at the housing trust, I—'

Silenced by his wife's kiss, Mike put one arm around her and shut the door with his other.

The kiss was full of intent. Evie meant business. She'd had enough of an arm's-length relationship. Time to wrench his mind back to *them*. Once they'd mattered; now they were way down the eternal To Do list in both of their heads.

'Oh, OK.' Mike smiled, against her lips. 'I see.'

He kissed her back, and she felt the hardness of his chest and the strength of his arms circling her. Evie and Mike could always go from nought to sixty when the lights were off. They had this to come back to, yet much of the time they forgot about the engine at the heart of their marriage.

Need of the most urgent kind, coupled with the tenderest feelings of love, made Evie's fingers a blur as she tore at the buttons of his shirt. Why couldn't she pin down these feelings on the page? None of Lucinda Lash's countless sex scenes could compare to this tingling anticipation, when the air was electric and her flesh jumped.

Afterwards, suffused with love for her sexy beast of a

man, Evie gathered herself. He had a right to know about the escape she'd planned: the betrayal. *This is it*, she thought. There would never be the perfect time to tell him – he could never 'understand', she knew – but this crystalline, intimate moment was as near perfect as she could hope for.

As she shaped her lips to speak, Mike whacked her hard on the bottom and bounded out of bed. 'Gotta floss,' he called over his shoulder. 'I've got breath like a badger.' The room was suddenly illuminated like Wembley Stadium and the atmosphere was chased away into the corners. Sticking his head around the bathroom door at his naked wife, who lay there wondering what had become of her afterglow, Mike said, 'And you might think about shaving those legs, love. It was like being jumped by a gorilla.' He disappeared, and then reappeared to add, 'A gorgeous gorilla, obviously,' in case she felt insulted.

Evie pulled the covers over what had been, just seconds before, a voluptuous woman's body quivering with sensuality, but was now, apparently, a gorilla.

She knew Mike felt able to make jokes like that because he knew she'd understand. But lately – and how long was 'lately'? a month? six months? – their closeness had been erratic, like the signal on an old radio. There'd been buzzing interference, then a burst of perfect music, then more static.

Would it kill him to pay her a compliment?

Clive's earlier comment about her top was utterly beyond her husband. Mike would have to subvert such simple praise – say that the colour matched her varicose veins.

Evie turned over huffily and closed her eyes. If she was envying *that* marriage, then she and Mike really were in trouble.

Outside an owl hooted, and Shen shouted something, very loudly, about noodles.

DAY 3
Thursday, 13th August

dear snowy
why cant cats go on ther holidays? i want yu here for
cudling i had an ant on my finger
i love yu

from your owner mabel

x

From a window Evie watched the agitated stranger in checked shirt and gumboots gesticulate at Clive and point at Zane, who was skulking guiltily, like Patch after one of his skirmishes with a full bin bag.

Phrases drifted on the morning air, already sluggish with heat. 'Led astray,' the man shouted. 'Broken headlight.' And, finally, most damningly, 'Young London fool.'

When Clive's wallet appeared, the other man calmed down, as if sedated by the sight of the Queen's face, and soon he was reversing his tractor down the lane.

Downstairs, in a summery dress that looked so much better on the website's gaunt model, Evie said to Clive, 'He had a nerve. That daughter of his didn't need much leading astray.'

'Trouble happens around Zane.' Clive was philosophical. 'I'm used to footing the bill.' A horn tooted outside. 'That'll be the guys who made the gate. They're giving me an estimate for the repairs.'

'Clive's a fast worker,' mused Evie, drawn to the kitchen by the smell of coffee. She looked around for Mike, who'd been absent when she awoke. Driven away, perhaps, by her primate legs? Perversely she'd decided to be proud of her hairy limbs; she might plait them later, tie in a few pretty bows. 'How'd he get hold so quickly of the people who made the gate?'

'Who knows?' Shen was airy. 'My husband works in mysterious ways.'

Just as well Clive didn't seem to expect gratitude: Shen expected high levels of husbandly performance. To Evie, such can-do was impressive: she was accustomed to issuing minute, step-by-step instructions if she wanted Mike to pick up milk on his way home. She'd guided him through many a minimart on his phone, ignoring his tetchy this-is-not-my-job inflection.

A true alpha, Clive simply got on with it.

'They reckon they'll finish the repairs by the time we leave,' said Clive, reappearing. 'The owner's not happy, but I've placated him and promised it'll be good as new.'

He must have been up at dawn, making calls, thought Evie. *And the expense . . .*

'Take it out of Zane's allowance,' said Shen, stirring a pot of porridge so worthy it was practically singing hymns. She tapped Miles's pudgy hand as it crept towards the bowl of chocolate-coated rice puffs that Mabel was flooding with milk. 'No, darling. You'll outlive Mabel if you eat my breakfasts.'

'Maybe,' said Evie, grabbing the cereal box, 'but he'll be bored rigid during those long, extra, crispbread years.'

'If,' said Paula, at the threshold of the kitchen, 'there's any planet left for these poor orphans to inherit.'

'What my wife means,' said Jon, behind her, 'is: *Good morning, everybody.*'

As the Wellcome Manor ad-hoc clan gathered for a lingering, multi-course breakfast, Mike pored over one of his stash of leaflets. 'There's a working seventeenth-century mill a few miles up the road.'

'An actual mill? You. Are. Kidding.' Evie's irony whizzed over his head.

'You can watch the water-wheel turn,' he said, awestruck, as if watching a wheel turn was right up there with Disneyland for the modern child.

'*You* can watch it turn.' Shen poured out a white liquid containing no dairy, no fat and no fun. 'I'll power-walk around the grounds.' She reached out to Fang, who was arriving in Elizabetta's arms, as clean and wholesome as a scoop of ice cream. 'Hello, you! Kiss your daddy!'

Clive bent for his cheek to be messily kissed, never taking his eyes from the financial pages. 'Good morning, Baby-pops,' he said absent-mindedly.

'Gimme, gimme!' Evie held out her hands. She'd anticipated much Fang-tickling and smooching on this break, but the child only appeared at set times, dressed in her best, her black comma of hair brushed fastidiously over her forehead.

The younger ones buzzed about, snatching food, pinching each other, complaining bitterly, exclaiming suddenly – the usual, in fact. Evie sensed Amber's eagerness to join in, but when the child finally worked up the nerve, she mistimed it. Just as she leaned in to the little horde, the throng moved as one and stampeded, knocking her to the ground.

'Man down! Man down!' called Clive, as various hands dragged Amber back to her feet.

Amber, snivelling, darted behind Paula, who made no attempt to coax her daughter back to the others, but simply recited, 'Shush' and 'There, there'. It was Tillie who put a gentle, many-ringed hand on her sister's thin wrist and guided her to a stool.

'Here,' said Tillie. 'Take some of my toast.' She broke off a buttered corner, which Amber took gratefully, like a squirrel.

Mabel said, 'We can play dead bodies later, if you like.'

Best not to ask, thought Evie, glad the little ones were back on-track.

'Where's—' Before she even said his name, Evie saw him, leaning against the door jamb, watching them all. 'Zane! Come and join us!' She shoved Patch off the chair next to hers and patted it.

'Naw. I'm not a morning person.' Zane's head dipped, his hands thrust into the pockets of his slashed jeans.

Among the dishevelled heads and yawning gobs, he was a thing of great beauty. Naturally polished and poised, he rivalled Shen for glamour. Was the melancholy in his huge brown eyes another affectation? Evie couldn't tell. He certainly loved posing. Was the pout natural? The boy intrigued her.

Zane moved to let Scarlett enter, jumping out of the way as if electrocuted. She glided to the table and took a seat unobtrusively, reaching out a freckled hand to slide the cereal box towards her.

'Nice of you to join us,' said Mike.

'Da-ad . . .' said Scarlett, drawling so that her father could guesstimate how boring he was.

'We're nearly finished. How come you can't get out of your pit to eat with the group?'

'The *group*?' laughed Scarlett. 'What are you, Oasis?' Chomping toast, she sneaked peeks at Zane, sizing up his boy-band posture. When she realized her mother was watching her watch him, she transferred her attention to the ends of her hair, studying them up close, as if wondrous things were to be found in her split ends.

Paula spoke hurriedly, compulsively. 'Was anybody else kept awake by the sounds in the bushes last night?' Her pasty face was hopeful.

'God, no,' said Clive. 'I slept like a baby.'

'Not like *your* baby,' muttered Elizabetta, eyes firmly on the floor.

'There's nothing in the bushes.' Shen gave Paula a look that the woman was too self-absorbed to notice. 'You're imagining things. We all get spooked at night.'

'Mmm.' Paula wasn't pulling her weight with putting the children off the scent. The other adults instinctively knew better than to put ideas into their heads, which might take root and cause trouble later.

'Let's,' shouted Mabel, 'investigate the bushes!'

As they scampered off like a pack of small, pretty hyenas, Mike bellowed after them, 'We leave for the seventeenth-century watermill in half an hour!'

'God, Dad,' said Scarlett. 'As if.'

'Who,' shouted Evie after the children, 'wants to explore the village?'

There was a chorus of yeses. Evie's brainwave had won hands-down. 'Sorry, darling.' She laid a placatory hand on her husband's arm. 'It's cos they know I'm a soft touch in a sweet shop.'

'It's just sad that they're missing out on the water-wheel,' said Mike, smiling bravely.

'It's sadder that you really do think that,' smiled Evie.

'Careful, you.' Mike wagged a finger and lowered his voice. 'Don't make me spank you, Lucinda.'

'You'd have to catch me fir— Oh!' As Evie pulled away from Mike, she careered into Zane who was – could it be true? – clearing the table. 'Sorry, Zane.'

'Leave that,' yapped Shen. 'You'll break them.'

The boy put down a smeared plate and loped out into the sun.

'Why do teenagers all walk as if they've got the world on their shoulders?' laughed Mike.

'Because they believe they have.' Evie watched the boy recede into the garden's shimmering greens. 'What I'd give to be that age again.'

'Not me.' Mike was terse, downing the last of his tea with a manly slurp and banging down the mug. 'Jon!' He hailed his partner in dull crime. 'You're up for the watermill, I bet!'

'Sorry, no.' Jon looked regretful.

In the right light, thought Evie, *Jon could be handsome.* He was standard-issue English bloke, tall and long-limbed, with thinning fair hair and blue eyes blinking behind his glasses. It was rarely the right light for Jon, however; he was too recessive, too keen on camouflage.

'I've planned a long walk,' he added, 'A solitary one' – just in case. He nodded his goodbyes and was gone, leaving Paula to stare after him like a mongrel tied up outside Lidl.

'Come on.' Evie took the woman's hand and led Paula out to the terrace. 'Where are these bushes?'

'There.' Paula pointed straight at a bed planted with wiggy shrubs of varying heights. Evie recognized conviction when she heard it; Paula was sure of very little, but about *this* she was certain.

'Let's take a look.' As Evie guessed, Paula hung back, allowing her to take the lead. 'Can't see any footprints.' Evie squatted, racking her brains, dredging up all the crime programmes she'd sat through. 'No broken branches. No sign of activity.' She straightened up. 'Can you think why anybody would want to lurk in the bushes?'

'To watch,' said Paula immediately, her face bloated, as if full of backed-up tears.

'To watch what?'

'Me. Us.' Paula shook her head. 'I can't make it sound sensible. Jon's right, I shouldn't try.' She bent her mouth into a horrible shape that might pass for a smile in a horror movie. 'You're right. Nobody was here.' She walked away, presumably aiming for a jaunty air, but attaining only demented.

Evie toed the dirt with her shoe. Avid watching of Scandi-noir had her half-expecting to find a crumpled cigarette packet or a clump of hair, but there was nothing, unless you counted one of Patch's curiously circular droppings, and she'd rather not.

'Come on, you lot, if you're coming!' Evie loved shouting for the children. They often complained that she shouted for them to come to the table when they were already seated. 'Zane!' she called, seeing the boy back away. 'You joining us?'

'Naw,' said Zane. 'I'll hang around here.'

'Hang around!' Shen harassed the porridge pot under the hot tap. 'That's all the boy can do.'

It occurred to Evie that Clive had yet to speak directly to his son.

'On the front step in ten mins!' boomed Evie.

'Mu-um,' said Mabel, from nipple-height. 'We're right here.'

The Wellcome Manor brochure was airy about the village. It was 'a few minutes' walk', apparently, down 'pretty country lanes'. With four young children in an untidy crocodile, the lanes weren't so much pretty as lethal. Country drivers put their pedals to the metal: cars zipped by so fast that the kids were flattened into the bushes.

'How much longer?' Mabel had been whingeing since they were still on the drive.

'Nearly there.' A handy maternal lie, this sprang easily to Evie's lips. 'Shall we sing something?' Imagining a hearty chorus of something traditional, she was overruled; they preferred pop songs. A mere two lines into each suggestion and Evie had to yell, 'Stop! Think of another one!' Their innocent voices trilling about 'ho's' and 'grinding' was too much to bear.

'Is this it?' Dan seemed disappointed with the village's Norman church, picturesque green and quaint lamp posts.

'What were you expecting?' Evie smiled.

'A lovely shopping centre.' Dan was dejected. 'These shops are all out in the weather, like the olden days.'

'Can we feed the ducks?' Mabel gurned desperately, her entire happiness suddenly dependent on duck-feeding.

Sweating in the rain jacket Paula had wrestled her into, 'just in case', Amber half-screamed, 'Not the ducks!', as if the feathered fatsos waddling around the village pond were man-eaters.

'Maybe later.'

The proper, traditional sweet shop shooed away all thoughts of ducks or malls. Even Evie fell into a reverie, going up and down the shelves, savouring the names of the sugary mood-enhancers. *Humbugs. Black Jacks. Sherbet Dip Dabs.*

In charge of the spending money, Dan was ruthless. 'You can't *afford* a million chocolate mice,' he told Mabel. 'You've got fifty pee.'

Coiled in a jar, emanating calories and straightforward joy, the liquorice shoelaces pitched Evie down a time-tunnel.

She hadn't believed that Mike, at the advanced age of twenty-one, had never eaten a liquorice lace. 'You serious?' she'd laughed, opening the crackling, cheap paper bag. 'Here.'

Licking it uncertainly, he'd risked a tiny bite, then wolfed the whole lot down. 'They're fabulous.'

'So you really never ate sweets, when you were little?'

In this blast from the past, Evie was all in black, a Nineties vixen in a bandage skirt, ruched top and clompy shoes. Mike was slim – God, *so* slim – and his hair was cropped, the better to show off the finely made bones of his face. His eyes . . . back then, staring into Mike's clear, slightly hurt-looking eyes had been her favourite hobby.

That was the moment he'd opened up about his childhood. On the pavement, outside a newsagent's. His shoulders lowered. His voice dropped to an urgent murmur.

When he'd finished talking, even though she was a gauche and fairly useless twenty-year-old, Evie had understood why the telling of his tale made Mike so emotional.

'There's no need to be *ashamed*.' She had lifted his chin with her finger and kissed his lips. Supermodel-plump, they tasted of liquorice.

'I like this village,' said Dan now, after they'd taken in the sweet shop and the fudge shop. 'Can we live here?'

'We have to live near Daddy's work,' said Evie. 'Ooh, look.' She pointed to a bow-fronted shop window. 'How about we pop in there?'

'No!' Dan backed away, a vampire confronted with a string of garlic. 'You can't make me!'

'Oh, but I can.'

The girls needed no prompting. They *loved* clothes shops.

'Come up, if you want, Zane.'

'I don't want.'

'Fine.' Scarlett giggled over at Tillie, who didn't giggle back. They'd brought some of Wellcome Manor's uncountable cushions from the house to the treehouse. They'd lit a candle, even though it was bright. Books were scattered. A bead necklace lay coiled like a cheerful snake.

'He really, really wants to come up.' Scarlett looked down at Zane meandering about the base of the tree, scuffing the grass with his spotless trainers.

'Why doesn't he, then?' The newcomer didn't seem to intrigue Tillie, although the fact that he intrigued Scarlett *did* intrigue her. 'I mean, either climb up or sod off, yeah?'

The thought of Zane sodding off grazed a sharp edge over Scarlett's good mood. She and Tillie hadn't talked much, yet. They'd merely, under adult scrutiny, herded together. She knew that Tillie attended a sixth-form college in London, and had been at a mixed comp back in the vague wherever that none of the Browns talked about, before Amber's arrival halfway through the spring term at St Ag's. To Scarlett, marooned in a girls-only sixth form, Zane was an exotic specimen, a gem glittering in the dreary fog of this dreaded fortnight. 'D'you think he's hot?'

'Do I what?' Tillie made a horrified face. A slapped-in-the-face-with-a-wet-fish face. 'I think he's an idiot!'

'Oh.' Scarlett had hoped for common ground.

'Why?' Tillie looked interested at last; she sat up on her cushion, alert. 'Do *you*? You do! You fancy him. Oh my God.'

'I don't,' said Scarlett quickly. Partly because this was the kind of information only to be shared with your bestest bestie – and Tillie wasn't even a worstie – but also because she wasn't sure what she felt about Zane. The sight of him made her tingle; she couldn't understand why everybody hadn't shouted in unison, 'Look at his amazing lips!' the moment he arrived. She'd already started working out how to discover if he had a girlfriend. But she hadn't really spoken to Zane yet. She needed to know more about him. Then she'd discover if he just made her tingle or if she wanted more. There was a difference. 'I think he's fit, though.'

'Fit?' Tillie wrinkled her nose. 'He's too busy looking in the mirror to notice us, Scar.'

Nobody ever called her that. Scarlett didn't correct Tillie, because she didn't know how to do it without being rude, and the careful, clever girl was spikey; Scarlett sensed that one comment could turn Tillie off for good. And Scarlett *needed* Tillie; two weeks was soooooo long to be surrounded by the hideously old and the ludicrously young. So she put up with her new nickname, even though it brought back memories she successfully suppressed.

Scar.

The treehouse trembled. Zane was climbing the rickety rope ladder.

'It looks lovely on you, Dan.' Evie was firm, ignoring the look on the face sticking out of the Breton-striped hoodie. 'We'll take it.'

The small pile of clothing on the counter was unnecessary and would have to be smuggled past Mike, but Evie found that spending twenty-four hours a day in the presence of Shen and her limitless wardrobe had affected her. The contrast between Miles's pristine blue dungarees and Dan's chain-store jeans was more apparent out here in the countryside, without other kids to bring down the mean average. A few pertinent, pricey purchases in this chichi boutique would narrow the gap.

'I love my new dress.' Mabel swished the crisp floral cotton, her Crocs clattering on the shop floorboards. 'Don't you wish you had a new dress, Amber?'

'Mm-hmm.' Amber nodded, consoling herself with a Dip Dab.

'I can't buy you clothes without your mummy's permission,' said Evie, in a gentle voice. This child was like tissue paper: she might tear, if handled roughly. 'But I can buy you *this*.' She popped a hairband, complete with fabric flower, onto Amber's head.

'Oh, it's gorgeouth!' The little girl wriggled happily.

'Can I have one?' Mabel was nothing if not predictable.

'No, that's Amber's special thing,' said Evie.

'You can lend it,' said Amber.

'You're a very kind woman,' said Mabel. 'I wish *I* wore glasses.'

As Evie pixelated the total and punched in her PIN number, she asked, 'Who's hungry?'

Every hand shot up, even the shop assistant's.

'Is there a sushi bar?' asked Miles.

'Maybe.' Evie hesitated. This was a truly evil step to take. 'But I noticed a burger bar . . .'

If the children had been strong enough to carry her shoulder-high out onto the cobbles, they would have done so.

All three of them looked resolutely in different directions.

Tillie looked out of the porthole that served as a window.

Scarlett looked at a mirror hanging on the raw plank wall, which gave her a view of the back of Zane's head.

Zane looked at the floor.

A tune hissed tinnily from an iPod.

'I like this track,' said Scarlett.

'S'OK,' said Zane.

When he spoke, his lips were, thought Scarlett, as plump as a bouncy castle. And they promised the same brand of bouncy fun.

Stop it, Scarlett! she told herself. *Stop it stop it stop it!*

'What was that whole thing with the tractor?' asked Tillie. She sounded amused.

'Something to do.' Zane shifted, looked her full in the

face. The effect was quite something, as if he was lit from within. 'I mean, this is nowhere, you know. It's dead here.'

'Don't you think it's beautiful?' Tillie, still amused, seemed immune to the full wattage of Zane's allure.

'Yeah, well, it's green and everything.' Zane looked at the floor again. 'I like cities, though. I like to run with my mates.'

'Me too,' said Scarlett.

'Yeah,' said Tillie, kicking her foot gently. '*You too*.'

Around the smaller ones, Dan regressed. With nobody to see him (his mum didn't count), he applied himself whole-heartedly to the swings and the roundabout and the slide, tucked away on the corner of the village green.

Her conscience troubling her – it was a busy creature, these days – Evie reassured herself that she hadn't asked Miles to lie to his mother, not exactly. She'd said, 'Shall we keep this from the others, in case they get jealous?' and Miles had agreed, along with the rest of them. Now they worked off their E-number energy on the playground equipment, and Evie nibbled a liquorice lace and recollected Mike's halting story back on 7 May 1995. She remembered the date, because later that evening he told her he loved her.

They'd been crossing an untidy London park, the sort that erupts in the midst of streets: a burst of tarnished green.

'I'm not like you,' he said, the collar of his leather jacket

– a maroon blouson thing, which Evie would soon banish to a charity shop – turned up.

'How d'you mean?' Evie studied his face, enjoying the firm grasp of his fingers. Mike wasn't one of those guys who'd pick up your hand and then go all sissy on you – he maintained a strong grip, as if she was a balloon and might fly away, if he faltered. 'You weren't born a woman or something, were you?' They'd been talking about light, silly things – their favourite Blur tracks, *Braveheart* versus *Sense and Sensibility* – and she didn't realize he'd made a U-turn.

'You're so confident. You're so brave.'

'Am I?' That was news to Evie. 'I chickened out of returning that cardi to Marks and Sparks.'

'You're brave in an ordinary way. You just get up and, I dunno, you *trust* the day ahead. I don't, you see.' Mike stopped and looked at her urgently. 'I don't trust. Didn't you notice that about me?'

'Not really and . . . *ow*!' Evie looked down at their entwined hands; her fingers were mangled in his.

'Sorry.' Mike released her, but she eased their hands back together.

'Explain, Mikey.'

How long was it since she'd called him Mikey?

'You're normal.' He ignored the face she pulled. 'Seriously, you are. You have a mum, a dad, a big brother, two little sisters. There's milk in the fridge and a *Radio Times* on the coffee table. You get told off if you get up late, and you moan when it's your go to wash up. All these things are gifts, Evie. Gifts from the universe, to help you know you belong. Me, I never had a home. I was *in* a home. It's completely fucking different.' He looked at her quickly. He rarely swore in front of her, and Evie guessed why: he feared she'd go off him.

'Mike,' she said softly, but he was barging ahead with his story, walking faster, so that she had to scamper on her thick-soled lace-ups to keep pace with him.

'My mum was sixteen or something, when she had me, and her parents threw her out, and she never said who my dad was, but they think he might have been Irish. Ha!' His laugh was horribly short and unhappy. 'Fancy that. I might be Irish, but I might not. I could be Turkish or Scottish, or from Mars. Anyway, I was taken into care when I was a week old, and I was fostered. Just until some lovely smiley couple came and carried me away to their mansion, you know?'

They'd reached an ornamental pond full of shopping trollies, but Mike strode on over the bridge, his audience beside him.

'Only that didn't happen. Eight different foster homes. Then the Mitchells took me in. They split up. I went back to the home. Then the Camerons fostered me. He lost his job and got depressed, and sent me back. It kept *almost* happening for me. So I lived in a big house with ten other children and our care workers. There was no abuse, there were no beatings. But nobody tucked me in. There was a lock on the fridge. The adults had rotas and couldn't wait to get away at the end of their shifts.' He halted suddenly and glared at Evie. 'Want to know when I'm most envious of normal people? When they say they're like their dad, or they have hair like their mum, or something. I have no idea whether I'm like my family. Because they're just . . .' He swallowed, looked up at the sky. 'They're not there.'

'You're as normal as me,' said Evie. 'You're ten times as kind as me. You're more thoughtful. You're . . .' It felt too soon in their relationship to say how much lovelier he was than any other boy she'd ever been out with. 'You're special.'

'Don't say that.' Mike sounded so sad. 'I don't want to be. I want to be ordinary. I don't want this information I've got.'

'What information?' He'd lost Evie.

'That the world is unkind,' he said. 'That there's no safety net.'

'Mum!' shouted Mabel now. 'It's all right if me and Amber tie Miles to the slide, isn't it?'

'No, darling, it sort of isn't.' Evie emerged from the past and stood up to reclaim her charges. 'Who's up for an ice cream on the way home?'

'And this is your life-line.' Scarlett traced the lightly etched channel. 'You're going to live a long, long time.'

'Tell him how many children he's going to have.' Tillie wasn't, apparently, reading the book she held; she was keeping an eye on Scarlett and Zane.

'You know how to do that, don't you?' When Zane demurred, Scarlett took his hand in her own. It was dry, warm. He gave off heat, despite his fey physicality.

Shoulder-to-shoulder with him on a pile of cushions, she fervently wished her mates could see her. 'Look. Beneath your little finger, here.' Their heads were close together. His quiffy black do and her blonde stack. 'See these upright lines? They're your children.'

'O . . . K.' Zane was dubious.

'Let's see. Three. Or maybe four.'

He closed his fingers over hers. She didn't dare look up. It felt way wilder than all the stuff she'd done with her last boyfriend.

Her only boyfriend.

'Your nails,' she said, noticing them, peering closer. They were bitten to the quick, ugly. She held on, as Zane tried to tug his hand away. 'You're not as tough as you look, are you, Zane Little? You're shy.' She risked a giggle, not sure if the boy was as haughty as his face alleged. 'You're a sensitive soul.'

With a *tsk*, Zane snatched his hand away. Then, gently, he put it back.

'Cassis,' mispronounced Dan. 'And meringue. No. Wait. Lemon sorbet.'

'I want chocolate,' said Mabel. 'But not horrid chocolate. Nice chocolate.'

'What's a pis-tar-shee-o?' Amber scratched her new hair-band in confusion.

The ice cream was available in endless flavours. Evie explained what stracciatella was. She explained what limoncello was. She didn't explain what maraschino was; she left it to the hair-netted young woman behind the counter, standing patiently with her scoop, and handed Dan a ten-pound note, saying, 'Pay up, sweetie, I'll be outside.'

Oh, the blessed peace. Four children feels like forty children, when you're the sole adult. Evie looked about her, savouring the village's super-Englishness: bunting, window boxes and, on a chalkboard in a frame: *We serve Devon's best cream tea*.

Even Devon's worst cream tea would be acceptable to Evie. The tables on the pavement were peppered with tiered cake-stands and pompous-looking teapots. Cream tea endured, unchanging and reliable. It was sweet, in both senses of the word. The eager, lip-smacking cream-tea disciples at each table covered the whole spectrum. Evie saw young people, oldish people and downright doddery people, all diving in, putting first dibs on their favoured sarnie, accusing their companions of hogging the clotted cream.

Seeing a familiar figure among the doilies made Evie squint. It *was* her. Miss Pritchett was everybody's favourite teacher at St Agatha's; renowned for her groovy, yet conservative clothes, today she was bare-shouldered as she dolloped cream and poured tea.

The kids'll scream! thought Evie, glancing back into the ice-cream emporium to see Dan picking up the change.

Miss Pritchett shaded her eyes against the sun and craned her neck to receive a kiss on the lips from a tall man, who took the seat next to her, scraping it along the pavement to get closer to her.

The children barrelled out, licking and exclaiming.

'This way.' Evie twirled them neatly in the other direction. 'Last one home's a pair of pants.'

It was easy to overlook Elizabetta. Shen would look up and there she was.

'How long have you been there?' Shen rose from her yoga mat on the brick stable floor.

'A minute, madam,' said Elizabetta from the doorway. 'Fang has her nap, and Miles is out with Mrs Herrera. Do you need me?'

'Go have some fun.' Shen rolled up her mat, tightly. 'Jump in the pool or something.'

'I bake some bread,' said Elizabetta, slipping away.

A burst of feminine giggles, and two girls fled past the stable door. Hot on their heels was Zane. He looked in, his hooded dark eyes on Shen's.

'Is Dad here?'

'In a gym? Hardly. Are you annoying Tillie and Scarlett?'

'You'd have to ask them,' said Zane.

He seemed to have nothing more to say, yet he didn't move. 'Have a go on the equipment,' suggested Shen, flinging a loose tee over her racer-back vest.

'Can't be bothered,' said Zane.

'Can you be bothered to peel vegetables for dinner?'

'No.'

'Shame. Because that's what you're doing. Move!'

Zane did as he was told. Over by the pool, Scarlett scanned the horizon for him, before finding his meek figure tailing Shen to the house.

'Come on!' shouted Tillie from the water, and Scarlett jumped in, fully clothed.

Fit to burst with her news, Evie scattered the children to the four corners of the property and went in search of her husband. She dashed into the kitchen and stopped short, staring.

A woman she'd never seen before, a stout woman in an apron, was bent over the sink, scrubbing a dish.

'Oh,' said Evie, and the woman turned around.

Evie would later blush at the fact that she'd suspected the cleaner of being a ghost. Wellcome Manor was so big and so old that it didn't seem fantastical to imagine a time-slip in the kitchen, but all the same. This woman, with her Metallica tee-shirt, was flesh-and-blood.

'Won't be a minute, love,' the cleaner said affably. 'Then you'll have the place to yourselves again.'

A skinny girl wandered out from the utility room, trailing a Hoover like a wayward pet. Beyond the glass wall, a man in overalls wielded shears.

'Thank you.' Evie bobbed back out. 'You're doing a great job.'

'Aw, thanks,' said the woman.

Spotting her prey mooching along the hall, Evie hustled

her husband into the home cinema. Taking him by the shoulders, she said, 'You'll never guess what I saw in the village. Not in a million years.' She paused before saying, 'Well, go on then: guess!'

'You said I couldn't.'

'I meant – oh, look, just guess.'

'Um.' Mike looked properly pained. Evie knew he was looking at the screen over her shoulder and wondering which brand it was. 'I don't know, Evie. A murder?'

'A murder?' She didn't stop to contemplate the stupidity of his guess. 'No, I saw . . .' She took a deep breath. The implications were huge. 'I saw Jon kiss Miss Pritchett. Outside a cafe. Proper kiss. Full on the lips. Like lovers.' It had been tender, sweet, *real*. And adulterous.

'Eh?' Mike looked dubious. 'Is this like that time you saw Matt Damon in Waitrose?'

'No, it is *not*.' Evie was sick of being reminded of that. Besides, it was more the shelf stacker's fault than hers: it's not fair to go around looking that much like Matt Damon. 'It was Jon. And it was Miss Pritchett.'

'Blimey.' Mike scratched his head.

'No, not *blimey*.' Men were so unskilled at gossip. 'Don't you see what this means?' She needed an extreme reaction to validate her own. 'Jon's cheating on Paula. With the kids' teacher. It's every brand of horrible.'

'Well, yes. But you said yourself there was something wrong. Maybe Paula knows, and they're working it out.'

'The only thing Jon's working out is his lips.' Dissatisfied with her wordplay, Evie was travelling too fast to come up with better. 'I don't think Paula knows. She probably suspects, though.' The woman's anxiety was explicable. 'It's terrible.'

'And none of our business,' said Mike. 'The watermill was fascinating, by the way.'

'More fascinating than the affair going on under our noses, behind our back?' Evie despaired of him. 'Doesn't it matter to you that your child's teacher is fooling around with a parent?'

'Maybe she does one dad a term,' suggested Mike, enjoying Evie's annoyance. 'I'll put my name down on the rota.' He yawned, rubbed his nose. 'Do you have any idea just how integral water-power was to the development of rural Britain?'

Before today, Evie had no opinion about watermills; now, as Mike chuntered on about interactive displays and the excellent coffee in the on-site cafe, they were her least-favourite topic of all.

'Breathlessly, she touches his . . .' *Nope. Maybe* 'her skin glows where his clever fingers had caressed . . .' *God, no. Sounds like a nut allergy.*

Lucinda Lash's muse was being coy. Evie sat back from the laptop, her lips in the grimmest of lines. Here she was, in paradise, with all the space and peace she could desire, her kids being tended by responsible adults, her chores managed by elves, with hot and cold running champagne, and she was suffering a terminal case of writer's block.

Back home, when she had to squeeze in her writing

around the nooks and crannies of her busy days, stories flowed. She could barely keep up with the 'screams of ecstasy' and the 'flurries of naked limbs'.

Deleting the page, Evie tried a different tack. She'd never written in the first person before, avoiding it because it felt too personal. Desperate times called for desperate measures, however: 'I look beseechingly at him and he knows what I am begging him for.'

Hmm. Not a bad opener. She typed on, slowly at first, then faster, then faster still, until – like her first-person heroine – she peaked and slumped back, exhausted.

Reading back over the racy scene, Evie realized she'd simply put down, word-for-word, what she and Mike had done last night in the wide, rumpled bed.

Dicing a potato slowly, methodically, was meditative. Evie relished Wellcome Manor's Japanese knives, their thin, deadly edges so unlike the blunt bastards she wielded at home.

Shen swept in. 'A potato,' she said, taking something beige out of the fridge, 'is basically a hand grenade.'

'I'm sautéing them,' said Evie defiantly. 'In lovely, lovely oil.'

'On your hips be it,' said Shen. Peering at a recipe on her iPad, she began to chop green things, and to peel other green things and grind yet another green thing with a pestle. 'Anything exciting in the village?'

'Various olde-worlde opportunities to spend money.

Lovely houses. Ice cream.' Evie hesitated. It was on the tip of her tongue to tell Shen about Jon and Miss Pritchett. She told Shen more or less *everything*, but a protective feeling towards Paula held her back. 'Standard chocolate-box stuff. It'd make you think: *God, I could so live here*, but if you swapped London for it you'd be on the cooking sherry in a fortnight.'

'Ha!' A cloud of cigar smoke announced Clive. 'True, true.' He ignored Shen's flapping, shooing hands as he nicked a sliver of green pepper. 'Fancy a snifter? I feel the need to open a bottle of something cold, after my hard day's sunbathing.'

A cork popped. Glasses chinked. *This*, thought Evie, *is Clive's soundtrack: the theme-tune of the good life.*

'Remember that, Wifey dearest?' He gestured at Shen's screensaver, a shot of their little family on a snowy mountaintop, all bobble hats and grins. 'Klosters. Last Christmas. We almost bought a chalet there.' Where other people brought home a souvenir tea towel, Clive nabbed real estate. 'D'you ski, Evie?'

'God, no,' said Evie. She was far too accident-prone to attempt winter sports; she'd break her leg simply phoning the travel agent. She leaned over to peer at the snap. 'Look at you all, up in the clouds,' she said dreamily. Far above mundane matters; far above poisonous secrets from loved ones.

'That's the top of the Rinerhorn,' said Shen. 'A really challenging ski run. I loved it.'

'She thrives on danger,' said Clive, admiringly, rueful.

'Tell me about it,' said Evie. 'I'd rather play Russian

roulette than accept a lift from her.' She scrutinized the photograph, bending over it, neglecting her dicing: Clive and Shen beamed toothily, Fang in her daddy's arms, Miles on Shen's lap, suspended in a cold, clean sky. Evie leaned in closer. Clive held Fang with the same insouciance as he bandied magnums of champagne, but the arm that Shen held around her son was tense, tight. Inside that padded glove, Evie knew, the knuckles would be white.

Shen always held on tight to what she valued. Her brand of love was red-hot, but Evie knew how safe it felt in the glow of its flames. Back during the turbulent year that Mike hated to mention, Shen had held onto the Herreras with the same ferocity that she held onto Miles in the photo, and with the same audacious style. *Who me?* said the smile in the photo. *Me, scared of heights? Me, scared to relax my grip on my son? Are you cray-cray?* Shen never admitted fear and she never harked back to 2009, when she'd propped Evie up.

Just as well the two friends had such history to lean back on, otherwise Evie would have brained Shen with a ladle as she said, 'That wooden chopping board you're using is more or less a dating website for bacteria.'

'Good,' said Evie. 'Bacteria deserve love, just like the rest of us.'

'I can't understand why the kids had no appetite.' Shen set down the glasses. The grown-ups' nightly terrace wine-binge was now a habit, no questions asked, with everybody taking up their usual position. Jon was the only absentee, still not home from his lengthy 'walk', and eagerly awaited by Paula with the same yearning anticipation Patch exhibited when the kids were due home from school.

'Odd,' agreed Evie, her face carefully shielded by her helpfully messy hair. All four little ones were excellent conspirators, not one of them letting slip about their lunchtime burgers.

'Be careful!' called Paula, as the eight-year-olds thundered past on their way to an assignation with a family of snails they'd discovered in one of the shrubberies and had named.

'They should put that on her tombstone.' Shen downed half her glass.

They should put 'Don't do it like that' on yours, thought Evie, also drinking deep of oblivion-juice. Every move she had made as they prepared dinner had been dissected. Criticism was to be expected with Shen; she was the type to take Jesus to task, for the shoddy way he plated up the Last Supper. Usually there was an escape hatch; Evie could stand up, announce, 'Right! Gotta get back to mine!' and flee the det. 6-bed for her own terraced 3-bed (slight subs'dnce). Here, however, the comments had just kept coming, like bats.

'Instead of salting the carrots, why not just shoot us all.'

'If you slice the cabbage thickly, it retains more vitamin C.'

'I've swapped the squash for mineral water. You'll thank me, when your children's teeth don't fall out.'

'Paula, darling!' Clive was jocular, man-of-the-house-ish, 'have a glass of wine. It's good for you.'

'No, no, better not, just in case.' Paula shook her head, as if he'd offered her pig's blood.

'Another possibility for the tombstone,' said Shen, out of the corner of her neat, pretty mouth.

'Lay off.' That came out a little more sharply than it had sounded in Evie's head. Perhaps if Shen knew about the affair, her attitude towards Paula would change, but Evie couldn't risk it. Instead, she made a bold move and stood up from her allocated spot and joined Paula, taking Jon's empty lounger.

'Look at them,' said Paula, without preamble, as if glad to share the jittery monologue in her head. 'Tillie and your girl and that Zane boy. Climbing down from the treehouse. I mean, think of the splinters. And you get Lyme disease from infected ticks.'

As Shen hummed 'Always Look on the Bright Side of Life', Mike called over helpfully, 'I'll inspect them for circular rashes if you like, Paula. I saw a video all about Lyme disease at the mill.'

Dreading tonight's pillow-talk, which was likely to be heavily mill-based, Evie looked at the approaching trio and, unlike Paula, saw no doom or disaster. She could see only three teenagers, flushed and happy, having the aimless fun their age group excelled at. Or, maybe, *two* teenagers having aimless fun. Tillie hung behind, arms folded, looking not scornful, not bored – what *was* that expression? It was veiled; the girl was hard to judge.

'Jon!' Paula stood, eyes gleaming, as if her husband had

returned from the Vietnam War instead of the village. 'Thank God,' she said.

'Hello, hello, all.' Jon made his customary curt greetings. 'I see you've eaten. I'll go and shower.'

Wash Miss Pritchett off your skin, thought Evie.

'He doesn't like,' said Paula apologetically, as her husband's footsteps receded, 'being around people.'

With an arched waxed eyebrow, Shen commented, 'Then he's on the wrong holiday.'

The teenagers reached the terrace. 'Dad,' drawled Zane, 'how come it's punishable by death when I get pissed, but you and *her*,' he cocked his head at Shen, 'get hammered every night?'

'Her?' Clive coldly repeated the word.

'Leave it, leave it,' muttered Shen, putting her glass to her lips, then hurriedly replacing it on the table.

'Get out of my sight, Zane,' said Clive. The lack of heat in his voice gave the command twice its impact.

'Fine with me.' Zane slouched off into the house, hands rammed even further into his low-slung pockets.

Scarlett flashed Clive a look that ricocheted off his sunburnt bald patch, then showily followed Zane, all stomp and elbows. She slowed by her mother. 'That's the first thing he's said to Zane all day.'

Hesitating for only a second, Tillie returned to the orbit of her own mother, who had already called Amber to her side.

'Am-*ber*,' wheedled Mabel. 'Come and play.'

'It's too late to be gallivanting,' said Paula, her arm tightening about the girl sprawled on her lap.

Gently Evie said, 'I really think it's safe out there, Paula. Nothing's in the bushes.'

'You don't know that,' said Paula, her voice a whiplash.

'Well, no, but . . .' Evie gave up for the moment. She was spinning various plates, and right now she had no energy to spend on this one.

Comings and goings on the terrace.

The children ran out of steam and flopped indoors.

Patch stole a bag of crisps.

Nuts appeared.

The elder Browns returned, their faces masks of counterfeit good humour.

The day dribbled to an end, and night draped itself about the shoulders of the trees and switched off the view of the hills.

His water-wheel facts finally used up, Mike went for a stroll. Shen plopped into the vacant seat beside Evie and said, low-voiced, 'Those brogues on Jon?' She nodded to where the man reclined, eyes closed. 'Three hundred quid a pair.'

'Your point?'

'That tweedy jacket? Savile Row. At least a grand.'

'I hope you intend to stop before you price his underpants.'

'I'm just saying,' said Shen, 'those understated clothes cost more than you think. A lot more than a *minicab driver* would spend.'

Refusing to rise to the bait, even though Jon was indeed the least likely cabbie she'd ever met, Evie said, 'They live very simply, Shen. You've got it wrong.'

'I'll tell you something I *haven't* got wrong.' Shen moved in closer; this was the good stuff. 'They don't sleep together.'

'You can't know that.' Evie wondered, fleetingly, if Shen bugged the bedrooms.

'Cleaners,' said Shen, tapping the side of her nose, 'know *everything*. Somebody slept on the chaise longue last night, up in the third-best bedroom.'

A loud howl came from the gardens, turning every head towards the darkness. Emerging from an outbuilding, Mike bellowed to the figures on the terrace, 'I found a snooker table!'

'I thought . . .' Paula sat back down and kept whatever she'd thought to herself.

'I'll give you a game.' Jon strode over to the barn as the others settled back into their positions, Evie pulling her chair close to Shen's.

'I've got a question.' Evie inclined her head towards Elizabetta, who was dangling Fang at Clive for a goodnight kiss. 'Why the sexy nanny? With Clive's track record for trading in wives for a younger model?'

'He'd never do that to me.'

'So he's changed?'

'No. He's well aware of my martial-arts skills.' Shen chopped the air. She took an aikido class twice a week and was given to boasting of how she could 'take' any man. 'He wouldn't dare cross me.'

Along with cellulite, and whether or not to open a

second bottle, their marriages were two of Evie and Shen's favourite topics for discussion. Evie shared the good, the bad and the frankly unsavoury. Shen, however, talked flippantly about her relationship. Evie often wished Shen would be more open, more *real*; she suspected there was more to know, and sometimes Evie felt she was failing Shen by not dragging it out of her. Buoyed by the holiday vibe, she pushed a little. 'Seriously, though. He's done it twice already. Divorce, I mean.'

'Exactly.' Black eyes gleaming, Shen was like a doll in this lighting. A doll with a head for commerce. 'And both times he was taken to the cleaner's. Clive can't go through that again.'

'That's the least-romantic reason for staying together that I can imagine.'

'Are *you* lecturing me on romance?' Shen dipped her chin. 'I see you, you know, jumping a foot in the air every time your phone buzzes.'

'It's a fair cop. But pull those claws back in, sistah. I'm genuinely interested.'

Eventually Shen said, 'Look, I know everybody thinks Clive has a roaming eye and I'm a gold-digger, but when we met, it was more than just sex and a black credit card. It was love. I fell in love.'

Did Clive? The question that sprang to mind was so immediate and so disloyal it took Evie by surprise. 'That's sweet.'

'No, there was nothing sweet about it,' said Shen, with a wicked movement of her eyebrows. 'It was hot and heavy. He pursued me.'

'I bet you didn't run all that fast.'

'He's out of shape, I didn't want to get him out of breath.' Shen sank back into herself, remembering. 'We couldn't get enough of each other. It was secret at first, obviously. Hotel rooms. A trip to Paris, where we never left the suite. We just *devoured* each other.' She blinked. 'God, sorry, Evie. TMI?'

'Nah.' Evie liked this red-blooded version of events.

'And then suddenly I was pregnant. I know what the Ubers say, but it really was an accident. There was no need to trap Clive. I already had him.'

'It sped things up, though.' Evie wondered how Clive had broken the news to wife #2.

'Yeah. Suddenly I was a wife, not a mistress.' Shen picked at her lip, a strangely inelegant tic for such a poised woman. 'And I remember thinking: were we ready, you know? Was *I* ready. It's a very different job description.'

'A lot less flimsy underwear,' said Evie.

'And a lot more hoovering,' added Shen. 'Not that I hoover,' she added hastily, in case Evie should get the wrong impression. 'I mean metaphorical hoovering. I decided to always be his mistress – make sure there's no gap for another woman to sneak in. So, I diarize sex.'

'Diarize? That's a boardroom word, not a bedroom word.'

Begging to differ, Shen ticked off the schedule on her fingers. 'We do it every other day, come rain or shine. Blow-job once a week. Something unusual once a fortnight. And on his birthday we—'

'Enough!' Evie held up a hand, closed her eyes, wondering how she could rinse her brain later. 'We've

strayed into TMI.' She hesitated. 'Do you enjoy it, though?'
A sex timetable didn't sound fun.

'I love it! Clive's adventurous and sensitive and far more
my type than some waxed gym-bunny. But, even so, I
never allow myself to be too tired or too preoccupied.
I never have a headache. The tasselled bra is always freshly
laundered. The stilettos are polished.'

'What if you just feel like a nice boxed set in your oldest
PJs? What if you just feel like a chat?'

Shen pulled a face. 'D'you think a woman could keep
a man like Clive with *chat*?' She shook her head sadly,
and looked at Evie the way Evie looked at RSPCA posters
– a mixture of pity and a desire to help the poor, knackered creature in front of her.

'If he loves you,' said Evie, 'you don't need the tasselled
bra.' She thought about that for a moment. 'Well, not
every other night, anyway.'

'If?' Shen bristled. The mood changed. '*If* he loves me?'

'I didn't mean there's any doubt. It's just a manner of
speech.'

Shen's expression faltered, then recovered. 'Of course
he loves me,' she said, with her best imperious toss of her
hair. 'Damn fool's too scared not to.'

The bench was not exactly hidden, but it was discreet. A
large palm shaded it from the hoi polloi on the terrace,
and Evie found Clive there, just like the night before.

'Oh, sorry,' she said. 'You're probably after some peace

and quiet.' She half-turned, but turned back again when Clive said, 'No, no, join me, please.'

They sat in silence that wasn't quite companionable; she didn't know him well enough for that, despite all the time she spent at his house.

'So,' said Evie at the same time that Clive said, 'Well.' They laughed. 'You first,' she insisted.

'I'm wondering,' said Clive, the tip of his cigar fiery in the dark, 'what you write on that computer of yours. I've seen you lugging it around.'

'Oh, that.' Instinctively, she lied. Just like she told the kids never to do. 'That's my diary,' she said, fast and unconvincing. She didn't want to go into the sexy aspect of her work; she'd learned that it could fall very flat.

'Really?' Clive looked puzzled and tickled; a very Clive-ish thing to look. 'You were in the summerhouse for . . . ooh, a couple of hours today.'

How come you know how long I spent in the summerhouse? 'Yeah, well, not just a diary. Kind of a fantasy. A daydream. A story.' She shrugged. 'I just like making up little stories.' Evie heard that and hated it; that was the subtext she detected when Mike spoke about her raunchy cottage industry. He called it 'your stories', and now she was joining in.

'Nice to have a hobby,' said Clive.

'Yeah,' agreed Evie, who barely had time to brush her own teeth most days.

Everybody was asleep. The dogs were asleep. The house was asleep. Even the moon had dimmed.

In a pocket, a mobile phone stirred: **if you were here I'd eat you alive. I'm coming (ha-ha) sniff the wind and you'll smell me xxxx.**

DAY 4
Friday, 14th August

Yo

Wish you were here and all that shit.

Dad's being a X@!***. The countryside is worse than maths. But, man, the ladies! I'm in love. Seriously.

Z

p.s. Seriously

The pool was a shattered mirror, chopped this way and that by swimmers.

Tummy permanently set to 'in', Evie was sticky with lotion and dopey with sunshine. The muzak of splashes and exclamations was soothing, once she got used to it. She drifted, drifted . . . until a stabbing finger in the shape of her mobile's text-alert poked her awake: **I know what we agreed but I'm starting to worry you've got cold feet. I'm relying on you. Am I mad to do that? xxxx**

Beside Evie, Mike was sunk in his book. From the look of the cover, it involved guns and lots of running about; she longed for something so brainlessly escapist to hide in. She was tethered to real life and couldn't get away long enough to nap.

'Mummy!' Mabel, resplendent in her new fish-patterned swimsuit, was at her side, dripping icy droplets on Evie's chest.

'Yes, sweetie-pie?' Evie was glad to hear Mabel's voice. The child had been sulking since breakfast, and nobody could fathom why.

Breathless with the urgency of her news, Mabel said, 'I've seen Miles's willy!'

'Oh,' said Evie, not sure how to arrange her face. Mothering felt too monumental at times. Would a misplaced word here affect her daughter's relationships for all time? If she laughed (as she was dying to do), would Mabel shy away from men's trousers for evermore?

Mabel absolved her from responding by carrying on, 'It was *'orrible*. I feel sorry for him.' She dashed away, untraumatized, calling over her shoulder, 'Imagine carrying that stupid thing around in your knickers all day!'

'At last,' Mike murmured, turning a page, 'somebody understands.'

'And I'm still sulking!' roared Mabel as she jumped into the water.

'Excellent, darling! Keep it up.' Evie shaded her eyes with her hand and watched the glimmering scene. The new swimsuits had been a scary price, but she was glad she'd splurged. Miles was on his fourth pair of trunks, and even Fang was in a new two-piece as she splashed, safe in the sinewy arms of her nanny.

Beside Shen, who'd teamed her white bikini with stilettos, Evie felt lumpen, as if Shen was a dainty schoolgirl leading a shire horse; whereas beside Elizabetta, who seemed to be part-sparrow, all sex-bomb, Evie felt like . . . well, she didn't know what she felt like, because she assiduously kept the length of the pool between her and the nanny at all times.

Her blow-dry sharp, her bikini destined never to be wet, Shen bent down and barked, 'Mabel Herrera! Here!'

Meekly Mabel doggy-paddled over so that Shen could splodge suncream on her barely-there nose.

'Ta!' called Evie.

'Happy to help,' called Shen, looking scathingly at Evie over her sunglasses. 'You just carry on sunbathing and ignoring the fact that your daughter's nose is redder than Rudolph's.'

The only place – apart from St Agatha's – that Evie felt entirely comfortable leaving her children was at Shen's house. There they would be cared for, looked after, scolded, loved. Mabel and Dan regarded Shen's all-mod-cons Edwardian pile as an extension of their own cramped, no-mod-cons terrace; the price to be paid for this relaxed to and fro was the occasional sermon. Evie could withstand that. By Shen's standards – and occasionally Mike's – Evie was a bad mother, but she herself knew she was a good enough mother and that she did her best.

Sitting up, Evie gave in. There was no point in forcing her brain to relax. Until she faced Mike, she would be on the run, her entire body itchy with guilt. She scrabbled for the notepad in her bag. *I might as well work.*

It felt sinful writing a scene involving handcuffs and half a tub of Lurpak a few feet from frolicking tots. Using the first-person approach had not just woken up her muse; it had put the crazy dame on crystal meth:

With agonizing slowness my tongue draws a lazy line down Clay's chest. His body melts at my touch as my lips carry on, until the scratch of his pubic hair—

Mike blew his nose showily, and the muse went for a little lie-down.

A figure approached, head down. Paula was defiantly fully clothed amidst the near-nudity of her companions. By now Evie recognized that stance and girded her loins – not easy to do in a tummy-control one-piece – for the next dose of paranoia.

'OK, OK, I know this sounds silly,' began Paula, before she even reached the pool.

All splashing stopped. All eyes were on her. The children, Evie noted, were agog. They *loved* Paula's odd fancies.

'Somebody,' Paula repeated the word, stressing it, '*somebody* finished the milk.' She held up an empty carton, like the Statue of Liberty in man-made separates. 'It was practically full. And they left the fridge door open.' She added, '*Wide* open', as if that was somehow much, much worse. 'This happened while all of you were at the pool. Just me in the house.' She looked from face to face, as if daring them not to take this latest atrocity seriously.

'Do ghosts drink milk?' asked Miles, his arms like pieces of string in water-wings.

'Apparently.' Jon didn't look up from his newspaper.

With an impulse to protect Paula from the inevitable ridicule, Evie said, as if translating from a foreign language, 'It's not really that unusual, though, is it? I mean, there's lots of us here, and one of us just . . . finished the milk.' She smiled, as if to remind Paula that an empty milk carton, while annoying, isn't life-threatening.

'But I was on my own in the kitchen,' said Paula, dogged in her attempt to weave a mystery around the milk. 'There was nobody there to drink it, and yet it went, and the fridge door was left wide open. All while I was sitting at the table, reading.'

The other adults were carefully non-committal, instinctively grasping her fragility.

Setting off on another leisurely length of the pool, Clive said, 'It'll be Zane. He drives his mother mad with exactly that manner of behaviour at home.'

All eyes looked to Zane. 'Yeah,' he said, his deep voice rippling with the rhythm of private schools and privilege. 'You can blame me, Paula.'

'Really?' There was something like disappointment in the slump of Paula's shoulders.

Normal service was resumed in and around the water. Mabel splashed her brother. Amber joined in. Scarlett clambered out, dripping. Jon, who'd unbent enough to take off his shirt, put it back on and reapplied himself to his paper.

Anointing her collarbone with lotion, Shen said under her breath, 'Jon will have to pick up the pieces, as usual.'

He's the one who broke the pieces. Another thought struck Evie. 'Hang on, isn't Zane . . .'

'Lactose-intolerant, yeah.' Shen put her finger to her lips as she reached under her gossamer kaftan to settle the gold chain that connected her bikini bottoms to her bikini top – an arrangement that only worked if your midriff was as firm as a drum. 'Clive wanted to put a stop to her Miss Marple impression, I guess. I mean, what does it matter? We'll buy more milk.'

'He didn't need to throw Zane in front of the bus.'

'He'll live.'

A tidal wave surged from the pool, drenching them both. Evie screamed, but Shen was silent. She was too furious to shout, her hair now a wet skullcap.

'Oops.' Zane surfaced. 'Guess the pool's too small to do a cannonball.'

'Clive!' Shen found her voice, and the doves all fled from the dovecote in a flapping mass. 'Tell him! Tell your son!'

Partway through another lap, Clive said, 'Sorry, darling. Your department. I do money. You do kids.'

Shen made a furious, razor-edged noise. 'Zane,' she shouted, 'you're an idiot.'

'He said sorry,' said Scarlett, righteously.

'Actually,' said Clive, climbing out, 'he didn't. The word's not in his vocabulary.'

Zane ploughed up and down the pool as his stepmother dug up clods of grass with her heels on her way back to the house.

'Scarlett seems to be warming up Tillie nicely,' said Evie to Mike, covertly watching the two girls draped on the grass on the far side of the pool. 'It's not a perfect match, but at least they're hanging out.'

'Tillie's a lot better than the airheads Scarlett usually follows around.'

'Her friends are perfectly nice, perfectly ordinary girls.' Evie was bored with Mike's worry that Scarlett would get in with a 'bad crowd', the spectral lurching mob of drug-taking, fag-smoking, teenage-pregnancy-making bogeymen that haunt all modern parents. 'We're supposed to think they're airheads; that's our job.' An idea struck her. 'Paula!' she called across the pool, now the setting for a water ballet involving Mabel, Amber, Miles and several drowning Barbies. 'How about a pub meal tonight? Stretch our legs?'

'But the children . . .' said Paula. The word 'pub' obviously wasn't having the miraculous effect Evie had hoped for (although, beside her, Mike had perked up considerably; 'pub' had worked its magic on him at least).

'We'll leave them with Elizabetta,' said Evie, suddenly appreciating how easy life must be for nannied-up women.

'I think it's a great idea,' said Jon, with a statesmanlike tone, as if speaking for himself and his little woman.

'What if . . .' began Paula, but her feeble dissent collapsed in on itself and she went back to staring at her fingers.

'It'll be fun, Mum,' said Tillie, raising herself up on one elbow. 'You're allowed to have fun.'

'I feel like a Playboy bunny,' said Evie.

'I feel like a boil-in-the-bag cod fillet,' said Mike.

They had different reactions to the hot tub.

Mike didn't get it. 'It's just a bath, outside, where everybody can see.'

'It's decadent, and it makes me smile.' It was louder than Evie had imagined. All that bubbling. Not the place to have a serious talk, she decided, letting herself off the hook yet again. 'I thought it'd make a break from lying by the pool. Not a sun-worshipper, are you, love?'

'You noticed?'

'The foot-jiggling. The sighing. The tutting.'

'Sunbathing is just wasting time,' said Mike, 'while being a bit too hot.'

'The sun sends me into a trance. Especially here, with all these acres around me. It's like we're lord and lady of our own personal estate.'

'The estates I'm used to aren't like this.'

'No junkies here.'

'No abandoned sofas.'

'Bet you miss all those burnt-out cars.'

'Jon's a decent bloke,' said Mike suddenly.

'Hmm. Would a decent bloke snog a woman who wasn't his wife?'

'I'd forgotten that.'

Evie marvelled at such forgetfulness; her own daily life involved myriad feats of memory, including which family members loathed Coco Pops, which family members didn't consider life worth living without Coco Pops, whose history project was due in, the date of the vet's appointment, Mike's inside-leg measurement, when her own period was due, where the scissors had last been seen, if there were any functioning glue-sticks in the house – and where her increasingly scattered marbles could be found.

'Innocent,' said Mike loftily, 'until proven guilty, and all that.'

'I saw him with my own eyes.'

'I *didn't*. And it's nice for me to have a mate, you know. I want to understand Jon, not just lock him up in jail and throw away the key.'

'You and your big heart,' said Evie, soft again. She'd forgotten, in the tumult of the past few weeks, how kind her husband was. Not in a namby-pamby way, but in a muscular, making-a-difference way.

He coughed. 'I don't have many mates.'

'Being married to a bloke for twenty years,' said Evie, 'you notice these things.'

'Well,' said Mike, scratching his head, 'sooner or later, when you're getting to know somebody, you have *that* conversation. The one where you talk about where you're from. Your background. Who you are . . .' He tapered off. 'And I'm not anybody.'

Such talk chilled Evie. 'You, sir, are Mr Michael Herrera of thirty-six Lambrook Road.'

'But that's *all* I am. I don't know if I have my dad's nose. I have no anecdotes about the cute things my grandma said. I envy you, because you have a photograph album,' said Mike suddenly, as if confessing a crime.

However choked he became, Evie knew there'd be no tears. He hadn't shed a single tear throughout their life together. Not when the babies came. Not even during the bad year. She realized that's how she thought of it: the Bad Year, as if it was in a tidy box, easily packed away. Which it wasn't.

'If you're going to envy me,' said Evie, 'at least envy me for my looks and wit and . . . um . . . skill at parallel parking.' Mike didn't smile. She was beginning to think of it as the Wellcome Manor Effect: feelings and reactions were exaggerated here. 'I don't think that particular conversation will ever happen with Jon.' She felt Mike's interest quicken. 'He's too private to open up like that. He doesn't want to chat about the old days.' This was a gentler way of saying that Jon was hiding something, just like Mike.

'Maybe that's why I'm relaxed with him. Why I'm overlooking the little matter of Miss Pritchett. I sense he's disconnected. It takes one to know one.' Mike looked down at the churning water. 'Can we get out now, please?'

A poolside game of Scrabble was in progress, led by Shen, in a new floaty kaftan thing and a complicated bikini.

'Where have you been?' Shen always wanted to know where everybody was, and didn't take kindly to people just taking off without prior permission. 'Join us!'

'Not a chance,' said Evie, settling down, locating a magazine, resenting her thighs. She'd played many a board game with Shen and had the bruises to prove it. The lady liked winning. The lady was also phenomenally bad at spelling; she seemed unaware of vowels. Scrabble could only end badly.

'Uh-oh,' said Evie. She nudged Mike as he settled down beside her, bracing himself for another stint of doing nothing. 'D'you see what I see?'

Mike looked up and around him, with trepidation. Twenty years with Evie had taught him that he rarely saw what she saw. 'I see Paula and Jon half-asleep. I see Clive gloating – sorry, *enjoying his holiday*. And Shen playing some game with the kids that involves lots of arguing.'

'First, look *there*.' Evie guided Mike's head by his chin.

'Zane,' said Mike.

The boy was, as ever, on the fringes. Head down, he chewed the inside of his cheek, as he squatted by the brick paving around the pool.

'Now follow his line of sight to the Scrabble game.'

Doing as he was told, Mike *did* see what Evie saw.

'Uh-oh.' He repeated her reaction, but with bells on. 'Oh, shit, Evie.'

'Quite.'

Zane was watching their daughter with the kind of concentration a lab technician might bring to a DNA sample.

Throwing up her arms in triumph, Scarlett let out a bellow of joy. Her nose was more freckled than ever, and her hair was dreadlocked from constant dips in the pool. The overall effect was much more charming than if she'd spent hours in a beauty salon.

'That's not her shirt,' said Evie, squinting at the cotton garment that hung down to Scarlett's knees and over her knuckles. She nudged Mike, who was treating the oblivious Zane to a full-on dirty look. 'She's wearing Zane's shirt. In some ancient tribes, that would mean they're married.'

She wondered why the boy wasn't sitting alongside the object of his affections; beside her, Mike wondered how quickly he could hustle his daughter to a convent.

Feeling his unease, Evie leaned in closer. 'She's seventeen, love. She's already had a boyfriend.'

'Don't remind me. Spotty so-and-so.' A right-on liberal to the ends of his fingertips, Mike turned Victorian papa the moment a male sniffed the air in the direction of his daughter. 'At least he wasn't some sub-James-Dean dickhead. That boy's trouble, Evie.'

'I'm not so sure.' Evie saw purity in the dark eyes trained on her little girl. 'Clive's very hard on him.'

'So would I be, if my son drove tractors through gates.'

'What if that was the only way he could get your attention?'

'Even so, I'd reserve the right to react badly to driving a tractor through a gate. Zane's a mess.'

'Somebody else has noticed what's going on.'

As if Tillie had heard Evie's murmured comment, she took her eyes off Zane and met Evie's gaze.

Without moving her lips, Evie said, 'And she's not happy about it.'

'What?' said Mike, wondering why his wife persisted in believing she could make herself understood without moving her lips.

'I do like beams.' The cottagey details of your traditional English pub soothed Evie. Those wonky pinkish shades on the wall lights, the gaudily framed bad paintings, the patterned carpet swirls and whirls that had soaked up much gin and gravy over the decades all conspired to take her to her happy place.

Not so Shen. She picked up a plastic table mat adorned with a hunting scene, all red coats and nervy steeds. 'Exhibit one,' she said icily. She picked up her paper napkin. 'Exhibit two.' She pointed at the barmaid leaning chummily over the bar, her low-cut blouse straining and her raucous laugh exposing the lipstick on her teeth. 'Exhibit three.'

'Actually,' said Mike, noting the contents of the blouse, 'she's exhibits three *and* four.'

'Enough *Carry On* humour.' Evie swatted him with the laminated menu. 'They do pies!'

'Pies,' said Mike reverently, the way some people say 'God' or 'Madonna'.

'The wine,' said Shen, 'comes from a box.'

'It still,' pointed out Clive, 'gets you drunk, darling.' He shushed her next comment by saying, 'When in Rome, do as the Romans do, Shen. We're not at Claridge's, we're in a pub.' He frowned at the menu. 'Shall I order you a lovely mixed grill?'

'What a nice pub!' said Paula, fidgeting in her seat as if she wanted to run out screaming. 'It's very nice. Really nice. A nice place with nice people.'

'Ooh,' said Evie. 'They do sticky toffee pudding.' She was anybody's for a sticky toffee pudding; she'd be sorely tested if somebody offered to swap her one for the kids. 'What do you fancy, Jon?' she asked, refraining from adding: *Apart from the children's teacher, you double-whammy pervert/adulterer.*

'More or less all of it,' said Jon.

'I won't have a starter,' said Paula timidly, as if having a starter was an internationally recognized sign of immense arrogance.

'Me neither,' said Shen. 'Everything on this menu is bad for you.'

'There's a salad,' ventured Evie.

'With croutons!' said Shen.

'Yeah, croutons, not severed hands,' muttered Evie, who'd forgotten how excruciating eating out with her friend could be. 'One stodgy meal won't kill you.'

'I watch my figure,' said Shen.

'So do I,' said Clive, raising his glass to his wife. 'And so do those fellows at the bar.'

Shen half-turned, a satisfied look on her face. 'Really?'

'Really, darling.' Clive leaned across and planted a proper smacker on her lips. 'They can look, but they can't touch. You're mine – all mine.'

'Oh,' said Mike casually. 'So you bought Shen, did you? I thought you married her.'

'There isn't enough money in the world to buy this work of art.' Clive batted away Mike's attempt to needle him. 'Now. Champagne!' He didn't seem able to envisage an evening without it.

Evie was going to burst. It had been that last Yorkshire pudding that had tipped her over the edge. She sat back and covertly undid her jeans, letting out a sigh of relief and happiness that was partly to do with her tummy's sudden freedom and partly with the arrival of the dessert trolley.

'Don't,' said Shen, as Evie's clammy paw reached out for an individual trifle. 'Consider this an intervention. I can't let you do this to yourself.'

'Get between me and this trifle,' said Evie, 'and our

years of friendship will mean nothing. I will hurt you. I will hurt you bad.'

'Don't come crying to me when they bury you in a grand-piano case,' said Shen, waving away the trolley as if it was loaded with nuclear waste.

'Should I have a mousse?' Paula looked as if she was making a life-or-death decision.

'Don't ask me,' said Jon, and then, more irritably, 'it's a mousse, Paula. Have it or don't have it.'

'Have it!' said Evie. 'Have two!'

Paula passed. Evie noticed how she watched the retreating trolley until it was out of sight.

'A toast,' said Clive, raising his glass.

'Another one?' said Mike, as if toasts were rationed by law.

'To our wives!' said Clive. 'Jon,' he remonstrated, 'lift your glass, man!'

'To our wives,' said Jon, obediently.

'Nice, very nice,' said Paula.

'Bill, *s'il vous plaît*.' Clive summoned a waitress as he pulled out his wallet. 'I wonder what's going on back at the house? Always risky, leaving Zane at home. I may need to flex my cheque-writing fingers.'

'Zane's fine,' said Evie. 'Last I saw of him, he was chillaxing with his harem. There was music. And Scarlett was over-laughing. Everything's tickety-boo.'

'Let's hope so.' Clive discreetly handed his credit card to the waitress, thanking her for the meal with, 'It makes a change from cooking.'

'Listen to him,' scoffed Shen, who'd overcome her wine-box prejudice, and then some. 'Anybody would think he made dinner every night. He can order food and he can eat it, but introduce him to an egg and he'd have no idea what to do with it.'

'Mike can do spaghetti,' said Evie. 'But only if I threaten him with a rifle.' The basic skill of cooking had somehow become a mysterious feminine superpower. Mike was no sexist, but put him anywhere near a saucepan and his belief system crumbled to dust.

'He's gonna need to work up some skills soon,' said Shen darkly.

'It's like we've walked onto the set of *Mary Poppins*.' Evie could see no strewn toys, no discarded trail of dirty clothes, no half-eaten doughnuts lying on open books, none of her shoes lying on their side after illicit involvement in a dressing-up game.

The house was hushed as Mike and Evie made their way to the attic for tucking in; Mabel had been clear on this: she couldn't be expected to fall asleep until they'd both tucked her in.

'I'm still sulking,' mumbled Mabel as Mike pulled the sheet over her. 'But I love you.'

'We know you do, silly knickers,' said Mike, kissing the tip of her nose.

A small voice sounded from the other bed crammed into the manor's eaves. 'Please could you please send my mummy in, please, thank you very much.'

'Of course, sweetie.' Evie called Paula, beckoning her in. 'Somebody needs a cuddle.'

'Oh, my darling.' Paula swooped on the bed as if visiting the dying. 'I know, I know,' she soothed the whimpering girl, sounding on the verge of tears herself. She was all emotion, a ball of empathy.

If the woman had a friend, thought Evie, a real confidante, perhaps she could be persuaded to override the empathy and downplay life's everyday agonies, for her children's sake. However would little Amber, so naturally fearful, learn to cope, if Paula agreed with her that every shadow held a monster and every separation from her mummy was a disaster?

Mike was peeling off his tee when Evie went to their room and shut their door. It creaked eloquently, as did the floorboards. As did Evie's knees when she sat on the bed.

Yawning, Mike said, 'I don't know how the idle rich take the pace. I'm not half as tired as this after a day dealing with alcoholic tenants and burnt-out bedsits.'

'Come outside with me.' Evie stood up, impetuous, determined. She held out her hand across the plateau of the bed.

'Naw.' Mike was scratching under his armpits, a disinterested monkey.

'Please.'

'Too tired, love.' He was under the duvet, then kicking it off. He punched the pillow, not hearing the pleading note in her second 'Please, Mike!' The click of his bedside lamp served as a full stop.

'Mike.' She said his name slowly, significantly – the approved method of opening a marital discussion of some importance.

He turned over, away from her, his voice muffled by the pillow. 'I saw the price label on that tofu stuff Shen buys. Amazing. I mean, it's not even *meat*.'

'Mike,' said Evie again, upping the implication. 'Darling.'

'And that champers we guzzle – I looked it up. Each bottle costs more than we ever spend on dinner.' A thought struck him and he turned, looking at Evie but apparently not taking her in, as he seemed unaffected by her tense posture. 'Fuck me, Evie, with a third of the cost of the house *and* the petrol down here, and all the extra bits and bobs I know you've bought, this isn't exactly turning out to be a bargain break, is it? I mean, shouldn't it be cheaper to stay in the UK than to go abroad?'

'Down at the side of the terrace, almost hidden by a palm, is a little bench,' said Evie. 'It's so pretty – just planks nailed together.' She found his face in the gloaming. 'We can talk there. Come on.'

'We've got ten more days to talk, love.'

'Pretty please? Please with knobs on?'

He smiled, a wide smile that was almost audible in the half-dark. 'We can talk any time.' He thrashed about, trying to find the perfect position. 'Was electricity included in the rate for this house, d'you know? If not, I start turning off lights tomorrow evening. The place was lit up like a birthday cake when we got back.' He exhaled, a long pre-dropping-off sigh, then said, 'Aren't you getting undressed?'

'I need some air.'

'No-o.' Mike sounded bereft. 'You've had loads of air. Too much air, if anything. I can't get to sleep unless I'm spooning that big old bum of yours.'

'Well, you silver-tongued charmer, you'll have to do your best.' *Keep it light*, Evie counselled herself, as she slipped out of the door. Sometimes she wondered if her husband saw pound signs above the children's heads.

The blackout of rural night was nothing like the eternal twilight of the city. At this lonely hour the acoustics were odd, as if everything lay under a deep coating of snow.

People are fundamentally the same, no matter when or where they were born. Evie felt sure she wasn't the first person to look up at the moon from Wellcome Manor and wonder and worry and – *ow!* – catch her ankle on a treacherously placed plant pot. Cursing softly, she limped down the steps, glad of the midnight drop in temperature. The springy support of the grass beneath her feet woke her senses, set them firing. It was time to wake up and kick some ass.

Except that she didn't want to kick Mike's ass. For one thing, it was such a nice ass. She wanted to *include* him, involve him. She wanted to reach past all the accumulated clutter of their marriage and speak plainly to him.

She reached the swing. How long was it since she'd swung – in the wholesome sense of the word, not the nipping upstairs with him-from-down-the-road sense of the word? She'd watched the kids kick off on endless swooping flights, but the swings in their local park were too narrow for Evie's behind. This wooden seat was magnanimously wide. Assuming the right position, she grasped the ropes and planted her feet in the earth that had been churned up over the years and pushed off.

No other word but *Wheee!* would hit the spot. Her hair flew back, then covered her face, then flew back again, her face washed clean by the moon.

Wearing herself out, Evie puttered to a stop, almost falling off. She'd never perfected that move; as a child, she'd always landed like a damaged Spitfire.

In the dark it was easy to imagine Mike beside her. The sweet, woody smell of his hair, the heat he gave off, the feel of his uniform of jeans and rumpled linen shirt.

'*Darling,*' she began. '*I need to flee. Don't panic. I only need to flee a little way and then I'll come back. But I'm suffocating for want of fresh air. Let me explain.*'

She raised her voice, warming to her theme.

'*You're the man I fell madly in lust with, the one I promised to love and honour (remember how we laughed at including "obey"?). I meant it. I also meant the sickness-and-in-health bit. As did you.*

'*But nowhere in the marriage vows did we mention that I would consent to being bored to death in order to keep you happy.*

'*You* don't *bore me. You couldn't. Not even when you're telling me for the fourteenth time why I should get into* Breaking Bad. *What's boring me is doing nothing.*

'Hang on, though. I'm not saying that running a home and bringing up three children is nothing. No, sirree!

'Being a housewife (which is what I am, and damned proud of it: don't you dare call me a "homemaker" or – strewth – a "family engineer') is tough. For a take-home pay of zero pence, it demands the practical skills of a carpenter/plumber/chef, the tact of a therapist, the steely attitude of a cop, the loving acceptance of a saint, the time-management prowess of a top executive, the story-telling talent of Sir Ian McKellen and, once the kids have been put to bed, the va-va-voom of Jessica Rabbit.

'I get no holidays. I can't call in sick; remember how I had to draw a manual on how to boil eggs from my flu sickbed? I'm the only one who knows everybody's shoe sizes, allergies, greatest fears. Which are, for the record: Mabel/snakes; Dan/serial killers; Scarlett/blowing off near a boy; you/something – anything – happening to me or the kids.

'Which is why I haven't been able to share my feelings. You love us so much, Mike, that you keep us in aspic. Or cotton wool. Sorry, my metaphors are going ape-shit.

'Staying at home isn't enough for me any more. I need something that's entirely mine, that I can point to and say: "See that not particularly important, yet quietly significant thing? I did that."

'When we met, my job impressed you and I liked the young woman reflected in your eyes. Apart, obviously, from the perm. You said, "I love telling people my girl-friend's in advertising", and I thought, "Oh my God, I'm his girlfriend", because I wasn't sure if the curries and pizzas and kisses in your ancient car added up to anything yet.

'By the time I left the agency, a teeny Scarlett firming up in my uterus, I was tipped for "great things" – whatever that means – but I hardly need to tell you that Scarlett had her issues, poor little thing, and it was a good three years before I felt able to leave her with my mum and get back to work.

'There was a job waiting. Less money than I'd been on, more junior, but with potential. And I was gagging for it, d'you remember?

'We never talk about this. It's as if it un-happened. But, Mike my love, it did happen. The morning I was due to go in and formally sign my contract and be allocated a desk and shown the kettle, you took me to one side and you said: "We need you."

'Now, I know you very, very well. I know when you say you don't want seconds of toad-in-the-hole that you're just being pious. I know when you say that you're squinting because the sun's in your eyes that you have a humungous migraine.

'So I knew what you were really saying was that you needed me.

'The abandoned little care-home boy couldn't watch the mummy of the house walk out of the door. Your past is always with us, Mike. I know you strive to feel "normal", and I know the children are the icing on our "normal" cake. I sense the satisfaction you get just from being around them, doing the little things like kissing a grazed knee. It *makes me well up, to have a man with massive reserves of feeling, who appreciates what we have.*

'D'you feel a "but" clearing its throat? Here it is.

'But . . . sometimes you smother us.

'Scarlett doesn't need to be collected from the youth centre. Dan can cross our quiet road. And I can return to work.

'I feel as guilty as if I have a lover. There've been assignations and secret texts and plans made behind your back. Remember Alex? She and I started at the agency on the same day. Now she runs the place. And she needs an assistant.

'She needs me.

'I could do it; I could do it well. It's not producing; I missed that boat. But it's a relatively senior admin post. The pay . . . it would make a difference. We might even be able to move. You could stop having nightmares about us all living in a cardboard box by the motorway.

'But the main difference would be to our daily lives.

'I've worked it all out, Mike, so the only change you have to make is your attitude. I'll work four days a week at the office, with Wednesdays working from home. Scarlett'll collect Dan and Mabel on Mondays and Tuesdays. I'll fetch them on Wednesdays. On Thursdays and Fridays, when Scarlett has after-school clubs, Mum'll take the little ones and feed them. Blimey, it sounds complicated, but we'll get used to it.

'There may be more convenience foods. I'll leave the house before you, so I won't wave you off, the way you *like me to. And now and then I'll have to travel, so you all will have to muddle along without me.*

'*I can already smell your panic. You once said, during the other time I almost left you, the time we call "the bad time", that you couldn't imagine the house without me. That, without me all aproned and ready in the kitchen, it would simply fall down, brick by brick.*

'*It won't, Mike. I promise. Meet me halfway. Try. I've been hanging on by my fingertips for quite some time now, only half the woman I was when we met: I want to be me again. And I want our honesty back: I shouldn't have kept this from you.*

'*Can you try?*

'*What do you say?*'

Evie dropped into an exhausted bow. It felt good to get it all out. She jerked up at the sound of applause.

'I say *yes*! What else could a man say to a speech like that?'

'How long have you been standing there?' she asked Clive, wanting to run.

'I came out to our bench.' Clive stopped, thought, smiled. 'It *is* our bench, isn't it? To see if you were there. I saw you on the swing, followed you down and, once you started talking, there seemed no easy way to pipe up.' Clad in a brocade dressing gown, the ornate leisurewear of a bygone age, Clive held out his palms apologetically. 'And then I was transfixed. Bravo, Evie!'

'I feel . . . exposed.'

'No need.' Clive's expression was hard to read. 'Talk to Mike with half the sincerity you just showed, talking to thin air, and he'll get on board. Nobody could resist such passion.'

'Really?' Evie felt her backbone rebuild itself, disc by disc. 'Passion?' Thanks to TV talent shows, it was an overused word. She liked it. 'Me?'

'Yes, you.' Clive struck a match to light his cigar and his face was bright for a second. 'Believe me, Evie. You were on fire.'

DAY 5
Saturday, 15th August

dear miss Pritchett
   our mummys made us rite this it is sunny we wish
you cud be our teacher forrever

miles mabel amber

X XXXX XOXO

Tillie preferred the shade to the noon sunshine. Like she preferred black to pink, and Stephen King to Jilly Cooper.

When she'd suggested to Scarlett that they escape the relentless sun by climbing up to their treehouse (it was *so* theirs by now), she knew Zane would follow. At a distance, but *there*.

As usual.

'Scar,' said Tillie. 'Bung us a ciggie.'

If Paula knew what went on up here, she'd faint. Evie would . . . Tillie wondered what Scarlett's mother would do. Shout, definitely. But then hug. And shout again. She was one of *those* mums.

A cigarette flew like a torpedo from Scarlett's hand.

'Ta.' Tillie didn't really smoke, but Scarlett did; some stuff you just *had* to do to fit in, so . . . she braced herself as she lit a match. They tasted vile, these stupid fags. 'Sorry to interrupt, lovebirds.'

Scarlett flashed her eyes at Tillie over Zane, stretched out at her feet like a pedigree pup, all health and gleam. 'Go on,' Scarlett nudged him with her foot. 'You were saying. About your last girlfriend.'

'She was mental.' Zane lay flat on his back, fingers inter-locked beneath his head, not looking at Scarlett, but at the untreated wood that was the ceiling. 'Bad reputation.'

'Like what?' *Maybe*, thought Scarlett, *I'll be an investigative journalist*. Investigative journalism was especially easy when the subject was as fanciable as this one.

'She was totally fit, but, man, she was crazy. Jealous. Always on my back. Bit of a slut too.'

A snort from Tillie.

'She *was*,' said Zane, those unfeasibly straight brows creasing. 'I'm only telling the truth.'

Scarlett knew she should tell the truth. She should tell Tillie she didn't smoke. It was a pain having to puff her way through one or two cigarettes a day. She'd been hiding them for one of her mates, but Tillie saw them and asked for one, and somehow Scarlett was now a fake smoker. *Jesus*, she thought, *life is complicated*.

'How many boys have you . . . you know?' said Zane, nodding meaningfully.

'He means,' said Tillie loudly, 'how many times have you had carnal knowledge of the opposite sex.'

'Yeah,' said Zane. 'Thanks, Tills.'

'You go first,' said Scarlett. She saw how he quickened when she looked coy. She was both pleased with herself for pleasing him and irritated for allowing it to matter. It was hard being a girl.

'Four.' Zane let her gasp. 'Actually, more like five. Yeah. Five – forgot that one on holiday.'

'You started young,' said Scarlett.

'Very.' Zane grinned. 'I can't resist the laydeez.'

'What's your type?' Scarlett was super-duper casual about this; she had no idea why Tillie was groaning.

'Kind,' said Zane. 'And hot, obviously. Good bod.' He closed his eyes. 'Sex is so amazing, isn't it? I mean, there's nothing like it, when you're in the groove with some amazing girl. If you're any good at it, I mean.'

'I wouldn't know,' said Scarlett. OK, this might put him off, but she had to say it. 'I've never done it.'

'You've never done it?' Zane sat up. A languid boy, Scarlett had never seen him move so fast. 'You told me you went out with some guy for five months.'

'I did. But I didn't love him.'

'That poor guy.'

Was Zane referring to the fact that the poor guy had endured five sexless months or that he hadn't been loved? Scarlett knew which translation she preferred.

'Didn't you ever feel . . . tempted?'

'Of course.' Scarlett remembered the yearning, taut feel deep in her tum and shifted on her cushion. 'But nobody will ever, ever convince me there's any point to sex without love.'

Zane stared. Rather than work out what the stare meant – she'd been working out what people meant ever since she'd turned thirteen, and it wears a girl out – Scarlett looked out of the rough-edged window.

One of them coming from the snooker outbuilding and one from the house, her parents were on a collision course. 'Oi, Dad!' yelled Scarlett. 'I hope you're going to tell Mum off about getting up so late! She's not a team player, dontcha know?'

Hands on hips, Mike stood beneath the treehouse and called up to her. 'Your mum deserves a lie in now and then. Besides, she's got a brilliant left hook.' He wanted to leap up the ladder. He wanted to shake Zane and say, 'Hands off my little girl!' He did neither of these things and he hoped Evie would notice and be proud of him.

Mabel said, 'I've stopped sulking.'

'Oh, good, darling,' said Evie. 'I'll alert the media.'

'Come and do my hair,' said Mabel. 'In here.' She led her mother into the narrow galley that housed the less-photogenic necessities. 'In the futility room.'

Typical of Mabes – a nester, a snuggler – to find the smallest room.

'Up or down?' Evie's hairdressing skills were limited.

'A plait all the way around like a crown, with bits hanging down, please.'

Crikey. Evie teased at the tangles gathered at Mabel's neck. 'Sorry!' she said in response to each tetchy 'Ow!'

'There's a swing,' said Mabel, truly, deeply excited. 'It swings!'

'Yes, darling, I suppose it would.'

'Amber won't get on it,' said Mabel, 'in case she falls off.'

'We all fall off things,' said Evie, soothingly. 'We brush ourselves off and get up again.'

'Unless we break our heads open, and our brains are all over the floor.'

'Well, yes,' agreed Evie, assuming this happy scenario was courtesy of Paula.

The trio of eight-year-old classmates had gelled into a gang, a solid, moving mass of childhood. *The Eights* was how Evie thought of them, as in *Where are The Eights?* or *Is that strange boinging noise The Eights on the trampoline?*

Dan had consciously uncoupled from The Eights. Neither Evie nor Mike dared to mention out loud that their middle child was engrossed in a book. The Greek myths that Evie had unthinkingly plucked from the bookcase and shoved at him, in answer to his 'I'm bored!' whine, had captured him utterly.

'It's like a film, but in your head,' was his best stab at describing why he now rarely lifted his eyes from Achilles, or the Minotaur.

'Nicely put,' said Evie.

'Amber still cries all night,' said Mabel.

'Bless her.' Evie began to plait. She didn't know where she was going with it; she simply set off. Right over middle. Left over middle. 'She's not as mature as you are.' Evie appealed to her daughter's rampant desire to be a big girl. 'Jolly her along when she's upset.'

'I could do my impressions!'

'Good idea.' *But please don't do one now, because you always put me on the spot by asking 'Who am I?' and nobody can tell your Lady Gaga from your Prince Charles.* 'There. All done.'

'It feels a bit funny.' Mabel put a wary hand up to the lopsided Heidi-do.

'No, no, it's great – off you go.' Evie patted Mabel on

the bottom and aimed her at the sun streaming through the door. A small face appeared, a question behind its wire-rimmed glasses. 'Shall I do your hair too, Amber?'

The girl's hair was fine; fairy tresses between Evie's fingers, compared to Mabel's thick kinks. A thought struck her: 'Will your mummy be OK with me doing your hair?'

'Yes.' Amber stood self-consciously, holding her head very still.

'How about a nice high ponytail?'

'Super.' The slightest of lisps. *Thooper.*

Bones like a bird, Amber was a slip of a thing and a contrast to Evie's own brood. She knew Scarlett sometimes kneaded the soft flesh of her tum and scowled at it; leading by example, Evie never commented on her own orange-peel or muffin-top or bingo-wings – Christ, female self-hatred had an extensive vocabulary! – and thus far Scarlett hadn't succumbed to crash diets or daft gym regimes.

'Can I wear thith?' Amber produced the hairband Evie had bought in the village.

'Of course.' Evie liked the shy girl poking out from her shell, a timid whelk in a sundress. 'Don't you look pretty?'

Drawn by the unmistakable plick-plock of table tennis, Evie followed Amber, who was frolicking – proper, full-on frolicking – across the grass. Her arms folded out of habit, Evie unfolded them, enjoying the sensation of swinging them as she crossed the gardens.

Her own garden was a glorified storage yard for trikes, bikes, a ladder and various empty pots. Nature in London was confined to parks; the one at the end of Evie's road was a place of almost daily pilgrimage, because of the swings and the slide and the sandpit. Evie never noticed the trees in that park, or bent to sniff a flower. She was too busy wishing Mabel and Dan would hurry up; only in adverts do parents stand adoringly by, while their children cavort. Real parents quickly get over the joys of the park.

The table-tennis match was just ending. Paula had beaten Jon. Rather, she had *demolished* him.

'Game, thet and matchbox!' shouted Amber.

Paula's atypical jig of triumph ended abruptly. She threw down her bat. 'That hairband.' She pulled the Liberty-print accessory from her daughter's head, knocking Amber's glasses off and catching the girl in the eye. 'Who gave it to you?'

Stepping forward, reaching the pair a moment before Jon did, Evie said, 'I did, Paula. Me. I did.' She wrenched the woman's attention from Amber, who was now, predictably, sobbing. 'It's just a present. It didn't mean anything.' Even as she gabbled her apologies, Evie wondered what on earth she was apologizing for.

Paula wasn't looking at Evie; she was looking over her shoulder at Jon, and whatever she read in his face changed everything. 'It's very pretty.' She turned the hairband over in her hands. 'That was kind. Thank you.' Belatedly she bent to Amber, and her face twisted at her daughter's distress.

'Can I keep it?' asked Amber, snot running into her mouth.

'Of course!' Paula, gentle now, replaced the hairband in Amber's thin hair and hooked her glasses over her ears. She led her child away, Jon tailing them.

The score stood at one game each. Mike and Evie crouched, bats firmly gripped, both determined to win and at least one of them thinking, *This is sexy!*

Evie liked the bead of sweat in Mike's exposed clavicle, and his provocative grunt when he hit the ball, almost enough to overlook his shorts. Now damp and clinging, they were somewhat improved. *Porn ping-pong*, she thought happily as she served for match point. Lucinda could get an entire chapter out of this.

Mike smashed it. There was no hope of her reaching it. He jumped in the air and she considered shouting, now, as he celebrated orgasmically, 'Oh and by the way I've got a job!'

But she didn't.

The gentle noise of the ping-pong ball was embedded in the house's soundtrack, but this time it was different. There was no space between the plinks and the plonks; the rhythm was ramped up, like a lovely old waltz reimagined as electro house.

Unable to challenge Clive on status, Mike had turned, inevitably, to table tennis.

It was intense. Much was at stake. And yet Clive still held his cigar fast between his teeth.

Evie knew just how much that would annoy Mike. And now she knew Clive well enough to know that was exactly why he did it. The old guy was showing the (slightly) younger guy he could take him, without even dropping his cigar.

'Out!' Clive held up his bat.

'It touched the edge of the table,' said Mike.

'It didn't.' Evie smiled from her seat on the grass.

'Whose side are you on?' Mike snapped.

'The side of justice.'

'Four-two. My serve.' Clive served the ball like a grenade.

'Four-three,' whooped Mike, returning the serve with a deadly forehand. He crouched, ready for Clive's next serve, which was unexpectedly dainty and had him diving, hopelessly, for the net.

'Five-three,' said Clive, not bothering to crouch. 'Your serve.'

'I *know*,' said Mike. When the shot whistled past Clive, he did what looked like a rain-dance.

And so it went on. Flash footwork. Aggressive smashes. Clive exuded a smugness so immense that it was probably visible from space, while Mike over-celebrated his every point.

Despairing of their macho posturing in such a paradise, Evie left them to it, suggesting over her shoulder, 'Why not just whack your willies on the table and measure them, boys?'

'Tell me again,' said Shen, slamming the car door more forcefully than was necessary, 'why we left our idyllic holiday home to come *here*?' The gesture she made to encompass the featureless business park was withering.

'The kids were bored,' said Evie. 'And yes, I know, at their age we were never bored, et cetera, et cetera; but even an idyll gets samey after four days.' The website hadn't mentioned that the Soft Play Centre was sandwiched between a discount tile-warehouse and a taxidermy-supplies outlet, but then it wouldn't, would it? 'Come on, Horrors.' The Eights teemed from the cars like an unusually cute invading army, Dan bringing up the rear.

'Are helmets supplied?' Paula scuttled in their wake.

'For gawd's sake, Paula,' said Shen. 'The clue's in the title: *soft play*. If they manage to hurt themselves in here, I'll give you a thousand pounds.'

As the children threw themselves off padded platforms onto each other's heads, Shen plonked down three murky coffees. 'This tip hasn't got a bar.'

'But it *does* have a crafting area,' said Evie.

'And there was me, thinking this was a waste of time.' If there was such a thing as a sarcasm-ometer, Shen's face would have blown it up.

Paula, immune to sarcasm, said, 'Let's make a comb-holder.'

'Ooh, yes, let's.' Shen scaled even higher peaks of sarki-ness. 'How have I managed all these years without a comb-holder? Hang on, that's right, *because comb-holders aren't a thing.*'

'I,' said Evie emphatically, 'really, really need a comb-holder.'

On the scratched Formica table in front of them were a loom band-bracelet, a peg bag, a crocheted flower brooch, a glittery pipe-cleaner spider, a stone painted to look like an owl and a pile of comb-holders.

The Eights had just been sent back, whining, to the soft play area.

'Shen,' said Evie wearily, 'the kids want to go home.'

'Tough!' Shen leaned over two rectangles of felt, sewing them together with embroidery thread. Her knees were up around her ears; it wasn't easy balancing on child-sized chairs. 'I need to make one more. Don't want Mike to feel left out.'

'You're ever so good at this,' said Paula, who only had a cross-eyed crocheted owl in front of her.

'You've found your vocation,' agreed Evie. 'You're the most glamorous crafter known to man.' She'd been amazed that Shen had allowed herself to be dragged to the craft area, but even more amazed when Shen had fallen into a craft reverie, churning out useless small item after useless small item. 'If Clive ever goes bust, you can sell bespoke comb-holders.'

'Shame they only have felt,' muttered Shen. 'Cashmere handles better.'

'Remember when we did stuff like this most days? I miss being a little girl,' said Evie. Little girls didn't juggle family needs and personal hopes in their miniature world of drawing and brushing dolls' hair.

'Me too,' said Paula with feeling, struggling to correct her owl's squint.

'It's almost as relaxing as knocking my opponents out at my aikido class.' Shen's needle plied in, out, in, out, as she asked with an oh-so-casual air that didn't fool Evie, 'So, Paula. You and Jon? What's your dating story?'

'Dating story?' Alarmed, Paula crocheted her owl a second beak.

'We've all got one. Evie here fell for Mike when he kept going to the same cafe as her.'

'And ordering the same thing as me,' said Evie, trying not to sound proud of her romantic history. 'Egg-and-bacon buttie.'

'Even though,' said Shen, 'he doesn't like eggs. Greater love hath no man, as the saying goes.'

'Jon and I don't have a story to rival that,' said Paula.

'You must have,' said Shen. 'Because that's one of the *dullest* stories I've ever heard.' She picked at a knot in her thread, then said, ignoring Miles's shrieks of 'I'm sick of this!' from a padded galleon, 'With Clive and I, it was love at first sight.'

'She saw his wallet first.'

'Evie's joking,' said Shen, unaware that Evie was mouthing, 'No, I'm not,' behind her back. 'I met Clive when I was on the bonnet of a Porsche at a car show. Apparently he turned to his friend and said, 'That's the girl I'm going to marry.'

'*Next*,' added Evie, enjoying herself. 'The girl I'm going to marry *next*.'

Loftily ignoring her, Shen went on. 'He chased me, Paula. I made him work for it.'

'How . . . um . . . nice,' said Paula, whose owl was looking lumpy.

'He says I'm the most infuriating woman he's ever met.' Shen preened. 'But he'd never leave me.'

Nobody had suggested otherwise. Evie watched Shen over the plastic tumblers of Ribena, realizing that Shen often insisted that Clive would never leave her.

'We have a deal, you know?'

'Not really,' said Paula.

'The terms of the deal mean that Clive's entitled to get in my way and dirty the towels, but he has to bring home the bacon. Which he does. Clive brings home *mucho* bacon. So I do *my* job to the same high standard.'

'I'm all ears,' said Evie. 'What *is* your job?'

'Looking good. Staying young. Being a trophy.' Shen threw a comb-holder at Evie when she grimaced. 'Shut your face, Germaine Greer. So what, if I'm a trophy? There are worse ways to live. I never welch on a deal. Why do you think I have so many clothes? You know, I'm a common-sense person at heart: nobody *needs* eight pairs of almost identical Manolos. The way I look reflects on Clive, and so I make sure I look chic twenty-four/seven.'

'Let me get this straight.' Evie had landed on a different planet. 'Shopping is your career? You over-spend on fur-trimmed thigh-high boots as a *job*?'

'I wouldn't put it like that, but yeah.' Shen nodded and the sheen on her jet hair strobed in the remorseless overhead lighting. 'I love Clive because he's generous and wise and powerful, and he loves me because . . .' She thought for a moment. 'Because I'm twenty-nine,' she said, with a flash of defiance at Evie.

'You won't be twenty-nine forever.' Evie wondered how, in all their hours of accumulated chat, Shen had never before been so baldly honest. Maybe it was the Wellcome Manor effect. Hell, maybe it was the comb-holders. 'And he'll still love you.'

'Hope so,' laughed Shen. 'We've had bumps in the road and we got over them. Like you and Mike, back in 2009.' Shen put a hand on Evie's arm, her short fingers slim and waxy, like a child's. 'I know you're superstitious about mentioning all that. You got through it by pulling together. By doing your *jobs* as partners. Isn't every marriage a deal?' She turned to Paula, who jumped. 'Are you madly in lurve, P? Is that the deal with you and Jon?' She barely gave Paula time to blush before adding, 'Am I right in thinking that Jon was seventeen and you were twenty-five when you had Tillie?'

Paula's colour deepened, from pink to ketchup. 'Oh, well, in a way.'

'He was seventeen in a way?' Shen kicked Evie under the table, and Evie kicked her back, much harder.

'Ignore her, Paula,' said Evie firmly. She was just as curious as Shen, but not as ruthless. 'Change the subject,' she said, even though a teenage Jon and an older Paula making a baby was a challenging thought.

'Yes . . . um . . . well,' said Paula, as Mabel shouted, 'I want to live with a different mummy who won't make me do soft play!' 'I did want to say . . . I really *did* see somebody outside last night.' She lifted some of her chins. 'I did.'

Not this again. A gloomy fog of déjà vu washed over Evie.

'By the swing. Pacing.'

The déjà vu dissolved. 'That was *me*!' Evie was glad to dispel the mystery, even though a realization came hard on the heels of her pleasure. If Paula had seen two figures, she'd have to reveal that the other was Clive. Explaining a moonlight tête-à-tête to the maniacally possessive Shen would be tricky.

'No, no, it wasn't,' said Paula, almost sadly, clinging to her nice comforting Peeping Tom.

'The pacing ghost was me. Brownie's honour. Were you ever a Brownie? No? Well, I assure you, a Brownie's honour is a serious matter. If I'm lying, Brown Owl will hunt me down and take me out.'

'Truly?'

Relieved that no shadowy 'other' had been mentioned, Evie had a bitter taste in her mouth at keeping something from Shen. 'Why would I lie?'

'There are many reasons people lie,' said Paula.

'Well, yes. But I'm not lying, honest.'

'Of course you're not.' Paula wiped a hand across her features. 'Listen to me. What am I like? Sorry, Evie.'

'Stop saying "Sorry".' All three women laughed as Paula shaped her mouth to say 'Sorry' for saying sorry.

The only other secret Evie had ever kept from Shen was how much she really weighed.

Oh, and Jon's cheating. She stole a sideways glance at Paula. 'Let's go home,' she said, 'and distribute all these wonderful comb-holders.'

Somewhere out there, as the smouldering day subsided, a rounders match was in progress; Evie had no idea who was winning and couldn't find a toss small enough to give about it, too busy feeling relieved that she'd finished cooking and serving roast chicken to six adults and eight children and had lived to tell the tale.

With only Mike to help (all the other Herreras were missing in action, popping up the moment the gravy was decanted), Evie had flailed. Mike hadn't known how to warm plates, or if the peas were done; he'd laid the table without knives. This lack of domestic skill perplexed her. He was proud of his capabilities, so why, when he washed up, did he leave the mucky casserole dish to 'soak' – that is, stand in tepid water until his wife caved and dealt with it? How had he passed forty-one summers on earth without amassing the wherewithal to set an oven timer?

Even as Evie thought these treasonable thoughts, Mike was in the kitchen carefully putting glasses back in the wrong cupboard.

Shen's dinners were always immaculately served. The plates and silverware stood to attention when she set them down. The woman was like a duck; all the activity was below the water line, invisible. Shen was as serene cooking a feast as she was wafting about in one of her kaftans.

Speaking of which . . .

'Another new floaty thing?' asked Evie, as Shen emerged from the house and took her customary seat and poured her customary large glass.

'Do you like it? It's Fendi,' said Shen. 'That chicken was divine.'

'Thank you.' Warmed by the compliment, Evie forgot for a moment to keep the lit treehouse window in her gaze;

she'd worked up a superstition that if she held it in her sights, nothing *too* disturbing would happen inside it. Mike emerged and put his mouth to her ear. Enjoying the warm rush of his breath against her hair, she expected a sweet nothing, but heard instead, 'Tell you what: if Jon *has* got Miss Pritchett holed up in the village, she's the most understanding mistress ever. The man hasn't been out for longer than it takes to buy a paper, for the last forty-eight hours.'

True, but Evie couldn't unsee what she'd seen. 'Isn't it nearly time for our nightly cuddle with the Fangster?' she asked Shen.

'Here she comes!' Shen's face broke into an uncomplicated smile; she was slightly goofy when she forgot to 'do' her smile, and it never failed to touch Evie's heart. 'Hello, Beautiful.'

'Say hello to Mama,' said Elizabetta to Fang, in that even voice that never rose nor dipped.

Clive took shape from the dusk, crossing the terrace, stepping over a discarded lilo and scattered towels and a ragged scrap, which just twenty-four hours ago had been Mabel's fancy new swimsuit, but was now one of Patch's chew toys. (Patch was the Gok Wan of the collie world; he never destroyed a chain-store garment, homing in instead on quality items.)

'You've got your daddy's nose, haven't you?' Fang looked squarely back at Shen, offering no opinion on the matter and managing to convey that she found the topic beneath her.

'No, she hasn't, Shen. Fang is the image of your mother, through and through, God help her.' Clive kissed Fang on her domed head; the baby pulled a face, evidently not being keen on cigars. 'Come back to me when you can talk, kid,' he said, kindly. 'I'll know how to deal with you then.'

'Yeah, you're *great* with them when they can speak.' There was an eerie disconnect between the ecstatic expression that Shen maintained for Fang's sake and her sarcastic tone. 'Ten out of ten for Zane, big Daddy.'

'Zane's not so bad.' Mike flopped on the chair beside Evie, eagerly snatching up the glass of wine she offered him. 'He'll grow out of it.'

'Into something even worse.' Shen shifted the baby to her other hip: Fang was round and bonny and *heavy*. 'I asked him his ambition, and he said to be famous. I said for what? He said it didn't matter.' She narrowed her eyes. 'So shallow. At his age I was working.'

'Me too,' said Clive.

'I like Zane,' said Evie. *I have to*, she thought, *as he's embarking on a summer romance with my daughter*. She smiled at Tillie, who'd climbed the steps to the terrace to snaffle some lemonade. 'Back me up, Tills. Zane's no nightmare, is he? Doesn't swear. Doesn't smoke.'

'There are other ways to be a nightmare,' said Tillie, taking a glass.

'Well, yeah.' Evie had expected solidarity. 'But you should hear about some of the boys Mike grew up with, what *they* got up to.'

A shutter clanged down over Mike's expression. He was sensitive to any mention of his history; as his wife, Evie knew this, and she kicked herself, grateful to Shen when she changed the subject.

Shaded by a weeping willow, right on the borders of Wellcome House's domain, The Eights were deep in debate.

'It's not *beg off*,' said Miles, with some of his father's confidence. 'It's *bog off*.'

'I always say *beg off*,' said Mabel, who had never said it. 'I think people say *you right tart* as well. That's a really bad one, though.' She felt ashamed and very happy, at the exact same moment.

'What about *up your bumhole*?' Miles did a jig with the sheer badness of that. 'I dare you to say that to your mum.'

'I've already told her to *bloody off*,' said Mabel.

'No, you haven't,' said Miles.

'*Whore*,' said Amber. '*Slut. Psycho-bitch.*'

The others were impressed.

Prunella and Patch joined in the 'fun' of rounding up the kids for bed. As soon as Mike grabbed hold of one small holidaymaker, another sprinted past, cackling like The Joker. The pug tripped him up; the collie ran into a tree.

'Show me this contract you mentioned then.' Clive sat alongside Evie on the bench.

Evie handed over her phone and he scrolled down the screen, reading intently. They'd gravitated to this corner when the bedtime rodeo began, as if they'd agreed to meet.

'Looks sound.' Clive peered over half-moon glasses that

Evie had never seen before. 'Nail down the date of your first pay-review, darling. Suggest three months; cheeky, but if you ask for six they'll up it to a year.'

'A crash course in business!' laughed Evie.

'Didn't you know I part-own a small ad agency?' Clive handed back the phone.

'No.' Evie part-owned very little; she was impressed. 'Blimey.'

'It does OK.' He spoke in bullet points, unlike his usual affable style. 'Right. My advice. Make yourself indispensable early on. Do more than they ask. Sniff around the creatives. Then you might get a crack at copywriting.'

'Really?'

'With your background? Of course.'

Of course? There were no 'of courses' in Evie's life. 'What background would that be?' It was quiet now, the children lassoed and indoors, the adults scattered.

'You did a few years in the industry . . .'

'A thousand years ago!' scoffed Evie. 'Things have changed.'

'And so have you.' Clive folded his arms, regarding Evie as if such an attitude puzzled him. 'You write novels. In other words, you pump out creative work to strict deadlines and word-counts.'

Put like that, the wilderness years with Lucinda Lash sounded like solid experience. 'I just hope I'm not nobbled by being a mum,' said Evie. 'You know, if one of the kids is sick, or I get in late because Dan misses the school bus.'

'So from now on, you all get up an hour earlier. Have your own mother on standby. Ensure Scarlett understands

that you rely on her. Get that husband of yours to understand he's in this too. Never let your home life interfere
with work. *Never.*'

Hurdles were no obstacle to this man; he vaulted over
them.

'I feel so guilty.'

Clive snorted. 'Pointless self-indulgence.'

'It's me who holds the family together. Now I'm pulling
it to pieces.'

'Bloody hell. It's just a job, Evie. Expect your family to
pull their weight and they will.' Clive nudged her. His arm
was bulky and hot. 'They owe you.' He stood. 'You can do
this,' he said, not like a motivational quote, not like a biased
mate, but like somebody who believed in her.

But why does he believe in me? thought Evie, as he left
her and made for the open French doors of the drawing
room. Clive had handed her the tools to tackle the job at
hand. So accustomed to furtiveness, it was heady for her to
feel energized and confident.

'Darling . . . darling!' Through the sheer curtains came
Clive's voice, trying to placate, but not doing very well,
given the tone of Shen's answering, 'Oh, stick it up your
arse, Clive!'

'As you wish, my little lotus blossom,' he called as Shen
punched her way through the sheers and stalked over to
Evie's corner of the terrace.

'Thanks.' Shen stood over Evie, a glass of wine in each
hand; a first, even for Shen.

'For what?'

Shen handed her one of the glasses. 'Taking some of the

strain.' She winked. 'With my old man. Literally. My old man *is* an old man. He does love to talk. And talk. Thanks for helping me out by letting him bang on.'

'He's a good listener too.' Evie defended Clive, but carefully.

'He's got no choice!' Shen let out a loud *ha!* 'With me around.'

The picture Shen painted of her other half was sketchy. Clive was kind; Evie was startled by her use of the word. She'd never thought of him as any soft and fuzzy adjective before.

Shen drained her glass and shook herself. 'Better follow him up. According to the schedule, it's sex tonight.'

'TMI!' yelled Evie at her receding back.

Out of the shower, standing before the long mirror in the dimly lit room, Evie regarded herself as Mike slumbered in the burrow he'd made of the bed.

Damp, she was naked in all senses of the word. No make-up. Her true feelings upon her face.

That woman looks unhappy, thought Evie, taking in the face that was a parody of the snapshots of her youth, as if somebody had Photoshopped puffy crescents beneath the eyes and a ladder of lines across the forehead. She touched her jaw; lately her jawline – a thing she'd never even noticed before – had begun to annoy her. It was sagging, yes; definitely sagging. She fingered it, as if touching it might encourage it to behave.

Turning, she confronted her bottom full on. On the whole, she ignored her bottom. *It's big and that's that*, she would think, getting on with life, making the best of it, enjoying how it upholstered cold bus-stop benches for her. Tonight she must face her bum.

Maybe it was the non-stop beauty-pageant parade of bikinis. Teenage girls in bikinis. A lithe nanny in a bikini. And Shen in a bikini.

Shen was so neatly made, as if turned out of a mould. Every inch of her was clean, unmarked, fragrant. It took some willpower not to feel like a sack of compost beside the much younger woman. The kaftans that floated on Shen would be sausage-skin tight on Evie.

Comparisons are pointless. This was Evie's line when Scarlett worked herself into a tizzy because she didn't, and never would, look like Rita Ora. Her own body had been through so much, had weathered such knocks and shocks, that it deserved respect and gratitude, not criticism. *Who cares what other people look like?* On the whole, Evie took her own advice, but what did Mike really think of the changes time and trauma had wrought on her flesh?

She glanced at him. He was twisted, heavy, as if he'd been thrown across the room into the tangle of covers. Surely the difference in inches and cellulite between herself and Shen didn't go unnoticed by him? As she went back to the shower room, Evie allowed herself a small sigh: just the one, for the matriarch can't afford to wallow too deep in these puddles; she has stuff to do.

Click.

The shower room went dark. Mike heard Evie's bare feet on the boards, sticking slightly, still damp. He stealthily laid down his phone, and its green glow died under the bed.

The mattress lurched. The sheet snaked away from him. Evie sighed; her customary exhalation before settling into sleep.

In front of the mirror, wet, hair all anyhow, she'd looked wild and exuberant. The ins and outs of her were a fairground ride – Mike wanted a ticket.

He pounced. They kissed. The kiss lingered. Evie made a swooning noise he particularly liked. They froze as a mobile phone announced the arrival of a text.

'Ignore it,' they said in unison, mouth-to-mouth.

Beneath the bed, unseen, unread, the message landed: **going mad in my empty bed thinking of you I want to devour you Mikey I want to tease you and maul you I WANT YOU don't make me come get you!!**

The treehouse smelled of Scarlett, of that perfume she wore. Roses. Something like that. Zane stretched out on the makeshift bed of cushions. How many had the girls dragged up here? And what was it with women and cushions?

He turned over. He could see the windows of the house through the jagged outline of the treehouse porthole. He was grateful for the heavy feeling in his limbs. Tonight sleep would just claim him; it wouldn't be one of those arid, wakeful nights. Perhaps he'd sleep out here every night of the holiday. It felt right, more *him*, on the edge of things.

What a bunch they were, these three families. They thought they were so discreet, good at hiding the important stuff, but the outsider Zane had X-ray vision and saw their secrets. He'd dreaded this holiday, done everything he could to squirm out of it. His usual techniques had failed him. Mum was adamant; so adamant that he'd been insulted. *Are you trying to get rid of me?*

But now . . . now he felt each day pass as if diamonds were running through his fingers and all he could do was watch them fall to the ground. And all because of a girl. It thrilled Zane whenever he imagined making his move. And then it oppressed him, because he couldn't ever imagine having such courage.

He turned on his side as a thought stabbed him: *Why did I say all that shit earlier?*

Zane had had sex once, two years ago, and he'd spent the twenty-four months since worrying that he'd done it wrong.

Beneath the tree, the garden slept. It wasn't silent; there were scurryings, slitherings. He sat up at a more emphatic noise. Was it the prowling cut-throat? Zane, keen to escape into sleep, decided it was a fox.

He looked up at her window, then closed his eyes, so it was the last thing that he saw before sleep. It was sacred.

DAY 6
Sunday, 16th August

Hi All Next Door,

Got your message. Please don't worry about the fish. I'll replace them and the kids will never know. We're on our fourth Finny and Bubbles already. And no, that smashed window isn't evidence of an attempted break-in – it's been like that since January ...

Evie x

Evie gritted her teeth. It would be easier to run a travelling circus, or invade a small kingdom, or herd cats through a dogs' home than chivvy everybody out of the house.

Mike had insisted, 'It's perfect picnic-on-the-beach weather!'

'No,' Shen had countered. 'It's perfect hanging-around-your-palatial-rented-house weather.'

Evie had wanted to add that she didn't feel great. She felt, to quote her grandma, 'a bit *off*'. Mike had noticed. 'You all right?' he'd asked gruffly.

The gruffness hadn't fooled Evie. The answer he wanted to hear – the only answer he could cope with – was the one she gave him: 'I'm fine, darling. Slept badly, that's all.'

For six years Mike had policed her every twinge. To him, they were all symptoms. She kept headaches from him, stoically bore a jippy tummy without complaint, in case he started feeling her brow, taking her temperature, *watching* her.

'Darling,' she'd said gently, just last month. 'It's not coming back. I feel ill because of the kebab that seemed like a good idea after the pub quiz.'

Eventually, somehow, Mike cajoled the kids away from the trampoline and the teens from the treehouse and Clive from his phone. 'Who are we waiting for?' He looked back towards the house. Timing was crucial; hesitate a moment too long and an Eight would need the loo, or Shen would realize she hadn't packed her picnic lipstick.

'Coming!' Paula was heffalumping through the front door, negotiating the steps awkwardly, with – they all saw it – *that* look on her face.

'You OK?' Mike put his hands on her shoulders.

'Not really.'

Shen's frustrated growl travelled out of the Ling-Little passenger window.

'My ring,' said Paula, twisting her finger as if trying to dismantle her hand. 'My wedding ring.' She appealed to Jon, already at the wheel of their BMW. 'It's gone.'

'Are you sure?' He was patient, but it was a rude patience, as if what he actually wanted to do was turn on the ignition and drive off, screaming. 'Because, Paula, last time this happened . . .'

'Can we go?' whinged Miles.

'I know I left it on the en-suite basin,' said Paula.

'Let me look.' Evie unbuckled her seatbelt and dashed back to the house as Mike shouted, like a hostage-taker, 'OK, nobody else move! And that means you, Shen!'

There was nothing on the basin except a sheen of soapy water. Evie checked the floor, the shelves, beneath the claw-footed bath. She tried not to clock the chaise longue on her way out, but had to look: the pillow and rumpled sheet backed up Shen's story about the Browns' sleeping arrangements.

Paula took the news stoically, and at last the cavalcade of cars jolted through the gap where the gates should be.

'Man, it's hot.' The windows were down, but Mike was suffering, wiping his brow. Tucked in between the kids on the back seat, Patch slobbered noisily; Evie knew how he felt.

'Why couldn't I go with Tillie?' pouted Scarlett.

'You mean,' said Mike, 'why couldn't you go with *Zane*.'

'What? Get off! No! God-duh.'

'You love him,' said Mabel.

'You want to snog him,' said Dan, biting his fist at the awfulness of that thought.

'Shut up! Seriously. Shut up.'

'Leave your sister alone,' said Evie.

'Thank *you*,' said Scarlett.

'Just because she loves Zane doesn't mean we should all go on about it.'

Over the laughter, Scarlett said, 'Mum! God! You don't know anything!'

'Hey!' Mike's sharpness chopped the merriment off at its knees. 'You do not talk to your mother like that, young lady.'

'I just did.'

Noo, thought Evie. *Not another one of these, please*.

'Who do you think you are?' said Mike, frowning into the rear-view mirror as Clive, car-hood down, overtook them, honking his horn.

'Shut *up*,' said Scarlett, as if dealing with the official most-stoopid guy in the world.

'What did you say?'

Neither, thought Evie, *will back down. That's the problem*. 'Can we just enjoy our day out?' she asked.

'That's what I'm trying to do,' said Mike. 'Madam won't let me.'

'Yeah, right, it's all my fault.'

'Scarlett, I mean it . . .'

All in all, the drive to the beach was a long ten minutes.

The kites bobbed fretfully high in the blue.

'I have to admit,' admitted Shen, 'this is fun.' She had a knack for flying kites, it turned out. Even with her hair blowing in her face and her heels sunk in the sand, she looked as if she was on a fashion shoot. 'It does exactly as I tell it!'

'As do we all, darling.' Clive was among the dunes, on a stunted picnic chair, which made him look like a circus bear on a tricycle. 'Did you remember the champers?'

'It's in the same coolbox as the sushi,' said Shen, in between hollers of joy as her kite looped-the-loop. 'The crystal glasses are in the hamper.' Her picnics were not as other picnics.

'There'd better be a sausage roll,' muttered Scarlett mutinously, wiggling into her swimsuit under cover of a towel.

Mike's kite dive-bombed the beach. '*Behave!*' he shouted, as if it could hear him. 'Dammit.'

172

'Swear!' shouted Mabel triumphantly, busy fashioning a seaweed bonnet for Patch.

Evie lay back on a towel and pretended she couldn't feel shells digging into her body. She had never felt able to confess her dislike of the beach. It was like disliking kittens, or honesty; *everybody* likes the beach. Maybe it was the sand, which got everywhere; she dusted it from her orifices for days afterwards. Or maybe it was the sea, which was noisy and wet and needy, constantly rushing at her.

Plus she could never get comfortable. She fidgeted and shifted, imagining all the tiny creatures using her as an adventure park. At shrieks from the water's edge, she shielded her eyes and saw Scarlett and Tillie braving the waves. 'Rather them than us, eh, Mike?'

'He's abandoned you.' It was Clive's voice. Hat on, shirt on, he too withstood the beach's siren call. Evie wondered if he'd ever be able to get out of that tiny chair; his bottom appeared fused to the webbing.

Clive nodded to where, a little way down the under-populated beach, Mike wandered, head down, phone to his ear.

'He's still manacled to the office,' said Evie. She understood that the demands of everyday life couldn't be stuffed in a box, no matter how seductive the charms of Wellcome Manor; earlier she'd spent half an hour composing an email to Alex, according to Clive's suggestions. To her delight, Alex had rolled over and agreed to every one of her demands. Hiding her jubilation from Mike made her feel seedy.

'Go over there,' said Clive, 'and biff him one.'

'Maybe later. I prefer to biff after lunch.' She lay back,

eyes closed. She didn't want to discuss Mike with Clive. Her mind wandered – another by-product of beaches, and one that could backfire – and recalled last night, when the 'outside world' had broken in on their lovemaking. It hadn't been the same after they'd heard that text arrive. Assuming (wrongly, it had turned out) that it was her phone, she'd stiffened, unable to concentrate. Mike, too, had stumbled at the noise, and she knew his body well enough to know he'd been going through the motions. When she got back to London, she'd have a word with his assistant; phoning late at night on holiday was a no-no, surely? She needed Mike to be thoroughly present. She winced at a sudden twinge of discomfort. Twice now she'd felt that spasm. *No need to take any notice*, she told herself, *until it's three times*. And it probably wouldn't happen a third time.

'I'm starving,' said Dan. 'Starving starving starving starving starving starv—'

'Stop it, darling,' said Evie.

'Me too,' said Mabel. 'Starving starving starving starving starv—'

'Stop it,' said Evie. Mabel noticed the dropped 'darling' and glowered.

'Amber!' Paula's voice was sharp. 'Have you been in the sea?'

'A bit,' said Amber apologetically. She was dripping wet from head to toe.

'Tillie, you're supposed to be watching your sister,' said Paula.

'I thought I was *supposed* to be on holiday,' said Tillie.

'Now, Tills,' remonstrated Jon mildly, as if dismayed by her.

'Proper plates?' Mike curled his lip.

'I'm going to stop believing in God,' said Dan, 'if there aren't any Wotsits.'

'Everybody, just shuddup and eat.' Evie's shout was the Herrera version of grace. Finally she was within fondling distance of a quiche Lorraine. They'd laid and relaid the tablecloth three times before Shen was satisfied, and even now she was adjusting her parasol and saying 'melanoma' under her breath. Prunella had stolen a California roll. Patch had walked in the hummus. Clive's chair had broken.

The beach had done it again.

Jon leaned in as Evie resmoothed the tablecloth and laid out the offerings to the Great Picnic God. 'Lovely spread,' he said.

'Thank you.' She felt a little better and was grateful to him for being neither smug nor manic – something quite beyond the other adults. She tuned in to Shen's latest complaint. 'What's wrong with paper napkins?' asked Evie.

'What are we – farmers?' Shen poured soy sauce into tiny glass dishes. The sushi was beautiful; Shen had a masterly touch. But it was all wrong for such a setting. The fish soon felt warm, and therefore suspect; Evie covertly unwrapped the mini pork pies. 'Where's Fang?' she asked, registering the absence of the smallest holidaymaker.

'Back at the house.' Shen, while not avoiding Evie's eye,

didn't rush to meet it. 'Elizabetta thought it would knock her schedule out, so . . .'

'But you employ Elizabetta,' said Evie, eyeing Mike's half-eaten sausage roll lasciviously. 'Not the other way around.'

'It's for the best,' said Shen, as if bringing babies to the beach was some newfangled notion.

Carefully separated from the boring grown-ups and the tedious kids, the three teenagers had set up camp further along the dunes. Clive motioned to them with his cigar. 'Love,' he said, 'is in the air.'

'Yup. 'Fraid so.' Evie smiled.

'At Zane's age,' said Clive, 'I was in love with my best friend's mother.'

'Ooh,' said Evie, scandalized. 'Did she know?'

'She knew all right,' said Clive, the look on his face hinting at X-rated memories.

'I wasn't allowed to date.' Shen flicked away a fly as if it were paparazzi. 'My parents wanted me to save myself for a nice Chinese boy.'

'That's me, by the way,' said Clive, bowing. 'I'm the nice Chinese boy she saved herself for.'

'They didn't like Clive,' said Shen, launching into an impression of her mother. '*Why you bring old man home?* Then she saw my engagement ring.' Shen held up a hand weighed down by a diamond like a meteor.

'Suddenly I was acceptable,' said Clive.

'I had boyfriends before Mike,' said Evie, recalling the procession of pimply oiks. 'And I thought I was in love. But then you-know-who came along and that was that.'

Mike looked at the ground. He didn't seem to have heard.

All eyes were on Jon and Paula, waiting for their story to complete the set. Finally Paula said, 'We seem to have known one another always.'

'That's sweet,' said Evie, even though Paula had said it as if something was wrong with the truth, but they hadn't had time to cook up a lie.

'Oh, we're very sweet,' said Jon, so bitterly that nobody laughed.

'Sweet's our middle name,' said Tillie, stealing up on them, her bare feet making no noise on the sand.

'Thmile!' shouted Amber, leaping into the middle of the cloth and brandishing a disposable camera.

Paula ducked as if Amber had yelled *Thniper!*

'Good idea.' Mike held up his phone, trained the lens on the assembled holidaymakers. 'Say "cheese".'

'No, I really don't, I mean . . .' Paula buried her head in Jon's shoulder. He sat immobile, as if he hadn't noticed her.

'Let's put it on Facebook,' laughed Shen. 'Show the Ubers what a great time we're having without them.'

'No!' Paula was fierce now, all her timidity vanished. 'Absolutely not. No!' She reached out and snatched Mike's phone. Only when she had it in her hand, and everybody was staring at her, did she come to. 'I'm sorry,' she said, holding out the camera like a naughty toddler.

'Facebook is dumb, anyway,' said Mike heartily. 'Who wants a game of footie?'

'Not,' said Shen, 'me.'

Evie's thinking went this way as she made her way through the whispering dunes in search of her daughter: *I have put in seventeen years of looking, of worrying, washing, cooking, reading aloud, spooning Benylin into you, holding your hand literally and metaphorically, nagging you into bed, then nagging you out of it; the least you can do is hang out with me at the beach.*

Scarlett didn't see it like that.

'Mu-um,' she said, 'go away.'

'No.' Evie stuck out her tongue, planting herself on the blanket spread on the velvety sand amongst the nodding grasses. She'd wondered what the teens were up to – like The Eights, they were now an entity – but, as ever, they were up to very little. They'd elevated lounging to an art form.

'We're, like, *talking*,' said Scarlett.

'I can do that.' Evie noted Zane roll onto his back, switching off; old ladies, apparently, were not his 'thing'.

'No, you really can't.' There was mild panic in Scarlett's voice.

Amused, Tillie said, 'We're talking about the Nyko Zoom Range reduction lens. You know, for Xbox. With Kinect.'

'Hmm.' Evie stole a sweet from an open packet. Its fizzy taste poked a hole in her past and she was momentarily a child again. 'Nope. Nothing to say on that subject. So, instead, tell me what you want to do with your futures?'

'Oh God, Mum, for God's sake,' spluttered Scarlett, sitting up. 'This isn't a bloody job bloody interview.'

Tillie took the question seriously. 'I'm going into the service industries,' she said. 'That's a massive market that'll keep growing and growing.'

Noting Scarlett's rude gawp at such collaboration with the enemy, Evie said, 'After university, I'm assuming?' She nodded at the face-down book by Tillie's knee, 'An English-literature degree?'

'Nope. I'm getting stuck in straight after A levels.'

'But . . .' A degree was the Holy Grail to the families at St Agatha's gates.

'What's the point? I'm going to work for myself. I'll begin by becoming a cleaner . . .'

Here Scarlett made an odd noise, then apologized.

'I'll take a bookkeeping course. Then, when I know what professional cleaning entails, I'll recruit staff and get stuck into refining the company. Eventually I see it as a concierge set-up, where we carry out chores for customers. Not high-end, particularly, so I've got to be careful about my price-points.'

There was silence as Zane and Scarlett stared at Tillie as if she'd just arrived from Planet Nerd. Evie wanted to kiss her. If children really are our future, as the song says, it was in safe hands with sensible, original Tillie. Plus, it would be tidy.

'I'm going to uni,' said Scarlett.

'And then, Scar?' asked Tillie.

'And then . . . not sure.' Scarlett lay back down with a

sigh. 'But, first, uni; so, to quote Dad, he can pay good money for me to sleep all day and get off with gits.'

'Never did me no harm.' Evie saw the others packing up hampers, folding blankets and winding in kites. 'Time to go.'

Lurching away and sinking in the sand, she felt an arm tuck into her own.

'I know that look,' said Evie, taking in her daughter's chewed lip.

'You do?'

'I know what's going on, Scarlett.'

'You do?' Scarlett was dumbfounded.

'Did you think you're being mysterious and elusive?' Evie smiled at Scarlett's lack of self-knowledge. 'It's written all over you.' Scarlett looked over her shoulder at Zane and Tillie. 'Both of you.'

'And you don't mind?'

'Why should I?'

'Well, Dad would . . .'

'Dad is Dad. He'll come round.'

'Mum, I know it wouldn't be your first choice for me.'

'No, no, you've got me wrong.' Evie wished Scarlett had been around when she defended Zane.

'Nothing's really happened.' Scarlett spoke in a rush. 'You know . . .' She faltered.

'I know.' Evie saved her daughter from elucidating.

'Maybe I'm not reading the signals right. We make some progress and then next day . . . back to square one.'

'Two steps forward,' commiserated Evie, 'one step back. All love affairs are like that at the beginning. It took weeks of going to the pictures to see films I didn't really want to see, before your father spelled it out in black-and-white.'

'Nothing like this has ever happened to me before.'

Evie envied Scarlett and felt afraid for her; she was on the threshold of a giant landscape that would more or less dominate her entire adult life: the pursuit and capture of love. 'Take it slowly. Baby-steps. If it's meant to be, it'll work out.'

'And Dad?'

'No – Dad's taken. I've got Dad.' Evie enjoyed Scarlett's snigger. Just because love is one of the great building blocks of a happy life didn't mean it couldn't be frothy and spar-kling. 'You'll always be Dad's little girl, even if you live to be one hundred and four. It's hard for parents to accept that their children are growing up. If you scraped your knee when you were teeny, I had to send Dad out of the room until I'd kissed it better and you'd stopped crying. The possibility of you being hurt in any way tears him up inside.'

'Just because I'm grown-up . . . it doesn't mean I don't love him.'

'Dad knows that better than he knows his two-times table.'

Bringing up the rear, Tillie said to Zane, 'Hel-*lo!* You can talk to me, you know. You don't *have* to keep your eyes on Scar's arse the *whole* time.'

'Sorry,' he said.

'Yeah, you sound it.' Tillie persevered. 'You know my ambitions. What are yours?'

'Same one I've always had,' said Zane. 'Living down to my dad's expectations of me.'

'Why not change the expectations?'

'Why should I?'

'You're screwing up your life to annoy your dad then, yeah?'

'You try having a dad like mine.' Zane sounded the closest he ever came to lively. 'You're lucky.'

'Tell me how I'm lucky, Zane.'

'Your dad loves you and lives with you.'

'My dad,' said Tillie, 'is a monster.'

Ahead of them, Scarlett and Evie sped up, until Evie broke into a run. Something about the way the other adults were dashing about, trampling the kites into the sand, bothered her.

'She's missing!' Shen, halfway to the treeline, turned. 'Mike's gone to the car park. Clive's doing the rockpools.'

'Who's missing?' Evie grabbed Shen's arm as Mabel's face, with its pointed chin and constellation of freckles, filled her consciousness.

'Ow!' Shen rubbed her arm. 'Amber. I'm sure she's just wandered off, but . . .'

'Amber?' Tillie streaked past them, calling her sister's name.

A veteran of 'lost child' panics, Evie counselled calm. 'Tillie, we'll find her. Mabel's wandered off a thousand times and—'

'Amber's not Mabel!' snapped Tillie, taking off down the beach.

'Amber!' hooted Dan.

'Amber!' shrieked Mabel.

'My little girl, my poor little girl.' Paula hugged herself as Jon darted off.

Torn, Evie decided there was sufficient manpower searching and put her arm around Paula. 'She'll be back in two shakes of a lamb's tail.'

Paula wasn't listening. Evie kept talking, willing Amber to pop up, sandy and happy. Paula's fear was infectious; the beach, benign and sunny a moment ago, now looked sinister. She saw Mike, hip-deep in the sea, scanning the water and she shuddered.

'I knew it'd come to this,' Paula murmured.

'Don't talk like that,' said Evie, just as Clive yelled, 'She's here!'

'Is she . . . ?' Paula looked up, evidently expecting to see a body, but was rewarded instead by Amber bouncing along on Clive's shoulders, waving a twig as if it were a wand.

Everybody's posture changed. Shen, who would never admit to panicking, slowed down on her heels. Mike waded back to shore. The packing up began again in earnest.

'She was up a tree,' said Clive, depositing Amber on the sand. 'Quite high up a tree,' he added, impressed.

'Did you speak to anybody?' Paula was on her knees, shaking Amber. 'Did anybody touch you? Tell me!'

'No!' Amber switched from carefree to horror-struck. 'I was looking for nests. Am I naughty?'

Before Paula could frame the *yes* she obviously wanted to, Jon took Amber's hand. 'No. Help me put the kites back in the car, eh?'

Nobody except Tillie heard Zane's whispered, 'He doesn't seem too bad to me.'

'You don't know the half of it,' she said. And she looked, suddenly, ten years older.

Wellcome Manor was large enough to enfold all three families, yet still seem serene. Evie was glad of the peace as she cracked on with another chapter:

> *'Why, yes,' I reply hungrily. 'I adore a cream tea.' Licking my lips, I undo a button and his gaze drops to my breasts. 'But a naked cream tea is even better.'*

Scone-erotica: Evie had discovered a new genre.

> *With his pointed tongue, Clay licks the jam from my taut tummy. I groan as he strokes the velvet skin of my inner thigh with a small cucumber sandwich, and when I see the size of his egg mayo I almost*

Any reader would surmise that Evie was more interested in the nibbles than the nipples.

> *'I want you!' I breathe, feeling his greedy erection hard against me. In a frenzy of desire, I sweep the tea things away and lie back on the table, pulling Clay's body against mine. I grasp for his*

His what? Evie was all out of smutty simile. To distract herself, she did a little literary housekeeping, tidying up her grammar and rewording clumsy sentences. Somewhere in the first few pages Roxana had said she longed to 'lay' with the hero; that bugged Evie. At that point Roxana was still a demure virgin – Evie would have crossed the road to avoid her – and there was no way she'd initiate sex until Clay had royally rogered her a few times. Using the 'Find and replace' tool, she found Roxana's use of 'lay' and replaced it with 'live': *I long to live with you* was more like something Roxana would say. Satisfied, she closed the document.

Writing about sex didn't turn her on, but writing about a cream tea made her ravenous.

Threatened with an early bed, The Eights were road-testing a strategy of being very, very quiet, in the hope that the adults would forget they were there. It was a tactic Evie remembered from her own childhood; she'd lie motionless on the sofa, dizzy with delight that *News at Ten* was on *and she was still up*.

There was a flaw in this plan; the children stayed so quiet they fell asleep, lying around the terrace like abandoned mattresses. Elizabetta stepped over them as she made her way from her eyrie above the garage to the kitchen in a pyjama-shorts set so small it was surely a child's size.

'Your turn, matey.' Evie nudged Mike, and he and Shen abandoned their cards and woke the eight-year-olds and cajoled them upstairs.

'I'll take Amber,' said Jon, rising with his trademark blend of politeness with a soupçon of martyrdom.

'Oh, thank you, thank you.' Paula was grateful; too grateful, considering that he was helping with the fruit of his own loins.

'Just you and me, then!' Evie was doggedly enthusiastic as she dealt another round of cards, even though she knew Paula found it hard to concentrate and often had to ask if they were playing poker or snap.

This time Evie heard the noise just before Paula did. 'What on earth—?' She got no further, because they both realized exactly what on earth they could hear from the bushes: two dogs getting jiggy with it. She and Paula avoided each other's eyes until the canine ecstasy abated and Pru waddled past looking, it had to be said, very pleased with herself.

'Onwards!' said Evie brightly. She noticed something as Paula reached out for her cards. 'Your ring!'

'Oh, that – yes.' Paula was as cagey as ever, as if Evie was an FBI agent. 'It turned up,' she said.

'Where?'

'Silly me, it was on the basin, right where I left it.' She laid down an eight of clubs.

'But I saw the basin. It wasn't there.' Evie pulled in her chin. 'Seriously, Paula, your ring definitely wasn't on the basin when we left the house.'

'Well, it was definitely there when I got back.'

'That means somebody put it there.' Evie felt it best to state the bleedin' obvious.

'No, it doesn't.' Paula closed the cards in her hand like

a fan. 'It really doesn't. I – *we* – just made a mistake.' She rubbed her eyes. 'I'm too tired to play any longer.'

'Me too,' fibbed Evie. 'Fancy some cocoa?' The soothing qualities of this magical drink worked wonders in the Herrera house, and Evie's belief in it was rewarded by a nostalgic glow in Paula's eyes.

'That would be lovely,' she said, as if she didn't expect such small kindnesses.

'I'll be back in a mo.' Evie realized she was using the tone she adopted when Mabel fell over or Scarlett had period cramps; Paula brought out her maternal side, even though the woman was her senior. Rubbing her eyes, she wandered into the kitchen. Clive and Elizabetta, close together, sprang apart.

'I warm some milk,' said Elizabetta, her face passive, 'for Fang.'

'I was helping,' said Clive.

'But of course,' said Evie, opening a high cupboard and scanning it for the cocoa tin. 'Warming milk. Definitely a two-person operation.' She reached up and winced.

'You OK?' Clive had noticed; he seemed glad of the change of subject.

'Fine,' said Evie, with a hint of edge. She softened. 'Sorry, Clive – yes, I'm OK.' He wasn't to know it was her third twinge.

I'll take them seriously at number four, she thought, revising her earlier decision. They were, after all, merely twinges.

187

It was so dark that Evie could have believed she was alone at Wellcome Manor. Or alone in the world. She shuddered, and was glad when Clive joined her at the bench.

'We need a plaque.' Clive sketched an oblong in the air. '*Our bench*.'

'I don't think of it like that.'

'I do,' said Clive. He hesitated, as if gauging her reaction to what he was about to say. 'And I think you do too.'

'Don't flirt with me, fella,' said Evie. 'Go find Elizabetta, if that's what you're after.'

'You have a suspicious mind.' Clive shook his head, as if disappointed. 'Is that how you see me? The bounder who gropes the nanny?'

'No . . .' At least, that wasn't how Evie *wanted* to see him. 'But, seriously, Clive? Helping her to warm some milk? That'd never stand up in court.'

'She said she had her hands full and she asked me to hold the pan, and I leaned across to put down my glass and somehow, suddenly, we were practically bloody entwined, and I remember thinking: *Christ, I hope nobody walks in on this* – and there you were.'

'So you weren't flirting?'

'No!' He looked pained.

'You were very close together.'

'*We're* very close together.' Clive paused. 'Are we flirting?'

'No!'

'Well, there you are then.' He was good at pauses, and he timed this one expertly. 'You're absolutely sure we're not flirting?'

'I'm not a silly young nanny, Clive. I know what I'm doing and what I'm not doing.'

'Good,' said Clive. 'Because I don't like silly young nannies.'

'Would you ever, though . . .' Evie fumbled for the right word, 'stray?'

'Stray? How?'

'You're pretending not to understand.'

'And I'll continue to do so. You're my wife's best friend, Evie. If – and I said *if* – I played away, why the hell would I tell you?'

'True.' Evie laughed. 'Forget I spoke.' It was something that Shen brought up occasionally, in an oblique way. 'Oh, Clive's working late again, and we all know what that means,' she'd laugh, prattling on before Evie could comment. Sometimes Evie felt Shen was laying a trail of breadcrumbs, but it was only here, on this holiday, witnessing the dynamics of her friend's marriage up close, that Evie began to suspect there was something truly rotten at the heart of it. She could only do friendship one way – honestly; if Shen needed to talk about this, then Evie would listen, but she needed the facts first.

'Why are you so interested?'

'I'm not *so* interested.' Evie felt the silence thicken. She could laugh off the conversation, steer it in another direction with a gag. Instead she said, 'Shen's my friend, Clive. I wouldn't like her to be hurt.'

'Would she be all that hurt?' Clive balanced on the slender line between serious and jocular.

'She'd be devastated.' Evie was astonished by his

189

astonishment. Did Clive really buy all that *I snagged my millionaire* hogwash?

'Your marriage is very different from mine,' said Clive. 'Different rules apply.'

Evie looked steadily at him, the way she looked at Dan when refusing to let him off the hook over a fish finger trodden into the rug.

It always worked on the kids, and it worked on him. 'I don't seem to be able to lie to you, for some reason.' Clive flung his cigar, harshly, as if it was his last ever. 'Yes. There – I've had affairs. Happy? I'll probably have more.'

Eventually Evie said, 'Why?'

'I've never thought about why.' He folded his arms, threw back his head. 'Because I can. Christ, that sounds shitty.'

'It does, a bit.'

'OK. Let's put it like this. Because I'm restless. I get bored easily. I like new things, shiny things. I like the chase. And I'm easily flattered.'

Evie wanted to say, 'You sound like a toddler.' Instead she said, 'But you have so much to lose.'

'I'm accustomed to losing things.'

'That,' said Evie, sitting up, 'is one of the saddest things I've ever heard.'

'Then you really need to get out more.'

'Ah. We're back to being light and witty again, after a brief detour into sincerity.' Evie was disappointed: this conversation was like a square meal after a diet. The frisson of not wanting to be overheard added a certain something. 'Do you ever fall in love?'

'That's a question only a woman would ask.'

Mike would ask; Evie felt sure of that.

'I'm very careful not to choose somebody I'd fall for. I like the look of many women, but love . . . that's something else entirely.'

'Clive, you're a closet romantic!'

'Rubbish.' He recoiled as if she'd struck him. 'I'm hard-headed. I keep everything in separate compartments. There's my life at home, with Shen. My *real* life, if you like. And then there's the other stuff.'

'The affairs.' Evie didn't let him off the hook. 'Let's call a spade "a spade".'

'The *affairs*,' he nodded, defeated, awarding her a sly, amused look, 'are with girls I trust to be discreet. They have a lovely time. We dine out. We go to dazzling places. There's some travel. I'm good at gifts. And then, when it ends – because it always ends – it's done gently, with affection and . . .'

'And?'

'I'm searching for a nice way of saying something that sounds damned seedy.'

'You pay them off.'

'Can you read my mind? Yes, I suppose that's what I do. It sounds sordid, but it's not. Well, I hope it's not. They're well provided for. It's not always cash. Sometimes it's a job, or an opportunity. I'm not a cad.' He seemed to rethink that. 'Not a complete cad.'

'Oh, you are,' said Evie.

There was another silence, then Clive said, 'Do you still like me, Evie?'

'Yes, Clive,' she said. 'I still like you.'

And she did. Even though he was a cheat. Even though he cheated on her dearest friend, a woman she was closer to than either of her sisters. She couldn't begin to contemplate how the Ling-Littles made this arrangement work, but this close to it, she appreciated that it was a complex, human thing. Being judgemental wouldn't help.

'You're the only person I've ever been this frank with.'

'I am?' To a woman whose honesty amounted to incontinence, this was puzzling.

'You're easy to talk to, Evie.'

'So are you.' Evie stood up. 'Time to seek out my other half. Ask *him* if he's having an affair.' She laughed at that – at how absurd it would be. For one thing, Mike didn't have the time.

'You know what lawyers say: don't ask questions you might not like the answers to.'

'This is different.'

'No marriage is *that* different.' Clive stared into the darkness. 'And, as you're so intent on honesty, we *have* been flirting.'

'You may have been,' said Evie, hoping she kept the fluster out of her voice. 'I haven't.'

'Sorry. My mistake.' Clive was amused again.

'Oh, shut up,' she said, taking advantage of this intimate new footing to insult him, the way she routinely insulted her husband. 'And goodnight.'

She wasn't sure if she was dreaming or not. Evie heard a whirr, like a small metallic creature waking. 'Wassat?' she slurred.

'Shh, nothing – just my phone. Go back to sleep,' said Mike.

Evie was slumbering by the time he finished the sentence.

when I see you I'm going to lick you all over every beautiful inch of you Soon soon very very soon then we can be together xxxx

DAY 7
Monday, 17th August

Hey,
Sorry but I had to leave.
One day I'll come back and explain.

love, Tillie x

Being first to the kitchen was a badge of honour. Evie bullied herself out of bed to get the kudos just this once, but Shen was there, humming, squeezing organic oranges.

'You're even in full slap.' Evie's own face resembled the unmade bed she'd just left.

'I've done a high-impact workout.'

'Urgh!' As Evie toasted and buttered, she noticed an enormous bouquet. 'And you even laid the table?' She took in the crisp white tablecloth, the cutlery laid out just so, the jug of orange juice, the napkins. 'My lot are lucky if I don't miss when I throw the cereal across the room into their bowls.'

'Nope, this was here already.' Shen tweaked a bloom. 'Clive was the last to go to bed, so he must have done it.' She hesitated. 'For me. He knows I like things to be . . .'

'Poncey?'

'I was going to say *nice*.' Shen flicked Evie with a tea towel.

'How romantic.' Evie was as chuffed as Shen at this husbandly gesture; was Clive's conscience finally pricking him?

'Even if you applied thumbscrews, Clive couldn't tell you where we keep the napkins at home.'

'I'd have to *buy* napkins, before Mike would be unable to find them,' said Evie. 'Maybe Clive's falling for you all over again.' Clive-in-London played a bit-part in Evie's life, but she understood Clive-in-the-country better. Not that this earned him a Get Out of Jail Free card; far from it. Clive was a cheat; *end of*, as Scarlett would say.

Despite this, Evie detected a note of deep yearning in Clive. 'One thing's for sure.' She hoisted herself onto a stool. 'These flowers ain't for me. The last time Mike surprised me like this was . . . let's see – *never*.' She saw a tiny card amongst the blooms and read it out loud: '*For my darling P.*'

'Who'd have thought Jon had it in him?' said Shen, impressed. She turned at a noise in the doorway. 'Oh, look, Paula! These are for you.'

Paula bundled up the tablecloth, parcelling knives, forks, plates and flowers. Dropping crockery, sloshing juice, she manhandled her parcel outside and flung it onto the lawn.

'Are you mad?' shrieked Shen.

Surveying the mess on the lawn, Evie mourned the loss of her photogenic breakfast; burnt toast tastes better off Royal Doulton.

'Disgusting!' Paula looked at the stained, lumpy linen as if it were a body-bag containing body parts. A change overtook her face. As if she saw what Shen and Evie could see. 'I'm not crazy,' she said.

'That's what all the crazy people say,' said Shen.

'If you knew . . .' Paula's face creased and wobbled, 'what I've been through.'

'Tell us,' said Evie gently, 'Perhaps we can help.'

'But that's it!' Paula was angry, as if Evie had sworn at her. 'Nobody can help.' She slammed into cabinets as she left, a demented pinball.

'The one time Jon *does* get romantic, she gets weird,' said Shen, adding defiantly when Evie frowned, 'It's the only word that fits.'

Spilling the beans about Miss Pritchett would help Shen to understand Paula's moods, but it would also mean letting a large and hairy cat out of the bag. Could she trust Shen not to blurt out something? To make a double-edged remark? Much as she loved her, Evie decided she couldn't tell Shen about this particular cat.

The extended, tenuously linked Wellcome Manor family trickled to the kitchen, lured by the smell of bacon and the *arf-arf* of Patch hoping for a tossed sausage.

Merrily frying an egg, Mike said, 'Shen, you can't intimidate me into muesli. I love this egg more than I fear you.'

'I'll quote that at your funeral,' said Shen, who, on the subject of nutrition, was an irony-free zone. 'Which will be ten years earlier than it should be.'

'Daddy,' said Mabel, attempting to smuggle a breakfast choc-ice out of the freezer, 'isn't allowed to die.'

'True, Mabes,' Mike smiled, 'and put that choc-ice back, you cheeky monkey.' He leaned over to Evie, who was awaiting her fried egg a little too keenly. 'Where's Dan?'

Evie, her eye on the pan, was at a loss. 'Dunno. Are we

neglecting our Danno?' She frowned; middle children were easy to disregard.

'Are we?'

'Maybe we need to spend more quality time with him.'

Locked in a mutual wince, both knew the other yearned to hear: '*Mais non!* The boy is happy! Let's get on with our lazy holiday and not worry that he's storing up emotional trauma that will one day erupt as binge-drinking and/or impregnating strippers.'

Miles wandered in. 'Mummy,' he began breathlessly.

Weighing quinoa with one hand, Shen handed him a folder with the other. 'Do ten Fun Maths questions before breakfast. Then we'll speak French for the rest of the day, yeah?'

Evie did her best not to smirk.

Dan, still in Spiderman pyjamas, tore in and fell over Pru.

'Dan's just fine,' said Mike.

'I have the number of that tutor we talked about.' Shen had created a balanced, wholesome breakfast that no sane person could want. 'She worked wonders with Miles.'

Where to begin? Not with *we can't afford it*, because Shen would offer to pay. Not with *Dan's doing fine without a tutor*, because to Shen nothing short of Potential Prime Minister could be classed as 'fine'. So she went with a simpler, 'I like kids to be thick, anyway. Makes 'em easier to control.'

'I fucking hate maths.' Miles threw down his pencil.

'Miles!' Shen swivelled to face him as the teens tried not to laugh.

'Sorry,' cheeped Miles. 'I meant *je fucking déteste le maths*.'

'Where did he hear such language?' spat Shen.

'Why ask me?' Evie put down her fried egg; this slur outranked her lust for crispy edges and yielding yolk. 'Not from my children, if that's what you mean.'

'I don't swear in front of him,' persisted Shen.

'What are you saying?' Evie felt attacked.

For an answer, Shen plonked a plate in front of Miles. 'That word is forbidden in this family.'

'Which word?' Miles hoped very much the word was 'maths'.

To save The Eights, Evie flung herself in front of the bus that was Mike's latest idea.

His eyes shone. 'The Thomas Hardy museum tells you so much more about the man than the books ever could!'

Evie begged to differ, staring at a waxwork Thomas Hardy sitting stiffly at a desk, while a waxwork Mrs Hardy with her wig askew regarded her hubby with an indecipherable expression in her crossed eyes. The commentary in her headphones kept sputtering out, as if boring itself to death, along with Evie. 'The great man was born in . . . He had a very . . . Of course, his new wife was full of . . .'

'Where's Jon?' She tore herself away from Thomas Hardy's actual waistcoat (the great man had been bang into green tweed, it would seem).

'The loo.'

'That was . . .' Evie glanced at her watch, 'ages ago. Unless Jon's got a prostate problem, he's escaped.'

Grimacing slightly – no man can hear the word 'prostate' without an involuntary *Oof* – Mike said, 'He's probably buying a souvenir.'

Yeah, cos he'll want to remember this golden day forever. 'He's buggered off to see Miss P.'

Mike rebuffed this theory, based on . . . well, very little, in Evie's view. 'God, you've got a suspicious mind.' He looked closely at her. 'You look tired.'

'Gosh, thanks.'

'How do you feel?' Mike scrutinized her face, much as he'd just scrutinized Thomas Hardy's long johns. 'Are you, you know, OK?'

'Yes. And unless your hand is an actual thermometer, there's no point putting it on my brow.'

'But are you *OK* OK?' Mike invested the inane word with intent. 'You know what I mean.'

'Yes, I do.' Evie heard herself become spiky. 'Because you constantly ask me, and I constantly know what you mean. So lay off.' She softened, regretful. '*Please.*' Before Mike could respond, she looked over his shoulder and called, 'Here he is!', hailing Jon as if he was returning from a war, rather than the Gents.

'See?' said Mike as they followed Jon to the car. 'All perfectly innocent.'

Evie did see. She saw that Jon's shirt was inside out.

Mike travelled light through life; he could pick up everything he cared about, if the house caught fire. Evie, Scarlett, Dan and Mabel. Everything else could burn and melt.

Oh. And Patch, obviously. Mike would have to carry Patch too.

He and the dog shared the egg-shaped hanging seat in a sun-trap corner of the grounds. It was so inviting, like one of the magazine pictures Evie brandished. Now, within its rattan embrace, he was less in love with it and its seasick motion. He was half-leaning, half-sitting, Patch curved around him like a bum-bag. Mike's philosophy of living light was proved correct; this covetable piece wasn't all it was cracked up to be.

Wellcome Manor was studded with want-able, costly, desirable . . . *stuff*. He couldn't find a more appropriate word; nobody would race from a burning building carrying an egg-shaped hanging seat.

He switched position again as Patch complained softly, before reapplying himself to his master's body, so close they were practically sharing the shorts.

Lunch had been spoiled by a specific magic trick that Evie could pull, whereby she ignored him while talking to him. She only said things that would be in any couple's script – *Pass the salad, there's mayo on your chin* – leaving out the quirky intimacies that made them *them*.

This oddness – slight but noticeable – pre-dated the holiday. She had been off-kilter for . . . Mike wondered how long. Weeks? Months?

Perhaps Evie was right and Mike didn't think enough about her – about them, that separate 'them' that was their marriage. Yet he thought about her and them all the time!

Had he allowed his wife to withdraw, inch by precious inch, because he was too wrapped up in the time-bomb he himself had set a-ticking? Paranoia that Evie might read an inflammatory text on his phone consumed Mike, until the couple who prided themselves on honesty were divided by half-truths.

He had a horrible suspicion he knew what Evie was hiding.

When Mike thought of 2009, he saw the entire year in black-and-white. It was a non-year, a gap in his life – the *real* life that had begun with Evie.

For longer than was sensible she had hidden her fears about her health. Mike would never forgive himself for not noticing the chasm in their closeness.

Even now, six years later – *six* already? – he couldn't say the word. Born on 30 June, Mike answered 'The Crab', when asked his star sign. All through Evie's treatment and its aftermath he'd avoided the six-letter word that described her ailment. It was 'it', 'the illness', sometimes even 'the enemy'.

The memories were as vivid as yesterday. The talk with Scarlett; only eleven, but she'd guessed something was up. Something bad.

'Will Mummy die?' she'd asked.

'No, darling, absolutely not.' Childcare manuals would berate Mike for that promise, but he couldn't tell his trusting little lamb the truth: *Yes, Mummy might die.*

They'd been open with Scarlett after that; he recalled her blunt and gentle fingers tracing Evie's new scar.

There shouldn't have been a scar. He'd kissed his wife's forehead in the hospital bed and reassured her. 'A laparoscopy,' he said, 'is *soooo* routine.' They had all the facts: a keyhole incision, the insertion of a tube that sported both a light and a camera, and then the removal of the pesky stones that had caused her periodic but intense stomach pains.

He knew she'd downplayed the agony, shutting herself away until the nausea, the sweating, the vomiting eased. It was Scarlett who'd outed her. 'Mummy!' she'd yelped one evening, as Evie bent to kiss her goodnight after another epic Peppa Pig tale, 'You've got horror-film eyes!'

All around the blue irises, Evie's eyes were a curdled, sick-looking yellow.

The particular blue-grey (or grey-blue) of his wife's eyes were stars in Mike's personal sky, yet he hadn't looked closely enough to notice the change. 'Doctor!' he declared. 'Tomorrow.'

Meekly, un-Evie-like, she'd agreed.

Before that first consultation, neither of them had given a thought to their gall bladders; they now became experts. 'Your gall bladder,' Evie had told Shen, 'is a small, shy, pear-shaped creature who nestles beside your liver, spending his days processing bile, a digestive liquid produced by the liver.'

The compression stockings had gone down a storm. 'Christ, I've never wanted you more!' Mike said, just as a nurse walked in to check that Evie had fasted for six hours.

Evie had nodded. 'I would quite literally punch my way through a steel door for a cheese-toastie.'

They'd bantered until the door swung open and a brisk orderly arrived with a wheelchair to take Evie to surgery.

Suddenly serious, she said, 'What if something happens?'

'Evie, Evie,' said Mike in the voice he used to reassure Scarlett about the werewolf who lived, apparently, under her bed. 'I'll see you back here, in no time, and you can have that toastie. It's just gallstones.'

Evie's face as she was wheeled away brought all Mike's latent superstition to the fore. *What if*, he thought.

Soon he knew exactly 'what if'.

The surgeon came out to talk to him. Mike had seen enough episodes of *Casualty* to know what that meant. He'd steeled himself not to turn and run, to listen as the surgeon used the word that turned Mike's insides to water.

The cancer, posh Mr Double-Barrel explained, had turned a straightforward procedure into a cholecystectomy. A more significant operation, it necessitated a wider incision. 'We've removed your wife's entire gall bladder.'

He'd imagined Evie's cherished body, ransacked.

'It's not a vital organ,' the surgeon said, as if people left their gall bladders on the bus every day. Everything else had to be repeated later by the nurse, a kind woman who understood the restorative powers of strong tea.

'She's lucky.' The nurse looked down at Mike, bent double on a plastic chair. 'Only one in four gall-bladder cancers is spotted this early. It's a grade-one.'

'What does that mean?' Mike cringed, expecting a blow.

'It's the least likely to spread.'

'So she'll live?'

'Of course she'll live.' The nurse laid a hand on his arm, but wouldn't be drawn on how long Evie would live. On whether or not 'it' would come back. They were questions even the GP couldn't answer, Mike was to find out.

Evie stayed in bed, no longer yellow. Mike was nostalgic for the yellow, now that she was so very white. The scar remained angry and red and raised.

Dismayed by her failure to thrive, nobody at the hospital could agree on treatment, wasting time debating radiation therapy. Mike was gruff and demanding with the professionals, barely able to stop himself screaming, 'But this is my wife!' while they hummed and harred and took yet more blood from her sore arms.

When Evie told the story, it was peopled with kind and heroic medics doing their best.

Mike never told the story at all.

When radiation was deemed unnecessary, Evie swooned with relief, but Mike wanted every possible treatment. He wanted armed guards around her internal organs. At the very least, he wanted a straight answer about the likelihood of recurrence.

This was not forthcoming.

Meanwhile, the house had changed. The clutter seized its chance and took over, the carpets became Patch-coloured. Accustomed to having their mum on tap, the children articulated their unease in tantrums and sudden aversions (Mabel's carrot-hatred was rooted in those days). Scarlett was sombre with her responsibility, telling the younger ones fairy tales when Evie took to her bed. The tales Mike told himself, as he lay awake beside Evie in the small hours, never had happy endings. He didn't dare think so far ahead.

Evie was lucky, people said; Mike never agreed. She'd lost a stone, along with her spark; his wife was not lucky.

'But I am!' she insisted, three months on, in another waiting room. (How they loathed plastic seating by now, and water coolers, and back copies of *Hello!*) 'I'm alive.' She'd pirouetted to prove her point. 'My scar isn't pretty, but frankly neither is my arse. OK, they can't tell how long I'll live, but they don't know how long you'll live, either! If the doc hadn't opened me up to remove those gallstones, the cancer would have taken hold before any symptoms developed. So, see, I *am* lucky.'

Mike had rehearsed how to tell his children their mother had died. He'd rehearsed what he'd say at her funeral. At the all-clear, he'd said nothing at all.

She likened it to being released from jail. 'Or,' she laughed, 'being given the all-clear from cancer!' Unfurling, like a tree in leaf, she could once more imagine the children's future without sorrow, inserting herself again into the family album.

'You can cry, you know,' she teased Mike after they left the surgery to wander aimlessly, dizzily.

'I don't want to.' He was projecting himself into the future; to when the angelic chord of the all-clear would morph into a low and ugly note of fear of those six letters returning.

Now, in the sunny calm of Wellcome Manor, Mike heard that growling note.

The swinging seat banged against his legs as he jumped up. He needed to hold Evie, to protect her. And beg her forgiveness. Without telling her what she had to forgive.

He wouldn't want to escape a fire without Evie in his arms; he'd simply lie down in the flames.

The vacant egg-shaped seat was colonized by the teens and their communal aura of shower gel, shampoo and body spray, strong enough to knock a grown man off his feet.

'Ladies first, Zane!' said Mike as he hurried away.

'Cool.' Zane hung back, letting the girls climb aboard.

'*Ladies*?' spluttered Scarlett.

Wandering towards the pool, Patch at his heels, Mike considered Zane's *cool*; the boy calibrated every utterance so that it could be either stroppy or polite. As if daring the world to think the worst of him.

Not that Mike distrusted the boy: he *recognized* him and his wary 'Am I welcome here?' look, which hardened into 'Well, fuck you anyway' the second he sniffed rejection. Mike and Zane had much in common.

Reaching the pool, Mike saw his red-faced wife wiggling into her swimsuit beneath a towel. He recognized her low-level panic as she desperately tried not to flash any pale flesh.

He loved that flesh. Mike could get drunk on his wife's thighs. The abundance, the generosity, the *home at last* feeling of her soft, strong body thrilled him. She was his personal adventure playground, and a kind of church too. *If I told her that,* thought Mike, *she'd assume she'd married a lunatic.* Evie's essential her-ness was intact: nothing much was wrong.

As long as she never found out.

'Come on in, yummy mummy!' shouted Clive from the water.

Smugly, Mike waited for Evie to fillet the porky mogul efficiently with some choice words.

'Oh, shush!' She smiled, as if batting away a cheeky pup, not a patronizing chauvinist.

Mike stretched out next to Shen, who was sunbathing with the same intensity she brought to everything; she was really, *really* sunbathing. 'Hi, Elizabetta,' he called casually, keeping his focus on her face, which lived only inches above her gravity-thwarting décolletage.

'Hi, Mike.'

Instantly he felt drawn into a conspiracy. He wondered if Evie noticed Elizabetta's subtle flirtatiousness; for the sake of his balls, he sincerely hoped not.

Whooping, Clive and Evie raced down the pool. Mike would have thrashed Clive, whose swimming style was best described as Walrus in Trouble.

'I can't compete with a young filly like you,' he panted.

Evie was many things, but she was no filly. Mike was surprised when she didn't pull a face at such eye-wash.

Mike was bursting with compliments. He admired so many things about Evie it would take a year just to jot them down, but they never made it out into the open.

Prunella licked Mike's fingers, then tried to jump up on him, her stubby claws vicious, even though her intent was friendly. 'Come up . . . Gorgeous.' He practised flattery on the flat-faced little creature. Prunella sneezed onto his legs.

Evie had loosened him up around the kids, saying, 'Flowers need sunshine to bloom.' He managed to force out 'Well done, Dan' or 'I'm proud of you, Mabes'. It barely did justice to his feelings; Mike *was* proud, but not of their achievements. He was proud of them for walking, talking, laughing; it daily blew his mind how he and Evie had *made* three whole little people. Three staggeringly beautiful little people, at that.

'You know how I feel about you,' he'd said once to Evie. 'Why must I keep saying it?'

'Because,' she'd answered, 'you must, sweetheart. You just must.'

She complimented *him*. All the time. *It's a good thing I'm level-headed* thought Mike, *or I could get a little cocky about my bum* (he was extremely cocky about his bum). When he'd tried to explain why he rarely reciprocated, Evie had thrown up her hands.

'So we're back at the care-home again!' she'd shouted, in a rare display of impatience. 'Can't we ever leave that bloody place behind?'

'Hey!' he called now to his wife, who was pushing her sopping hair back from her face. 'Prunella's putting on weight! But, Evie, *you* haven't!' *No time like the present*, thought Mike, *to start complimenting your missus.*

'Eh?' Evie kneaded chlorine-angry eyes.

'Put on weight. If anything, you've lost a pound or two.' Why was she staring like that? 'Not that you need to. Not that anybody needs to. A woman's weight is her own affair, even if she's twenty stone. Which you aren't. Not now, anyway. Now you're quite . . .' Mike tailed off. This flattery lark was tricky. 'Thin,' he ended, quietly.

'Jesus, Mike, you're an idiot,' said Evie.

Another magnificent meal. Evie was so impressed with Shen's dim sum that she forgot it was good for her.

As she filled the dishwasher, Miles ambled past, saying, 'Psycho-bitch whore' experimentally to himself.

'That's not a nice thing to say, sweetie.'

'I know!' said Miles gleefully.

Toting a pyramid of dessert plates, Evie said, 'You're a *brilliant* cook.'

'Thank you,' said Shen.

'Zank you,' said Elizabetta.

'Eh?' Evie paused. 'No, hang on, Elizabetta, don't go just yet.' The nanny halted in the doorway, her back to them, Fang's outraged baby-face peeping over her shoulder. 'You both prepared dinner?'

Elizabetta stayed mute.

'Yes, yes, Elizabetta made it,' said Shen, exasperated. 'Sue me, why don't you, for prawn-fraud?'

'Madam pays me extra,' said Elizabetta, escaping.

'Madam's a cheat,' said Evie.

'Like just about everybody in this house,' murmured madam.

'How d'you mean?' said Evie.

'Have you told Mike?'

'You don't get to do that. Swerve like that. We weren't

talking about . . .' She threw a wary glance to the terrace, but Mike had vanished, 'my job.'

'I know.' Evie could tell Shen was sorry, but she didn't know that word in any of her four languages. 'Go, Evie. I'll finish up here.'

Out on the terrace the only available company was Paula. After a moment or two of silence, Evie Made An Effort. 'Are you sewing something?'

Paula held up a tiny dress, just centimetres long.

'That's exquisite!' Evie examined the tiny stitches.

'It's for them.' Paula gestured to The Eights on the floor at her feet, engaged in their interminable, open-ended doll game. Even Miles had become engrossed and, pooling resources, they'd created a doll family. The Barbies, Kens, Sindys, with a couple of Bratz, an Action Man and a wing-less Tinkerbell, were every bit as mismatched as their Wellcome Manor human counterparts.

Mabel's Barbie talked in the same emphatic deep voice as her owner: 'I'm off to buy a massive cat.'

A Bratz doll dressed like a prostitute had Mabel's lisp, 'Letsh call it Russell.'

'Gerroff, Patch.' Miles rescued Action Man from the dog's grasp. Tiny plastic hands were irresistible to Patch; most of Mabel's dolls had mangled stumps.

'Would you like to sew something?' Paula handed over a half-finished minuscule yellow ra-ra.

'I'll try.' Evie cack-handedly employed a needle. 'This is quite meditative. Has it helped you feel better about . . . earlier?' She didn't know how to describe Paula's demolition of the breakfast table.

'Yes, sewing calms my nerves.' Paula peered closer at a tiny seam. 'But it was Jon who straightened out my thinking. He's used to my silliness.'

'Hmm.' *Is it silliness to blow your top because your husband's shagging somebody else?* 'Peaceful here, isn't it?'

'Mmm.'

'It's nice, after London.' This stuttering conversation was like a bad first date. 'All those sirens.' She cast about for another archetypal London noise. 'Fox-sex.'

'It was like this where we used to live,' said Paula. 'Nobody else for miles.'

Another person would enlarge, but Paula had to be prompted. 'Did you move for Jon's work?'

'Hardly. He's a cab driver.' Paula was as close to sharp as she could get.

'So what made you move?'

Paula's face was hard to read, but Evie sensed cogs whirring. 'Well, there were . . . issues with our house.'

'Issues?'

'Jon was happy, but . . .'

'But?'

'I made him up-sticks. That man's a saint.'

At their feet, Miles adopted a squeaky voice for the scantily clad doll who was, for the purposes of the game, a mum of eight. 'Look at me, I'm your mummy!'

'Mums don't say that,' scoffed Mabel, disappointed with his doll prowess.

'Have her crying,' suggested Amber.

That evening's card game started up behind them. It was shaping up to be a double-hander, just Clive and Shen.

'You. Are. Cheating,' said Shen.

'No, my little Venus Flytrap, I. Am. Winning.' As ever, Clive sounded amused; as ever, it bugged his tipsy wife.

'If I'm a Flytrap, you're the fly, sonny Tim.'

'*Jim*, darling. Sonny Tim doesn't exist.'

Shen dealt another hand, smacking down the cards like insults.

The doll action became increasingly surreal.

'Whee!' Miles dropped the mother of eight from a great height. 'I'm dead!'

'Let's rescue her!' Mabel tucked a Monster High doll and Tinkerbell into Prunella's collar. 'On our magic doggy!' They had reached the stage of the evening where they communicated in exclamation marks. 'Quick! Ken!'

Amber's Ken doll seemed not to mind that the magic doggy was sniffing its own private bits.

'These games,' said Evie, 'are daft, bless them.'

'I love listening in,' said Paula.

This irony-free conversation began to relax Evie; she and Shen got very arch round about the second glass. 'Eight's a great age.' *Although,* thought Evie, watching Mabel valiantly try to extract Prunella's nose from Prunella's bottom, *all ages are great*.

Using Ken's hard head, Amber knocked both of Mabel's dolls out of Prunella's collar.

'Hey!' protested Monster High.

'Thut your thupid face!' Ken jumped up and down on Monster High. 'I with I'd never thet eyeth on you, you ugly cow!'

Both Evie and Paula managed to pretend neither of them had heard.

'Amber, darling,' sang Paula, 'Come and help us sew.'

'Mummy!' Mabel's face folded, like a flower dying. 'Amber said—'

'Run and get my glasses from the kitchen, sweetie.'

'What?' The little girl's wrath wiped her indignation clean away.

'Chop-chop.'

'I'm just a slave,' muttered Mabel, dragging her feet.

'Room for one more?' Mike pulled over a chair, whispering to Evie, 'Here come the lovebirds,' as Scarlett and Zane meandered, in that drifting way of young folk, out to the terrace.

'Come *on*,' Zane was pleading. 'Let's go to the treehouse.'

'It's dark,' pouted Scarlett in a baby-voice. 'What if somebody really is hiding out there?'

Zane reached out his hand. 'You're safe with me.'

Evie and Mike looked at each other. Evie shook her head in a *No* at Mike as he half-rose.

Scarlett looked down at the hand being held out to her. The fingers tapered; the wrist was all bone; the skin was the colour of the husk of an almond.

Zane said, 'I won't let anybody hurt you.'

Scarlett glanced towards her parents, who hurriedly looked away, humming, clearing their throats, looking as guilty as hell.

'OK.'

Evie sensed the air ripple as the hands joined. Her

daughter's retreating outline softened and disappeared in the twilight. Scarlett had crossed a momentous line.

So had somebody else; Mike had managed to stay in his chair, instead of flying out of it, pinning Zane to the ground and giving him a crash course on How to Treat My Daughter.

Nursing a not-hot-any-more drink, Evie wandered the dark downstairs, looking for her laptop. The house was bright with the blueish light of the moon falling in stripes and squares across the velvets of the drawing room. Spotting her mac on the coffee table, she tucked it under her arm and opened the French windows. Evie stepped out into the night just as Scarlett skipped up the steps from the lawn.

'G'night, Mum.'

'Night, love.' Evie searched her girl's face for signs. *Like what*? she asked herself. *I JUST DID IT tattooed on her forehead?*

They'd had 'the talk', of course. They'd discussed love and sex and the whole damn thing a few times. It was vital to Evie that her brood set sail with a full understanding of the facts of life, both biological and emotional. She and Scarlett had always had a frank, buoyant relationship.

Evie had always known that at some point her daughter would set sail on her personal sex life, but for some reason it clutched at her gut. Her own sex life was a source of happiness, pleasure, longed-for babies, yet the idea of her naive and lovely Scarlett getting into the sexual nooks and crannies of adulthood was disquieting.

A rift had cracked between them when Scarlett dated that fool of a boy for five months – he was Not Good Enough – and now it yawned into a gulf. It felt wrong not to know whether her own daughter was still a virgin . . . And yet, when she was honest with herself (it happened if the wind was in the right direction), Evie accepted that it truly wasn't any of her business.

Many seventeen-year-olds were sexually active. Evie wasn't a maiden aunt: hell, *fourteen-year-olds* were on the pill these days. She never judged these children (for that's what any fourteen-year-old is); instead she wondered how they coped with their early membership of the adult world.

Ah! Good. He was there.

Pulling her dressing gown tight, Evie took her seat beside Clive.

'Evening.' He smelled of cognac.

'We punched above our weight last night.' Evie rushed her words. 'It got a bit personal. Bop me on the nose with a newspaper when I get too nosy.'

'I liked it. You listen. As if what I say matters.'

'But everybody listens when you talk,' laughed Evie. 'You heap-big important man.'

'Almost everybody listens.' Clive filled in the blanks when Evie held back. 'Except my wife.'

'If wives went around listening to their husbands, we'd all be in big trouble.'

'Bet you listen to Mike.'

'Nope. Couldn't tell you what his voice sounds like.'

Clive said, 'You and Shen almost had a spat about the dim sum. Not like you two to snipe at each other.'

'This house's brochure should carry a warning that paradise can be more fraught than real life. All this free time puts stuff into sharp focus and . . .'

'Perhaps it's better when we all just muddle through. When we don't talk,' said Clive.

'Maybe,' agreed Evie. She stood up.

'I thought . . .' Clive's woebegone expression didn't suit him; he was designed to look regal. 'I thought we might sit out here for a bit.'

'Tillie left her book in the treehouse. I said I'd fetch it.'

'Really?'

'No, I'm making it up. Yes, really!' Evie giggled, wondering at Clive's intensity. Too much cognac, she decided.

Out in the blank darkness it was easy to imagine Paula's pet monster in the rustling garden. There were no landmarks, as if everything had melted, and Evie felt she might topple off the end of the garden, if she went too far. Feeling for the rope ladder, she held one hand out in front of her.

Back at the bench, Clive spotted her laptop, a techie version of Cinderella's glass slipper. His mouth framed to shout Evie's name, but he stopped himself and instead slipped back into the house with the computer.

Not especially nimble, with her dressing gown flapping like a sail, Evie climbed the treehouse ladder. Scrabbling around for *Catcher in the Rye* on the dark floorboards, her fingers encountered something both soft and hard. A knee.

'Oh, shit God!' Evie sprang back.

'Sorry, Mrs Herrera.' Zane firmed up in the shadows.

'You could have said something!' Evie sat back on her haunches. She glanced through the window that he sat by; the light in Scarlett's and Tillie's window was still bright. 'Keeping an eye on the ladies?'

'No!' said Zane, far too rapidly for it to be true.

'You're allowed to like people, you know.' Zane's thoughts and deeds were criminalized; some support might be welcome. 'I know about . . .' She wondered what young people called it. Assuming whatever she said would be wrong, she went with what she'd called it way back when. 'I know about your crush.'

'Dunno what you're on about.'

'OK. Sorry.' She moved and knelt on a book. 'I've got what I came for. I'll leave you be.'

The ladder shuddered as she descended. Zane was coming after her. Keeping a careful distance behind her on the grass, he spoke softly, as if chatting to the still night air. 'You disapprove. Obviously.'

'Nope.' Evie guessed the rules of this game and didn't look back at him.

'Really?' Zane's voice leapt upwards. Correcting it to its usual bass, he said, 'You don't think I'm out of my league?'

'Well, I'm biased, obviously. But people fall for people. That's the way the world turns. But listen, Zane,' Evie cranked up the seriousness; this was important. 'Be gentle. Go slow. Be a gentleman, yeah?'

'Yeah! Of course. Of course!' His meticulous cool fell away with a clang. 'If I had a hope in hell! If I was getting anywhere!'

Evie habitually went where angels fear to tread. 'She likes you, you idiot.'

'She *does*?' Zane stopped dead. 'No, man, don't do this, yeah? She is, for real, properly interested, like?'

'Properly.' Evie added 'bro', but managed not to add 'innit'.

Zane laughed. It was like firecrackers.

'That you?' Mike was four-fifths asleep as Evie slipped in beside him.

'No. It's Dolly Parton.' She stroked his hair back from his forehead. 'Of course it's me.'

'I don't think you're fat,' he mumbled sleepily. 'I think you're just right. For me, I mean.' He groaned, eyes still closed. 'Did I spoil the compliment again? I mean, you look fine. No, not fine, more than fine. You . . .'

'Back to sleep, Mike, before you make me swoon with your fancy words.'

In the womb-dark of their room Evie couldn't ignore it any longer. That insistent, gnawing mouth inside her. A feeling that was familiar to her. A symptom.

It could be a symptom of eating too much. It could be a symptom of some dodgy ingredient in the evening meal. It could be a physical reaction to the strain of keeping secrets from Mike.

She punched her pillow. Evie knew exactly what it was.

DAY 8
Tuesday, 18th August

Greetings, slaves!
   Having a great time. Loads of pics of Thomas Hardy
museum to share. COMPLETELY RELAXED!!!
                                    Boss man a.k.a. Mike x
                        p.s. Remember monthly figures are due.
                        p.p.s. Remind architects we need plans.
                        p.p.p.s. Use petty cash to buy new kettle.

A man of the world, Clive wasn't easily shocked, but the words scrolling down the screen made him whistle. Darting looks at the door, in case Shen's Spidey senses sent her in, he sat on the bed and read more of Evie's diary, or fantasy, or whatever she called it.

Deep down in the very pit of my soul I want this man.

Clive squirmed a little on the silk bedspread. 'Crikey, Evie old girl.'

Watching him is torture. His body sends signals direct to my panties. How can I concentrate on what he's saying, when all I want is to tear at his belt and see if the bulge in his trousers lives up to my feverish daydreams?

The innocent sounds wafting up from the garden came from a different world. In Clive's present world, people were smearing nipples with clotted cream.

Clive knew which world he preferred.

Guiltily, knowing he shouldn't, he tore through the rest of Evie's story.

'I want you!' I breathe, feeling his greedy erection hard against me. In a frenzy of desire I sweep the tea things from the table and lie back on it, pulling Clive's body against mine.

Clive stopped dead. He reread the last line, then read it again. He pinched the bridge of his nose, but the wording didn't change.

Reverentially he closed the laptop and stared at the wall for a while. Then he laughed and rubbed his hands together, and skipped – yes, skipped – out of the room.

Just along the corridor, Mike was reading something just as erotic: **I think of you and my whole body smiles my naughty lovely Mikey-man come get me lover!!! xxxx**

The teenage Evie had scoffed at her mum's assertion that things look better in the morning, but her mother was proved right. Again. (She'd been right about Evie's legs; they *were* just like her granddad's.)

With not a twinge, not an ache, she leapt out of bed like a kitten, albeit a fairly elderly kitten with a slight hangover. She had sailed through the morning and now she lay on a lounger, soaking up the warmth that the sun spilled so generously, feeling at one with the world. *Perhaps*, she thought, *I overreacted. I do that. I overreact.* She'd once threatened to leave home because Mike couldn't see what was so great about George Clooney.

'Christ!' Mike loomed, blotting out the promiscuous sun. 'You really look rough, Evie.' He jumped back as she sat up. 'Just saying.'

'Well, don't just say!' It irritated her when Mike treated her like one of the lads, as if years of cohabiting had stripped her of all femininity.

'OK, OK.' He held up his hands as if she was levelling a machine gun at him. Which wasn't a bad idea. 'Bad mood. Christ! Sorry I spoke.' His showy sigh said, *I put up with so much.*

Huffily Evie rammed her feet into her sandals and dragged on the aged cardigan that was her version of Shen's kaftan. She *did* look rough; she hadn't overreacted – those symptoms hadn't lied. 'I'll be indoors, looking rough, if anybody wants me.' If she stayed on the lounger, Mike would study her, examine her, pretending all the while that he was doing nothing of the sort.

Hard facts were needed. Evie's fears must either be confirmed or pooh-poohed before she allowed Mike anywhere near the situation. Asking him to hold her – as she longed to do – would provoke apocalyptic predictions.

Collaring Evie, Shen was in her white ninja-style Lycra aikido gear. She panted, fresh from practice, 'I know just what we need!'

Just this side of testy, Evie paused on the steps. 'Do tell me, Your Majesty.'

'We need a girls' night out.' Shen readjusted her hat, a cream satellite dish that protected her from the sun, and added a small 'Woo-hoo!'

'We do?' Evie didn't feel like a girl; maybe she needed an old bags' night out.

'And the boys,' said Shen, 'need a boys' night in. To bond.'

'Those three? It'll take more than a few beers and some peanuts.'

'They can . . . oh, watch some sports thing.'

'Clive hates football. And Jon doesn't seem the sporty type.'

'It's happening,' said Shen, 'We'll all dress up – even if I have to sedate Paula – and hit the nearest flash bar. Shush!' She held up her hand as Evie spluttered. 'Talk to the hand, because the face knows exactly what you're going to say, and the face is bored already.'

'Is this yours?' Paula held out the sleek silver rectangle.

'Thank you!' Evie almost grabbed the laptop, delirious to see it again. 'Where was it?'

'Just there.' Paula motioned to the hallway table.

'But I know I didn't . . .'

'At last,' said Paula, picking fluff from her shoulders in the enormous mirror, 'I'm not the only one whose stuff mysteriously disappears and reappears. Don't tell anybody, or they'll think you're a nutter!'

'Nobody thinks you're a nutter.' Evie regretted brushing the back of Paula's sundress as the woman leapt.

'Oh, you do,' said Paula. 'And I'm starting to agree.' She slumped, staring at Evie in the mirror, holding her gaze in a way that was usually beyond her. 'I just saw somebody, honestly, in the shade of the willow.'

'Come! Now.' Evie held out her hand. 'We'll look together.'

'What if I'm right?'

'*If* you're right? I thought you were certain?'

'I am, but . . .'

When Evie took her hand, Paula docilely allowed herself to be led through the kitchen, past The Eights, who were frozen mid-pilfer at the fridge.

'That's it. Nearly there.' Their shadows were stunted in the midday sun.

Paula stopped, dug in her heels. 'I can't.'

'Then wait here.' Evie approached the trailing branches of the willow, greenly translucent like seaweed. The space beyond the leaves seemed other-worldly, as if it was too quiet in there, too dark. She saw something. A startled movement.

Slowing, Evie couldn't back out with Paula watching her. Putting out her hand to part the fronds, she saw a darting motion at the corner of her vision, like a deer or a rabbit. But a human-sized one.

The branches closed behind her, and she saw a woman backed against the tree trunk. The woman looked easily as terrified as Evie was shocked.

'Hello.' Well, what else does one say to a petite woman lurking in the grounds of one's holiday home?

'No,' said the intruder nonsensically, on the verge of tears.

'Listen.' Evie took a step towards her.

That galvanized the woman and she slipped behind the tree, and the great bushy clumps beyond it swallowed her up. Evie pushed her way through, emerging into a glade of slender trees that marked the garden's eastern border. She was alone, and a wooden door in the wall stood open.

'Well?' Paula's shout was querulous.

'You were damned right.' Evie retraced her steps. 'You're not a nutter, Paula, and I'm going to make sure everybody knows that.'

'Did you see him?' Paula was incredulous, as if she'd wanted to be wrong.

'*Her.*'

'Her? What do you mean? Who was she?'

'She was nobody,' said Evie. 'Some girl from the village, trespassing for the hell of it. So you were right about somebody being there, but wrong about them being dangerous.'

'Her,' repeated Paula.

'Haven't you started getting ready yet?' Shen looked at Evie with mingled annoyance and pity. 'You know how long it takes to domesticate your hair.'

'Shen, we don't all have your perception of time,' Evie replied, looking around the master suite. A print jumpsuit was hanging up, with shoes standing primly by. Hair-straighteners were plugged in and ready. An arsenal of potions was massed on surfaces. 'I refuse to spend all after-noon prepping myself to sit on a bar stool.'

Shen swept her with a look that said *Hmm*. 'This place I've found is pretty luxe. Don't wear your black thing.'

'I wasn't going to wear my black thing,' said Evie, who had been going to wear her black thing, because it covered her arms and understood about her bottom. She went on impatiently, wondering how Shen always lured her down conversational rabbit holes, 'Have you see Jon?'

'Why?' Shen was vexed, as if people could only ask questions she approved of.

'Because – oh, never mind.' Evie's phone jumped in her pocket.

'Is that Alex?'

'Yup.'

Soz to spring this on u. Can u make meeting with head honcho 9.30 a.m. 25th? x

The real answer was: *Are you mad? That's the morning after I goad my family plus dog cross-country to London. I'll be up to my hips in laundry, wading through red bills, hating my house for not being Wellcome Manor, and dealing with Scarlett's Zane-withdrawal symptoms. And I have nothing to wear to meet a head honcho!*

Even an entry-level honcho would be unimpressed by Evie's wardrobe. However, she texted a cheery acceptance, suppressing the knowledge that she might well spend the twenty-fifth in a doctor's office.

'There's Jon!' Shen, slathering her arms with moisturizer, nodded at the window. 'Run and you'll catch him.'

She ran. And she caught him. Evie didn't know where to start.

'Um, yes?' Jon was half-turned away, taken unawares by Evie's hollered 'Stop!' 'In a bit of a hurry, so . . .'

'Your girlfriend was here earlier.'

He became still, his eyes locked on hers. They were lovely close up, a changeable green. 'I'm not sure what you mean.'

'Let me spell it out for you.' Evie held his gaze. 'Miss Pritchett is Paula's monster in the bushes.' When Jon didn't speak, she continued, 'I saw you and Miss Pritchett in the village a few days ago.' A tremor crossed his face. 'Just now I humoured Paula by checking out the garden. She's been right all along. There was somebody there.'

'Jane,' he said, very quietly.

'If that's your mistress's name.' Evie couldn't resist the slight sadism. 'Yes, Jane.'

Jon shrank, as if all vitality had been sucked from him. 'This sounds trite, but . . . it's not what you think.'

'What do I think?'

'You think it's a grubby affair. That I'm a bastard! But I'm just trying to save my own life.'

Evie hadn't suspected Jon of such melodrama. 'What I think isn't important. But your mistress shouldn't—'

'She's *not* my mistress.' Nostrils flaring, this was a different Jon from the fogey she knew.

'I won't debate technicalities.' Perhaps Jon hadn't slept with Miss Pritchett (in her head Shen trilled, 'Yeah, right!'), but she was still the 'other woman'. 'Paula's fragile.'

Jon's eyes flickered, as if he was tired of hearing that.

'She sees peril everywhere and your . . .' *Bit of fluff* would be too incendiary. 'Your *friend* will tip her over the edge, lurking like that. Me too, actually. None of us want a voyeur standing in the shadows.'

'Point taken.' Jon lifted his head, until he literally looked down his nose at her. 'I didn't know she was here, I swear. It won't happen again. And as for Paula,' Jon moved away, 'you're not paranoid, if they really are out to get you.'

They were walking, talking clichés.

The women were dolled up, high heels and clutch bags.

The men sat, legs splayed, beers lined up in a row.

'No hookers, OK?' warned Evie.

Mike snorted. 'And no dancing around your handbags.' As Evie leaned to kiss his cheek, he hissed, 'Don't leave me with Clive!' just like Dan, on a play-date with the class brat.

'Be good,' said Shen, without irony. 'Talk to each other. Bond!' Hands on hips, she said, 'Get cracking! *Bond*, you idiots.'

In the taxi – once Paula had hobbled over the gravel in borrowed heels, like a pantomime horse – Evie said, 'It didn't look promising. They're just sitting there, monosyllabic. How can the poor gits bond, when they have nothing in common?'

'*Us*.' Shen broke off from haranguing the cabbie about the route. 'They have us in common.'

'Jon doesn't talk about me,' said Paula.

'I don't think Mike talks about me, either.' Evie knew that Mike, always cautious about revealing himself, would never confide in Clive.

'They can listen then, while Clive goes on about me,' said Shen.

'I'm sure he'll say lovely things.' Paula winced as the borrowed Spanx dug into her personal bits.

Shen smoothed her already super-smooth black hair and sprayed enough Chanel No. 5 to make the driver gag. 'He'll whine, Paula. For hours.'

'So.' Mike raised his beer.

'So,' said Clive.

'I don't really like beer,' said Jon.

'This can't be right.' Shen surveyed the cool night-spot.

'It's right,' said the driver, tearing off, his tyres screeching like a getaway driver.

On home turf Shen's antennae sought out the chicest bars, full of naughty potential and populated with A-list faces. The West Country pollen count had bunged up her feelers: this was a boozer.

'What'll it be?' The bar staff were cheerful, considering their lack of teeth.

'Euthanasia, please.' Shen turned. 'Let's go.'

'I like it.' There was a dare in Evie's smile. 'Very . . .

um . . . louche.' She approached the bar, grateful for a venue where her trousers were *too classy*. 'A bottle of your finest white wine, please.'

'It in't cold. That awright?'

'That's wonderful.'

Paula said, 'This place isn't so bad,' adding, 'the people seem friendly' as a 1,000-year-old man fell off his stool trying to look down Evie's top.

Evie confiscated Shen's phone. 'We're staying,' she said. 'It'll do you good to see how the other half live.'

'What about that match, eh?' Mike leaned back.

'Which match?' Jon frowned.

'I've no idea,' said Mike.

'We won't stay out late, will we?'

'That's not the attitude, Paula!' Evie offered her a stale crisp. 'This is a girls' night out.' She nudged Shen, who was rod-backed on a cracked leatherette stool. 'I like the ice bucket.' They stared at their bottle, wedged in a wellie filled with ice.

'I imagined a shabby-chic vibe,' said Shen. 'Not actual shabbiness.' She shuddered as a dart thudded into a board. 'Darts!' she squealed. She caught Evie's eye and said it again. 'Darts!'

That set them off. Shen went first, her eyes creasing to

nothing. Evie threw her head back, mouth full of crisps as she hooted. Even Paula wasn't immune. Like three schoolgirls, they laughed and laughed until the laughs slowed to sighs and ended on a long *Aaaah*.

'Who's for pork scratchings?' asked Evie.

'So we've decided,' Jon ticked off the list on his fingers. 'No politics, religion, money.' He bit his lip. 'Doesn't leave much.'

'The women,' said Mike, 'won't have paused for breath. Evie and Shen could talk around the clock without sleep.'

'But that's girl-talk.' Clive lit his fattest cigar yet. 'Hair. Nails. Does my bum look big in this?'

'That's not all they talk about.' Mike felt the slander, on his wife's behalf. 'They talk about feelings. What they want from life. They laugh too. A lot. And they talk about us.'

'Relationships,' said Jon, 'are strictly off-limits.'

The silence that fell was like an old friend by now. An old friend you were rather sick of.

'Stuff this sewage-water.' Clive said and tossed his beer bottle into a flower bed. 'I'm opening the good stuff.'

'Sssh, Paula!' Shen was sharp, but warm, in a way Evie couldn't achieve. 'You're harshing our mellow. Tillie and Amber will be fine. Enjoy yourself. For one night. That's an order.' She stood up, unsteady on her red-soled Louboutins. 'What's your favourite song?'

'I'm partial to Michael Bublé.'

'Aren't we all?' Shen nodded her approval. 'I'd be very grateful if he gave me an hour of his free time and decided it was too hot for clothes.' She squawked in a way that Evie recognized as she headed for the jukebox; Shen was tipsy.

A drunk Shen was more than the sum of her sober parts. A drunk Shen was a teeny powerhouse of terrible ideas.

'It's delicious,' said Clive.

It was like drinking nectar from Scarlett Johansson's slipper. Not a furry slipper, like Evie's, but a satin one. This was the moment Mike realized he was pissed; when he began comparing slippers. 'It's gorgeous.'

'Worth the money?' Clive was redder than usual. Cardiac-arrest red. 'Admit it.'

'I can't!' Mike banged the table. 'The price of that claret could keep a family for a month. It's obscene.'

'It's obscene with a vanilla bouquet and a spicy finish, though.' Clive poured out three more goblets. 'Come on, laugh, you bastard.'

And Mike did. He laughed. *With* Clive. Not *at* him.

'I rather think,' said Jon, upending his glass, 'we might be bonding.'

'I do!' said Shen. 'Honest!' There was a hair – just the one – astray on her gleaming head. And her bra strap was showing. By her own standards, she was a slutty mess. 'I envy your marriage, Evie.'

'Bullshit!' said Evie loudly. So loudly that the barman gave her a warning look. 'You never envy anybody, and if you were to take up envying as a hobby, you wouldn't bloody start with my bloody marriage to bloody Mike.'

'Mike's lovely,' protested Paula. She'd located her inner drunk, talking earnestly to a point over Evie's left shoulder. 'He's a lovely man and you're a lovely woman and I'm a lovely . . . Where's the bog?'

As Paula toddled off – Evie had no confidence she'd ever see her again – Shen leaned in and spoke in a loud whisper that the man asleep on the carpet could probably hear. 'I do envy you. You're normal.'

'That's what Mike says.' Evie pouted. 'Why can't people say I'm amazing or I've got incredible boobs?'

'You don't care what people think.'

Even through the haze of *vin du welly*, that sounded like one of Shen's double-edged compliments. 'Eh?'

'You're yourself around Mike. I'm . . .' Shen gestured up and down her body. 'Perfect. Young. I have to smell great. My abs have to be, like, really abby. I mustn't have a stomach. My thighs must have a gap. If Clive really loved me . . .' she tried to focus, 'then he'd adore me even if I had no abs. Like you. And a big old stomach. Like you. And thighs that—'

'I get it,' said Evie hurriedly. 'This deal of yours – was it Clive's idea?'

'Not really.' Shen shook her head and an earring flew off. 'But believe me, he expects high standards. It's tiring.' She slumped a little, and her couture playsuit looked like glitzy wrapping on a modest present.

'Shen, you're more than good enough, without the flat tum and the gel nails.' Evie fell prey to an attack of drunken sentimentality. 'Remember . . . then?' She nodded encouragingly, when Shen looked blank. 'The bad time? *My* bad time?'

'Oh, when you had,' Shen lowered her voice dramatically, 'cancer?'

The word slapped Evie's face. 'You were the best, Shen. The bestest. You let me talk, and you let me cry. Mike was so fragile and he thought I was this Amazon, holding myself together, but it was all you. You held me up.'

Shen held up a finger. 'We don't talk about those days.'

'I'm drunk. I can break the rules.' Evie heard herself say *rule-sh*, but ploughed on regardless. 'You've never let me properly thank you and I have to say it now: thank you Shen my lovely lovely friend.' She was bawling.

Shen was bawling.

They bawled in each other's arms, eyeliner only a memory until the barman tapped Evie on the shoulder.

'I hate to disturb you,' he said. 'But I think your mate's locked herself in.'

'You're a gentleman and a . . .' Mike searched for the word. Where had all his words gone? He seemed to have only about eight at his disposal. 'And a gennulman!' He toasted Clive royally, glass aloft. He left it aloft for a while before remembering what to do with it, and bringing it to his lips. He'd never realized how moreish shamefully expensive booze can be.

'Thank you, kind sir.' Clive dipped his head and his cigar fell onto his lap. 'Ouch,' he said mildly.

'Christ, it's dark out there,' said Jon. His hair stood on end. He looked as if somebody had reached out and tousled his whole body.

'Don't you start,' said Clive. 'It's bad enough with your bloody . . . I mean, your good lady wife banging on about prowlers, without you doing it.'

'I didn't mean . . .' said Jon. 'Are we ruining this holiday?'

'Noooo!' Mike was effusive. He sounded fake to his own ears, but he couldn't stop. 'Not at all! No! God, no! Not in the least!'

'This is a strange time for us,' said Jon. His watery green eyes might have been tearful, but the other men couldn't focus enough to be sure. 'Paula has her demons.'

'We noticed,' said Clive. 'Those are not quiet demons, Jon.'

Not listening, Mike suddenly wanted Patch. He needed to tell Patch how much he loved him. 'Oh, Patch,' he whimpered, as Clive said, 'Ladies, eh? Can't live with 'em, can't . . . what's the rest of that damn saying?'

'Shoot 'em in the head?' offered Jon.

'Give me your take on this, team.' Clive stubbed out his cigar. 'Man-to-man.'

'I love Patch,' said Mike.

'I'm sure you do,' said Clive. 'But this is about a woman. Now, I'm not proud of this, but there have been women. Other women.'

'That's bad.' Mike forgot all about Patch. He wasn't sure if he had a dog at all. 'Bad Clive.'

'I've never been able to resist temptation.'

'I can resist everything,' said Jon, 'except temptation. Oscar Wilde said that. I love Oscar Wilde.'

'Is Oscar Wilde your dog?' asked Mike.

'This woman's different,' Clive went on. 'She's under my skin. I keep women in compartments. You know.' He shaped boxes in the air with his hands. 'Wife. Lover.' He dropped his hands. 'But this one won't fit in a box. She's unique.'

'How,' asked Mike, trying to focus, 'does this unique lady feel about you?'

'That's it.' Clive shook his head, delighted, disbelieving. 'She has feelings for me. She *wants* me. If you know what I mean.'

'Oh, I do know.' Mike winked at Clive. He didn't know what Clive meant.

'This isn't like the others. I can't pick her up and put her down. This is real.' Clive was taken aback by the word.

'Go for it!' Jon looked entirely different when he was passionate. 'You have one life, and what's the point of . . .' he windmilled his arms, 'all this . . . without love? Do it. And hang the consequences.'

'Hold on!' Mike was high-pitched with consternation.

'You made vows, Clive. Shen's a great woman.' He thought of Shen and shuddered. 'Bit terrifying and bossy, and Jesus Christ – the obsession with tofu; but she's a good person. Think about this.'

'But what if she's the one?' Before this evening Clive had never used that expression: talk of 'the one' was for Zane's age group. 'What if I dare to be true to myself?' Here Jon applauded, but Clive, intent on Mike, didn't hear. 'Even if innocent bystanders get hurt? What if none of them – not even her husband, who's a nice enough bloke – matter, when you imagine a life with her?'

'You can't do it.' Mike was immovable. 'Have some backbone, man. We all need to stand for something. Otherwise we're just babies, grabbing at whatever sparkles.' Abruptly he stopped, as if somebody had pulled out his plug.

'You look as if you've seen a ghost,' hiccupped Jon. 'Or one of my wife's ghosts.'

Suddenly sober, Mike missed the warm fuzziness of a moment before. 'I shouldn't preach on this subject.'

'Why?' Jon's hiccups stopped. 'You're Mr Happily Married.'

'Am I?' Mike sighed and told them everything. He showed them the texts, and the photos on his phone. He recounted conversations. He left nothing out. 'What do I do?' he asked. 'What the hell do I do?'

'You know what to do,' said Jon. 'You tell your wife.'

'She'll . . .' Mike imagined what Evie would do. Even the best-case scenario involved a future without testicles. The worst-case scenario involved a bedsit, and visitation rights.

'Listen to a pro, mate.' On familiar ground, Clive's chest swelled with confidence. 'Don't come clean. Carry on.'

'It's killing him.' Jon was empathetic. 'Lies can destroy you.'

'Bollocks!' Clive was brusque. 'Deny everything. It'll blow over. I've been in your position more than once and I bluffed my way through.' Clive lit another cigar and puffed contemplatively. 'Although, on second thoughts, maybe you should 'fess up.'

'Really?' Mike tried to process this U-turn. 'But you said . . .'

'Forget that. Tell Evie. Tomorrow. She'll understand.'

'She'll understand I'm a weak-willed bastard,' said Mike.

'You're just a man,' said Jon. 'Trying to get by.'

'Tell her,' hectored Clive. 'Do you promise me?'

'Of course I don't promise you,' spluttered Mike. 'Why are you so keen?'

'Because,' said Clive, 'we've bloody bonded.'

DAY 9
Wednesday, 19th August

Dear Mother,
  No idea why people write postcards.

Clive

Like a knight and his lady on a medieval tomb, Mike and Evie lay apart, not touching. A hangover is a hangover is a hangover; linen sheets make no difference.

'My head,' said Evie, not moving her lips in case they, too, hurt.

'My guts,' said Mike.

They had withstood a spirited 'Good morning' from Mabel, who'd launched herself from the door to land cleanly, like an Olympic athlete, first on Evie's solar plexus and then on Mike's groin. All they had to do now was withstand until the hangovers wore off. They were withstanding nicely, until doors started slamming on the ground floor and Shen's raised voice reached them.

'I will kill you!' she raved. 'That's a promise!'

'Should we see what that's all about?' Evie wasn't sure about the whole being-upright-and-walking thing.

'S'pose,' said Mike.

'Oh God,' they yowled in unison as they stood up and the second-best bedroom tilted like a galleon.

A whirlwind of rage, Shen couldn't stand still. Clive, by contrast, was motionless, standing legs apart in the hall, arms folded, grim forbearance on his features. 'Welcome,' he said to Evie and Mike as they descended, 'to the madhouse.'

On the doorstep Elizabetta was almost unrecognizable in clothes and without Fang hanging from her like a koala. Shen held the baby as she harangued the nanny, to a rapt audience of the teens and the Eights.

'You're so selfish!' Shen shouted.

'My *nonna* has died,' said Elizabetta calmly.

'I'm so sorry,' said Evie, touched.

Eyes blazing, Shen yelled, 'Don't be! *Signorina* here has run out of *nonnas*. At the last count, both of them had died. They were helpful enough to kick the bucket when Elizabetta wanted a holiday, but I let that pass.'

Evie found time to admire Shen's exquisite outfit; neither hangovers nor defecting nannies got in the way of her grooming. She'd turn up for the Apocalypse with a French manicure.

'There's such a thing,' said Tillie, 'as step-grandmothers. I have one.'

'I'm sure she's a lovely woman,' said Shen. 'But don't waste your sympathy on Elizabetta, because one look at her emails told me all I wanted to know.'

There was a communal intake of breath at her attitude to piffling niceties like privacy.

'How you know my password?' Elizabetta didn't look so pretty with her mouth hanging open.

'Oh, *please*,' scoffed Shen, as if this was kindergarten stuff.

'You had no right,' said Elizabetta.

'And you have no right to bugger off to Mustique with Françoise!'

Evie gasped. It was an Uber plot.

Shen threw up one arm, playing to the crowd. 'Françoise offered more money, so Elizabetta's off this minute to join her in Mustique. So, *cara*,' she said to Elizabetta, 'unless your beloved *nonna* keeled over in the infinity pool, you're defecting.'

'*Spies* defect, darling.' Clive joined them. 'Nannies *leave*.'

Elizabetta took off with her case towards the taxi at the end of the drive. 'I miss you, baby,' she called to Fang, whose starfish arms shot out traitorously. 'And sorry, madam.'

'You will be!' yelled madam. 'When Françoise makes you work weekends and listens to your phone calls!'

'*You* make me work weekends and listen to my phone calls,' called Elizabetta.

'That's not the point,' yelled Shen.

Lying on the mile-long sofa in the cool drawing room, glad of the respite from the insistent heat, Evie heard Shen roam from room to room making calls.

'I understand – sure, bye.' She let out a frustrated

scream. A pause. A drumming of fingers. Then, for the eighth time, 'Hi, it's very short notice, but I need a nanny for the next six days . . . Devon, near Seaton . . . Six months old . . . No, no, right away, like today . . . OK, I understand, bye.'

In the pause while Shen dialled, Evie called out, 'We'll look after Fang together.'

'Now,' said Shen, 'is no time for humour.'

'What's that wailing noise?' Scarlett, her arm through Tillie's, wandered in from the garden.

'Fang.' Evie kept her voice low. 'She's been crying for . . .' she looked at her watch, 'fifty years. Or that's how it feels.'

'But Fang never cries,' said Tillie.

'Only because Elizabetta danced attendance on her.' Evie clamped a cushion over her ears, noting that the girls were without their minder. 'Where's Zane?'

'Dad made him help move the cot from over the garage to the master suite. Did you hear,' Scarlett turned to Tillie, 'what your mum was saying?'

Tillie, with a resigned sigh, nodded: '*Make sure you've locked up properly.*'

'Yeah!' Miles popped up. 'That's in case murderers hide in the garage and stab us up our bums!' He paused, added, 'The fucking fuck-men' and ran off, cackling.

'When I've sorted this,' Shen wearily stabbed another number into the phone, 'I'll sort that.'

There was much sighing and grunting and general *Look at me – I'm a real bloke* noises from the hallway as Mike, Jon and Zane manoeuvred the massive cot towards the stairs. Clive oversaw matters, carrying Fang as awkwardly as if she were the Olympic torch.

'Is this cot made of cement?' Mike's face was a vivid crimson.

'Can we rest?' Zane, quiff wilting, sounded tearful.

The cot banged down on the black-and-white tiles.

'I've discovered,' said Mike, 'that putting your back out cures a hangover. So, that's something.'

Evie laughed, nice and loud, so he would hear. She noticed he was leaving rooms as she entered them.

The howling rose and fell, like a police car approaching a riot. 'Ssh,' cooed Clive, patting Fang's narrow back as she hollered her message of doom, gloom and nappy rash. 'I don't know what she wants.' He held her at arm's length, gazing into her puckered face, as if she might announce, in perfectly modulated English, 'Actually, Father, what I want is . . .'

'Have you checked her bottom?' Mike recalled his own years on the baby frontline. 'Is she hungry? Thirsty? Does she have wind?'

'How do I bloody know?' said Clive, as Fang regurgitated many rusks down his shirt front. 'Oh, for—!'

'Come on, *mate*.' Mike bent to take the strain of the *Game of Thrones*-style cot. 'Don't tell me you can't cope with one teeny baby.' He shook his head, saddened by such ineptitude. 'She's trickier than a business deal, isn't she?'

Clive's good nature had followed the nanny out through the gates. 'I can handle my own baby daughter, thanks.'

'What made Elizabetta behave like that?' Mike, as ever, tried to understand.

'Maybe,' called Evie, 'she was punishing Shen for, you know, taking advantage.' She added, 'You *did*', when Shen treated her to a look that could turn a lesser woman to stone.

'It's all my fault, then?'

Moving swiftly on, Clive said, 'Elizabetta's gone. That's that. She was a capable nanny, but Françoise shouldn't leave her alone with that drippy husband of hers.' He looked down at Fang. 'I hope you know how to change your own nappies, kid.' He thrust the baby at Shen. 'Take her.'

Recoiling as if the baby might be red-hot, Shen snapped, 'I'm busy! Nobody can start straight away. These nanny agencies don't understand the meaning of the word "emergency".'

'I need,' said Clive, with clenched-teeth calm, 'to sponge the sick off my shirt. *Darling*.' He doggedly held out Fang, her chubby legs dangling.

Crossing her arms, Shen said, 'Hold her until I've engaged a new nanny. Or,' she pulled an ironic face, 'shall we look after her ourselves?' Her brittle titter illustrated the lunacy of this idea.

'Ooh, no.' Mike was inching up the stairs beneath the cot. 'Clive couldn't handle Fang twenty-four/seven. He might break a nail. JESUS!' he yelled as Zane dropped his side of the beast.

'Put your phone away,' said Clive. 'If there's no nanny, so be it. How hard can it be looking after a baby?'

Evie called to them from the sofa. 'From personal experience, extremely hard indeed.'

'It's all about organization,' said Clive. 'You women make heavy weather of it.'

'After I've sorted the nanny problem and the Miles-swearing problem, I'll sort the putting-a-hatchet-through-your-head problem.' Shen hit 'Redial'.

'Put the phone away,' repeated Clive. 'Five days. One Fang. It'll be a doddle.'

It had been tricky tussling Fang out of Shen's arms.

'I don't need help, Evie,' she'd insisted, jiggling the noisy dumpling.

'I want her, though,' Evie had said. 'I've hardly seen my god-daughter this holiday.' Grateful for Fang's uncomplicated companionship, she took off on an aimless tour of the garden, half-expecting Clive to follow. He was the opposite of Mike this morning; catching her eye, gazing meaningfully at her. Thankfully he remained at the house, and Evie soothed Fang with a stream of gentle nonsense until the child's head drooped onto her shoulder.

The gesture touched her. It was without guile – the way babies are.

Then one of her own babies, albeit a large one, approached. Dan careered over, calling out, 'It's disgusting!'

'What is, darling? Keep your voice down. Fang's all snoozy.'

'Snogging! Proper snogging!'

Evie gulped.

'In the treehouse!' spat Dan. 'I hate Scarlett. My sister's disgusting.' He stormed past, propelled by prudery.

'Grab a lolly from the freezer, love.' Most of Dan's troubles could be soothed with the application of a Mivvi.

'I'm full.'

'Eh?' Dan hadn't been full since birth.

'I'm going to lie on my bed and read my myths.' Another bombshell: Dan choosing reading over playing.

'Dan, sweetie, don't be hard on Scarlett. Teenagers like kissing, you know.'

'Not in front of me!' he yelled, disappearing into the house, anxious to put as much space as he could between himself and the snoggers.

'One day,' shouted Evie, enjoying herself now, 'you'll want to kiss a girl!'

'Urgh! Never! Shut up!'

Evie, with Fang curled about her, delved deeper into the garden, reaching the wild patch. The edge of the known world. A deep restlessness wouldn't let her sit down, even though she was tired.

Too tired. *Suspiciously* tired. She resented how easily it came back, that physical self-policing, that acute attention to detail. Is this sore? Is that tender? Is this normal?

From the terrace, Mike called her name.

Evie turned back. 'What?' Grateful that he'd stopped avoiding her, she didn't, however, want to speak to him right then. She could feel something coming, an avalanche building in the hills. Her resilient, sturdy husband was neither resilient nor sturdy on this topic, so until a kindly doctor patted her hand and said, 'You big silly, there's nothing to worry about', she must hug her worries to herself.

'I'm taking you out for a treat!'

Evie's brow lowered.

'Well, look pleased!'

One of the nicest things about a cream tea, or afternoon tea, or whatever you want to call it (Evie just wanted to eat it) is that there are no choices to make. 'Cream tea!' you say gaily to your waitress, closing the menu with a snap. 'And be quick about it.' Your waitress will forgive your rudeness; she knows that women can't be kept waiting for a cream tea, in much the same way that they can't be kept waiting for a naked Channing Tatum.

Even though this cafe had been the venue for Jon's extracurricular kiss, Evie would forgive it anything, if it came up with the cakey goods. 'This place is so *right*,' she said, all her senses sated. There were swaggy curtains, there were cushions on the spindly chairs, there were fussy jugs and spoons and cake-stands on every surface. In short, it was stuffed with li'l-ole-lady tat that she normally hated, but which was just right for the taking of cream tea. 'Look!' she said, delighted. 'They have horrific dried-flower arrangements on every table!'

Fidgeting with the scalloped edge of a doily, Mike said, 'See, I do listen sometimes.' He cleared his throat, as if about to make a declaration, but all he said was, 'I couldn't let you go through the whole holiday without a cream tea.'

'You get many, many merit points for this. I know it's your idea of hell.'

'Kind of.' He almost, but not quite, achieved an authentic smile. 'I mean, the table has two tablecloths on it.' He coughed. It was a punctuation mark. It said: *Prick up your ears.*

The trolley arrived before he could speak. Blood rushed to Evie's head as a three-tiered cake stand, gilt-edged, shapely, was laid on their undersized table.

The waitress pointed to the different storeys. 'Them's cucumber sandwiches and egg-mayonnaise sandwiches and, hang on . . . oh yeah, chicken-and-pesto.' She allowed herself the tiniest of smug chin-tucks at such sophistication. 'And in the middle you've got your cream horn and your Battenberg and your lemon-drizzle. And on the bottom—'

Evie butted in. 'Scones,' she said, the way some men (admittedly not the ones you'd want to hang out with) say, *Breasts.* 'And clotted cream. Is the jam made here?'

'Of course.' The waitress set down a dignified teapot, a large and curvaceous item that has seen Brits through generations of war and peace and recession and booms and births and deaths and weddings and funerals and *Midsomer Murders* omnibuses. She laid down a strainer in a drip-bowl, two cups and saucers, teaspoons, a jug, a sugar bowl and a pair of tongs. And she left without a word, because she was accustomed to her female customers entering a trance-like state.

'So,' said Mike, his voice the dusty one he reserved for bad news. 'Before I say this, I want you to know that—'

'Hang on.' Emerging from her reverie, Evie poured out two cups of tea, relishing the novelty of straining out the leaves. 'I can see you have something to tell me, love, and this cream tea is to soften me up.' She put a dash of milk in her cup, a slightly bigger dash – a dash and a half, maybe – in Mike's. 'You think you're going to upset me no end, I can see that from your face.' She picked up and dropped the tongs, smiled at their olde-worlde daintiness and picked them up again. 'So, before you spoil this wonderful spread . . .' *Plop!* One sugar in her tea. '. . . allow me to say that I already know everything.' *Plop! Plop!* Two sugars in Mike's tea. 'I know all about it, and it doesn't matter, and can we please start eating because that cream horn is, frankly, giving me the horn.'

'But you don't know.' Mike was agitated, his whole body a frown. 'You can't.'

'I can and I do.' Evie sat on her hands to stop herself ravishing the Battenberg. Taking a deep breath, she spoke rapidly, getting it over with, 'Mike, darling dearest Mike, here is what I know. When I was ill and we were at sixes and sevens and we were scared and you were trying to look all manly, but underneath you were Bambi, you went to a staff leaving do because back then you could afford staff, and you drank too much and suddenly you weren't worried any more because you were as high as a kite and could barely pronounce your own name.' Evie broke off to take a sip of tea. 'Am I on the right track?'

Dumbly, Mike nodded.

'Excellent. So, there you were, plastered and emotionally unstable, and suddenly Haley – who's the one leaving – appeared. Haley with the foofy hair and the tendency to cry in the loos. You can't really remember what happened next, but you think it went like this: you were randy and you suddenly fancied her and you kissed her when you both went outside for a smoke and you led her on and you took advantage and you made her believe there was a future for you as a couple. So, when she began calling and texting and emailing and generally scaring the bejaysus out of you, you felt you owed her something and you tried to let her down gently, by listening to her crying and carrying on. Haley upped the ante by threatening to tell your wife – i.e. *moi* – even though I was sick. You begged her not to. Finally she met a guy and, hallelujah, the silly cow got engaged and told you fiercely she was deleting your number and you were a pig, et cetera, et cetera.' Evie took another sip. Her tea was getting cold, so she sped up. 'Fast-forward to this summer. Haley's divorced – surprise, surprise – and she's texting you again. You're baffled, because she behaves as if you have this great love that she can't leave behind. She's insisting you dump your wife – me again – and you're worried she'll talk to me and I'll believe her, because she's so convincing that some-times *you* think you've had an affair instead of one drunken kiss you'll regret until you die.' Evie sat back, spent. 'Am I right?'

Mike nodded again. 'How?' he began slowly.

With one eye on the scones, Evie said, 'How do I know?

When you're bonding with your bros, Mike, you should keep your voice down, and double-check that the ladies haven't come home and crept upstairs. I lay in bed last night and listened to you telling Clive and Jon.'

'Why didn't you say something?'

'I wanted you to tell me yourself.'

'You believe me?'

Evie laced her fingers together and wondered how to put it. 'Listen, I had no idea this Haley creature is bugging you. But I did know about the other time – the first time.'

Mike looked as confused as Evie had when she slept through the middle of *Homeland* and woke up for the climax.

'Because Haley came good on her threat. She came to see me.' She added 'in hospital', just for the fun of seeing Mike's eyes widen. 'I told her to bugger off. I know her type. Drama-queens who churn up the water and watch everyone drown.'

Evie recalled the faux-tears at the end of her bed, the knowing face gauging her reactions, the *I'm sorry, I know you're ill, but you should know the kind of man you married*. Evie had retorted that she knew *exactly* the kind of man she'd married – that is, not the kind of man who would look twice at a schemer who'd pull a sick stunt like this. 'Mike, your assistant told me all about the kiss, the morning after.'

'Barb did? You're kidding.' Mike's past rearranged itself.

'She couldn't stop laughing. She'd watched the whole thing unfold and gave me a heads-up, in case there were repercussions. She'd seen Haley's type before. You were easy prey, running on empty. Clever old Barb tailed you when you went out for a smoke – and this is another reason why you were right to give up the fags, by the way – so she saw the lunge and the clinch and the taking advantage. Haley took advantage of *you*, love. Barb was tickled because you were too drunk to notice that Haley sat beside you all night, trying to hold your hand. It was a narcissistic fantasy, Mike.'

'Good old Barb.' Mike looked as if he'd been though the spin cycle in a washing machine.

'She's a diamond. But even if she hadn't told me, I would've said the same thing to that bunny-boiler.' She moved the milk jug and took his hand. 'I would've told her I trust my husband.'

'Christ!' said Mike. 'I'm so relieved. I want to shout.'

'Don't shout,' said Evie. 'Eat.'

As Evie sliced, diced and filleted, Fang's caterwauling grew louder, then diminished, only to grow loud again as her parents walked her desperately from room to room. The child, understandably, missed her nanny.

'Thanks to you,' said Evie to Mike, who was 'helping' prepare dinner, 'we've got poor Fang's howls as a backing track.'

'Thanks to me?' Mike was aggrieved.

'You taunted Clive, and he took the bait.'

'I had a point. *We* managed without childcare.'

'*I* managed, you mean. You were at work.'

'Don't say it like I was in a strip-joint, tucking tenners down strippers' bras.' Mike assumed the face he used for doing his tax return. 'I mucked in, didn't I?' He considered himself to be a New Man. He distinctly remembered hoovering with Dan strapped to his front. Once.

Hands deep in a bowl of crumble mix, Evie paused, looking over at Mike and back into the past. 'Remember when we took Scarlett out in the car to lull her to sleep? Driving around like zombies at 3 a.m.?'

Mike's shoulders softened, recalling those drives through slumbering streets. 'Dan always dropped off on top of the tumble-dryer.'

'Happy days,' said Evie, attacking the crumble again. 'Exhausting days.'

'If we can do it, so can Shen and Clive.'

'Well, they're not us,' said Evie.

'Is that a compliment to us?'

'Sort of. Why didn't you offer to help?'

'Because it's *Clive*,' said Mike, as if that explained everything.

'Now you're being childish.'

'Ouch!' said Mike.

'I might need you to be grown-up quite soon.' Evie's face was hot, and not just because of the steam from the dancing pots and pans.

'But I am grown-up.' Mike sounded sulky and not particularly grown-up. 'I have a job. I wear long trousers. I can open safety caps on tablets.'

'True.' She was grateful for his lightness of tone. 'But . . .'

She had to be more realistic. 'Life changes, Mike. You may not always be able to rely on me so much.'

'What're you trying to say?' Like Patch sniffing under the kitchen door when sausages hit sizzling fat, Mike knew something was in the air.

'I'm trying to say . . .' Evie quailed, 'never approach a woman making crumble. That's when we're at our most dangerous.' She sensed him wondering whether to press her, and exploited his hesitation to say, 'Make me a Martini. Dry. With an olive.'

Mike started for the den and the comprehensively stocked cocktail cabinet that secretly intimidated them both, with its polished shakers and strainers and row of gleaming glasses. 'How do I make a—'

'Google it!' roared Evie, sick of being her family's personal encyclopaedia.

A phone buzzed and she jumped, before realizing the noise came from Mike's mobile, lying on the worktop. As she read the message, her eyebrows disappeared into the undergrowth of her fringe: **I think of you and I bite my lip I'm on heat mike come and fill me up DUMP HER NOW xxx**

Evie typed a reply: **Hi Haley! Evie here. Nice to hear from you again. You sound hot, you poor thing! Why not open a window instead of bombarding my husband with poorly punctuated smut? If I were your friend, I'd urge you to talk to a professional about why you're pursuing Mike. But as I'm Mike's wife, I'll simply delete your number and leave you with the knowledge that you have no power over him, because I know all about this correspondence and your threats. Goodbye.**

When you nurture – when that's what you do, day in and day out – it's hard to be brusque with somebody so damaged. After some hesitation, Evie pressed 'Send'; Hayley must reach out for the help she needed.

'One dry Martini.' Mike was back, proffering a triangular glass.

Evie slung the crumble into the oven. It was majestic, made with pears from the orchard she'd discovered in a far corner of the garden; another gift from Wellcome Manor. Taking the glass from her husband, she thanked him and left the room, with an autocratic 'Keep an eye on the potatoes.'

'I thought it was for you . . .' Mike watched her cross the terrace to Clive and trade his painstakingly mixed drink for Fang.

'Here. A medicinal Martini.' It was a relief to talk to somebody that Evie was neither married to nor keeping secrets from. 'I heard you grumbling about dinner being late.'

Taking the Martini like a bear stealing a taco, Clive said, 'You're an angel.'

Fang fidgeted grouchily in Evie's arms. Clive gazed at her. 'So small and yet so powerful. And so very, very full of shit.'

'Not in front of the baby, Clive. Elizabetta never used such language.'

'Elizabetta knew where Fang's off-switch is. It's beyond me.' He regarded Evie over the rim of his glass, smiling slyly. 'Done any writing today?'

'Haven't had time.' She was riveted by Fang. The damp curl on her forehead. The bulge of her putty nose.

'Waiting for inspiration to strike?'

'This place inspires me.'

'And . . . me?'

She laughed. 'Everybody inspires me.' She drew back a little; his gaze was very intense. 'Are you all right, Clive?' She moved closer, murmuring, 'Fancy a lie-down?'

He looked startled. And pleased. 'Darling, come on – it's the middle of the day and Shen's about, you naughty girl.'

'Shen won't mind. She'll understand.'

He was taken aback. 'Are you mad?'

'Please yourself.' Evie held out Fang and took the glass, wondering at Clive's clumsiness, not letting go until their fingers touched.

'Just imagine,' he said in an undertone, 'if we'd gone to the Maldives, this would never—' He straightened up as Mike approached and carried on, more heartily, 'Can't believe I shelled out Maldives-style money to stay in the English countryside with baby-sick in my ear. Literally,' he said, with something like awe, '*in my ear.*'

The slinky motion of Mike's arm sliding around Evie's waist made her shudder happily as he said, 'The Maldives would cost twice what we paid for this place.'

'This place is no bargain,' said Clive. Evie, sensing what was coming, willed his lips to close, but no, he kept going. 'I paid twice what *you* paid, mate.'

Mike withdrew his arm. 'Evie, is that true?'

'Well . . .'

Taking that as confirmation, Mike said, 'Thanks, love'

as he walked away. 'There's nothing I enjoy more than being made to look stupid.'

'Oops.' Clive looked penitent. Or as penitent as he could look. 'I should stop rubbing your husband up the wrong way, shouldn't I? For both our sakes.'

'Clive,' sighed Evie. 'I should put you over my knee and spank you.'

'*Now* you're talking!' said Clive.

The Eights didn't notice the atmosphere at the dinner table; they were too busy interrogating Evie about their food: 'So this pig definitely had a happy life and then just dropped dead of old age?'

Similarly the teenagers were too absorbed in their own psycho-drama to police the oldies: Scarlett watching Zane; Zane pretending not to watch Scarlett; Scarlett watching Tillie watching Zane. The permutations were endless.

Evie saw it all. She noticed Mike's seething indignation. She noticed Shen struggling to stay calm, as Fang writhed on her lap and put her hands in the food. She noticed that Paula was on Planet Paula, that unreachable distant sphere. She saw Jon pick at his meal. And as for Clive – she reminded herself to find the Optrex. The poor man was suffering from some form of pollen allergy. Either that or he was winking at her every time she looked his way, and obviously he wouldn't do that.

'Let me take Fang,' she said to Shen, 'so that you can eat.' Having cooked and served the meal, Evie didn't really want to hold the baby, but clearly nobody else was going to offer.

'It's fine.' Shen's eyeliner was smudged; a detail as discordant as the Queen sporting a Hitler moustache.

'Just hand her over and—'

'Leave it, Evie.'

'But . . .'

'Are you saying I can't cope?'

'Darling,' said Clive warningly, 'Evie said nothing of the sort.'

'Don't you start.' Shen trembled with manic energy as she shifted Fang to her other knee, giving the child easier access to the pearls around her neck. 'Oh no, Fang, why?' she groaned as a small fist closed around the necklace and pearls scattered all over the dinner table.

'Pearls before swine!' shouted Dan. 'I don't know what that means!'

Mabel stuck one up her nose, without further ado, as if she'd been waiting for a pearl to roll past so that she could do just that.

'They're real!' said Shen, despairingly.

'Mabes!' Evie jumped up. 'That's a hundred quid you've stuffed up your hooter!'

'If your mother says it's worth a hundred pounds,' said Mike, lifting a pearl out of his mash, 'It's probably worth two hundred.'

Fang kicked over Shen's glass.

'Clive,' she said, in a metallic undertone, 'I could do with some help here.'

'Sorry, darling. What?' Clive stopped studying Evie and

slapped his forehead. 'Sorry, Angel. I'll get you another glass.'

'I mean, help with your daughter.'

'One of your many daughters,' said Zane.

'But I'm eating, my love.'

'I'll take her,' said Evie.

'No, thanks.'

'Dan . . .' Miles ate greedily, unaware of the pearl amongst his peas, 'why'd you sleep with the light on?'

'I don't,' said Dan hastily.

'You do,' insisted Miles. He had the table's attention; without Evie and Shen conducting the conversation, the adults were quiet. 'Mabes said, and everything.'

'I didn't!' Mabel burst into tears. Amber, this being her area of expertise, joined in. 'That's not true, and it's a secret!'

Fang burst into empathetic, even louder tears, as her mother crammed her own mouth with food like a famine victim.

'It's Dan's business.' Mike eyed The Eights sternly, as Clive finally accepted Fang from Shen's grasp like the prize in a grim game of pass-the-parcel.

Dan's bottom lip was jelly.

'Whoa, Dan.' Zane slouched over the table towards him. 'Never had you down as a cissy, man.'

'Zane . . .' Scarlett, looking hurt, put down her fork.

'You afraid of ghosties? Even girls sleep with the lights off.'

'Even girls?' said Tillie. '*Even* girls,' she repeated, leaning over to Fang, who stopped crying and plonked two mash-smeared hands on her cheeks.

'It's a bit gay, Dan.' Zane was bubbling, as if ill will had fermented within him and pushed out the words.

'I want him to be gay.' Mabel's tears were magically dry. 'But he won't be.'

'*You're* gay,' said Dan to Zane.

'No, you're gay,' said Zane.

'Nobody's gay,' said Evie. 'Well, statistically somebody probably is. It doesn't matter. But Dan isn't,' she added, as her son's face filled again. 'For God's sake, Zane.' Goading a ten-year-old with homophobic crap was beyond her patience. 'Stop it.'

'He never picks on somebody his own size,' said Clive languidly.

'Nor do you,' said Zane. 'But then, there isn't anybody your size. Except a gorilla, maybe.'

The Eights laughed uproariously. Having recovered, Dan did a creditable gorilla impression.

Shen foamed with anger – only some of it, in Evie's opinion, rooted in her stepson's rudeness. 'Zane! Get out!'

'No, leave him.' Clive grunted with frustration as Zane jumped up, threw down his napkin and stalked out. 'Let him insult me, darling.'

'At least,' Tillie poked her food around, mouth pursed, 'he says it to your face.'

'Tillie,' cajoled Paula, 'dear, we don't talk to grown-ups like that.'

'Grown-ups, Mum?' Tillie stood too. She didn't have

Zane's knack for posturing and caught her trailing skirt in her chair as she made her exit. 'Like Santa, I don't believe in them any more.'

In her bijou home (bijou being estate-agent speak for 'too bleedin' small'), Evie always knew where her personnel were, give or take an inch or so. Wellcome Manor absorbed and hid people. She could have been alone in the house as she crept downstairs.

There were distant sounds. A chuckle. A bang. Footsteps. Presumably The Eights were in bed, but they'd become so feral and self-reliant they might well be sacrificing peasants by the pool.

'Sh-en!' she called, moping through the rooms. Shen wasn't in the quiet, on-standby kitchen, or in the womb-like cinema room, or in the hoity-toity drawing room with its ankle-deep carpet. In this posh commune Evie was accustomed to constant access to Shen and high-quality gal-pal chatter.

Gauzy curtains fluttered at the French doors. Evie saw the teens canter past, holding in their laughter, up to no good. Zane, who seemed to have something under his shirt, reached for Scarlett's hand with an insouciance that suggested they were an established item.

Stepping outside, Evie called to Paula, who was upright on a chair. 'Remember when you were that age?'

'Not really.'

Conversation-killing skills like that are rare. Evie had

no comeback as she took the next chair. 'Still checking out the bushes?'

'No,' lied Paula, who scanned the horizon avidly, like a sailor's wife waiting for his boat to appear out of the mist.

'Good. Cos there's nothing out there. Apart from our scoundrels, off to their treehouse.' She wanted to go further, and say Miss Pritchett wouldn't dare creep near them again, but that would open up a can of conversational worms. Spotting Shen tottering towards them in patent heels, her body-con dress outdoing Evie's khaki and Paula's Crimplene pleats, Evie said, 'Bloody hell, are you off to a soirée?'

'I'm sick of being a human wet wipe.' Shen drank from a wine bottle without the customary glass middleman. 'I need to feel human again.'

'Very few humans look like that.' Evie took in the sweep of hair, the translucent powder across Shen's clavicles, the bling at her ears. 'I couldn't look like that if a crack team worked on me for six months solid.'

'You could.' Maybe there was truth-serum in the Chablis, because Shen added, 'Well, no, you couldn't.'

'None taken.' Evie was accustomed to Shen's bare-knuckle honesty. 'Did Fang go down OK?'

'Yes,' flashed Shen. 'Christ – I can talk about other subjects, you know.'

Less than twenty-four hours with her own child and Shen was reduced to a level of savage rudeness that Evie only reached on the evening of Christmas Day with the extended family. Evie understood: Shen's experience of motherhood wasn't half as hands-on as most women's. Shen had never battled and sunk and risen again, to doggy-paddle through another day. She didn't yet know that she would be fine, just fine, once she hit her stride.

Evie had watched Shen dash upstairs with Fang each time the baby coughed up a gobbet of goo, returning with an immaculately groomed child, only to repeat the process within an hour. She'd watched her wipe Fang's chin after each mouthful. She'd watched her wash Fang's hair when Prunella got too licky. Fang had been camera-ready all day, but her mother had ended up crushed.

'Do you think your priorities are a bit orf?' If Evie hoped her comedy pronunciation would soften Shen's reaction to what could be construed as a criticism, she was wrong.

'Do you want to see me scream? Is that what you want?' Shen was an inch from Evie's face.

Evie drew back. 'What sort of person would want that?'

'Your sort,' said Shen.

'Shen, shush.' Evie smiled.

'No, *you* shu—' Shen slumped, gave up. 'I can't even argue properly. Just fight with yourself, while I get on with drinking this lovely, lovely, much lovelier-than-ever-before wine.'

'I'll happily make personal remarks about my clothes, if you're too tired to do it.' Evie relished Shen's frazzled giggle and looked companionably to Paula, but the other woman wasn't laughing. Instead, as ever, she stared out at the dark.

'Go and snatch some zeds, Shen. I hate to be a party-pooper, but Fang won't magically change overnight. Tomorrow will pretty much be Groundhog Day.'

'No, I want to party.' Shen wiggled her shoulders. 'Be *me* for a few hours.'

'Then let me help with Fang tomorrow. That's what friends do. They pitch in.'

Shen shook her head. 'Christ, she's just a baby. *My* baby. Why don't we whack on some music and have a boogie? Find the guys and get them on their feet?'

Evie knew Mike only danced when drunk. It helped if the onlookers were also drunk. 'Paula,' she said, to winch Paula's attention from the Miss Pritchett-free gardens, 'does Jon dance?'

'Never!' She almost laughed at the question.

'Well, he's gonna dance tonight.' Shen made it sound like an ugly threat. 'Where is Jon, anyway?'

'Around,' said Paula. 'About.'

'Get Mike. Get Clive. Get the bloody useless teenagers,' commanded Shen, upending the bottle, savouring the last ambrosial dregs. 'We're going to get down with our bad selves. We're going to start a disco inferno.'

Within twenty minutes Evie had tucked Shen into bed and was downstairs again, to find herself alone. Jon's car was missing from the forecourt and Evie's own husband was also AWOL. With so many corners and hidey-holes in Wellcome Manor, Evie didn't know where to begin looking for him.

One spot more or less guaranteed some company.

'Ah, there you are.' Clive patted the bench beside him.

'I'd almost given up. I brought supplies.' An ice-bucket gleamed in the moonlight.

'Clever old you.' Evie left a healthy space between them on the slats. There was no other word for this than flirting: she hadn't flirted since 1994, but she knew it when she saw it. If it stayed light-hearted, something to do with the long evenings, *fine*. Her co-flirter was a man of great experience in such matters.

'Silence!' Evie cocked her head. 'The mighty Fang sleeps at last.'

'That kid sure can cry.'

'Welcome to the coal-face of parenting. You were present when she was conceived; It's only fair you're around to wipe her botty or let her stick her fingers in your eyes.'

'Good point.' Clive made a wry face. 'If Shen put it like that, maybe we'd get somewhere.'

The Ling-Littles weren't a natural team. There was no harmony, just point-scoring. Even so, Evie had to say, 'Don't diss my homie.' She felt Clive scrutinize her again, as if searching her face for clues. 'Guess what I did this afternoon?'

'I never guess. Why do women make men guess all the time?'

'I had a *cream tea*.' She spun out the words, lingering on them, gooey at the memory of the crème pâtissière, the compote, the – oh God – ganache.

Clive's weariness evaporated and he sat up. 'And we all know how much you love a good *cream tea*, don't we?' If the lady diarist wanted to talk in metaphors, so be it.

'Don't I just!' Elated to have found a fellow-enthusiast, Evie hugged herself, cooing, 'I wanted to *roll* in it!'

Clive licked his lips. 'Were there . . . scones?'

'So many.' Evie winked.

Clive let out a moan. 'You're driving me mad.'

'I haven't even started on the finger-sandwiches.'

Looking as if he hardly dared ask, Clive said, 'What . . . did you do with them, you naughty girl?'

'What do you think,' purred Evie, 'I did with them?'

'Knowing you,' said Clive, 'I can guess it was good.'

Remembering how nicely seasoned the egg mayonnaise was, she had to agree. 'Oh, Clive, there's nothing better than a good, long cream tea.' She could see that she had his attention. Time to exploit it. 'Do you ever treat your *women* to cream tea?'

'Endlessly,' said Clive.

'Your ladies get a lot more out of the affairs than you do.' Evie saw how the change of topic side-swiped Clive, who looked confused. And disappointed. She pressed her point; these bench rendezvous were an unmissable opportunity to carry out light repair work on the Ling-Little marriage. 'They visit nice hotels and swanky restaurants, with a handsome pay-off at the inevitable end, but you only get X-rated memories and another wedge between you and your wife. Stop seeking happiness *out there*.' Evie waved her hands vaguely at the great outdoors. 'Start looking for it nearer home.'

'*My* home?'

'Well, not *my* home!' laughed Evie, nudging him.

'No, obviously not. Not with Mike there.'

'Concentrate on one woman.' She hesitated, knowing from her family's complaints that she could be preachy: Archbishop Herrera, they called her. 'Aren't we all searching for meaning?' That question resonated with her. 'Isn't *connection* what we crave?'

'Connection.' Clive nodded rapidly. 'Plus a damned good cream tea.'

'Absolutely!' laughed Evie. *Good old Clive.* 'Right.' She slapped her lap. 'I'd better find my husband and make up with him.'

Clive was rueful. 'I dropped you in it, didn't I?'

'Yup.'

'Sorry. I should be more careful from now on. Make an effort. I'm sorry . . . darling.' Clive scattered *darlings* willy-nilly, but this one had weight.

'No probs, *darling*.' Evie stood and kissed his forehead, moved by what she took to be real contrition on his face.

'You're right, Evie. I've ignored the special woman right under my nose. She deserves to be treated like a queen.'

'That's beautiful, Clive!' Evie was better at this advice-lark than she thought; she might go professional at some point.

'The only question is,' said Clive, 'does she feel the same?'

When he went puppyish like that, when his face became a needy question mark, Evie saw Zane in Clive's features. 'You know the answer to that,' she said quietly.

'I do.' Jubilant again, the old Clive was back. 'Goodnight.'

'Goodnight.' Evie left him, calling over her shoulder, 'I hope you dream of a damned good cream tea!'

'What was that?' Evie sat bolt upright, wide awake, all her senses flashing red. She prodded Mike. 'Something smashed downstairs. Mike! Somebody's in the house!'

All urban males develop a finely honed fight-or-flight reflex and have, at some point, leapt out of bed ready to wreak hell. Mike felt for the baseball bat that lived among the dustballs under their bed, but came up with a towelling slipper. Realizing where they were, he said, 'Evie, there are loads of "somebodies" in this house.'

'It's 4 a.m. Everybody's asleep.' She jumped at a loud crash downstairs, like somebody falling through a door. 'It's burglars!' She concocted a small-hours scenario where they were imaginatively slaughtered.

'They're bloody clumsy burglars.' Mike crouched, his ear to the door, at another clatter. He laid down his slipper. 'And they're happy in their work.' Maniacal laughter echoed up the stairs. He opened the door and grimaced at something on the landing. 'Great,' he sighed. 'Just *great*.'

Scarlett staggered in, her hair in her face, her grip on a brandy bottle still strong. Falling to her knees, she whimpered, 'Mum, I feel—'

'Oh, yuck!' Evie's shoulders hunched to her ears as

Scarlett bent over and added more swirls to the pattern on the rug.

DAY 10
Thursday, 20th August

Hi

   Mental night last night. Think I'm dying. Quite like Devon now.

Scar xxx

pee ess there's stuff to tell . . .

Fang's reign of terror had turned the master suite into the sort of room seen in blurry images on CNN, where hostages are kept without basic facilities. An armchair was overturned, towels lay around like corpses. Even the Picasso print seemed to be crying for help, with its one eye.

Shen despaired of the bottles. They were reproducing. She kept washing and sterilizing, but dirty ones leaned against each other like drunks, on every flat surface. She shuffled to the four-poster – a chaste bed, despite its wanton untidiness – with a nappy wrapper stuck to her slipper, and asked her husband in the hushed tones they used in the rare intermissions when Fang slept, 'Why did you turn away the cleaners?'

'This room is beyond their powers.' Clive's fancy dressing gown was as dejected as a charity-shop buy. Settling himself like a dishevelled sultan against the bank of creased pillows, he whispered, 'I'm starting to enjoy the anarchy. I mean, why let the clocks have it their own way? Why *not* stay up all night singing "Mary Had a Little Lamb"?'

'You *would* say that!' hissed Shen, 'You can sleep all day. I have to get Miles up, feed him, scrape the mud off him,

feed Fang, bathe her, while you take over for the easy bits.'
She dragged bedclothes over herself, too tired to arrange
her limbs. The aikido session she'd planned was out of the
question. 'And today I have to scream at your son for leading
the girls astray and getting pissed. Because, as usual, you'll
duck out of disciplining him.' She closed her eyes. 'Wake
me up when Fang goes to university.'

'Evie can help. She dotes on Fang.'

'Don't you talk to me about Evie.'

Clive wouldn't put it past Shen to bug the bench; his
wife's intelligence-gathering skills were beyond the CIA's
wildest dreams. 'Don't drop off, darling,' he murmured. 'I
have calls to make.'

Looking pained, as if somebody had stirred a knife in
her gut, Shen sat up slowly. 'I'll have a shower. That might
help.' She rose like a statue coming to creaky life. 'Don't
wake Fang,' she ordered hoarsely.

'Do you think I'm a bloody idiot?' Clive reached for his
mug on the bedside table, catching his dressing-gown sleeve
on the tray. It plunged to the floor, along with the milk jug
and teapot.

The noise of the tray's suicide would wake the dead, never
mind a fractious baby. Fang's wail propelled Shen into the
bathroom, where she whacked on the radio as soon as the
door slammed.

'Oh, come here, you big silly.' Clive negotiated Fang out
of her cot, his ham-hands gathering her into his lap. He
looked her in the eye. 'Do what your daddy tells you. Sleep!'

Fists at her chin, Fang stopped crying, her expression
hard to read.

'Sleep! You know you want to.'

Fang stuck out her lower lip, a signal that Clive now recognized.

A quick crossing of his eyes and Fang's pout curved into a smile. She fidgeted, her plump feet cycling, and then she fell asleep – *bam!* – as if knocked out by an invisible cartoon frying pan.

'Good girl.' Frightened even to rock her, Clive held her to his chest. 'Always do what your daddy tells you. Even though your daddy's an imbecile.'

Far from those inviting pillows now, but afraid to roam all the way up the mattress with his touchy little passenger, he sat on the edge of the bed and thought about last night. And Evie.

As if their holiday was a Richard Curtis movie, the weather cooperated with the mood. The reliable dazzling sunshine had hardened into a heavy heat that lay over the house like one of Patch's blankets. Out in the distant hills, a storm was on its way. According to the local news, it would be a humdinger.

In the drawing room a storm had already arrived. Hurricane Shen.

'I hope you're all ashamed of yourselves.' Shen paced, her face a mask of disapproval, before the teens lined up on a brocade sofa. In her arms even Fang looked stern, a by-product of trapped wind. 'You've let us down, and you've let yourselves down.'

The other adults backed her up, muttering and nodding from their positions around the room. Only Mike, suppressing his laughter, seemed unimpressed by the gravity of the situation. Evie silently thanked the hungover juveniles for distracting him from her white lie about the cost of the holiday.

'You should be ashamed to look us in the face.' Shen was an old-style teller-off. None of this *Do you want to think about what you've done?* She went for the jugular. 'What example are you setting the little ones?'

'Sorry.' Scarlett's head was down, her foul and matted hair over her face.

'Ooh, it speaks,' said Shen, at today's preferred volume of Extremely Loud. 'What was that?'

'Sorry.' Scarlett mumbled a little louder.

'That's fine then. You're sorry. Let's forget all about it. Not!'

'My head hurts.' Zane held his forehead as if it was made of bone china. 'Could you keep it down?'

'Why, of course,' simpered Shen, before bellowing, 'Did you keep it down last night when you were blind drunk?'

'We're very, very disappointed,' said Paula, looking at Tillie as if she'd never seen her before.

'And a bit jealous,' murmured Mike. He turned to Shen. 'Shall we get to the consequences of the kids' actions, Shen?'

'Yes! Let's work out how many years they're grounded for!'

'Tillie,' said Paula, with defiant meekness, 'has never ever even sipped alcohol before.'

'Oh, Mum,' said Tillie. 'Of course I have.'

'What? Oh my God. Are you hearing this, Jon?' Paula looked at her husband, one hand clutching her heart, the other around Amber. 'What else don't I know?' Her voice cracked. 'We promised. No secrets.'

'No, Mum,' said Tillie. '*You* promised. I had no choice.'

Amber said jauntily, 'We have loadth of thecrets.'

'No, we don't.' Paula shook her. 'We . . .' The sentence fell on its knees and Paula relinquished the spotlight to Shen.

'You.' Shen pointed to Zane. 'And you.' The silicon nail picked out Scarlett. 'And you, Missy,' she included Tillie in her wrath. 'All of you are in big trouble. Big. Trouble. Really big.' She hesitated, nodding vehemently. 'The biggest.'

Even though her role was to look stern, Evie smothered a smile, all too familiar with Shen's predicament. She too had often set off on a comprehensive bawling-out before deciding on the punishment to fit the crime; it left her opening and closing her mouth like a goldfish. Just as Shen was doing now. The truth was that it's tricky to punish teenagers; there's only so much the vengeful mum can do.

Undaunted, Shen gathered herself. 'First, you'll replace the booze you *stole* from the drinks cupboard.' The beautiful piece of Edwardian mahogany stood open, its interior ransacked. 'I totted up the bill and it comes to . . .' she hesitated. Evie knew the figure: a mind-boggling £500. (The Wellcome Manor drinks cabinet was in a different league from the Herrera one, which was a kitchen shelf supporting a small bottle of Tesco whisky and a green liqueur they'd never had the nerve to open.)

'A thousand pounds!' shrieked Shen. 'What's more . . .'

She wavered, before sticking out her chin. 'Zane, you're going home this minute!'

Their faces sharp with shock, the girls looked at their accomplice. 'Oh no, please,' begged Scarlett.

'In that case, send us all home,' said Tillie, her face a peculiar colour.

'Believe me, I'd like to,' shouted Shen. 'You girls can make dinner every night and go to bed early and get up early and . . . and . . .'

'Perhaps you'd like us to lick your feet?' asked Tillie with total seriousness.

Zane sniggered, then said, '*What?*' in answer to his step-mother's withering look. 'Are you going to send me home even more?'

Clive put his oar in. *And*, thought Evie, *what a predictable and unhelpful oar it is*. 'I should never have let him come in the first place.'

'Yeah, right, Dad,' said Zane. There was a flicker between him and Tillie, as if he drew energy from the girl's grit. 'Don't forget to polish your Daddy of the Year Award.'

Before Shen could draw breath to roar, Jon strode to the rug and put an arm around her. 'I think these three are idiots,' he said soberly. 'Absolute idiots. I think we were probably all idiots at their age.' Evie almost raised her hand and said 'A-men', before reminding herself she was neither from the Deep South nor in an Oprah audience. 'They're ashamed and embarrassed, as they should be.' Jon craned his neck to look closer at each in turn. 'If they've any sense – and they have plenty of sense – they'll learn from this and it won't happen again. At least, not in front of us. I suspect their brains are like throbbing, rotten cabbages right now.'

Three heads nodded in agreement, then stopped as their owners regretted such extravagant movement.

'Jon's right.' Mike slapped him on the shoulder. 'Don't send Zane home, Shen. Do something far worse to the boy.' He lowered his head and looked penetratingly at the accused. 'I vote for a fate worse than death.' He rubbed his hands like a panto-villain. 'Crazy golf!'

The pace of holiday life is slow; for Evie, forty-eight hours ago was another era, the good old days of relative peace before the turmoil of modern times. *Why did I make such a fuss about revealing my new job?* From her present perspective, as another spasm made her wince, that barely qualified as a problem.

Standing under the shower, grateful for the abundance of hot water that never sputtered or went cold when she had suds in her hair, Evie absent-mindedly fingered the scar on her abdomen, a pink memento of something she'd rather forget.

Not all the memories of 2009 were ugly. There were nuggets of gold amongst the murk. Like Shen casually handing over a rectangle of paper, saying, 'This is for you', as she unpacked a carrier bag full of organic goodies.

'But this is . . . I can't take this!' Evie had fingered the cheque and noted the noughts. 'Seriously, Shen, it's lovely of you, but I can't accept it.'

'People only say that in films,' Shen had laughed. 'It's my contribution. It's only money. It's simpler than having to sit here and watch you in pain. I already do that, so please let me do something easy, for once.'

That cheque had helped Evie jump the queue. It may have saved her life. Driven out of the shower, she found her phone and closed the door against the noise from the master suite.

'This is your territory, Shen!' Clive was shouting.

'She's not territory – she's a baby!' Shen was shouting. 'Change her bloody nappy while I have a bloody nap or I'll cut your bloody balls off and bloody feed them to you!'

'Hello,' said Evie into her phone. 'I'm not one of your regular patients, but I need an appointment.' She swallowed. 'Yes, it's urgent,' she finally conceded.

It was too muggy for anything energetic. Tillie and Scarlett stayed in their room, suffering, waiting for the after-effects to wear off.

In the driveway Zane cleaned his father's car.

'Hot work.' Evie wandered out to him with a cold drink. 'Did Clive order you to do this?'

'Nope.'

'Is it your way of saying sorry without using the word?'

Zane looked affronted. 'I've nothing to be sorry about.'

'Last night's behaviour wasn't very responsible.'

'You lot . . .' Zane rubbed at the bonnet. 'If you knew what the guys at my school get up to.'

'I don't want to,' said Evie hurriedly. 'Scarlett's been tipsy, but never as slaughtered as she was last night.' She rewound Scarlett's short life, seeing her as a ten-year-old, as a six-year-old, as a dot. Mike always warned her to be wary of sentimentalizing childhood, of looking at Scarlett as a snowy piece of paper for life to scribble on.

'It was my fault. Dad was right about that.'

'Like all seventeen-year-old girls, my daughter doesn't need leading astray. She's halfway there already.' Evie took back the empty glass. 'Why do you do all this this petty rebellious stuff, Zane?'

'Dunno.'

'*Dunno.*' Evie mimicked him. 'Yes, you do.'

Zane buffed a headlight. 'Something to do, isn't it?'

'You could collect stamps or learn French. No need to push the self-destruct button every time.' Evie wondered where this empathy and eloquence went, when she dealt with her own teenager.

'Stamps are boring, and I speak fluent French.'

'Maybe it's to impress a certain lady then.'

'Hardly,' said Zane quickly.

'I'm right. When you're right, you're right. And I'm right.'

'I just do what I do,' said Zane cagily.

'Pulling girls' hair to get their attention is out of date,' said Evie. She'd seen Scarlett's baffled pain when Zane teased Dan about his night-light. 'Why not try a little kindness? Girls like that stuff.'

'Secretly, they like having their hair pulled even better.'

'You won't get far with that attitude.' Evie wondered why she had such patience with a boy who spurned advice and

Claire Sandy

rampaged through life, his sense of entitlement so pronounced that it took a seat beside him on public transport. 'Girls aren't an alien life-form. They have the same needs and hopes as you. You don't have to be cocky, but you do have to be *nice*. That's a lame word, but it hits the spot.' She had a sudden urge. Since phoning the doctor she'd felt light-headed, with a hunger to be happy right here, right now. So she gave into her urge. 'Come here, you twit.'

Zane resisted the hug. The hugging didn't stop, however, and he had no choice but to surrender. His head found Evie's shoulder.

If somebody had hugged Mike at Zane's age, his teen years might have been very different. Zane's arms tightened around her and Evie realized she needed a hug just as much as the boy did.

'Sure you don't want to come to crazy golf?'

'Mike, have you ever met me?' said Evie. '*I'm sure*.'

'But you love crazy golf.' He was slack-jawed with shock. 'We've played crazy golf loads of times.' He went white. 'Are you telling me you never enjoyed it? Not once?'

'Now that I've shaken our relationship to its core, I'll tootle off and run some errands in the village.'

'What else are you keeping from me?' laughed Mike as she walked away.

282

Another hole-in-one. Clive retrieved his ball from the giant plastic duck's custard-coloured beak. 'I believe I'm winning,' he said.

'Winners. Losers. Who's counting?' Mike lined up his shot.

'The winner is counting.' Clive leaned on his club. 'Where did Jon go?'

'He's around somewhere.' Mike concentrated hard. Clive had been unbearable since his first hole-in-one had hurtled over a miniature bridge. 'Damn!' It was too muggy for crazy golf; he felt as if the sky hung just above his head.

'A hole in . . . twelve,' said Clive.

'This is shit!' shouted Zane, from the far side of a toy farmstead.

'Language, please,' said the man in the ticket booth. 'There are children playing.'

The children were The Eights and they had yet to hit a ball, preferring to explore the strange, small world of the course. 'Mummy, look!' shouted Amber. 'A loop-the-loop!'

'Yes, dear.' Paula was distracted. She'd been stuck at the windmill for what felt like years.

The woman in the mirror was a stranger to Shen. The determined, shapely chin was the same. And the demure nose and the large forehead. But this poor cow had mascara smudges beneath her eyes and her hair was unbrushed.

She wasn't accustomed to being this bad at something.

She was an achiever. She blazed trails and set standards. Yet here she was, two days into full-time motherhood, and she was a wreck.

The baby who'd conquered the house with one shake of her rattle, who had more energy than a fleet of cheerleaders, who made Shen's heart lift with joy and her brain wilt with fatigue, was asleep. Shen thought of Fang's naps as something delicate, made of the same stuff as bubbles. If she thought too loudly, she'd wake Fang and the whole cycle would begin afresh.

Clive had whistled a tune on his way out to crazy golf. He was still in the parallel universe she'd recently left, the one where this was a holiday. For Shen, Wellcome Manor had become an endurance test.

It had come to this: Shen Ling-Little was envious of people playing *crazy golf*.

Alex, just seen the doc. It's as I feared. This changes everything. I can't take the position after all. I'm so, so sorry. I know I'm letting you down. We'll talk when I get home. But for now, please start looking for another assistant. E x

Bypassing the front door, Evie rounded the side of the house. Since leaving the surgery, a sheaf of pamphlets in her bag, she'd pelted along at full tilt. At some point she would stop and, when that point came, she would need to talk. To talk and talk and talk to somebody who understood, somebody who cared and would let her burp up all the fear, and then hold her while she cried.

That person, however, mustn't be Mike, so she was relieved to find the jalopy still absent from the drive. Shen was what Evie needed. Ferocious, you'll-get-through-this-because-I'll-kill-you-if-you-don't Shen.

The house was quiet. Evie hoofed from room to room, until she heard a smothered snuffling coming from the drawing room.

Propped up on cushions, Fang slept. Kneeling beside her, her head sunk into the sofa, Shen sobbed into the velvet.

'It's playing the game that counts,' said Mike as they handed over their flimsy clubs at the kiosk.

'But winning is nice,' said Clive. 'Who wants an ice cream?'

You little traitors, thought Mike, as The Eights gathered around Clive as if he was the Pied Piper.

Shen felt the sofa shift. She jerked her head to see Fang's waxy soles rise in the air, as the child was lifted up and spirited away through the door, which closed with barely a thud.

She sat up, rubbing sore eyes that felt like tiny button-holes. She hadn't cried like that in years and was surprised at how fresh and clean she felt now. And tired.

On the coffee table was a tray. A percolator of coffee stood, its plunger flirtatiously begging to be pressed. On a plate sat a slice of organic, gluten-free carrot cake.

Shen ate greedily. And gratefully.

The house's empty spaces filled up with noise. Five minutes back at Wellcome Manor and each teen was already accessorized with a bowl of cereal.

'Mum,' said Scarlett, 'Dad puts the "crazy" in crazy golf.'

'I heard that.' Mike looked hurt at this slur on his miniaturized sporting acumen. 'You have real promise, Scarlett,' he said nobly, generous despite his daughter's rudeness.

Scarlett locked eyes with Evie. 'I can die happy,' she said, through a mouthful of Cheerios.

'Here she is, my favourite lady.' Clive breezed into the kitchen.

'My wife or your daughter?' asked Mike wryly.

'I leave that entirely up to you.' Clive winked at Evie, but the wink was lost as she thrust the baby at him, leaving him no option but to embrace Fang.

'Yours, I believe,' she said, in a tone of voice that Mike knew well. Even though he wasn't in the line of fire, it made him want to duck.

'Could you hang on to her, darling?' Clive held Fang out again; the child was a human relay-baton. 'Just until I've opened a bottle of something glorious.'

'No, darling, I couldn't.' Evie crossed her arms as Fang dangled.

Clive looked at her as if she was a gadget that had suddenly short-circuited. He leaned in, lowered his voice. 'You look fabulous when you're angry.'

'What? No I don't.' Evie stepped back. She needed the people around her to be rock-solid, to be ordinary, not odd. 'Clive, Shen's worn out, and I have things to do.'

'Like what?'

Like digesting the universe-tilting news from the doctor. Like planning the assault course of the rest of my life. Like telling my happily oblivious husband he's just escaped one man-trap, only to step into another. 'Your daughter's nappy needs changing and you're the only available adult – you do the maths.'

'I don't do babies,' said Clive.

'You do now.' Their stand-off – *Is Clive enjoying this?* thought Evie, irritated – was curtailed by a full-throttle scream from the terrace.

'Paula,' they said in unison, and bustled out to see Paula pointing at the ground as Jon tried to pull her away.

Shen, her hair on end, ran out, Mike behind her, holding Mabel and Amber by the hands. Tillie rushed up like a paramedic.

'What does this mean?' Paula was mad-eyed.

Picked out in pebbles on the stone flags was a name: *Paula.*

'It's starting again!' she screamed.

'No,' Jon battled to keep her hands from clawing at her scalp. 'Please, Paula.'

Tillie went to her mother, dwarfing her, wrapping her

long brown arms around her, but to no avail. Paula screamed on.

'I was out here five minutes ago.' Evie bent to examine the pebbles. 'There was nothing here.'

'It's the murderer!' Dan, late to the scene, caught up quickly.

'I love the murderer!' yelled Miles, high-fiving Dan.

Mabel burst into tears, welding herself to her dad's leg.

'Quiet, boys. You're making it worse,' sighed Evie.

'You all think I'm cuckoo. Even you, Tillie, who should know better.' Paula shook her daughter off. 'I'm the only one who knows what's going on. We have to leave. *Now*. You!' She wheeled at Jon, jabbed her finger so close to his face that he had to dodge her. 'You broke your promise!'

'Mummy!' Amber's voice was a screech. Everybody looked at the little girl. 'I'm thorry, Mummy!'

'Was it you?' Mike hunkered down, eye-to-eye with Amber, his voice gentle. 'Did you spell out your mummy's name?'

'Yeth!' cried Amber, as if confessing to a homicide. 'It was me!' She stamped her foot, losing control. 'It was a thurprithe, Mummy!' She was tormented, as if she wanted to jump out of her eight-year-old skin.

Paula sank to her knees. 'Amber,' she began, breathless.

'No!' Amber roared into her mother's face. 'You're always being mean. And we never do anything bad.' She raced off down the steps, almost taking flight in her desire to get away.

Tillie followed. After a second's hesitation, so did Scarlett, shooting a reproachful look at Paula.

'Again.' Jon shook his head, took off his spectacles, massaged the bridge of his nose. 'You've done it again, Paula.'

'Look, let's all—' Evie got no further, and the arm she reached out to Paula found only thin air as the woman lurched away, as hysterical as her eight-year-old.

'I know you hate me, Jon!' Her diction was distorted by tears and spittle. 'I know you want out!'

Like a man walking to the gallows, he followed her into the house.

The argument was circular, endless. Nobody dared rap on the Browns' bedroom door to tell them that, with the window open, every bitter word was telegraphed to the whole of Wellcome Manor on the still, pregnant air.

'Just go!' Paula said that over and over.

Jon's answers were various. Sometimes he shouted, 'Where the hell would I go?' Sometimes, 'I don't want to go.' About an hour in, he snarled, 'I've given up everything for you. What more do you need? Do you want blood, woman?'

He ran out of steam earlier than Paula, resorting to, 'Paulie, how about a nice lie-down?' while she was still telling him he had no feelings and had always considered himself above her.

Whacking up the sound system, Evie enticed The Eights into an impromptu dance session, which always went down well at home; watching Mummy wig out to The Saturdays was a perennial crowd-pleaser. Whether it was the oppressive weather crushing down on them or the backdrop of marital carnage, today's danceathon didn't catch fire.

'Amber.' Evie took the little bundle onto her lap. 'All mummies and daddies argue. It doesn't mean they don't love each other.'

'My mummy doesn't love my daddy,' said Amber, matter-of-factly. 'My daddy loves my mummy too much.' She sighed. 'How can you love thomebody too much?'

'I think too much is just the right amount.' Evie squeezed her and Amber giggled. The child was thawing, with the awe-inspiring resilience of little ones.

From upstairs Paula yelled, 'Don't you think I'd love to walk away from this mess myself!'

Twilight swooned over the house, like a damp blanket. Waving Mike and The Eights off in search of a chip shop – the rota had gone to pot; dinner wasn't happening – Evie wished the storm would just get on with it. This charged feeling of something eternally about to happen exaggerated the mood of the house. A natural blurter, she wanted to shout her news.

She needed to hear Shen chop it into manageable chunks. Within ten minutes her eyes would be dried and a To Do list written.

That's how the old Shen would deal with it, thought Evie. The new, dead-eyed and hostile model would probably shrug.

The Browns were quiet up in their room. Hopefully they were making up, although they might have resorted to miming their insults. As Evie put the terrace to rights, scooping up a Frisbee, a Barbie and some rogue sunglasses, a shout broke the sullen air.

'For God's sake, you insufferable female!' It was Clive's voice, thick with irritation.

Evie straightened, earwigged.

'Out!' That was Shen. She was angry. Properly angry. Her rage was top-of-the-range stuff, more powerful than generic brands. 'Out, *now*, Clive, before I strangle you with this nappy!'

Evie could have sworn the house said *tsk*. Sick of all this argy-bargy, Wellcome Manor was a class act. Historically people had suffered in well-bred silence within its walls; they hadn't chucked teething rattles through windows.

'Jesus H. Christ,' snarled Clive, emerging onto the terrace and trying to light his cigar with a match as uncooperative as his wife.

'What does the H. stand for?' asked Evie.

Clive goggled at her, then laughed, his self-righteous anger punctured. 'Who knows? Herbert?'

Dumping her armful of tat, Evie said, 'Come and sit down.'

Evie and Clive. Together again. On their bench. It was comforting, in a day of revelation and discord, to reprise a habit.

'You heard?' queried Clive. 'Of course you heard. The whole of Devon heard. I shouldn't have shouted like that.'

'Shen can take it.' Besides, Shen *was* an insufferable female.

'I wasn't shouting at *her*.' Clive dragged deep on his cigar as if it was an antidote.

'You were . . .' Evie looked askance. 'You yelled at little Fang like that?'

'Yes.' Clive wasn't proud. 'She just drove me mad – the way they can, you know.'

Evie did know. Every parent or aunt or uncle or friend knows. 'But, Clive . . .'

'I can oversee an international merger without breaking into a sweat, but my daughter does a poo on my laptop and I lose it.'

'Yeew. Was it one of those strange runny ones?'

'It was *orange*!' Clive looked horrified by life's cruelties. 'I knew,' he turned to her, 'you'd understand.'

'But I don't.' Evie was brisk; with pressing troubles of her own, she wasn't in the mood to absolve Clive for buckling under his petty woes. 'Three wives and umpteen kids in, it's time you got on top of this stuff.'

Clive exhaled morosely. 'True.' He leaned back, put his hands behind his head, reminding Evie of the moves that school boyfriends had pulled at the cinema. 'Surely you screamed at your old man when he helped you, when the kids were babies?'

'Nope.' Evie was adamant.

'What, never?' Clive was rudely sceptical, even as he looked intently at her mouth.

Evie wondered if she had food stuck to her lip. 'Not once.'

'I had you down as feisty.'

'I never screamed at him, because he never helped me out.'

'Rubbish! I see Mike in a pinny – no problem.'

'Me too. But he didn't *help* me.' Evie waited for, and got, comprehension in Clive's eyes. 'He did his duty.'

'So you *did* scream at him?'

'Obviously. My hormones were playing musical chairs. I was getting by on eight minutes' sleep. Motherhood was nothing like what Angelina Jolie leads us to believe. And there was Mike, putting talc on the baby's head and plonking Scarlett in front of a horror movie, instead of *Tellytubbies*. We were both overwhelmed and at times he didn't pull his weight, but I never felt I was in it alone.' Evie had a strong suspicion: time to air it. 'Are you cocking up chores on purpose, so you're never asked to do them again?'

'No. Maybe.'

She swatted him with her hand. 'You should be ashamed of yourself.'

'Oh, I am, I am.'

'You're not.'

'No, I'm not.'

Evie rapped him smartly on the knuckles. Tonight, with a storm humming in the hills, the house braced for the onslaught, and her own news heavy within her, was a night to take liberties.

Clive evidently agreed. He blinked hard, a tic that Evie had never noticed. 'I don't let anybody else talk to me like you do. But nobody else does talk to me the way you do. Nobody,' he shifted nearer, twisting so that he leaned towards her, 'makes me feel the way you do.'

That was a cue to dart off like a spinster aunt, but instead Evie became absolutely still.

'Our heart-to-hearts at the end of the day,' said Clive, 'are the only times I feel properly alive.'

Evie held up her finger to shush him, but he took her hand in his paw. She tugged. He held on harder. 'Clive, my hand, please,' she said ever so politely and he relinquished it. 'You shouldn't be saying this.'

'It's burning a hole in me. And don't pretend – not now.'

'Who's pretending?' Evie gestured to her face. 'This horn-swaggled expression is the real deal. We'll just forget this, Clive. You're tired and you—'

'Not too tired for a nice cream tea.'

'Well, now you're just saying whatever comes into your head.' Evie frowned. Had she missed something?

Clive leaned closer. She leaned back. She was almost horizontal (and somewhat impressed by her own suppleness; Clive had achieved what Pilates couldn't) as he said, 'I'm really into Battenberg too, by the way.'

'I'm very glad for you,' said Evie. She straightened up, relieved when Clive did the same. 'I'm not sure a shared love of cake is any reason to—'

'Do this?' Clive put one hand around her neck and pulled her face towards him.

'Get off!' Evie pushed against his chest, electrified by the proprietorial way he laid hands on her. 'What the hell are you doing?'

'Clotted cream!' breathed Clive. '*Cucumber sandwiches!*'

'This is now officially scary.' Evie stood up.

'I read your story. Your little fantasy.' Clive allowed her a moment to catch up. 'You and me and a cream tea?' He brimmed with wickedness, all fatigue forgotten. 'Let's make it a reality.' He took in her dumbfounded face. 'Forgive me. I shouldn't have looked at your laptop without your permission.'

'My password,' said Evie. 'How'd you . . . ?'

'It was your birthday, darling. Patch could have worked it out.'

Clive had read her erotic prose; Evie shuddered as if he'd riffled her knicker drawer. (If he *had* inspected her underwear he'd have snow-blindness from the expanse of big white control pants, and this conversation would not be happening.) 'That's not fantasy, Clive. It's certainly not about you . . .' She tapered off, as a small, rarely used cog turned at the back of her brain. 'Oh, shit,' she said with feeling.

Slowly, clearly, Clive said, '*With his pointed tongue, Clive licks the jam from my taut tummy.*' He closed the space between them.

Evie opened the space again. At this rate she'd soon be flattened against the house. 'I know I said it was a diary, a fantasy, but it's not. It's my sideline. I write erotic books.'

Clive looked ecstatic. 'You put me in a saucy book! You hussy!'

Glancing neurotically towards the house, Evie gasped, 'I did *not*.'

'I get it. You're frightened by what's happened between us.' Clive held out his arms. 'Take a leap, darling. I'm here.' He disregarded the strange, tortured sound Evie made. 'Don't think this is some grubby affair I'm offering. This is different.'

'How many times have you said that?'

'Dozens. But this time I mean it.'

'How many times have you said *that*?'

'Never.' Now that Clive was in earnest, he seemed younger, less entitled. As if he feared a slap. 'This is unfamiliar territory. I feel . . .' He laughed, as if afraid of sounding foolish. He grabbed for her hand. 'I feel brand-new.'

Acutely aware of how visible they were in the dusk, Evie tried to pull away her hand. 'Please stop it. Shut up, please.'

Holding on tight, Clive said, 'When we talk, I don't bullshit. I don't try to impress you. You're always your lovely self with me. Don't force me to do without that now. I can't.'

'When I said *shush*,' said Evie, 'I didn't mean go on and on and on.'

'When I'm with you I see life in primary colours. Everything seems simple.'

'Everything *is* simple.' Today she believed that more than ever before. She wrenched away her hand. 'Clive, we're all striving to feel OK, to feel like we're home. Stop searching for happiness in other women.' Evie was now an Other Woman: that sickened her. 'I promise you that you already have what you're looking for, in the palm of your hand. And I'm always right, remember?'

'Not this time. But listen, if you and I do this, we don't discuss Shen, darling. That's a rule, yeah?'

'Eh?' She found time, amongst various overlapping feelings, to marvel at his chutzpah. 'We're not *doing this*, Clive. There is no *this*.'

'That's not what your subconscious is saying.'

'It's saying goodnight.' She ran out of things to say and left him, wondering if she should round up her family and sneak off in the middle of the night.

'Goodnight, Gorgeous.'

Evie was an experienced huffer and puffer, but never had she huffed and puffed so much as on that short stomp back indoors. She passed the kitchen door to avoid Shen, so was startled when she stepped through the French windows and came across her friend in the drawing room.

Shen's sticky fringe was vertical. 'I know your little game,' she said.

'You do? You don't!' Evie tried to hold her nerve. 'Do you?'

'You've been out there with Clive.' Shen sighed. 'Trying to talk some sense into him.'

'Was I?' Evie registered relief and a deep, deep need to be far away. 'I was,' she added firmly. 'I really was.'

'He'll never get why I need him to help,' said Shen. 'But thanks for trying.' She peered at Evie. 'Are you feeling all right? You look off-colour under your sunburn.'

'The expression is sun*tan*, Shen.' Evie managed to smile. 'I'm fine,' she said.

'That you?' Mike's voice was soaked in sleep.

'No. It's Nigella Lawson.' Evie put out her hand to steady herself as a gush ran through her body, a ripple of feeling that almost toppled her. 'Oh no-oh!'

'You OK?'

'Yup!' Evie climbed in beside him. 'I'm fine.'

DAY 11
Friday, 21st August

Dear Spa reception,
   Book me in 9 a.m. on 25th for anti-ageing facial/full-body massage/bikini wax/pedi/mani/cut/blow-dry.

Shen Ling-Little

The air hung heavy as leftover stew. Specifically, Evie's leftover stew; there tended to be a lot left over of the impromptu casseroles knocked together, after a long day of kinky composition.

By the pool, the adults lay in neat formation, as still as if posing for a portrait. Even the younger members of the Wellcome Manor squad were affected by the lethargic climate and lazed in the water, leaning on the tiled edging.

Fang was now a fully paid-up member of the holiday. The sluggish pace of holiday time meant they barely remembered those distant days when she had descended upon them at set times in Elizabetta's arms. Now she was on her father's lap, pulling his chest hair.

No merger goes smoothly at first, thought Clive, attempting to watch Evie through his sunglasses without his wife noticing this covert surveillance. 'Ow, darling,' he said softly to Fang, who found that terribly funny and pulled harder. The adorable tot had a sadistic sense of humour.

First rule of business, he said, telepathically, to his daughter, *is keep going*. History is made by the people who bother to turn up; Clive would keep turning up and keep facing the put-downs, if it meant winning Evie.

He peered surreptitiously at her. How had he never noticed that face before, when she dashed in and out of his house in that quicksilver way of hers? She'd merely been Shen's BF, somebody for his wife to talk to, someone to distract Shen from going through his phone or querying his late-night meetings.

He'd overlooked a jewel, believing it to be paste. Evie's blurred jawline spoke of ageing, yet those merry eyes bewitched him.

Willingly, Clive gave in to her spell. He was good at infidelity; she need have no worries on that score. She could continue her friendship with Shen. They could both continue their marriages. Everybody's happy. 'Happy!' he said to Fang.

Fang liked that word. She gurgled like a drain. Then again, she liked all words, if said brightly enough. He tested her: 'Crematorium!' Yup. That got a huge smile.

Then Fang was on the move, lifted away by Mike, and Clive's lap felt cold, even in that leaden sunshine.

'Take a break,' said Mike chummily. 'Let me look after her.'

'Thanks,' said Clive, not sure if he was grateful.

'Hello, little lady.' Mike spoke over-loudly to the baby as he lay back and let her drum her feet on his chest. Had Evie noticed his gesture? He bloody well hoped so; he wasn't helping Clive for the sake of it.

Sleepily Shen said from her position two loungers away, 'A baby suits you, Mike.'

'Ooh, not any more,' he laughed. 'Been there. Done that. Bought the vomit-flecked tee-shirt.' All the same, it was all sorts of delightful when Fang snuggled into his shoulder with that I'm-welcome-everywhere confidence of infants.

'Why isn't your godmother talking to me?' asked Mike, his mouth to Fang's tiny, perfect ear. Evie had stayed on the periphery of his vision all morning. It was worse than out-and-out avoidance, making their interactions just that: *interactions*. Evie was polite, but she wasn't warm. This wasn't about crazy Haley; when Evie put a subject to bed, it stayed there. This was about something else. 'I'm racking my brains, Fang,' he told the child. 'Why won't she talk to me about it? There's nothing me and her can't talk about.'

Except for one thing.

Realization hit, and everything around Mike sharpened up. With newly keen vision, he saw through Evie's striped swimsuit to the bones and the meat of her. Her body no longer a fascinating map of curves and dips, wonderful to warm his feet on and even better to hold, but a collection of hazards. He bored through her and saw her gall bladder glow like kryptonite.

Even a lioness like Evie would baulk at telling him about a relapse.

Jerkily, as if he was trying out new legs, Mike stood, foisting Fang onto the nearest human, who happened to be Zane.

'Hey!' complained Zane, but Mike staggered off, leaving his paperback behind, not even turning his head. 'Here. Somebody take her.' Zane held out the curiously heavy baby – was she made of cement? – to Tillie, who laughed in that superior way that infuriated him.

'No way. Don't bung her to me just cos I'm a girl, Zane.'

'I wasn't.'

'You *so* were.'

But he so wasn't; he was giving her to Tillie because he'd never held Fang before and this felt all wrong. The baby was a rival, an adversary, a fellow heir to Clive's dubious legacy. He looked around for Scarlett, but he knew she wouldn't help. Every bird in Britain was a bleedin' feminist these days. Personally, he blamed the Spice Girls. And Mrs Thatcher. Whoever she was.

'Blaaaaaaaah!' guffawed Fang.

'Yeah. Whatever.' Zane's arms began to ache. 'You'd be useful down the gym, for weight-training.' He brought Fang to his chest. 'Can it swim?' he asked of the world at large. Tilting his head awkwardly, he went on, 'So . . . um . . . hi.' Fang listened, rapt. 'I'm your brother.'

'Half-brother.' Clive corrected him sleepily.

Zane pursed his lips and Fang copied him. 'When you're all grown-up,' he told her, loudly, 'come and find me and we'll talk about *him*. How he fu . . . screwed us up. But don't worry,' he added, 'he'll pay for our therapy.'

The little thing, slippery and plump and exploding with good humour, was cute, close up. Zane had imagined she'd smell sour like milk, but she smelled of something indefinable, something between vanilla and wool and summertime.

Watching Zane pretend to bite Fang's fingers and tickling her feet, Tillie said, 'You're being a bit obvious, dude.'

'Did somebody speak?' Zane said it in the coochy-coo voice he'd used to ask Fang if she was *lovely-wovely*. 'Did somebody speaky-weaky or did somebody farty-warty?'

'You want *her* to think: *Jeez, he's amazing with babies*, so that her womb melts and she falls for you.'

Zane wibbled his lip with his forefinger, with Fang looking on as if he were a comedy genius. 'I don't know what the silly lady's talking about, Fang!'

'You think you're getting somewhere, but you're not. Not really.' Tillie flipped over, fidgeting with her straps, offering herself to the clammy sunshine.

Dropping the baby-talk, Zane said, 'That's not what Evie says.'

'You've talked to Evie about it?' Tillie's careful composure fractured.

'Evie's cool. She's broad-minded. She's not like other mums.'

'She reckons you've got a chance?' Tillie seemed stupefied.

'She says they've talked about it. I'm doing OK. If you didn't have a book in your face the whole time, you might notice what real people are actually doing.' He lifted Fang into the air, and she cackled with happiness. 'Hey! Scarlett!'

'Aww!' called Scarlett. 'That's so sweet!'

'Jesus Christ!' said Tillie.

Patch shot through the kitchen and cowered under the table.

'That means there's thunder and lightning coming,' declared Dan. 'Patch always knows.'

'It's the only thing he does know,' said Evie, slipping the daft bugger a corner of her eggy-bread elevenses.

'I'm proud of how stupid he is.' Mabel's glass-half-full attitude would stand her in good stead.

'Why is Fang crying?' Miles's bland, peachy face was troubled.

'Is she depressed about politics?' suggested Mabel, stealing a major portion of her mother's eggy bread.

'Or maybe she did a murder,' suggested Amber, 'and she'th thcared the police will come for her.'

'Get out, children,' said Shen, in a quiet way that Evie recognized as dangerous.

'Come, kiddiwinks.' Evie stood and The Eights followed her to the cinema room, where she pressed random buttons on a remote the size of a tea tray until the screen flared into life.

'*Frozen*!' yelped Mabel. 'I want to live in a ice palace! I like the horse in it too!'

Knowing how quickly a mob of Eights could turn ugly, Evie asked, 'Is *Frozen* OK for the rest of you?'

'S'pose,' grumbled Dan, who secretly knew all the lyrics to 'Let It Go'.

'Great.' Evie shut the door on them, silently thanking Walt Disney for all his babysitting over the years. When she returned to the kitchen, Shen had done a bunk, and in her place was Clive, holding Fang and jiggling her far too fast.

'Ah,' said Evie.

'We need to talk,' said Clive, in the hush suitable to church or library. Or a woman you're trying to have an affair with.

'We've talked. We're done,' said Evie hurriedly, hearing Mike and Jon in the hall. She sat at the table and pretended to read Shen's *Vogue*, while Patch quivered against her leg.

The other men were keen to help out their buddy, it transpired. All three of them manhandled Fang into her high chair. After some discussion and a few interesting theories about how the restraints worked, they buckled her in safely.

'So. Food,' said Clive, a born leader of men.

'Carrots,' said Jon adamantly. Then, more tentatively, 'Carrots?'

'Yeah, carrots.' Mike had the air of a man with plenty of carrot experience.

'Do we cook the carrots and then . . . um . . . what is it – purée them?' Clive stroked his chin.

'No, no, we . . .' Jon lost faith in his fledgling hypothesis. 'Oh, hang on, yes, cook them first!' His face lit up, only to fall again. 'But how does one purée?' He looked pained.

'With a mashy thing?' Mike was right there with a plan, rooting through the nearest drawer. 'Our one at home is a disc shape with holes in it.'

'No, no.' Clive's brow was like a newly ploughed field. 'Doesn't it involve a small machine of some kind?' Helpfully he did an impression of a stick-blender.

All in all, it only took an hour to purée the carrots, and Fang's mewling subsided at last as she accepted the sloppily wielded spoonfuls.

'Good girl.' Clive beamed. 'Good, perpetually wide-awake little girl.' He appealed to the others. Evie noticed that he treated Mike exactly the same as ever, with no trace of guilt about his attempted seduction of Mike's wife. 'How in the name of God does Fang stay awake for so long? Is she fitted with Duracell batteries or something?'

'She should sleep tonight,' offered Mike sagely.

'I bloody hope so.' Clive wiped his daughter's mouth with the cloth Shen kept for cleaning the guck out of Prunella's prominent eyes. 'I think we should let her cry. You know, not run to her every minute.'

'Shen disagrees?' Jon was rueful.

'Obviously. My good lady wife disagrees with every word out of my mouth.'

'Don't,' interrupted Evie, without looking up from *Vogue*, 'call her your "good lady wife". Just saying.'

'Shen agreed we'd experiment,' said Clive, 'by not picking up Fang the moment she wails, but then she gave in and grabbed her.'

'Highly illogical,' said Jon.

'Highly,' agreed Mike. Evie could tell he had nothing to add, but wanted to keep 'in' with the chaps.

'So we pick her up, we put her down, we check her nappy, we have a row, I shout, Shen shouts, Fang screams, we put her down, we pick her up, and so on and so forth.'

'Lunacy,' said Jon. 'Sheer lunacy. You need to pull together.'

Ironic, thought Evie. *Coming from him.*

It would take more than a fortnight for Wellcome Manor to offer up all its secrets. Evie discovered a new room, a small hexagonal chamber papered in a pattern of larks and leaves. It was cosily dark, thanks to the clouds slowly obliterating the sky, like bullies spoiling for a fight. Patch slipped in alongside Evie and slid under an antique desk.

The only light in the room came from the screen of Evie's laptop as she read Alex's email. It read breathlessly, as if Alex had typed her raw reaction with no editing, no diplomacy: **You've let me down. Thanks for nothing.**

Whatever the outcome of her diagnosis ('I can put the wheels in motion immediately,' the sympathetic doctor had said, suggesting that Evie might curtail her holiday), she'd burned her bridges with Alex. The gorgeous sparkly job that had sustained her with its promise of a different, better life was dust.

The door squeaked open. Clive was there, and the room felt claustrophobic.

'Actually, I'm working . . .' Evie kept her eyes on the screen, on the vitriol: **You've really landed me in it. Did you even stop to think how stupid this makes me look?**

'It can wait.' Clive closed the door and leaned against it.

Grateful that he didn't approach her, Evie turned to face him in the spindly bentwood chair that felt like doll's-house furniture beneath her; Georgian bottoms were evidently on the small side. 'I'm very flattered by all . . . this.' Her voice sounded dry and tired. 'But you have to drop it.' She would never add that she simply didn't fancy him. It was beyond her to be so pointlessly cruel. Moreover, it wasn't that Clive wasn't her type, but that Mike – and only Mike – *was* her type.

'I'm not listening,' said Clive, unperturbed. 'I'm going to wear you down, Evie. One morning you'll wake up and you'll want me. I'm not some stud flashing his pecs, and this isn't some fling. I've started to need you.'

'You don't need me.' Evie was exasperated.

'I need to hear you talk. I need you to listen to me. I need you to take me down a peg or two.'

'A man who's married to Shen,' said Evie, 'already has the services of a professional taker-down of pegs.' She shrugged. 'What can I say, Clive? I seem to be wasting my breath, but you really do have everything you want in Shen. She's intelligent. She's a great mother. She's fiery and funny and passionate and gorgeous. Be a team. Stop thinking of ways to get one over on each other.'

'A team.' Clive considered the word. 'Like you and Mike, you mean? I've been watching you both today.'

'Lovely, and not creepy at all.'

'You're giving him the same cold shoulder you're giving me.' Clive perched on a dainty chaise longue. He looked uncomfortable, as if regretting his decision to perch. 'It's a very nice shoulder,' he said. 'But it's cold.'

'That's personal.' Evie hoped she sounded duchess-like, but suspected she sounded like Mabel. 'It's between me and Mike. I can't take any more of these conversations, Clive. How many different ways do you need to hear "No"?'

'I'm not giving up.'

Evie threw her hands in the air. She saw Clive's expression brighten, as if he saw any reaction as progress. 'I'm not being coy so that you chase me. This *attraction* is based on a misunderstanding.' She faltered. She hadn't planned to shoot him down like this. 'Clive, the hero of my current novel is called Clay. A stupid name, which is mandatory in my genre. While I was editing dialogue, I used the "Find and replace" tool to replace the word *lay* with the word *live*, but I—'

Clive's arms unfolded as he interrupted. 'Oh God,' he said. 'You made it find and replace *all* instances of "lay" with "live", which—'

'Changed Clay to Clive, yes.' Evie nodded. 'The universe played a joke on us.'

'So, you don't want to smear cream on my—'

'Nope!' Evie cut in. 'The cream-smearing was all in a day's work.' Now that he was deflated, she longed to reach out and comfort Clive. *Best not*, she thought. 'One day we *will* laugh about this, I promise.'

'I'm a fool. But I don't take a word of it back. I'd cross this room in a heartbeat to take you in my arms.'

It was so sad, the way he said it. Evie let the silence lie between them for a while before saying, 'I'm very flattered, because you're a man of taste. You married my favourite woman in the world.'

Clive scoffed, disconsolate.

'What with a demanding wife and a sudden, second chance at fatherhood, you don't have time to imagine yourself falling for me.'

'I'm doing my best with Fang,' said Clive, with a hint of impatience, as if they'd changed topics before he was ready.

'I meant Zane.' She saw his eyelids waver at the mention

of his prodigal boy. 'Having a close relationship with your children is like . . . like . . .' Evie fell over her words in her desire to convince him, 'it's like a never-ending magic trick that keeps amazing you. It's something that gets deeper by the hour. It's the one subject in life that never bores you.'

'Oh, come on, I'm not letting you get away with that. There is *nothing*,' said Clive, 'as fucking tedious as people talking about their kids.'

'Yeah. *Their* kids. But not your own. Zane's waving his heart at you, if only you'd notice.'

'Waving his heart?' scoffed Clive. 'Bollocks!'

'Just talk to him, touch him every now and then. Eye contact will do, for starters.' Evie saw his face harden. 'Zane's being very generous. Why don't you stop leaving a trail of baby mamas and take the opportunity he's offering you?'

Clive stood up, ruffled his hair, puffed out his chest. 'You can be damned preachy, Evie.'

They were back in the playground. *I didn't let Clive catch me playing Kiss Chase,* thought Evie. So *he's pulling my hair.*

Napping was for other people. Shen had never got the hang of it. She sat up, irritated with herself.

The only role she could pull off was Queen Bee; blow-dried, accessorized, droll one-liners ready in her statement handbag; Worker Drone was beyond her. Over-tired, below par, she wasn't capable of doing the job at hand.

What made it unbearable was that the 'job at hand' was Fang. The chip off Shen's old block – so like her, and yet so intriguingly different – was wearing her out. She shifted in the tousled bed; a plastic building block dug into her coccyx.

I'm not a real woman. She was a fake, like those bags Evie bought hopefully on eBay, and which turned out to be Prarder or Channel.

Motherhood was something you had to learn. Your baby arrived, squawked at you, and you interpreted that squawk and produced a soft toy/your breast, as appropriate. Shen's first attempt at mothering, with Miles, had been a limo-ride. Whenever she'd drooped, she simply handed him to a trustworthy, salaried adult. She'd slept deeply and woken refreshed, unaware that other women slept like sentries: one eye open, one ear cocked for that unique cry.

It wasn't that her beloved schedule was disrupted; there *was* no schedule. Even if she could muster the energy, there was no time to exercise. Her daily wash and careful blow-dry was only a memory, and her armpits had sprouted little fur gilets.

The depth of the fury she felt at Clive astonished her. True, theirs was a partnership built on squabbles and jibes, but this was different. Her nagging of Clive, her remorseless reminders that he was damned lucky to have her, were hot air. She knew he liked a volatile woman and that their arguments fuelled the sex, so she bitched and carped for fun. But this low-level resentment towards him, always audible in the background like Sky News, was different.

Why didn't Clive *notice*? How come he could enjoy a long shower, smoke on the terrace and read the papers while she did a thousand-and-one tiny, thankless tasks?

But worse, why couldn't she appeal for help in a plain and simple fashion? Shen had long suspected there was a component of their marriage that was on the blink, like a rusty carburettor on a car. The missing constituent was intimacy. And the easy communication that came with it.

Sometimes she had a mental image of herself on a conveyor belt in the factory that churned out Clive's Wives. 'Number three of three' was how she archly referred to herself, but what if she was not the last, just the latest?

In bed they communicated, but that timetable was also shot to hell. Today was the twenty-first, so that meant . . . she sighed as she realized she should be prepping her basque.

Another uncomfortable truth reared its ugly head, blinking in the light. *I don't fancy Clive any more*. True, he would never win a Mr Universe pageant, but Shen had never been drawn to good looks. Meeting Clive, she'd felt a primal tug. He was so very *there*. *He* was an alpha, a silverback and fizzingly alive, compared to the younger men she'd hung out with before his reign. She'd sensed his power and respected the frank way he pursued her.

It was impossible to respect the Clive who sauntered away without a backward glance, forcing her to take up the slack; the Clive who only picked up Fang when forced to.

Those divorce gags weren't funny any more. As Fang's air-raid wail started up again downstairs, Shen stood up, pulled her rat-tails into a plait and thought vehemently, *If it happens, I won't take a penny. Not one single penny.*

The sky foamed with angry clouds. Evie sat in the silent kitchen, lit by the eerie acid glow that presages a storm. She heard a voice, low and authoritative.

'I need more documentation before I can consider green-lighting such a dramatic overhaul,' Clive was saying. It was business double-Dutch, meaningless to Evie's ears. She crept towards the half-open door of the drawing room.

On a split computer screen two earnest male faces frowned, while a watery voice floated from a speaker. 'Sure, but we need to avoid reneging on our contractual commitments.'

The chair swivelled and Clive's bulk blocked the screen, jabbing the air as he pontificated.

It was Clive's prerogative to ignore her heartfelt advice, to leave Shen to soldier on with Fang somewhere in this vast house. Evie closed the door.

Hearing a faint click, Clive swung around, but no, there was nobody there.

'Listen, guys,' he said, 'I've made my position clear. Either we do as I say and make piles of cash, or you ignore me and I sue you. Goodbye for now.'

He pressed a button decisively, as if it needed a damned good pressing and Clive Little was the man to do it.

'Such utter bollocks, all of it,' he said. 'Pardon my French, darling.' He leaned down towards Fang in a Moses basket beneath the desk, her comma of hair neatly combed, her face shining with the exertion of trying to nab the feather that waved tantalizingly just out of her reach.

Laughing, Clive took the feather from between his toes and handed it over, grateful to it for keeping Fang contentedly quiet throughout the conference call. 'There you go, Princess.'

It had landed. The feeling Evie had struggled to describe had blossomed, as Fang lay against his chest in their like-a-bomb-hit-it bedroom.

Their eyes had met. And locked. It was the thousandth time he'd looked at Fang's face, but the first time he'd seen her.

How had he never noticed before his daughter's incredible eyes? They were wise and ageless, and sort of like his eyes and sort of like Shen's. Something had passed between him and his daughter, a bolt of pure empathy.

Clive had always known that Fang belonged to him, but until today he hadn't realized that he belonged to her.

'I wondered,' said Evie, 'where you'd all got to!'

The Eights trooped in, teens bringing up the rear, Paula skirting them like an old sheepdog. She'd taken them to the village, and hoped that was all right?

'More than all right!'

'We're staying up to watch the storm,' said Dan.

'The chap in the newsagent's,' said Paula, throwing teabags into the pot, 'reckons it'll be a corker.'

Surprised that Paula even knew where the teapot lived, Evie fussed around with mugs, slapping away the children's efforts to snaffle biscuits, and muzzling a smile when Jon said, good-naturedly enough, 'And everybody knows news-agents make the best weather forecasters.'

He was as brightly brittle as his wife, the two of them striving for 'normality' – never an easy task for the Browns.

'Mr . . . um . . . Jon,' said Mabel, her eye on the multi-pack of Orange Club biscuits that her mother had moved to a place of greater safety, 'where did you go?'

'How d'you mean, dear: where did Jon go?' Paula smiled, unpacking a granary loaf and a slab of cheese and a weepingly cold bottle of white wine. 'He was with us.'

'Not when we were at the museum of local history. Which was very boring, by the way. I hate local history now. Did you,' Mabel asked Jon, 'go to the pub?' She had an unshakeable belief that all men, whenever they left the house, went 'to the pub'.

'I . . .' Jon measured his words. 'I went for a little wander.'

'He does,' said Paula, 'love his little wanders. Don't you, dear?'

'I do, dear,' said Jon, as if chewing staples.

Dinner was *odd*. Not the food; the chicken and the spiced rice were delicious. Everything else was slightly off-key.

Eating indoors after days of balmy al-fresco meals meant

the acoustics were different: forks scraped on plates and glasses thudded on the table. The overhead lighting wasn't half as poetic as the lantern's flattering flicker, which had bonded them against the tightly knit dark beyond.

'It's the weather,' said Mike, when Clive commented on the monastic quiet of the table tonight. 'This is the quiet before the storm.' He nudged Evie. 'Isn't it?'

'Mm.' She sensed him watching her, putting two and two together. At some point she'd have to congratulate him on getting his sums right.

'I'm sick of this storm,' mumbled Shen. 'And it hasn't even arrived yet.'

When Fang griped from her basket, Shen slumped, as if attached to the child by an invisible cord. 'Quiet, please, sweetheart,' she said, a little desperately.

Clive laid a hand on his wife's arm. 'She's fine,' he said. 'C'mere, little 'un.' He fetched Fang and propped her on his lap.

'I'll never have a baby,' said Scarlett.

'You'll change your mind,' said Zane.

'Shut up,' said Scarlett, reaching over him for the salt. Zane shoved her away, ducking as she fought back.

'We're eating,' said Clive.

' And?' Embedded between his women, Zane was cocky.

'*And*,' Clive's face puckered into anger, 'I wish that boy would stop messing about. He's not ten.'

'*I* am,' said Dan.

Zane muttered something to Scarlett and she sniggered, turning it hastily into a cough.

'Guys, don't be rude,' said Mike.

More indulgent than her husband, Evie was grateful the teens had shaken off the prevailing lethargy, and glad that Scarlett no longer took Zane at supercool face-value. Once a girl kisses a boy, the game's up; they both know who's *really* in charge.

Zane flung a crust of bread at Tillie. His father responded, in character, by scolding him.

'God, Zane, grow up,' said Tillie.

I bet Scarlett's glad she came, thought Evie as her daughter's freckled shoulders shook with merriment. *She's found a boyfriend* and *a friend.* The affinity between Scarlett and Tillie had bloomed while nobody was looking. *Lucky Zane,* thought Evie, cosy between his honeybunch and her new BF.

'Yeah, grow up, little Zanie,' giggled Scarlett. 'Your baby sister is embarrassed about you!'

'Her?' Zane pointed a fork at Fang, who was sifting through Clive's rice like a forensics expert. 'I'll probably never see her again after this holiday.'

Clive said, 'Zane, stop being a prick.'

'Mummy!' Mabel almost screamed, in her haste to alert her mother to this terrible crime. 'Clive sweared in front of me and I'm only a kid!'

'Shit, Clive,' said Shen.

'Well played, Shen,' said Mike, helping himself to more rice.

'You'll live, Mabes.' Evie chucked the child's cheek.

'What *is* a prick?' asked Miles.

Paula slammed down her fork.

'Oh God,' groaned Shen.

Jon got as far as 'Look, let's just—' before being interrupted.

'Everybody,' shouted Clive, his arms outstretched, 'shut up.' He resumed eating. 'Thank you.'

As if night had barged in before its appointment, the garden was dark when they finished eating. Evie was first on the terrace, staring out into the black, impatient for the rain. She wanted thunder, lightning, a whirlwind; so that the drama within her body matched the one outside.

A striped awning, neglected up to now, was tugged into place.

No longer still, the air was full of rolling, churning activity. The leaves bristled, their customary susurration growing louder until it turned into a different sound altogether.

A deep-throated rumble boomed around them.

'It's starting, kids!' called Evie. The awning creaked and complained as the striped sail rolled out of its niche. She put out a hand, palm up. 'Where's the rain?'

Shen scuttled to stand beside Evie. She was every bit as superstitiously afraid of thunder and lightning as Prunella and Patch, both of whom had disappeared.

The teenagers swarmed out, glasses in hand, like visiting celebrities, and made for the balustrade. 'Did you hear that!' squealed Scarlett, as the sky growled again.

'What's with the leaves flying about?' Zane picked a twig out of his coiffeur.

'It's a mini-typhoon,' laughed Tillie.

A mischievous wind gusted, support act for the head-lining tempest. Small branches, torn leaves and dust snatched from the earth reeled and rolled.

'Confetti!' shouted Dan.

'Come under the awning, darling!' The wind snatched away Evie's words.

Always keen on his rights, Dan shouted over the booming and the whooshing, 'You said we could get wet!'

Appearing with Fang in his arms, Clive's shirt-tails blew in the air and, behind him, Mike squinted against the wind.

'We really do need the garden lights tonight,' griped Mike. 'I'll demand a refund. The brochure promised lights.'

The olive trees in their pots waggled their pale arms, adding to the surreal nature of the night.

'I don't like this.' Paula stepped out from the kitchen. 'Jon!' she ordered, peremptory for once. 'Pull the glass doors shut, or the house will be full of debris.' Her skirt flew up, exposing pudgy knees. 'I don't like this at all.'

'So you keep saying, Paula. Let's just go with it, for once.' Jon yanked on the doors and guided her, like a long-suffering maître d', under the awning. 'The rain should arrive any minute.'

Out in the dark, a giant hand shook the garden. When Evie said, 'Isn't this fun?' she wasn't sure if she meant it.

A blinding silver line tore from the sky to the earth. It was rewarded by a communal scream.

'I'm off inside,' said Shen.

'Me too,' said Paula.

'Hang on.' Mike took off towards the steps. 'I've just realized: the garden light switches must be in the garages.'

'Of course,' said Evie.

'It won't be half as scary if the garden's lit up.' He jumped down into the blank black beyond the steps, making for the row of whitewashed garages to the side of the house.

'Stay, Mummy.' Miles slipped his hand into Shen's. There was no way, Evie knew, Shen could withstand Miles's use of the long-abandoned 'Mummy'.

'OK.' Shen sniffed. 'I can smell . . . what can I smell?' Damp vegetation was on the air.

'And what's that noise?' screeched Scarlett from the edge of the terrace, keen to ramp up the drama.

'Rain, silly.' Tillie banged her shoulder against Scarlett's. 'Lots and lots of it.'

The rain – sheets of it – pounded into the dry earth, drawing near to Wellcome Manor's jurisdiction. Bilious clouds hung over the house, like a heavy fringe on its brow.

'Where's Mike?' fretted Paula. 'He should be back by now.'

Just as Evie felt spooked – Paula's fears were contagious in this volatile setting – a far-off shout placated her.

'Found them!'

Like a slap in the face, the rain hit. Wellcome Manor, no longer a fortress, was a shaken snow-globe.

'Hang on!' Mike's voice found a way through the noise and the wet. 'It's a bit stiff!'

'Oo-er, missus,' shouted Scarlett, cowering under the jacket Zane held over their heads. Tillie apparently preferred a soaking to his gallantry.

Dark, wet blots blossomed on the stone. The dogs' dish

bowled past on its side. Dan jumped to avoid it. Paula tugged Amber beneath the awning, which jerked and jumped, as if desperate to fly off like a striped bat. Evie's hair whipped over her eyes and she put an arm around Mabel. The little girl was shaking.

'OK! Tell me if this works!' Mike's voice was a reedy note in the tumult. 'TA-DAA!'

Hidden lights, squirrelled into corners and crevices, flashed on just as lightning ripped a wound in the sky.

The screams competed with the furious clap of thunder. They screamed partly for the crescendo of noise and light, and partly for the man it lit up on the lawn.

Tall and broad, his balaclava made him the stuff of nightmares. As flummoxed as his audience by his sudden illumination, he stood, arms by his side, motionless.

Evie had one thought, diamond-bright and megaphone-loud: *Paula was right*.

The man charged. Like a bull. Like a lorry. From standing start to breakneck speed. His roar could be heard above the crashing of the storm.

'Inside!' Evie dragged Mabel to her with one arm, Shen and Miles with the other. Dan, soaked to the skin, adhered to his mother like an Elastoplast. Propelling her blob of whimpering humanity as best she could, Evie headed for the glass doors as if they were the gates of heaven.

'Let me go!' Paula fought Jon, who was trying to drag her along with him. 'Let me go to him!'

Knees pumping, the dark man grew bigger than the sum of his parts, as he pounded over the sodden ground.

'Move!' Clive, almost choking on his own spit, foisted

Fang on his wife. The beloved baton was almost dropped as they fumbled, but as Shen's arms closed around the baby, Clive barrelled off towards the steps, almost colliding with Tillie, who was dodging through the scrum, reaching out to Paula.

'Mum,' she rasped. 'Mum, it's happening!'

'Inside!' shrieked Evie again, as her older daughter followed Tillie across a terrace suddenly transformed into an obstacle course of bodies. 'Come on!' Everybody was accounted for, as she herded her unwieldy charges towards the doors. Except one.

'Where's Dad?' mewed Scarlett, her face close to Evie's.

She looked back to see Mike tear out of the garages. Her stomach dropped away as she realized he was on a trajectory to meet the creature hurtling across the grass.

'Inside,' she repeated; the only remnant of her vocabulary left to her, it seemed.

There was a collision in the squall as Clive hurtled into Zane, who was also heading for the steps. 'No, you don't.' Clive turned the boy neatly, but Zane spun on his heel.

'Let me!' he yelled.

'Zane!' Shen found her voice, as she, Evie and the children reached the glass doors. 'Zane!'

A shove from Clive sent Zane towards the house. Clive leapt down the steps, almost stumbling.

The bifold doors were never closed. And yet they *were* closed. Evie's wet fingers slipped on the long chrome handle.

'Mummy, quick!' Dan's stubby fingers were in the way, as Mabel and Amber made wordless noises, beating the glass with their fists.

Wiping her fingers on her jeans, Evie batted away Dan's hand and tried again.

'What's the problem?' Jon sounded at breaking point as he pinioned Paula, who bucked like a Bedlam inmate.

'It won't . . .' No point in wasting breath. Evie, children clinging to her like baby monkeys, peered through the glass; Dan's manic rattling had clicked the latch shut. 'Are the French windows open?'

'What?' screamed Shen, holding the wriggling, shrieking Fang to her chest.

Evie turned, desperate to see what was happening, desperate not to see it. Still the man bellowed, his mouth a wet gash in the woolly slit of his mask. He surged, solid and unstoppable, now only a few paces from the foot of the steps. A damp bundle lay in the grass behind him. Her husband.

Evie pushed Mabel away and sprang. Yet she got nowhere. 'Get off me,' she spat at Jon, who'd relinquished his grip on Paula to hold Evie back.

Jon was stronger than he looked.

Lightning sputtered again. Liberated by Jon's pounce on Evie, Paula streaked over to the bench, hair flattened, expression savage. 'You can have me!' she shouted.

Now it was Evie who turned jailer, to hold onto Tillie. 'French doors!' She crawled crab-wise, with Tillie strait-jacketed in her arms, The Eights huddled around her. They stopped, shocked, as Clive and the stranger met at the foot of the steps. At speed. There was no finesse to this; Clive's plan seemed to be to topple him with his sheer bulk.

A hand on Clive's chest fended him off, as if he was a

ballerina. Clive's spine met the edge of a step with an audible crunch.

The man took the steps two at a time. When Zane broke away to run at him, he was met with an elbow in the nose and he, too, went down.

The body count was rising.

'I'm here!' shouted Paula, her hands in the air, like somebody greeting a relative at the airport. 'I'm all yours!'

As if remote-controlled, the man changed direction at the top of the steps. He turned away from Evie and the children, towards Paula.

Jon flew off the ground, but his tackle was met with a casual shove, almost an aside. As Jon hit the floor, Paula bowed her head, awaiting the inevitable.

Something warm and rounded was pressed on Evie.

Fang was in her arms, and Shen was dashing through the downpour. As the apparition lunged for Paula, Shen launched herself at his shoulders and hung there, as if glued.

He staggered and pirouetted, but Shen clung on. Her hands went to his face, blinding him, tugging at his nostrils.

The tenor of his howls changed, from fury to pain.

'Yes!' shouted Evie, keeping Fang's face to her chest.

The man lost his footing and crashed to the floor, with Shen as his buffer. Her *Ooof!* brought an answering moan from Evie. Dan threw a plant pot. Shen, however, didn't need their assistance; she sprang up, skidded and righted herself and, with a movement that was both elegant and fierce, faced him with both her tiny hands up, their pale palms out.

He did the same, but with no elegance, flying at her as if to flatten her.

Deftly Shen grasped the assailant's raised right wrist with her left hand and pulled it down. It went smoothly, it *folded* in fact. With the same grace, she used her other hand to press against his elbow. The huge, bulky, bogeyman followed his arm, like a good doggy doing a trick, as she bent it backwards to the floor. His nose hit the flagstones. He was still suddenly, all his violence neutered.

The picture made no sense. A dainty woman standing over this Minotaur.

Tillie stepped forward, too close for Evie's comfort.

'Dad, it's over,' she said.

DAY 12
Saturday, 22nd August

Dear Mum,
    You were right. This holiday <u>is</u> better than I thought
it would be! Last night we almost got murdered!

Zane

Sitting on the loo, bracing herself for the post-mortem of last night's extraordinary events, Evie was planning.

She liked to plan, and this would be one of her proper set pieces. It would happen tonight, with no watchers in the woods, no heart-stopping violence. There would be candles and tranquillity. Children would be a-bed. And she would tell Mike everything, and they would work out how to proceed, and her burden would be halved. Well, perhaps not halved. But it would be shared.

She remembered now, from the last time, how this calm had descended. She was grateful for it; one of the body's coping mechanisms, she supposed. Evie would talk Mike through the options, and he would say, 'Don't worry' and she would agree with him that they could cope. *Because*, she thought, tapping her bare toes on the tiled floor, *we have to*.

His face still muddy from his lie-down on the grass, Mike broke one of the cardinal rules of their marriage and barged into the bathroom.

'Hey! I'm on the loo.'

He was naked and agitated. 'I'm right, aren't I?'

'About the earth being round?' Evie tore off some plush toilet paper; even the loo roll was posh at Wellcome Manor. 'Get out, Mike! You know I prefer to wee in private.' Even the kids respected that law.

Mike was nervy, practically jogging on the spot. He wasn't really there with her, Evie realized; he'd jogged back to the past and he didn't like the scenery one bit.

'Darling,' she said, 'I can't talk on the toilet, OK?' *Not about this, anyway.*

'But I'm right, aren't I?'

'No comment,' said Evie, eventually.

'Christ!' yapped Mike. '"No comment" means *yes*.'

'It means "No comment". That's why the phrase exists.' She shifted. The toilet seat dug into her thighs. 'It means I don't want to comment in the midst of a peaceable wee-wee. Surely you understand that?'

'"No comment" means *yes*. PR people say "No comment" when they're asked if their celebrity client has sex with monkeys.'

'In that particular case, "No comment" would mean *yes*. But not in mine.' Evie wasn't at her best with her knickers around her ankles. 'Can we, you know, continue this later? In a room without a cistern?'

'I'll support you, Evie.' Mike, still wired, sounded lost, despite the valiant words. 'We'll go to the doc together, the minute we get home.'

'No comment, Mike.'

He was beyond making a game of it. 'We coped before. We'll cope again.'

'Seriously, Mike, later.'

Mike backed away. 'But I'm right?'

With her big toe, Evie slammed the bathroom door. Why must he always muddy the water, disrupt her carefully planned scenes?

He had previous convictions in this area. Most nights he whacked on the overhead fluorescent tube, so that its glare cancelled her artfully placed candles on the dinner table. He squirted ketchup all over her made-from-scratch Pad Thai. And the gossamer nightie purchased for its concealing qualities would be pulled off, to unmask her cellulite, before she'd struck a single sultry pose.

The late breakfast was a free-for-all. Toast and cereal and butchered fruit on the kitchen island, alongside scraped-clean Ben & Jerry's tubs and packs of salami. The adults' hive-mind concurred: *let the little mites eat whatever they want.*

Taking a cup of the strongest coffee that the machine could muster, Evie went to the terrace, the setting for last night's drama and last seen bristling with stab-vested police officers, the beams from their torches striped with rain, and the static from their radios crackling.

All was spick and span, every trace of the commotion washed away by the last of the healing rain. The sun was back, taking its rightful place at the centre of the heavens, warming the house and the gardens and Evie's grateful, upturned face.

Butterflies redoubled their efforts in paying court to the

delphiniums, and bees buzzed pompously through the lavender. Wellcome Manor had risen above the scandal: if two world wars couldn't bring it to its stately knees, one furious git in a balaclava stood no chance.

The Eights careered out from the house, pulling at each other, shouting, looking nothing like hapless victims. Even Amber was lively this morning; *perhaps*, thought Evie, *seeing her own personal hobgoblin do his worst and fail is just what she needed*.

Expecting a request to sleep in her bed, Evie had been relieved when Mabel and Dan had crawled off to their own berths. She braced herself, however, for some manner of psychological hangover. They'd witnessed real violence for the first time. She remembered Paula's shrieks, and Amber trying to run to her.

'Hi, you lot!' Evie stalled their mad dash.

'Mabel hurt my face,' said Amber immediately, as if grateful to find an authority figure to report to. 'She put a thpoon on it and it was completely marmaladey.'

'That,' said Evie, 'is disgraceful behaviour, Mabel.'

'Thank you,' said Mabel proudly.

'Dan,' called Evie, flapping her hand to summon her escaping middle child, 'all of you: you know, don't you, that you can talk to me or any of the grown-ups any time about – well, anything?'

The blank faces told Evie she needed to be more specific. 'About last night.'

'Oh, *Daddy*,' said Amber. 'He was a pig.'

'That's your daddy, though,' said Mabel. 'You kind of have to love him.'

Funny how the weeny ones cut straight to the heart of everything.

'We were frightened last night,' said Evie. 'But we're all safe now. If you feel scared or unhappy, that's fine too.' Her audience were earnest, giving her their full attention. 'Do you have any questions?' She scanned their faces. 'Anything at all. I'll answer it.'

'Well, I've been thinking . . .' Mabel pursed her lips. 'Which one's your favourite eyebrow?'

The drawing room looked like the last act of an Agatha Christie play, when the country-house guests assemble to hear whodunnit.

Everybody was there, from the titchiest to the tallest. Nobody said it out loud, but they needed to be together.

The oil paintings of long-dead gentry stared down at the tea things scattered over the inlaid table, the open drinks cabinet, the baby lolling like a drunk on the silk rug. Those who were alive stared at Jon, who stood in front of the fireplace.

'Before we go any further,' he said, 'I want to formally thank Shen for what she did.'

Applause broke out. Evie felt tears prick her eyes. She tended to cry at sudden applause, like she cried at guide dogs, speeding ambulances on their way to help the sick, an old lady being offered a seat on the bus; it was a wonder she managed to get anywhere, some days.

'Bravo!' she shouted.

In crumpled sweats, Shen closed her eyes and shook her head, as if it was a case of mistaken identity. 'It was just an aikido move. I do it every week at my class,' she said. The enormous armchair she'd chosen dwarfed her further, and its tasselled splendour emphasized her bedraggled state.

'I saw a new side of you last night, darling,' said Clive, his ham-like hands making plenty of noise.

Shen stirred. 'You did?'

I didn't. Evie had always known what her pitbull-in-a-chihuahua's-body friend was capable of.

'Thank you,' said Paula, the word lost in Shen's ovation. The red upholstery of the sofa unhappily matched her eyes, which were sore and swollen. She'd sobbed through the hour cloistered with the police, sobbed all the way up the stairs to bed and was still going, a tissue held to her nose. Dan had asked if she was trying to get into *The Guinness World Records.*

'Paula,' said Jon. 'I think these people deserve an explanation.' Altered magically by the night's events, he was, Evie realized, *relieved.* He took a deep breath, but Paula interrupted him.

'Let me,' she said. 'It's my story, Jon.' She honked into her hanky and took Jon's place by the mantelpiece, blinking away his reluctance.

Mabel stage-whispered, 'This is better than a film', and Paula began.

Each word came out well chewed, as if she'd contemplated for a long time how to say this. 'That was Carl out there last night. We've been married for almost twenty years. Jon was at the wedding. Just a teenager then, he was fourteen.

In a velvet suit.' She looked at him and he nodded, still wry about the hated suit.

'One expects some sartorial humiliation,' said Jon, 'as the bride's little brother.'

Evie looked at Shen who looked at Clive, who looked at Mike, who looked at Patch, who was chewing his own leg.

'Yes, Jon's my younger brother. We've always been close,' said Paula, oblivious of the *You're not kidding* lift of Mike's eyebrows. 'I turned to him when . . . but I'm getting ahead of myself,' she went on, and began her tale.

Marriage to Carl had been happy, to start with. He hadn't worn a balaclava in those days, presumably, and they'd got on well, fancied each other, shared the same dull but wonderful goals: a house; babies in that house; a nice holiday once a year; overspending at Christmas. There'd been a corkboard in the kitchen covered with snaps of the new baby and reminders for NCT coffee mornings. Carl was a police officer, good at his job, respected in their small community.

'Where did you live?' asked Mike.

'Warwickshire.' Nothing much happened in their sleepy town. 'Carl was no front-line copper. He was a neighbourhood-beat officer, ticking off truanting kids, then giving them a lolly.'

'Sounds idyllic,' said Clive.

'Oh, it wasn't,' said Paula. She and Carl were two separate couples. There was the public Paula and Carl, who held hands, took their daughters to the park and were stalwarts of the PSA. The other couple lived amongst sharp angles and deep shadows, as Paula waited for Carl to erupt.

He could 'go' if his dinner was too hot. If Tillie didn't look him in the eye when she spoke to him. If the weather report forecasted rain. When there was an R in the month; when there wasn't.

Paula summed up her Carl. 'He's a very angry man.'

'Amen to that,' muttered Clive.

'I could give you reasons for it.' Paula shook her head, dispirited. 'But nothing explains the rage. His life was no harder than the next person's.'

'So he was violent towards you,' said Mike, grimly.

'Actually, no. He didn't need to be.' Paula glanced at Tillie in the window seat, head down. Scarlett and Zane flanked her, each holding one of her hands. 'If he'd attacked me, or the girls, it would have been easier.' Paula put out her arms. 'Amber, do you want to come to Mummy?'

Amber shook her head, twisted her body so that she curved around Mabel, who patted her absent-mindedly.

'Have you ever seen an elephant at a circus?' asked Paula.

'Um . . . yes,' said Evie.

'Did you notice the chains around its ankles? They're delicate, thin. The elephant could raise her foot and break free. But she never does. Because she's been chained up since she was a baby, and she believes that chain will still hold her back.'

'You're an elephant,' said Evie, before thinking how that would sound.

'I'm an elephant,' agreed Paula. 'Bit by bit, Carl dominated me. Telling me exactly what was wrong with everything I did, or wore, or said. Nobody, he said, except him would put up with a fool like me. Useless. Ugly. Boring.' She shrugged. 'If I stood here all day I wouldn't run out of his insults. I had to stand and listen until he was finished.'

'In front of the girls?' asked Mike.

'In front of the girls,' confirmed Paula. Now that she'd found her voice, it grew stronger. 'He'd always been a fusspot; I used to tease him about it, but something changed when Tillie was born . . .' Paula frowned as if still unpicking this conundrum. 'Carl became compulsive about order and safety, going far beyond fitting baby-gates. A video camera above Tillie's cot recorded twenty-four hours a day. He checked out the neighbours' police records. Visitors wore cotton gloves to pick up Tillie. I had to list each mouthful of food, and he'd go quiet if I'd had to improvise and cook something not on his approved list.'

'What happened,' asked Evie, 'after he went quiet?'

Paula looked to the ceiling. 'Hours – all-nighters – of relentless character assassination while he made me scrub and rescrub the floor, or wash every window in the house, or bleach all the cutlery. Don't get me wrong. It wasn't all like that. There were times when we were . . .' she offered the word apologetically, 'we were *good*. We had fun. We went to the coast. All the conventional stuff. And then, out of nowhere, something would catch his eye. I'd hustle the kids away. Brace myself. And it would start. Tillie began to . . .' Paula looked over at her older daughter. 'You began to stick up for me, didn't you, darling?'

'Of course,' said Tillie curtly, clearly suffering to see her family's filthy linen aired in public. 'He's a bastard,' she added.

'Tillie . . .' Paula was reproachful.

'Well,' said Clive, 'he *is* a bastard.'

'He's also her father,' said Paula.

'Not any more,' said Tillie, loud and clear.

'Well, darling, technically . . .' Paula stopped, gave up on that one for the time being.

The complexity of her situation dawned on Evie. She felt guilt slip its blade between her ribs; she'd been the first to label the Browns *weird*.

'Paula.' Zane held up his hand as if at school. With all eyes upon him, he was timid. 'I'm not being funny, I don't want to be mean, but . . .'

'Why didn't I leave?' Paula exhaled heavily. 'I did. But he found me. Every time.'

'How many times?'

Before Paula could answer, Tillie said, 'Five.'

'Each time you went back,' Evie guessed, 'it was fine for a while. Then . . .'

'Much worse.' Paula wrapped her arms around herself. 'It's hard to hide from a police officer. He has eyes and ears everywhere. He has access to all kinds of information. I went to a refuge once. Oh God, that was the worst. I mean, it's been bad, but that time he went berserk because somebody might have recognized me, and his bosses might have heard about our home life . . .' He never bullied the girls.' Paula stressed this. 'I don't think he ever would.' It was his wife he blamed for everything. She was stupid, she was thoughtless, nothing got through her thick head.

During their favourite television programmes he whispered that she was ugly, old, a slag.

'For the love of God,' murmured Mike.

'Quite the charmer, our Carl.' Jon went to a window and looked out, lips gummed together.

'It got worse and worse, until the scenes joined together to make an unbroken line.' Paula looked startled as she rehashed those days, as if they'd happened to somebody else. 'It was my very own hell. No bars on the windows, yet I was trapped.' Carl controlled the money, doling out an allowance each week and demanding comically detailed expenses. Friends became an impossible luxury; the strain of double-think was too much. As Clive drove her to the supermarket – she wasn't 'permitted' to walk such a distance alone any more – she envied the ordinary lives behind each lit window.

'The police . . .' began Clive.

'The authorities weren't an option; Carl *is* the authorities. He drummed it into me that, however far I ran, he'd never stop looking. And he'd find me.'

'I convinced her to leave,' said Jon from the window. '*Rubbish!* I said. Carl's a local bobby, not Batman. If she went to London, say, it would be impossible to track her down.' He sighed. 'I can still hear myself saying it.'

'I wanted to believe Jon, to believe it was possible,' said Paula. 'But Carl had access to my social security numbers, my driving licence – all sorts of records. He swore he'd find me.'

'And then?' said Mike, with the therapeutic voice he

used to talk to the damaged people who came to him for shelter.

'He'd kill me.'

'No,' said Evie, the word automatic.

'Yes,' said Paula.

'But if he was never violent before . . .' said Clive.

'He told me he'd kill me,' said Paula. 'And Carl's a man of his word. If I hid, I had to stay hidden forever.'

'What made you finally decide to leave?' Shen asked this so avidly that Clive gave her a sideways glance.

'Carl was on lates. The night before, I'd commented on a TV presenter's shirt and he'd exploded. My orders were to clean the bathroom with a toothbrush. He said he'd dust for fingerprints when he came home.'

'What?' Evie had to let it out.

'Fingerprints!' said Miles. 'Brilliant!'

'I reached under the bath with this mangy old toothbrush and I thought: *No.*' Paula quivered, reliving the force of that short word. 'Just bloody no. Pardon my French.'

Tillie pushed her hair back and spoke. 'Mum got us out of bed. Told us we were going. Told us to pack a small bag.' She turned to Scarlett. 'Imagine that: packing a bag, knowing you can never come back for what you leave behind.'

Scarlett shuddered. Evie imagined the internal tug of love between her daughters' hair-straighteners and her diary. Evie thought of the tea set her gran had left her, the bed she'd given birth to Scarlett in, the framed Beatles posters in the sitting room.

'We had to leave Tippytoes,' said Paula. 'He was grey

– a rabbit, I think. Fake fur. Amber slept with Tippytoes every night. And I left him there, on her bed, because I was this close to hysterical, imagining Carl's key in the door. She still looks around for Tippytoes when she's upset.'

Poor Tippytoes, thought Evie. *Poor Amber.*

'We didn't even ask why,' said Tillie. 'We just fled. Mum,' she leaned forward, 'you did the right thing.'

'Well . . .' Paula threw up her arms and let them drop; she was unconvinced.

'They came to me,' said Jon. The physical similarity between him and Paula was obvious now; both had a gentleness of expression, a recessive quality that ran right through to their unobtrusive colouring. 'She asked if they could stay.' He told her *no*.

'You what?' Mike looked as if he hoped he'd misheard.

'I'm not proud of it, but Paula and I were estranged when she turned up on my doorstep.' He pushed his palm across his features. 'You see, I couldn't watch, I couldn't stand by . . .'

'Everybody fell away,' said Paula. 'We were toxic and impossible to be around. And of course I made excuses for Carl. I drove you mad, Jon, insisting it would get better.'

'I should have *been* there.'

Evie knew Jon would take that guilt to his grave.

'She'd stayed with me before.' Jon knew the drill. Paula and the children would camp out in his flat, ignoring Carl's texts, which spanned a predictable range from tearful to incandescent, then back to contrite sniffles. Carl would approach the kids at the school gate with little presents.' Noticing Evie sit up, he said, 'Yes, that's why Paula had a fit over the hairband you bought for Amber; why she imagined the worst, when Amber wandered off at the beach.' Finally, Jon went on, Carl would turn up with flowers and promises, and Paula would find herself believing, because that was so much simpler than the alternative.

'The truth is,' said Jon, 'Paula believed Carl's tripe because he indoctrinated her to believe that she couldn't survive without him.'

'It wasn't all tripe.' This exchange had the feel of a well-worn debate. Paula tried to explain; life after Carl would be so neurotic, so stressful, it was easier to carry on living with the horror.

'Better the devil you know,' said Evie.

'Exactly!' Paula looked grateful to be understood. 'You,' she said to Jon, 'kept going on about how he wasn't some all-powerful god, how he couldn't track me down if I went far enough. And now . . .' The facts spoke for themselves.

'I have the rest of my life to regret being so naive.'

Mike stood. 'This is Carl's fault – nobody else's. Don't go taking the blame, Jon.'

'Easier said than done,' said Jon.

'Almost everything is.' Mike looked at Evie, and she was wrenched away from Paula's story and back to her own.

'Anyway.' Paula described how they'd sat up all night, going backwards and forwards over the same barren ground, until they'd trampled her emotional landscape flat.

'And the moral of the story is,' interrupted Jon, 'never make an important decision at 4 a.m.'

'Big, anonymous London,' said Paula, 'seemed the best

– the *only* – place to hide. We had to think of a new name.'

'You're not really a Paula?' asked Zane.

'I am, but none of us are Browns.' Paula fiddled with an earring. 'We kept our first names. Amber couldn't cope with remembering them.'

'So, who are you?' Clive almost smiled at his preposterous question.

Jon bowed. 'I'm Jon Thorpe.'

Tillie said, 'And I'm Tillie Delgado.'

'What a brilliant name,' said Scarlett.

'I used to be a Thorpe, of course. My little brother never married.' Paula added, 'To be precise, he's not married *yet*.'

Evie thought of the kiss outside the cafe, Miss Pritchett's vigil beneath the willow. Tectonic plates shifted. No longer a philanderer, Jon was simply a man who knew a good woman when he saw one.

Guiding her listeners in baby-steps through the decision process didn't detract from its folly. 'We thought Carl would search for a single mum, not a couple. It would buy us time – time to burrow deeper into our hiding place.'

'Besides,' said Jon, 'I couldn't let them go alone.'

'So,' said Clive, 'sister and brother became man and wife.'

Paula winced. 'We never shared a bed, or anything icky like that.'

'We know,' said Clive, 'thanks to my wife's sleuthing skills.'

'Oh.' Paula and Jon shared a non-plussed look. 'Then what did you think . . . ?'

'We thought you'd had a tiff,' said Mike. 'Like married couples do.'

'Why Brown?' asked Shen. 'Why not a more glam name?'

'What?' Clive screwed up his face at this left-field interruption. 'Why not call themselves Cuthbertson-Twigge and *really* blend in, you mean? Next time I'm on the run in fear of my life, remind me to leave you at home, darling.'

'Brown felt ordinary, realistic,' said Paula. Once they'd reached London, the capital proved expensive. They lived on Jon's savings, but 'I wouldn't let him use a hole-in-the-wall. I made him drive miles to obscure branches to take out bundles of cash.' Money was just one of the numberless hurdles. 'We had to convince our landlord that we'd lost our papers in a fire, in order to lease our tiny flat.' They weren't registered with a doctor or a dentist: 'too many forms to fill in'. They kept their heads down, lived as simply as possible. 'The girls know better than to ask for treats.' Paula glanced at Amber, still as close to Mabel as a Siamese twin.

'My income's erratic,' said Jon. 'I'm not cut out to be a cab driver.'

'No shit, Sherlock.' Shen's head was back, her eyes closed.

'I am – was – a lecturer.' Jon couldn't take a position in academia: one Google search and Clive would be upon them.

Evie said, 'No wonder you're a bit paranoid, Paula.'

'A bit?' Paula hinted at a dormant GSOH, as Scarlett would call it.

From the window seat came Scarlett's hopeful voice. 'Jon, you can go back to your job, right? Now it's over?'

'I burned my bridges, walking out like that. Leaving my students in the lurch. It doesn't really matter.'

Everybody heard how much it mattered.

'How did Carl find you?' asked Mike. 'Out here, in the back of beyond?'

'My fault. Again,' said Jon. 'According to the officers last night, Carl fed my name into the PNC, the Police National Computer. When I broke the speed limit last week and showed my driving licence to the local police: ping!'

'You need a good reason to use police computers,' protested Evie, clinging to a belief that the world was run by the good guys. 'He'd lose his job for that, surely?'

'You scratch my back,' said Clive, confusing Evie for a moment, who *really* didn't want to scratch his back, 'and I'll scratch yours. He probably bent the rules for one of his colleagues, and they did the same for him. It's how everything works.'

'Carl's been at Wellcome Manor,' said Paula, 'since the very beginning.'

'Yup,' said Evie. 'Your missing wedding ring?'

'Typical Carl. To move something, so I thought I'd lost it, then replace it and tell me I was a lunatic.' Paula was sad, horribly sad, as she said, 'This was no holiday for me.'

Shen said, 'He laid the breakfast table and put those flowers in a vase.'

'Did he,' asked Mike, 'drink the last of the milk?'

'That was one of his favourite tricks,' said Paula. 'Nothing's too petty for Carl. That's why I assumed the worst, about the pebbles spelling out my name.'

'What was his plan?' asked Clive.' Did he even have a plan?'

'Don't underestimate Carl,' said Paula.

'You sound proud, Mum,' scoffed Tillie.

'Sweetheart, no,' said Paula, tenderly. 'I've learned not to underestimate him.' The police had found Carl's well-equipped camp beyond the walls. He'd come and gone as he pleased, using the foliage as cover in the sunshine, stealing audaciously near at night. He'd kept everybody under surveillance, all the while intimidating Paula in their personal language. 'That's how he gets his kicks, knowing I couldn't convince a rational person that all these innocuous incidents were threats.' He was letting her know he could strike when he chose.

'I'm puzzled,' said Clive. 'He could hardly pounce on you in a house full of people. If Mike hadn't forced his hand by illuminating the garden, what would he have done?'

'S'obvious.' Tillie spoke when her mother seemed too uneasy to answer. 'He meant to get you on your own and kill you, Mum. He hates you. He hates me as well, and her.' She motioned, with an offhand gesture, to her little sister. 'He hates everything and everyone. You were right to escape, Mum. You're my heroine.'

'Am I?' Paula's hand went to her mouth. When she began to cry, something broke in the room. One by one they stood and wrapped their arms around her, until she was invisible in a rugby scrum of goodwill, and her tears had become slightly claustrophobic giggles.

He was on 'their' bench. Evie had never seen Clive as animated as he was now, playing with Fang.

'No cigar?' she queried.

'The little lady doesn't like it.' He widened his eyes at his daughter. 'Do you, Fangy? Do-you-do-you?'

Fang squealed and shook all over with the fun of life.

'She's her old self again.'

'In the nick of time.' Clive carried on pulling faces for Fang's benefit. 'Social workers were ready to swoop.'

They were both exuberantly friendly, ever so normal. Evie guessed a switch had been thrown; Clive would not mention his declaration again.

Slowly Shen approached them.

Evie said, 'You were astounding last night, girlfriend.'

'Was I?' Shen sounded bored, as if she was no fan of compliments, and that was one of the most tedious she'd heard.

'I was so proud when you flattened that brute. None of the men had a hope, but you—'

'Clive!' snapped Shen. 'How many times? Suncream!'

'Ahem.' Pinkie cocked, Clive held up a tube.

Disconcerted that he was in the right, Shen pointed at Fang's sippy cup. 'That better be—'

'Sugar-free. But of course.' Clive put his head to one side. With Fang on his knee, he looked like a music-hall ventriloquist. 'We've established that you're the best in the family at disarming intruders, darling, but clearly I win at childcare.'

'It's not a contest.' Shen stepped back from Evie, who'd closed in on her. 'What are you doing? Get off!'

'I'm hugging you,' said Evie, doing just that. 'It's what we earthlings do, when one of us is being a prat and refusing to accept gratitude for bravery that may have saved more than one life.' It was like embracing an ironing board. A really pissed-off ironing board. But Evie persisted. 'You illustrated the real meaning of girl-power to our daughters.'

Why, wondered Evie, *isn't Shen relaxing, giving in?* This was a common enough scenario between them, and Shen always capitulated, squeezing Evie back.

'May I go now?'

Evie sighed and pulled away. 'Yes, you can go now.'

Shen went to the gym in the stable, to run and box and spin away the envy that nibbled her soul. *What's the point*, she asked herself, programming a Himalayan route into the running machine, *of being able to slay giants, if you can't nurture your own baby?*

'Ooh, lovely!' Evie, her arms in the sink – even in paradise, there is washing-up to be done – felt Scarlett's arms tight about her. 'This hasn't happened in a while.'

'Remember I used to jump in and snuggle you in bed all the time?'

'Remember? It's half your lifetime ago, but to me it's the blink of an eye.'

'Mum, I have to tell you something.'

Evie turned, drying her hands.

'I knew.' Scarlett wound a lock of hair round and round the nibbled skin beneath her nibbled fingernail with its remnants of blue varnish. 'Tillie told me about her dad. Are you angry with me?'

'About what, darling?'

'For not saying anything. I mean, that was proper dangerous last night. When Dad disappeared, I . . .'

The memory jabbed at Evie's beleaguered innards. 'Scarlett, I'm proud of you.'

'Really?' Scarlett squirmed with pleasure. 'Why?' she asked, with that naked need for affirmation that children only show their parents.

'You're a good friend. Being a friend is a skill, and you have it.' Evie kissed Scarlett's forehead and gave her a damned good cuddle. 'Tillie's lucky.'

Boundaries were being relaid. Scarlett was moving her tepee and pitching it elsewhere. Close by, but not within reach of Evie's arms. Such change was wholesome and right, but oh, it was hard. Evie prolonged the cuddle.

She'd got so much wrong this holiday, misinterpreted so many signals. She thought she'd made a friend in Clive. She thought her body was ticking over. She swallowed the Browns' cock-and-bull story. And now she was, somehow, estranged from Shen. Scarlett began to pull away. 'A few seconds more, please.'

'I have to get back,' said Scarlett, 'We're taking special care of Tills today.' She was gone.

Same pool. Same personnel. But much had changed. No longer grumpy dad of two, Jon was now heroic martyr. Paula, returning from the police station, was a domestic-abuse survivor.

'How did it go?' Evie tugged self-consciously at her swimsuit gusset. Were there outward signs on her body of its betrayal? She missed the compliments that she'd come to rely on from Clive.

'Fine,' said Paula. 'If you like that kind of thing!'

Maybe, thought Evie, *the real Paula is witty.* 'Thank goodness it's over.'

'It'll never be over,' said Paula.

'Mummy!' Mabel sprinted out of the undergrowth. 'Come and see! It's really funny! Pru is trying to give Patch a piggyback!'

Wincing at the orgasmic grunts emerging from the greenery, Evie held onto her daughter. 'Let them . . . um . . . play on their own for a while.' Patch and Pru seemed to think they were in a *Carry On* film, taking every opportunity for rumpy-pumpy. *I'll have a word with him later*, laughed Evie to herself. *Make sure he's treating Pru right. Calling when he says he will.*

When Jon rose, saying it was his turn to make a formal statement, Evie asked him to wait for her. The man beside her, as they walked to the house, was a stranger; for a fortnight she'd believed him to be a sadistic cheat.

'We were a very unconvincing married couple,' said Jon. 'Always rowing.'

'That was the most convincing part,' said Evie. 'It was more what you *didn't* do.'

'Was I,' he asked, 'a horrible husband?'

'You went – *wham!* – from bachelor to family man. Just add water. Whatever kind of husband you were, you're an amazing brother.'

It was hard to tell, but Jon seemed moved. 'I learned a lot about having children.'

'Mainly that you don't want to have children?'

Relieved to hear such heresy, Jon laughed. 'I adore those girls, but, ye gods, sometimes we couldn't get out of the front door because Amber was having hysterics about the colour of her knickers.'

'Welcome to my world,' said Evie. 'I've been unable to leave the house without incident since Take That were in the charts first time around.'

'All parents deserve medals.' Jon rubbed the back of his head. 'You saw how often I lost my temper. I'm not proud of it.'

'Oh, come on! You were under intense pressure, living a lie.' Evie felt honesty was the best policy. It generally was. For other people, that is; for herself and Mike, avoidance seemed to be the best policy. 'A saint would lose their temper with Paula.'

'When she was younger, she was cheerful and sweet and . . . well, *happy*.'

'Perhaps that's what attracted Carl. Some people see a bright light and want to snuff it out.'

'The worst of it is she constantly tries to please *me*. Knotting a scarf around my neck, triple-checking the food's to my liking. Like a demented geisha. Paula became Carl's creation, a colourless drudge too timid to air an opinion. I want my sister back.'

'That process has started. She insisted on driving herself to the police station.'

'The trial will . . .' Jon let out a long, tired sigh. 'It'll take over our lives. Paula will have to give evidence. If she's up to it.'

'She'll be up to it.' Evie felt sure of that.

'One hears tales of deals, of sentences being commuted. Carl might be out in a year. Then what?'

'I don't know,' admitted Evie. 'But something had to give. Your fantasy family was coming apart at the seams.'

'The thing is,' said Jon, in a confessional tone, 'I should have taken Paula's fears about the ogre in the bushes seriously, but lately I've taken my eye off the ball.'

'You fell in love,' said Evie as they reached the back doors.

Jon was silent for a moment, as if he hadn't been sure that she'd bring this up and didn't quite know how to proceed now that she had. 'Jane's mortified you saw her. She usually waited by the gates until I could get away, but curiosity got the better of her. It was lonely in her bed-and-breakfast. This hasn't been the nicest summer holiday she's ever had.'

'I'm *loving* your understatement, Jon. Has she known from the start, about you and Paula?'

'Not right from the start. We had quick chats when I dropped off the girls. Mundane stuff, really.'

'But you liked her,' said Evie, keen to get to the good stuff.

'She's so *interesting*,' said Jon. 'I couldn't stop thinking about her. But how could I ask her out? I was a dad.'

'Some dads would do so,' said Evie.

'It's tricky communicating complex emotional information over the heads of eight-year-olds hitting each other with lunch boxes, but one morning I suggested a coffee and I said, "It's not what you think; please say Yes" or something like that. She assumed I wanted to discuss Amber's dyslexia. I blurted it all out in Starbucks. Foolhardy, but I sensed I could trust her.' With easy, natural gallantry, Jon let Evie go out through the front door first. 'It's been tough. We behave as if we're adulterers. She walks a hundred yards ahead of me.' He sighed. 'It was Jane's idea to come to the village. I knew there'd be trouble. When you found her, lurking like a spy, she was trying to steal ten minutes alone with me. Madness!'

'She must like you, Jon,' said Evie, 'to go through all that for you.'

'She does,' said Jon, with a smile shocked out of him. 'She likes me.'

'And you?'

'Oh, I love her,' said Jon, as if it was general knowledge, like the capital of France. 'That's why I've been so distracted. And Paula paid the price.'

'Love's supposed to distract you. That's love's job. And if you'll permit me to stick my big nose in, go to her. No, *run* to her.'

'Can't,' said Jon simply. They'd reached his car and he climbed in. 'Paula and the girls need me.'

Watching the car bump away, Evie waved after a fine example of a dying breed: the English gentleman.

As befitted a day with no rules, lunch was a sprawling open-air affair, at the point where striped lawn gave way to wild flowers.

Half a Dairylea sandwich mashed and visible in his mouth, Dan shouted, 'Who's this?' He bunched up his shoulders and bellowed.

'Carl!' Mabel, overcome by Dan's comic genius, jumped up and joined in, until they collapsed, laughing, onto Patch, who was so engrossed in waiting for an escapee Scotch egg to roll his way that he barely noticed.

Segueing seamlessly into a cancan, Mabel yelled, 'Wait till I tell everyone the baddie was tied up with my skipping rope!'

The Year Four *What I Did in My Holidays* essays would be interesting this September. Mike joined Evie and Paula, who were conspiring on a crumpled rug.

'Howdy, gals.'

They ignored him. 'Agreed?' said Evie.

'Agreed.' Paula heaved herself up. 'There's no time like the present.' She left the Herreras together.

'What's going on with you two?' said Mike.

'Nothing.' Evie fluttered her eyelashes.

'And us?' he asked, as The Eights rolled in the remains of the picnic. 'What's going on with us?'

'We're the same,' said Evie, 'as we always are.'

Shen heard the lunch posse return before she saw them, trailing blankets, whooping at the dogs. She returned to the lentil and butternut squash she'd blitzed to a fragrant mush. 'Ooh, yum!' she said to Fang. 'Delicious!'

Fang bought the hype and reached out for more. *Mush*, her demeanour suggested, *is where it's at*, dude.

Footsteps passed the open doors. Screams and sudden eruptions of childhood. Lower, wary tones of adults. All at a remove. All *out there*.

Accustomed to the spotlight, Shen found it chilly in the wings. And lonely.

She had always felt different from the people around her; not better, even when it came across that way. Just different.

Well . . . maybe a *little* better.

She'd defended the tribe. And she'd do it again. (Hopefully she wouldn't have to; her shoulder throbbed.) That didn't mean she felt comfortable, or accepted – one of them.

Evie made it look easy. She saw the good in people, and liked them all the more for their shortcomings and quirks.

Had Evie seen the good in Clive? Was that why he had engineered those humiliating tête-à-têtes he thought Shen didn't notice?

After nine years together, she thought, *Clive should know I notice* everything *about him*.

Perhaps he did know and he didn't care.

With perfect comic timing, Fang stuck her finger up Shen's nose. Even while she laughed – hard not to – Shen saw the gesture as proof of her lack of power. *I don't even have dominion over my own nostrils.*

To make matters worser (as Miles would say), Clive had proved to be a pro at Fang-handling. *I'm not a proper woman*, Shen rebuked herself. No wonder Clive looked elsewhere.

Yuk! Shen's eyes watered at a familiar perfume, even more pungent than the one Evie had bought her for Christmas. Fang needed changing. Again. *One more mind-less task can't hurt.* She was a robot now, with no desires of her own. She lived to serve.

'Come on, you, let's sort out that nappy,' she whispered to Fang, whose head nodded heavily against Shen's chest as she hoisted her out of the high chair. Breathing through her mouth, she let out a small exclamation at Fang's productivity. She removed the nappy, bagged it, threw it away, wiped her daughter's bottom, fastened up a fresh nappy and swung the little girl into the air. 'Who's my best girl?' she asked.

Out on the terrace, Clive was on the phone. 'Today, Maureen!' he said. 'It has to happen today.'

Everybody danced to Clive's tune. Shen didn't have a tune any longer.

'Making a formal statement' had turned out to be a disappointment for Evie. The police station smelled of Cup a Soup.

A jaunty two-seater overtook her on the drive as she returned to Wellcome Manor, honking a cheerful salute as it slowed in front of the house.

The front door opened. Paula appeared, beckoning to somebody behind her.

Jon emerged into the brilliant sun, hesitant at first, then breaking into a run down the steps.

Stepping out of her car, Evie recognized Miss Pritchett. Jane.

'It's you!' Jon shouted.

'It's me,' laughed Miss Pritchett, who was considerably foxier out of the playground.

'Jon!' Paula brandished a suitcase. The children had congregated, and Evie would remember with pleasure the amazement on their faces. Seeing their favourite teacher out of context was exciting enough, but add to that witnessing her soundly snog one of 'their' adults, and you had three stunned eight-year-olds straggling down the steps to mob their Miss P.

Within minutes Jon was gone, laughter mingling with exhaust fumes as the racy little car tore off.

'You did it, Paula!' said Evie.

'I've learned a thing or two about being sneaky these past months,' Paula said. 'I ferreted out Jane's number and asked her to come right this minute and rescue Jon.'

'That was brave.' Especially as Paula was the least can-do person Evie knew – more a can't-do person. 'You rely on him.'

'He deserves some ordinary happiness.' She looked – really looked – at Evie. 'The sort you have.'

Evie wondered when she last thought of herself as happy.

'I'm a single parent,' said Paula. 'I'd better get used to it.'

'You've got *us* now.' Evie slipped an arm through Paula's, disregarding the tense physical reaction. 'We look useless, but you'd be surprised.'

'You've got your own lives.'

'You're part of them. Give in,' said Evie. 'You have friends, and they know the worst and they're still your friends. Did Clive tell you he's briefed his lawyers on your behalf?'

'He's so kind.'

'He's probably showing off; but, yeah, he *is* kind.' Evie wanted to muss up this woman's hair, goose her. 'Carl's locked up, Paula, but you're walking about in the sunshine. Why not enjoy the feel of it on your face?'

'Yeah,' said Paula with what, for her, passed as defiance.

Another car turned up. Pink, gleaming, with *Beauty by Maureen* emblazoned on the side, it disgorged a small women with a toolbox. This was Maureen, and she announced that a nice man called Clive had hired her to 'do' three ladies. 'Manicures, facials, massage – the lot!'

Her satanic feet de-callused, her hands soft as Fang's bum, her shoulders back from their extended trip to the top of her ears, Evie floated down to the pool to whistle up Maureen's next customer.

'Shen,' she said, 'you'll never guess what's waiting for you in the house.'

Wordlessly, Shen got up and went indoors.

'I prefer it when you shout at me,' called Evie, tired of the cold shoulder.

'Give up,' said Clive. 'She's freezing me out as well.' He rubbed noses with Fang as he wrestled her into water-wings, providing Fang's dialogue as well as his own. 'I'm a wubbly lidl baba!'

'I don't think,' said Amber from beneath fourteen layers of suncream, 'Fang would talk in that thoopid voice.'

The holiday had healed over the wound. Zane dunked a noisily protesting Scarlett in the water as Tillie looked on, rolling eyes that by now must be almost rolled out.

The other teens took their cue from Tillie. Evie worried that Tillie – so skilled at bottling up and putting her best foot forward – wasn't showing her true feelings. The violence they'd witnessed was the tip of an iceberg. Tillie would need careful care.

Evie sat and picked up Shen's discarded *Vogue*, noting that Zane didn't lay hands on Tillie. *Sensitive boy*, she thought, as she popped on Shen's Moschino sunglasses.

Twenty times as expensive as her own pair, with exactly the same sights through the lenses.

Zane flopped down, shedding water like a dog. 'Stepmama likes her luxuries, doesn't she?'

'She's probably suffering Botox-withdrawal symptoms.' Their local beautician depended on Shen to put her children through private school.

'Not that she needs it.' Zane lay back.

'Oh, and *I* do?' Evie enjoyed his twitch. 'I'm teasing, Zane.'

'I took your advice. Did you notice?'

Young people's healthy sense of self was breathtaking; as if she had time to notice Zane. 'Sort of.'

'It's hard, taking it slow and steady.' He spoke low, eyes closed, as the girls swam lazy lengths. 'I want to tell her how I feel, you know?'

'I do know.' Evie felt, briefly, seventeen again.

'I have so much shit to say, but none of it makes sense and she's the only one I want to tell, but I can't tell her.' Zane opened one eye to look at Evie. 'I wrote a poem. My mates would die laughing.'

'Bet you anything your mates write poems.' Evie riffled through the magazine, past leggy anorexics and ads for miracle cream and features about finding yourself: she normally *found herself* at the fridge. 'Girls love that stuff, Zane.'

'Even *her*?' he scoffed, shading his eyes to watch Scarlett attempt an underwater handstand.

'I know her pretty well, and she'd melt at a poem.' *So would I.* Evie found mental space for a little outrage that nobody had ever written her a poem. Looking down at her thighs, she reckoned she'd passed her poetry-inspiring window.

Zane covered his face, desolate, in pieces – your average young lover. 'Trust me to fall for a goddess.'

'Get in the pool and strut your stuff, Zane.'

Desolate no more, he sprang up and jumped into the pool, knees hugged to his chest.

'Zane!' shrieked Scarlett.

'Idiot!' shrieked Tillie.

Clambering out with Fang in his arms, Clive sent paternal evils Zane's way, as he patted the baby dry with all the fussiness of an old lady drying a poodle.

Head lolling, Evie closed her eyes, welcoming the attentions of the sunshine that slid along her skin like a lover.

She patrolled her body, taking an inventory. How did that bit feel? What was that sensation in her tum? Was her head a little fuzzy because of the heat, or because of what was going on inside her? Each sensation was suspect. They could be innocent, or they could be foot soldiers of the invading army that was currently conquering her.

'Early to bed, early to rise, makes a man healthy, wealthy and wise,' Evie had recited, in response to Paula's exclamation, when she'd excused herself, yawning, halfway through a game of pontoon. 'And a woman, too, hopefully.'

The real reason for her early night wasn't hope of health or wealth. Evie toppled like a tossed caber onto the bed and lapsed into a sleep so deep it verged on a coma. She was drained. Parts of her hurt; other parts were revving up to hurt.

Woken by a muffled 'Shit!' from the pitch-darkness, she knew by that concise syllable that her husband had taken a little too much firewater. She pretended to be asleep.

'Don't pretend to be asleep.' Mike sat heavily on the bed and shimmied awkwardly out of his shorts. 'Do you realize, Mrs Herrera, we haven't said a word to each other all day?'

Evie made a non-committal noise.

'Have you been avoiding me?'

'Have you been avoiding *me*?'

'Definitely.'

'Well, there you go.'

'No, Evelyn Herrera, there *you* go.'

'What does that even mean, Mike?'

'We need a serious talk. Like, a serious, *serious* talk about serious . . . um . . . matters, but off you toddle to bed. You always do this.'

'I don't *always* do *anything*. Besides,' Evie pulled the covers petulantly and tipped Mike onto the floorboards, 'you always do this.'

'What?' Mike scrabbled about on the floor, knocking over a pile of paperbacks. 'Which *this* do I always do?'

'You get drunk when you want to talk. There's no point discussing anything with you in this state.'

'You're the one in a state, Evie. I'm fine.' Mike stubbed his toe and she sensed his deep need to scream.

'Goodnight,' said Evie frostily. She carefully nurtured

her irritation; if she was irritated, she could turn away and go self-righteously back to pretend-sleep. If she dug deeper and diagnosed why Mike was drunk, she'd have to put on the light and talk.

Mike stuck his foot in the small of her back as he climbed into bed and bashed his elbow in her ear as he pulled off his tee-shirt.

DAY 13
Sunday, 23rd August

Dear All Next Door,

The gerbils too? That *is* disappointing. RIP Mrs Hairybum and Keith. Yes, as you suggest, leave them out for the binmen.

Evie x

p.s. I'm a bit tearful now

The second-last day of a holiday is too late to embark on anything too ambitious, but too early to pack. There was a pointless feel to the breakfast Evie cobbled together from what was in the fridge.

Day thirteen of a fourteen-day break was, more or less, an ending; Evie didn't like endings.

'My mum,' said Tillie, manfully attempting the Brie-and-fried-egg sandwich, 'is already making piles to go in the suitcase. She won't let me wear my favourite top, because it's folded.'

'I'm wearing these knickers for the second time around,' said Scarlett.

'I counted out enough for the fortnight,' insisted Evie hotly. Any slur on her daughter's knickers was a slur on her own maternal skills.

'Well, Mother dearest, your knicker-maths needs work,' said Scarlett.

'What are you youths up to today?' Evie made Patch dance, by holding up a nugget of Brie. She dropped it for the silly hound, which was as bad at dancing as he was at guarding, or not eating shoes.

'Climbing,' said Zane.

'Maybe.' Scarlett was schoolmarmish. 'We said *maybe* climbing.'

'We found a quick way to the beach.' Zane ploughed ahead. 'On foot. Right by the back-entrance.'

'What back-entrance?' Evie's antennae quivered. She wasn't sure she liked the teens venturing beyond the boundaries. Hastily she suppressed her fears: *Venturing beyond boundaries is what teenagers do.*

'This old door in the wall at the bottom of the grounds,' said Scarlett. 'I don't like heights, Zane.'

Zane leaned over, eye-to-eye with her. 'It'll be cool.'

'Sounds way cool,' said Evie, watching Prunella effortlessly intercept every Brie bogey she tossed for Patch. *That's* why the little dog was growing plumper. She hoped.

'Oh, Mum, don't,' said Scarlett.

They dribbled out, then dribbled in again, while Dan and Miles dribbled past, and Amber and Mabel dribbled up and down the steps. The day's feet were stuck in molasses. Mike, looking as if he'd been dredged from a canal, haunted various rooms, curtains drawn against his hangover. Clive, his drinking partner, bustled about, industrious.

In the kitchen Shen oversaw the teenagers' preparations. 'Why put your lunch in a horrible carrier bag when there's a lovely wicker hamper?'

'Why don't you come with us?' said Zane.

'Yeah,' said Scarlett, under her breath. 'So you can tell us we're eating our sandwiches all wrong.'

'Have you even remembered blankets?' Shen shook her

head at their picnic-ignorance. 'You can't just sit on the sand like . . . like . . .'

'People enjoying themselves?' suggested Tillie.

'Like homeless people, I was going to say.' Shen snatched the knife from Zane's hand. 'You're using too much butter. Let me.'

Tillie and Scarlett shared a smile, and Evie, loitering by the door, barged in on the end of it. Scarlett leaned up to tie the taller girl's scarf more securely around her up-do.

'Go, go!' Shen clapped her hands impatiently as the last cold can was dropped into the bag. 'Here.' She shoved a rolled-up blanket, blue-and-white chequered mohair, at Zane, who was already carrying most of the food. 'And don't complain,' she said as his mouth framed a whine. 'You're a man. Act like it.'

Tillie reached out and took some of Zane's burden. 'He's a man, not a butler.' She sounded amused. 'I don't need anybody to carry my stuff.'

'I do!' laughed Scarlett. 'Zane!' She clicked her fingers. 'Heel!'

'See?' Zane shook his head sorrowfully, his voice low, as he shuffled past Evie, laden down. 'She doesn't take me seriously.'

'Nonsense.'

'And besides, she's in love with somebody else.'

'Nope.' Evie shook her head, sure of her facts. 'That other guy? Over long ago, and never really amounted to much. Not really. He means *nada*.' She lowered her voice. 'It's an old ploy, exaggerating a rival to make you try harder.'

'Come, slave!' shouted Scarlett from the terrace.

Scarlett's tummy churned. 'I don't like this.'

'Come on,' said Zane, his salesman-teeth gleaming. 'Never had you down as a wimp.'

For the past thirteen days the house had dominated, a friendly star omnipresent in her sky. Scarlett regretted losing sight of it, of going over the edge where the lovely solid earth ran out and plunged down to a curve of beach below. 'The sun's disappeared. We're too high up. I don't know where to put my feet.' Skewered, helpless, on an expanse of crumbling white rock, she refused to cry. She *refused*.

A few feet below them, Tillie called up, 'Wait there. I'll climb back up to you and help you go back. Zane, you're moving way too fast for her.'

'Freaks.' Zane descended, surefooted as a goat, carefree as a tampon ad; to all intents and purposes, he was a goat in a tampon ad.

'S'OK, s'OK.' Tillie was placid as she helped Scarlett place her hands and feet.

Flat to the ground at the top of the cliff, Patch sniffed his encouragement, tail thumping.

'That's it. Slowly does it.'

'You're good in an emergency,' said Scarlett, as she hauled herself back onto scrappy grass, grateful for its horizontal nature and the reinstatement of Wellcome Manor on her horizon.

'In my family,' said Tillie, 'you get a lot of practice.'

A holler from the beach. 'Scar! I've found a cave!'

'I love caves,' murmured Scarlett, peering over to see Zane waving frantically. She had a few small, secret places in her own home – a place that seemed like a dream now. Hadn't she'd always lived out of doors, with the sound of the surf competing with the hymns of bees and the swish of trees?

'There's an easy way down,' shouted Zane, pointing to steps hacked into the cliff face. He'd dropped his cool. He liked caves too, apparently.

Tempted, Scarlett looked to Tillie. 'The steps look do-able, even for me.'

'But we're supposed to be looking after The Eights.' Tillie turned to go.

'Come on!' yelled Zane. His patience was tissue-thin.

'I don't know . . .' shouted Scarlett.

'I'm waiting!' shouted Zane.

Dan, watching from a handily flat, head-height branch, wondered if there was a way to stay aged ten forever. He dreaded being a teenager. They spoke in code all the time, just like adults.

Order was returning, bit by bit, to Shen's life. Thanks to Clive's newfound vocation as a daddy, she'd had time to hit the gym/stable with a clear conscience.

It had been a good session. As she stepped out into the sun, her hair wet and her muscles singing, she felt as if the tired extremities of her body had woken up.

Tousled, a touch of the hobo about him despite the cost of his clothes, Clive was leaning against a greenhouse. When he spotted Shen speeding towards him, he shook his head, smiling. 'Sorry, darling, you can't tell me off for anything. Fang is fed and happy and in her godmother's arms.'

Shen pumped her arms, power-walking.

Clive stood straighter. Pressed down his uncombed hair. Tried to shoot his cuffs, but they were too limp to comply. 'Don't start, Shen.'

As Shen neared, determination blazing in her beautiful warrior face, he took a step backwards, holding up his hands.

'In there!' she ordered, pointing at the greenhouse. '*Now*,' she added as he stared.

She sprang at him, just as she had on their first date. Shen's legs hooked around Clive's waist, her mouth covering his as he staggered slightly to steady himself, and his hands found her bottom.

They grappled the greenhouse door shut with fumbling hands. They tore at the relevant parts of each other's clothing, lust calling the shots as they welded their bodies together. It was old-school sex, the way they remembered it from a distant past. They gasped. They growled. They knocked over some geraniums. They came simultaneously, with a fury that was all the more intense because neither dared cry out.

Panting, they clung together for a while, their bodies cooling, their expressions asking, *Where the hell did* that *come from?*

A scratchy sound disturbed them. Prunella looked out from behind a pot. Her eyes told them she'd never feel the same about them ever again.

'Somebody's happy,' commented Evie, as Clive approached her on the staircase, singing like one of the nuns in *The Sound of Music*.

'Somebody *is*,' he agreed, skipping past.

'Could you keep the noise down?' Mike walked across the hall as if illustrating how a very, very old man might walk across a hall.

'How much did you drink last night?' Evie was intrigued; to work up a hangover of this calibre, she'd need a wedding reception.

'All of it,' whimpered Mike, inching towards her. 'All the drink in the world.' Sandpapered eyes lifted to hers. 'But I'm not too hungover to talk, love.' His radar beeped and jumped. Evie mocked his early-warning system, reminding him that 99 per cent of the calamities he prophesied never came to pass. But that nasty 1 per cent had a way of over-shadowing everything.

Plimsolls squeaked to a halt on the tiles, as Mike and Evie regarded each other, both unwilling to fire the starting pistol on the conversation. Dan threw himself between them, red-faced, barely able to enunciate what he was trying to say.

'Slow down, love.' Evie crouched, her face near to Dan's. 'Breathe.'

'I know I shouldn't be watching. But they're trapped.' Dan gulped a lungful of air. 'I know I was bad.'

'Trapped?' Mike's hangover dissolved. He said, clearly, dad-ishly, 'Dan, who's trapped and where?'

'Scarlett. It's cos of the snogging. I couldn't help watching.' Dan started to cry. 'It was disgusting, but I wanted to see. They kiss all the time in the treehouse.'

Evie shook Dan, a little more roughly than she meant to. 'Where is she? Speak slowly, darling.'

'In the cave. She went in there to kiss and she didn't know I was there, and then Zane saw me and shouted, "Go away, you little creep" and now the tide's coming in and Scarlett's screaming and it'll fill up and Scarlett will—'

'She won't, Son.' Mike put a hand on Dan's shoulder. 'I promise. Find The Eights and take them to Paula. Tell her we've gone out and she's to look after you until we get back.' As Dan dashed away, glad of a job, Mike cupped his hands to his mouth and yelled, '*Shen! Clive!* NOW!'

Instructed by Dan to head for a tree 'all bent over, like it's dropped its lunch money', the rescue party (for that is what Evie, Mike, Shen and Clive had reluctantly become) left Wellcome Manor's polite gardens and raced over the scrubby terrain.

Under strict instructions from Paula to send Tillie back, Evie envied such small-scale anxiety. 'Tillie!' she called as they neared the tree, with Shen, of course, in the lead, Evie plodding in everybody's wake. *Why haven't I been out here before?* The landscape was unkempt and exciting, an obvious lure for youngsters; she should have checked it out. Scarlett, at seventeen, was old enough to have sex or get married, yet it felt too young to be arsing about in caves.

In Evie's mind's eye, Scarlett was small and vulnerable in the face of nature's indifference, like an ant on Everest.

'I knew something like this would happen.' Mike's words kept rhythm with his steps, as he ran. 'I should've put my foot down about Scarlett and that boy.'

Clive stopped, and Mike stopped too. '*My* boy, you mean.'

'She didn't want to go. This was Zane's idea.'

Clive squared up to Mike. 'Your kids are no angels, Herrera.'

Shen, now well ahead, called back, 'Guys, I've got an idea! Why not have a punch-up? Instead of, say, *rescuing the children*?'

Rescuing shocked a whimper out of Evie. She endeavoured to think of it as *making everything all right*. She'd always made everything all right for Scarlett, from a dropped lolly to a tangled ponytail. This would be no different.

Catching up with Shen, Evie peered over the edge. The wind snatched her extravagant curse and bore it away.

During a pleasant ramble the cliff would be a medium-rise, rugged corner of England crumbling into the Channel. To Evie, in these circumstances, it was high enough to qualify as heart-stopping, and its pockmarked face was brutal.

Clive puffed to a halt. 'Tide's right in.'

The bay was a wobbly U, narrow at the top, with a small gap for the sea to rush through. The tide had already reduced the pebbly beach strewn around the foot of the cliff to a pale, shallow margin against the dishwater sea.

'Where's the . . . ?' As she said it, Evie spotted the cave and pointed. 'They're in there.'

The cave was shaped like an eye, blind and dark, the sea already encroaching upon it.

'Look!' They all followed Shen's pointing finger, and Evie's stomach fell down a lift shaft as she saw the blue-and-white blanket borne up and down by the waves, a pretty rag mimicking a drowned body.

Clive bent down. 'Plenty of footholds. Quite an easy climb.' He straightened up. 'I can do it.'

'Clive, *don't*,' said Shen, as he got to his knees. 'You haven't done anything like this for years.'

The horizon was tranquil, a vicar's tea party compared to the thrash-metal mosh pit of the water within the bay. Something about the angle at the neck of the inlet angered the water and set it churning. Persistent thoughts of Scarlett's fear of deep water reared up at Evie. *I need to think efficiently.* She must gather up her scattered self. 'There's no point climbing down.' She cast around her wildly for what she needed. 'There's no solid ground between the cave and the scrap of beach that's left. We need a boat.'

'But there's no boat,' said Mike.

As he was speaking, Shen called, 'There!' and shot off, Evie hard on her heels.

Both of them had spotted the sign – *Trips around the bay in real Devon fishing boat £15* – and the steps carved into the rock-face.

Why, oh why, am I in flip-flops? Evie's feet slipped as she strained to keep up with Shen, who flew, inches from the edge, in trainers. At the top of the steps Evie hesitated. Shen was speedily tiptoeing down, but Evie's senses were assailed by the height of the cliff, the narrowness of the steps and the booming of the sea. With Mike and Clive right behind her, she only had a second to suppress her vertigo and grope her way down the steps as fast as she could, which was not as fast as she would like, but was better than lying down, which was what her body wanted to do.

'There's Tillie!' Shen stopped, halfway down the steps, and pointed to a smudge partway up the cliff, jaunty chiffon scarf flapping like a pennant. 'She's stuck. Clive,' she called back up to her husband. 'You'll have to help her. You said you could do it.'

'But . . .'

'Leave Zane to me.'

Irresolute for a moment, Clive snorted and turned back. As the others carried on down to the sea, he called, 'Tillie! I'm coming!'

A hut, held together by salt and hope, stood on a ridge that, apparently, was never swallowed, even by this greedy sea. Upturned boats rutted in a mass of nets and oars. One small wooden vessel bobbed maniacally in the water, tethered by a stout rope.

'In!' ordered Shen, and Evie did as she was told, leaping over the frothing water to land and slide on the slick floor, her bottom meeting – a touch too smartly – the wooden slat fixed across the width of the boat.

'We can't just steal it!' Mike held back as Shen leapt in.

Evie tried to estimate how many yards of unfriendly water lay between her and her daughter, but gave up, leaving it at a dismal *lots and lots*. 'Scarlett!' she hollered, her words whipped away. *If only Scarlett would come to the mouth of the cave, show herself.* 'Mike!' she snapped. 'For God's sake, get in!'

'We should leave some money.' Mike was scrabbling in his pockets, unfolding tenners.

Baring her teeth with the effort of untying the thick rope, Shen shouted, 'Evie, can you see life jackets?'

'Nope.'

'Oh well.'

'Mike,' said Evie, leaning over to help with the rope, which had claimed Maureen's manicure. 'Get in!'

'Really, though,' said Mike, 'we should leave the bloke a phone number.'

'Mike, your daughter's over there!' Evie pointed to the dark, disappearing cave.

Snapping out of it, Mike threw a shower of ten-pound notes into the sea. 'We need oars.' Ransacking the pile, he cursed. 'They're all different sizes.'

A cry of 'Help!' rose above the clamour of the sea.

Both Evie and Shen stiffened. Shen threw back a square of dirty tarpaulin to reveal an outboard motor. Just as Mike brandished two oars in triumph, she pulled on the greasy lead and the boat bucked like a bronco and took off.

The boat's nose rose in the air, tipping Shen and Evie backwards, slamming Evie's head hard against the side.

'You OK?' called Shen. She crouched by the motor, taming the boat. It obeyed her, and after another false start they carved a clean line through the water, making straight for the cave. Behind on the little stone jetty, Mike shrank.

As the cave grew more distinct, they saw the water already slopping into its belly.

'Evie!' Shen's voice was a sliver of noise above the tinny brouhaha of the engine, 'we'll get them.' When Evie nodded, Shen shouted her name again and Evie turned to look at her, to look properly at the dark teardrop eyes squinting against the spray and at the salt crusted on the flat bridge of Shen's nose. 'I said, we'll get them.'

'I know we will.' Evie held out her freezing hand and Shen grasped it with her free one. *Thank God*, thought Evie, *for my Shen*.

Up on the side of the cliff, Clive reached his huddled target. Down below, the boat neared the cave.

'Slow down, Shen,' warned Evie.

Shen tinkered with the motor. Evie felt her willing the boat to conform.

Two pale, stooped figures hung back in the gloom.

'Shit!' blurted Shen as the boat convulsed, dashing itself against the treacherous, half-visible rocks. To a chorus of screams from within the cave, the vessel tipped, flinging Shen the length of it.

Hooking her legs under the bench seat, Evie braced herself and caught Shen around the waist. 'Got you,' she breathed, as the boat righted itself.

As the two women battled to steady the boat, it rose and fell in tune with the steady, disgusting slurp of the sea water that was steadily claiming the cave. It was an ancient place, pitiless and dark, and Scarlett was in there, only a few feet away, but out of reach.

'We're here!' called Evie, her face numb with spray.

'*Mum!*' Relief; fear; a deep need for the endless comfort

the title conveys – it was all there in Scarlett's desperate shout.

The heavy rope in her cold hands, the boards slippery beneath her flip-flops, Evie leaned over the side of the boat, searching for something to lasso. *If we ever get back to dry land,* she vowed, *I'll never leave it.* Not even to go upstairs.

A column of rock, sticking straight up, flipped Evie the finger. She aimed the rope at it, but it slithered off as the boat reared like a roller coaster.

Looking helplessly behind her, she saw Shen chivvy the rudder. 'Try again!' she yelled, as the tide slapped them against the cave and snatched them away again, as if enjoying itself, as if sarcastic.

From the cave, the lovers hoarsely yelled encouragement.

It worked. The skin on her fingers raw, Evie hung on, looping the rope around the blasphemous finger of rock and managing to make a scrappy, unreliable knot.

'I'll keep us as steady as I can.' Shen glowered with concentration, her hair flat against her head. 'You reach out to Scarlett and Zane.'

'Come on, guys!' Evie braced herself to lean right out. She had to. So she did. 'Now!' There was a perfect moment when the wave swelled and held the boat level with the cave, when the rope was taut, when the stern was tucked in neatly, bringing them parallel with the rock. Arms out, Evie felt a surge of strength. The last time life had demanded such physical resilience was during childbirth; now she carried out a labour in reverse, pulling her daughter towards her, landing her like a fish, so that Scarlett sprawled, gasping, drenched, alive, in the belly of the boat.

Despite its current state of emergency, Evie's body hadn't let her down.

'Zane!' she hollered as the boat shuddered and dropped. She knew when the next window of opportunity would open; she didn't know how many they had left. 'When I say "Jump" . . .'

As the wave swelled, as the boat rose, Evie saw a figure shape up, taller than Scarlett as it waded through the swampy cave.

The gap between boat and cave widened and closed. '*Now!*' Evie stretched out her arms – and Tillie fell into them, both of them falling backwards, a cold tangle of limbs and hair.

'Where's Zane?' Eyes wild, Shen shoved Scarlett's shoulder. 'Where is he?'

'That must be him.' Evie pointed to the top of the cliff. Two figures were outlined against the sky, as the scarf that Zane had earlier stolen from Tillie fluttered free and soared out over the sea.

'Can we go home?' asked Scarlett, coiled up and shivering.

'You bet,' said Shen, as Evie untethered the boat. She turned them around, navigating as if born to it.

Wet, and in dire need of as much tea as Devon could muster, Evie prescribed showers for – well, pretty much everybody apart from the smaller children, who were already re-enacting the rescue with the pressganged, uninterested dogs.

I wonder, she thought, *if Mike has realized?*

Ungallantly first in the attic-floor shower, a clean and warm Zane emerged and sought out his father.

'Dad.' Like a vampire who can't enter without permission, Zane wavered in the doorway of the master suite. This room was not his territory. It smelled of aftershave, of milk, of his stepmother.

Clive jumped, then waved his son into the room. 'Any shock symptoms yet? Shen keeps checking my pulse and asking if I need the toilet. Charming!'

'You won't tell everyone, will you?' Zane, bare-chested, felt small beside his lion of a father, a man who procreated each time he sneezed.

'Tell everyone what?' Clive had picked up a cigar and was looking at it with longing, as a man in a strip-club stares at boobs he can never touch.

'Well, not that I was stuck.' Zane scowled at the damp sketch that his feet had made on the floor. 'They know that already.'

'Help me out here, boy. Who am I not telling, and what am I not telling them?'

Zane twisted a towel between his fingers. 'Don't say I was too scared to move.'

Clive shrugged. 'Fine.' He turned away, then turned back. Zane wasn't finished.

'I feel so stupid. Having my dad rescue me, and everything. I was the one going for help. We'd sat on the beach for ages. Then the tide came in, and the beach was disappearing and the steps were underwater. The girls were in the cave, and I said I'd go and get help. I was meant to be the knight in shining armour, but I ended up getting saved myself.'

'Son, you're in the wrong family if you want to be a macho-man. Some girls just don't need saving. My little wife has bigger balls than the average grizzly.'

'Dad, please.'

'Fine, fine – your secret's safe with me, you little pillock. I'll say it was a tricky climb, and I only managed it because of the adrenaline. Something like that.'

They both stood, then moved at the same time, away from each other. Some moments scream *hug*, but this father and son were deaf.

Zane padded down the hall.

Clive remembered looking over the edge, to see his child sobbing against the rock-face. Whatever fear Zane had been going through, it was nothing compared to the terror that rocketed through Clive. Zane's fear of falling had paralysed him; Clive's fear of loss had galvanized him.

'Zane!' shouted Clive.

He was out of earshot.

Another calm after another storm.

Evie was glad to see the light disappearing down the plughole of the day. She needed peace.

Out in the lavender dusk, Zane wandered, headphones on. Evie waved to him as she tidied the kitchen, wiping the worktop, putting tops back on bottles. She was self-soothing;

the house at home was only truly tidy when she was in need of comfort.

'Should we,' she asked Mike, his back to her at the sink, 'talk to the girls? We should, shouldn't we?'

'Are you freaked out by it?' asked Mike, giving up all pretence of cleaning the sink and throwing down the sponge. 'I mean, I don't want to be dinosaur dad – the only one freaking out.'

'Then don't. Freak out, I mean.'

'But I have to. I mean, don't I?'

'Tell her how you feel. That's all you can do.' As she pulled back the great glass door, she laid a hand on his arm. 'How you *feel*, Mike, not how you think you should feel.'

'I didn't realize,' said Mike, 'that you actually have a *degree* in armchair psychology.'

Like two pieces of a jigsaw, Scarlett and Tillie curled around each other on a wide sun-lounger. They'd lain like that many times during the holiday, but now Evie saw it differently and wondered how she'd missed it before.

'So, girls . . .' began Evie, dragging over a lounger for herself and Mike to perch on.

Scarlett looked apprehensive. Tillie's face was strenuously impassive. 'We're in love,' said Scarlett, a little too loudly.

'This'll make you laugh. Me and Dad,' said Evie, with a wry *what-are-we-like?* look, 'we thought Scarlett and Zane were the ones falling for each other.'

Scarlett spluttered so fruitily she practically blew a raspberry. 'What? Me and Zane? I mean, he's lovely and everything, but come on!'

'Guy's a joke,' said Tillie.

'But we like him, don't we?' Evie waited for Tillie's nod. 'It's just that, while you're chatting to him, you realize he's looking at himself in the nearest mirror.' She pulled in her shoulders, wincing. 'I'm not being mean or anything.'

All through her school days, during all the petty friendship wars, Scarlett had lived in fear of the terrible sin of 'being mean'.

'I *am* being mean,' said Tillie. 'No way is Zane good enough for you.'

'You *would* say that, though. I shouldn't diss him. If I'm honest, I did have a crush. A crush-*ish*. A tiny crushette. I mean, he's gorge, for God's sake. But Tillie really *interested* me. I wanted to know what she thought about everything. Didn't I?' She nudged Tillie. 'But, Mum, you and I talked about Tillie. About a week ago. You said it was written all over me.'

'Crossed wires.' Evie smacked her forehead with her hand.

Mike asked, 'So, Tillie, have you always been . . .'

'A lesbian? Yeah, pretty much. I mean, I'm only eighteen, it's not like I have loads of relationships behind me. But I've always known, yeah.'

Scarlett held up her fingers to count. 'Let's tot up your relationships, eh? Ooh, *zero*, that's right.' The girls laughed, utterly in harmony.

This was first love. *That's why*, thought Evie, *they fit so snugly together*. It's why they shone. It's why she envied them. This fortnight, no matter what might happen to them later as a – *gulp!* – couple, would never fade in the girls' memories. It would retain its sunshine colours, jewel-bright forever, because it was the first time.

Mike coughed. 'Your mum and I,' he began, triggering a shot of alarm through his wife. *Oh gawd, what's he going to say?* 'We wish you'd told us, love. To find out about . . .' evidently unable to use any of the proper words, Mike opted for no word whatsoever, 'halfway through a life-or-death situation isn't the best way to break this type of thing to your parents.'

This type of thing. The lame expression hung in the air between the four of them, with all the charm of a dead fish.

'Learning about this type of thing during a life-or-death situation,' said Tillie, 'does put this type of thing into perspective, though.'

Evie said, 'She's got a point.'

'She has,' agreed Mike.

Tillie carried on. 'Life-or-death situations are nothing new to me.'

Scarlett squeezed her hand; the compassion on her face made her look mature. Evie saw traces of the woman Scarlett would become, and she liked that woman. 'I want,' said Scarlett gently, 'to make it all right for Tillie.'

Tillie barely opened her lips. 'You do.'

Mike stood, as if bitten suddenly. 'Well, yes, great, lovely – glad we cleared the air, girls . . . um . . . ladies, I mean, women.'

'Wait, Dad!' Scarlett fell into step with Mike as he marched through the French windows, boxing with the gauzy curtains, knocking petals from the drowsy roses climbing on either side.

Alone with Tillie, Evie contemplated how to approach this girl, who seemed to be made of elbows. 'You don't need my blessing, Tillie,' she said eventually, when both of them had looked out at the garden for some time. 'But you have it. I can see you and my daughter are bonkers about each other.'

'You're wrong,' said Tillie. 'We *do* need it. Thank you.'

Evie smiled. Slapped her knees. The tricky bit was done. 'Hot chocolate?'

'Great,' said Tillie. 'They say hot drinks are good after a shock. But even though I almost drowned today,' she bit her lip, 'you might need it more than I do.'

As the milk warmed, Evie snooped by the open drawing-room door. It wasn't big, it wasn't clever, but it was irresistible.

Please, she prayed to whichever god was on duty, *help Mike speak from the heart!*

Scarlett was talking, in that intense gabble she used when something was important. Important to *her*, that is; Scarlett didn't always fall into step with what the world considered to be important. 'Thing is, Daddy,' she was saying, making Evie nod admiringly: *Nice move. Call him 'Daddy' and he's putty in your hands.*

'Thing is, Daddy, what *is* gay, anyway? I don't know if I'm gay. I just really, really like Tillie. Well, actually, I love her. *Aaargh!*' Scarlett let loose the scream she and her friends reserved for the highest grade of embarrassment/ excitement/new trousers. 'That feels so weird. But I do!' She was a pendulum, swinging from juvenile to adult. 'I don't feel right when she's not with me. And she can't bore me. Even when she goes on and on about politics. If I make her laugh, I swear I grow a full inch.'

Mike's voice was rumbling ballast to his daughter's hot-air balloon. 'You're young, Scarlett. You'll meet other people who make you feel that way.'

'Oh my God, Dad, are you homophobic? After all that shit you say about—'

'Scarlett!'

'Newsflash! I say "Shit" all the time. Shit,' said Scarlett. 'Shit shitty-shitto.'

'Very clever. Glad the education isn't going to waste. And of course I'm not homophobic, you brat. I'm just saying—'

'You're just saying,' Scarlett cut in, her voice full of the tears that were always hot on the heels of her anger, 'you're disappointed in me.'

Mike sounded tired. 'Don't be silly.'

'See! I know that voice. This is another disappointment.'

'Another one? What do you mean?'

'Oh, that Scarlett,' said Scarlett, 'she's always late. She's the last out of bed. Does her homework at the last minute. She argues. She swears. She cries. She screws up. She's an idiot, and she's always been an idiot.'

That's your cue! Evie implored her husband, through the door.

'Where's all this coming from? You *are* a disappointment, if you believe that.' As the crying went up a notch, Mike said, 'Joke, Scarlett. Joke!'

'It's not funny. Get *off* me.'

So a cuddle had been attempted. *Bad timing, sir*, thought Evie.

'Hang on. Don't go. Love, listen. Are you listening? It's

hard to know, cos you're biting that thumbnail so viciously and staring at it as if you hate it.'

'Just get on with it, Dad.'

'I don't know how to put this. I was the first person to clap eyes on you. Mum was zonked by the effort of pushing you out, and I cut your umbilical cord – it's much thicker than you'd think, by the way – and then you were handed to me. I took a good long, hard look at you. You were covered in goo, and one of your eyes was sealed shut with gunk, and your forehead had a dent in it from the forceps. The midwife said, "She's perfect." She meant you had all your fingers and toes, but I said, "Yes, she is" and I meant much more than that.'

Evie stayed very still.

'And I still think that when I look at you. I think: *She's perfect.* Nothing has changed that, and nothing ever will.'

There was a pause for some snuffling.

'Scarlett, you don't disappoint me, because you can't. If I nag you, it's only cos it's my job to prepare my daughter for the big bad world, where she's just another person – not my precious, incomparable Scarlett. Being your dad is the most satisfying job I've ever had. I love you, Scarlett, just the way you are. And, for the record, I think Tillie's amazing.'

Major snuffling.

'*I've* disappointed *you*, I see that. But when I was growing up it was harder to live as a gay person, and my gut reaction is to make everything easy for you. I don't care if you fancy boys, girls or pot plants.'

More snuffling, plus a snotty giggle.

'Are we clear on this matter now? Because I don't know

if I can say it all again. I'm just your stupid dad, you know. This'll have to last you for the next ten years or so.'

There was a lot of talk from Scarlett after that. Most of it Evie couldn't decipher, through the tears and the nose-bubbles and the laughing, but she heard her call Mike 'Daddy' just as the milk boiled over.

'I want one of these,' murmured Evie, watching the moon from the gurgling hot tub. She might as well want a unicorn. 'I'd live in it, if I had one.' She held out her glass and Shen refilled it. They were alone. Shen had set up the tub, then beckoned Evie out to it, without alerting anybody else.

'I'm glad you and I seem to be . . . *us* again,' said Evie.

'Me too.'

'What the hell happened? Why did we fall out? We—'

'Evie, with the greatest respect in the world, shut up.' Shen's maquillage was once again perfect, despite the damp. '*We* didn't do anything. I lost the plot for a while.'

'It's Wellcome Manor. It's all this perfection.' Evie looked around at the spotlit, impeccable grounds. 'It feels ungrateful and petty to be unhappy here, but the truth is we packed all our problems in our suitcases.'

'It's not the house's fault, it's mine.'

'OMG,' mouthed Evie. 'Is this an *apology*?'

Shen blew out her cheeks. Exhaled heavily. 'I. Am. Sorry.'

'I should have caught that on-camera. But I don't need a sorry, Shen. We lost our way a bit, that's all. No inquests, eh?'

Off the hook, Shen nodded. She'd envied her friend, instead of crying on her shoulder. Now that Shen had come down from the ceiling she could accept they were different people with different strengths. Her recovery – her return to being 'her', as Evie put it – had begun when Clive's jibes petered out. There was no rivalry over Fang now; in fact, Clive was possessive and wouldn't let Shen do the little practical chores that had flummoxed her.

The pivot had been that romp in the greenhouse. It had reignited something between man and wife, turning them back into lovers after years of stage-managed sex. She fancied the ruffled bear of a man who looked after his family, who was tired, but not too tired to have his missus among the lawnmowers and the compost.

'So,' Evie looked over the rim of her glass with mock-horror, 'you ravished him in the greenhouse with your gym kit on?'

'Put like that, it sounds like pervy *Cluedo*, but it was *hot.*'

'Got it. No need to say any more. Sounds like you and Clive have found your rhythm, just as Mike and I have lost ours. Ships that pass in the night, and all that.'

'You'll be fine.' Shen was airy. 'You always are.'

Her confidence was reassuring; *but*, thought Evie, *it's easy to be confident from afar.*

'So,' said Shen. 'We finally have a lesbian in the family.'

'You sound as if you've been looking out for one for months. Like when you go on the Louboutin waiting list.'

'I love lesbians.'

'Oh God, Shen, listen to yourself!'

'Well, I do.'

'No, you don't. That's patronizing. You're saying you love lesbians because Scarlett's in love with Tillie.'

'No, I've always loved lesbians.' Shen was affronted by Evie's doubt. 'They're so chic. They're so *now*. It's very trendy to be gay. I'd do it myself, if I wasn't so fond of willies.'

'Don't look at *me*. I'm spoken for.'

'As if I'd go out with you,' scoffed Shen. 'I'd want a younger girlfriend. A model or an actress. No offence.'

'Lots taken.'

'Give it a decade and we'll have a queer Queen.'

There was no point picking apart that assertion. 'Do you think Scarlett and Tillie are a bit young to make such a big decision about their sexuality?'

'I knew from the age of six I wanted to marry a millionaire.'

'I suppose, come to think of it, I *did* define myself at a young age. As straight.' Evie rubbed her streaming eyes; she'd gone off the hot tub. It was like sharing a hot bath with someone who was constantly, vigorously breaking wind. 'Scarlett's a wise kid, once you delve past the *whatev*s and the *duh*s. But you know how it is, Shen. We worry about them.'

'You're thinking about her going back to school, yeah?' With a ghetto-princess snap of her fingers, Shen dismissed the shadowy playground bigots. 'Fuck 'em!' she declared. 'Scarlett is who she is, and besides, she's *ours*. And so is Tillie. Nobody messes with our girls.'

'Amen to that.' Evie raised her glass. Shen's forcefield was up and humming again, wrapped around them all. She would put iron in Scarlett and Tillie's blood, protect them from the trolls. It would be up to Evie, however, to protect them from Shen's newfound enthusiasm for all things lesboid.

'We said no inquests,' said Shen, 'and I agree. But can we promise never to lose our way again?'

'Please.' Evie couldn't do without Shen; Shen couldn't do without Evie. Their shaky ecosystem worked. 'Oh, look at the dogs,' she said, soppily. 'They want to get in with— Oh, Jesus!'

Prunella and Patch took her smile as an invitation. Leaving them to it and retreating to the terrace, Evie looked back at the two faces, one bug-eyed, the other barking, in the bubbling water. *So it's not just a sex-thing*, she thought, approvingly. *He takes her out on dates.*

'I know you're awake, Mike. When you're really asleep, you don't make those dainty little sheep-noises; when you're asleep, you sound like a masturbating hippo.' Evie kissed the edge of his ear, one of the few surfaces of her husband sticking out of the duvet and available to her. She lay along the bundled-up length of him, needing the beat of his blood.

'I *am* asleep, honest.'

'Our powwow is off the agenda then.' It had been buried beneath the avalanche of the day's events.

'It's been a hell of a day. My daughter could have drowned. My wife could have drowned. Our family has one more lesbian in it than it did when we got up this morning.' Mike burrowed deeper. 'I went nuts, when you and Shen took off without me in that crappy little boat.'

'Sorry. You know how Shen is. She can't bear to waste a second.'

'I felt so impotent. I thought, *What if I lose them both*?'

'You didn't, though. You don't always have to be the hero, darling. I'm here to take up the slack.'

Mike's head and shoulders appeared. 'Answer me truthfully, Evie. Did you know? About Scarlett and Tillie? Did she confide in you?'

'Cross my heart, I'd have told you.' She was dismayed that he suspected otherwise. 'I tell you everything.' The lie slipped out so smoothly; she absolved herself, because soon it would be the truth. 'Why would Scarlett tell me before you?'

'Because I'm the ogre who's disappointed in her.' Mike slammed back onto the bed, as if he'd taken a knockout punch. 'Because she thought I'd be ashamed of her. Christ!'

'No, no, no.' Evie was having none of that. 'She spilled her heart out to you. She needed you to know all about her, about how she felt. It's pretty *cool* – to use a forbidden word – that a teenager needs that connection with her daddy.'

'That's true.' A half-smile scribbled across Mike's face in the scant moonlight. With a sudden half-turn of his head to look at Evie, he said, 'Hold on. How do you know what she said to me?'

'How d'you think?' Evie was busted. 'I have an O level in Eavesdropping, to go with that degree in Armchair Psychology.'

'You nosy old bag.'

'I love it when you talk dirty to me.'

'We were such mugs. We totally bought the idea of Scarlett and Zane, just because it was the heterosexual option.'

Evie's clothes felt restrictive suddenly. She needed to be naked, to be her undiluted self. 'Poor Zane. I was mentoring him. I thought he was getting somewhere. His little heart must be breaking.'

'Zane looks fine to me.'

Men, thought Evie. 'I'll have a word with him tomorrow. Take his emotional temperature.' As she stretched out, Mike shuffled his body towards her, drilling his bottom gently into her torso. They often slept like that, but tonight Evie gave a slight start and pulled away.

No, she lectured herself. *Relax*. Evie let her limbs liquefy and spooned Mike, her skin against his, for the full length of their bodies. After tomorrow he would be too anxious, too careful, to bump against her like that; she remembered his hyper-awareness of her body last time. He'd thrown a cordon around it, in case he hurt her, in case he made things worse.

Hmm. I really should get one last shag out of him, before he goes all respectful on me. Evie kissed Mike's ear. 'Maybe this liking-girls thing is just a phase.'

She turned the kiss into a nibble, then added an exploratory flick of her tongue on his neck.

'Oh.' Mike turned, smiling with his whole body. 'I see.'

Against his mouth, Evie said, 'My parents still think you're a phase.'

DAY 14
Monday, 24th August

Dear Wellcome Manor,

THANK YOU for this extraordinary holiday. For letting us swim in your pool and play in your treehouse and go wild on your lawn. And thank you for helping us put things into perspective.

Love,

Evie, Mike, Scarlett, Dan, Mabel & Patch xxx

The noise at the end of the drive woke the whole house.

Clive padded down the gravel in slippers and shook hands with the foreman of the small working party replacing the gates. He handed over a cheque and jogged back to the house, baying for breakfast.

'The last croissant.' Evie lay it reverentially on his plate. The house was alive with comings and goings, pitterings and patterings, just like the first exploration fourteen days ago. Now their little army was retreating.

'Where's my rucksack?' hollered Mabel from the top floor.

'Can we steal the telly?' called Dan from the den.

'Not so sunny today.' Evie joined Shen on the terrace with the half-glass of orange juice that was left.

'It knows we're going home.'

'How like you, to assume the sun is your personal celestial body.'

'Oi!' A happy squeal from a top window. Evie squinted up to see Scarlett and Tillie crammed into the frame. 'Fry us a bacon sarnie, Muvver!'

'No bacon!' shouted Evie.

'No bread!' shouted Shen.

It occurred to Evie that Scarlett and Tillie had shared a room since day one. She closed down that line of thought: the sex lives of other generations are a no-go area. She remembered the spine-tingling mortification of the realization that her own parents must have *done it*, and Scarlett's loud gagging if she saw Evie and Mike kiss, however chastely.

'This,' said Evie, taking in the picturesque sweep of the garden with early-onset nostalgia, 'will probably be our last family holiday. I can't see Scarlett wanting to come away with us next year.'

'She and Tillie will have broken up by then.'

'Possibly.' Evie elbowed Shen for her lack of romance. 'But I didn't necessarily mean she'd go away with Tillie. She's turning into a woman. She'll have some other love interest, or a bunch of friends. This is quite a historic occasion.'

'Yeah,' said Shen, unimpressed. 'Let's all get a tattoo of the date.'

'Soon other people will take possession of Wellcome Manor,' said Evie to Clive as they strolled down the drive to inspect the finished gates, Fang jolting along in her pushchair, and Patch variously way in front, way behind or right under their feet.

'Do you know what you are?' asked Clive.

'Well, that's an odd question.' Evie smiled. 'Let's see, I'm a woman, English, five-foot-five-ish, allergic to conversations about mortgage rates, over-fond of Cadbury's Creme Eggs.'

Clive said, 'You're my first ever female friend.'

'Am I?' The thought pleased her.

'Never had one before. Turns out, it's useful and – well, *nice*.' Clive shook his head. 'I must be getting old. Enjoying *nice* stuff.'

'We're all getting old.' Evie's age – and how much future she had – was on her mind.

'Peculiar to think we barely knew each other just two weeks ago. Now I feel as if I know you better than most other people. Dear God, woman, don't look so nervous! I'm not about to declare myself.' He paused, and added, '*again*'.

'Good. I can only take one declaration per holiday.'

'You're not the only female I got to know at Wellcome Manor.' Clive bent down towards his daughter, currently kicking her legs like a chorus girl in her Bugaboo. 'I also got to know this small, over-emotional, incontinent but thoroughly charismatic person.'

'And Zane?' Evie gestured to the young man, currently defying expectations by helping the workmen load tools back onto their flatbed truck. 'Still a menace to society?'

'Hey!' Clive saluted his son. 'What's all this? You wouldn't help *me* if I begged you!'

'Nice to have something to do.' Zane dragged a tarpaulin over the load.

'Classic. All this opulence, paid for by the sweat of my brow, and he's bored.'

'Oh, Clive,' said Evie. 'Don't pick him up on everything.'

'It's for his own good. I won't always be here to pay the bills.'

'Ignore him, Zane.' As Clive's certified Only Female

Friend, Evie felt qualified to meddle. 'Fathers are handed a pamphlet of annoying phrases when their kids are born. My dad had the same edition as yours, by the sound of things.'

'I don't mind him saying irritating things.' Zane patted the side of the truck, as if it was a good dog. 'He hardly says anything at all.'

'I can't win,' said Clive, examining the gates.

'*I* can't win,' said Zane, as the lorry sped away.

'Actually, I think you'll find it's mums who can't win,' said Evie. 'It's been scientifically proven.'

Trotting up to join them, Scarlett suggested, 'Maybe nobody has to win, eh?', widening her eyes in an *hmm, interesting* way. 'Listen, Zane, sod off. I need to talk to your dad for a minute.'

Zane sodded off back to the house, just like that; *still under her spell*, thought Evie, heart swelling.

'I have a confession.' Scarlett twirled a lock of hair that had escaped from the scarf around her head. She would have won first prize at a fancy-dress party as Tillie: baggy dungarees over a rainbow vest, earrings dangling, bangles jostling.

'Ye-es?' Evie and Clive took a gate apiece, closing them slowly through the ruts they'd worn in the earth.

Taking Fang out of her buggie, holding her fondly but awkwardly, Scarlett said, 'You know when we – like – got, you know, a bit drunk?'

'A bit?' said Evie, as the gates clanged together. 'You were speaking in tongues.'

'Well, yeah, whatever, the thing is . . . it wasn't Zane's idea.' She moved Fang to her other hip. 'He kept telling us not to, but me and Tillie egged each other on, and then we made Zane join in.' She turned to Clive. She bit her lip. 'I didn't stand up for him when you blamed him. But I should have.'

'Yes,' said Clive. He seemed rattled. 'You should.'

'He took the rap for us.' Scarlett overdid the amazement, for Fang's benefit, and was rewarded with loud giggles. 'He was brilliant. Why would anybody do that?'

Because he loves you, you dozy child-woman, thought Evie.

'Zane!' The board members of Little Associates wouldn't recognize their MD, who was scuttling breathlessly around the side of the house. 'Wait up, Son.'

'What?' The habitual exquisite boredom was present and correct in Zane's expression. 'Dad, what?' he repeated, when Clive just looked at him.

'I . . .' Clive was never at a loss for words; language did his bidding at all times. He gestured to Fang. 'I need your help. With your sister.'

'As she's my half-sister,' said Zane, 'how about I half-help?'

'It's time this family stopped doing things by halves.' Clive turned the pushchair, its handle towards Zane. 'Go on.'

'What do I do with her?' He advanced fearfully, as if taking charge of a stallion.

'Amuse her. Offer her a sippy cup of something.' Clive folded his arms, as Zane crouched to put his face near Fang's. It struck him for the first time that Zane and Fang were alike: something about the way their hair grew, something indefinable about the planes of their faces, something they'd both inherited from *him*.

'Dad, she stinks.' Zane recoiled.

'I'll show you how to change her nappy.'

The unconvincing repulsion didn't cloak the pleasure on Zane's face. Clive had thought he'd left it too late; maybe, where your kids were concerned, there was no such thing.

Fated to be eternally out of step, Paula tackled the steps into the pool just as the others finished their last dip. Evie, towelling Mabel's hair, wolf-whistled.

'See!' she said to Paula, as Mabel darted away like a feral child returning to her orang-utan foster family, 'Told you my swimsuit'd fit. You look fab.'

'Oh no, gosh.' Paula hurried into the concealing water.

'You're *Baywatch* material.'

Laughing in the shimmering water, Paula was shedding her old skin, layer by layer.

'When we get home,' said Evie, stooping to pick up discarded water-wings and foam batons, 'you can come to the leisure centre with us and the kids. They have huge slides and everything. Amber'll love it.'

'Sounds nice,' said Paula.

'Don't let Shen challenge you to a race, though. She does ten lengths by the time I've buttoned up my swimming hat.' Now that Shen had renounced the dark side, she'd not only reiterated Evie's pledge to support Paula; she'd taken over. *We'll take Paula shopping*, Shen gushed. *We'll bully Paula into doing Pilates*. Between them, they would launch her into school-gate society.

Paula had seemed reluctant, as if her murky half-life should continue even now there was no need for it, but Evie would persevere. It was time for Paula to face up to a host of practical and emotional problems. Evie, despite her own situation, would be *there for her*, as Jeremy Kyle might put it.

'Oh!' squealed Paula. 'Oh-oh-oh!'

'What?' Evie wheeled around.

Paula let out a loud *phew*. 'Nothing.' She smiled. 'Just thought I couldn't touch the bottom with my feet.'

'But you can,' said Evie, liking the metaphor.

Her husband was at the car, doing the mysterious, pre-long-journey things that men do at cars. Evie saw him out of the window as she helped Shen pack: twenty minutes in and they'd barely made a dent in the wardrobe.

'What sort of holiday did you think this was?' Evie held up an evening gown. 'You could cruise around the world and not wear the same thing twice. I've been in the same jeans for the past five days.'

'I know,' said Shen darkly. 'Oh God, *underwear*,' she groaned, opening a drawer.

'I can see a garter. I don't even own a garter, and you brought one on holiday.'

'Three, actually.' Shen stuffed them into a small holdall. 'I'll have to put the whip on the roofrack.'

The most banal holiday fixes its year in the memory; 2015 would forever be when they went to a very big house in the country. The photos would nail that year's haircuts, trouser lengths and heel heights. Mabel's children would laugh out loud at Granddad's car, and Mabel would grow wet-eyed at the sight of Patch, tongue lolling, one ear up, one ear down, and say, 'Patch was a good dog.'

Evie looked out of the window and saw, framed in the stonework, a vignette of Mike letting Dan pretend to drive the not-yet-old-fashioned car. Everything became unbearably dear to her, like somebody about to leave a party and realizing what fun it's all been.

'Catch!' Shen balled something up in her hands and chucked it Evie's way. By the time it had unfurled in mid-air and landed on her face, it had revealed itself to be an ivory silk cardigan. 'Want it?'

'God, yeah!' It was simply cut and elegant. 'Thanks.' She thanked Shen not only for the typically offhand generosity, but for bitching and joking and whining as usual.

Without thinking, without planning to, she told Shen everything, with one short sentence.

Shen's hands flew to her mouth. She began to cry. She locked her arms tight around Evie. 'Oh God,' she said. 'Oh God, Evie, oh God.' She promised to help. Whatever happened. 'And Mike . . . how's Mike?'

When Shen discovered that he didn't know, she wiped her eyes. 'Go tell him,' she said. 'Now!'

Plodding up the drive, wiping his hands on a rag, Mike spotted his wife on the steps and halted. Her expression told him that the not-knowing-for-sure was about to end.

Evie reached for his hand and led him around the house. Together, in step, they passed through the garden and went through the wooden door in the wall, which delivered them to the outside world where nature did its own thing. They settled down, backs against the sun-warmed brick, still hand-in-hand.

Evie abandoned the opening gambits she'd rehearsed. 'You know what I'm about to say.'

'I do,' said Mike, tonelessly.

She stole a look, sideways, at him. As she'd feared, his face was twisted in panic.

Mike said, 'Please, don't say the words. I can't bear to hear it.' He cringed at her dismayed intake of breath. 'I know, I *know*. Just give me a minute to absorb it, and I'll be fine. I'll manage. I'll look after you. And them. All of us. But don't make me listen to the words.' Jackknifed with unhappiness, his head sank between his knees.

Her most colourful fears hadn't gone this far; Evie was too disappointed to speak.

'To think you got in that bloody boat yesterday, in your state of health.'

Tired of the melodrama – just plain *tired* – Evie said, with none of the delicacy or understanding she'd planned, 'Don't start that. I'm pregnant, not ill.'

His head shot up, as if yanked by a sadistic puppeteer. 'You're not pregnant!' It was a statement and a question, all at once.

'Then what are we talking about?' Evie drew back, her face screwed up in confusion.

'Your cancer's back.'

'It is *not*,' she said, affronted, as if he'd accused her of bestiality.

'Isn't it?'

'Christ, no. Don't even say stuff like that, Mike.'

'I don't get it.' Mike looked helpless.

Evie, in a flash, *did* get it. She put her hand over her mouth, then on the side of his frightened face. 'You thought my cancer came back?' She almost enjoyed how toothless the dreaded word was at this moment. 'You're wrong, darling. Wonderfully, brilliantly wrong. I'm pregnant.' Allowing his features time to regroup, for his jaw to undrop, for his eyes to deglaze, she went on, 'Well, actually, *we're* pregnant. I didn't do this with a turkey-baster.'

Mike opened his mouth. 'This is . . .'

Evie willed him to say *marvellous* or *wonderful* or *fantabulous*.

'A bit of a shock. We . . . but you, for God's sake – the pill?'

Evie had had a lot of time to work it out. 'Remember my food poisoning? That bad whelk in Brighton?' Mike nodded; nobody who was there could forget. 'And then we went to my Aunty Gloria's eightieth the next day? And made the beast with two backs in the B&B?' *Free bar + no kids is a heady combination.* 'We didn't realize I'd thrown up

402

my pill that morning.' She shrugged, looking down at her tummy. 'Not the most romantic story, but probably the way most of the human race starts off.'

Mike was pale. Very pale. Practically see-through. Mildly aggrieved that she had to do so, Evie yammered on, to cover his silence. She was the one carrying the baby; all Mike had to do was say something. *Anything*. 'I know, I *know*, it's not planned. Our baby-years are over. We can't afford another mouth to feed. The house is bursting at the seams, as it is.' Never mind the small matter of her own abandoned dream of a job.

'So,' said Mike, as if he'd only just learned how to speak, 'you're really not dying?'

'The opposite. I'm making another life.' Putting it like that, Evie impressed herself.

'I thought . . .' And that was as far as Mike seemed able to get with the whole speaking thing.

It was clear he needed time to get used to the idea. *But*, thought Evie, *I wasn't given time to get used to it, and it's inside me and all over me and sharing my blood*. She needed Mike to come through. As she awaited his next utterance, fingers splayed on a stomach not yet swollen, something worked itself out, like a knot untying. Love for this baby landed squarely in the centre of her.

Mike said, 'We can't afford it. I work flat-out as it is, and Lucinda Lash doesn't bring in much.'

Evie had forgotten all about Lucinda. She realized she'd have to crank up the old *Rude Word Thesaurus* again; they needed the saucy old bat.

'And,' said Mike, 'it'd be eighteen years younger than

Scarlett. Not to mention that – well, come on love, you're *mature* to have a baby, to say the least.'

'Gee thanks.'

'You'll be forty-one when it's born.' Mike began to breathe shallowly. 'And sixty when it's nineteen.'

'Nice to know you can still do simple arithmetic, even while you're blowing a gasket.'

'Where will it sleep?'

'Dunno. Biscuit tin?'

'I'll be at retirement age when it starts university.'

'If it ever gets to university. Remember, it had a very disadvantaged start in life, sleeping in a biscuit tin.'

In her bleakest prophecies Evie hadn't imagined this blind pessimism. But she'd forgotten about the see-saw dynamic of marriage. The more Mike foresaw catastrophe ('We'll have to move house!', 'You're knackered as it is!'), the more buoyantly confident she became. She brushed aside his fears, deciding on the spot not to share with Mike the 'options' the doctor had outlined. The time frame – any termination would have to take place before twenty-four weeks – was meaningless. No longer was the countdown written in flame before her eyes; the countdown was a slower one, giving them months to come to terms with the demands this new-comer would make of them.

The 'problem' was already a Herrera. This conversation was its first taste of just how maudlin its dad could be.

Mike chuntered on. He stood up and began to pace. 'There's no safety net,' he said.

Evie joined him, enjoying how he hastily stuck out his hand to help her up. She brushed her bottom free of grassy hangers-on and led him back through the door, back to the tidy borders, the precise lawn and the waiting house.

'There *is* a safety net,' she said, in the gentle, no-nonsense tone she used for sore throats and cancelled play-dates. 'It's made of human relationships, knitted together with love and respect. The minute we met, it started to form itself.'

They reached the soft, sandy path that looped past the treehouse, skirting the pool.

'Your safety net was strengthened,' Evie went on, 'when we made some more humans, who rely on us just like we rely on them. You're not the solitary boy I met. You're a man, embedded in a far-reaching framework of affiliations and bonds and friendships. Even though Shen drives you mad, she's one of *your* people. And now so is loopy old Paula. Don't you get it? There's a safety net, and you're a vital part of it. If you weren't here, there'd be a gaping, Mike-shaped hole in the world, and I wouldn't want to live in a world like that.'

More than quiet, Mike was mute now. Evie experienced one of those abrupt energy dips she recalled from her last pregnancy. Time for her other half to clamber back on the marital see-saw. She needed to hear him say something. Something very specific. 'Mike,' she said, 'do you want this baby?'

Mike looked at her. All the pent-up, unshed tears of chilly spare rooms, local-authority bedsits began to fall. 'Do I want it?' he asked, wild-eyed. Out they came, the tears he hadn't cried at their no-budget wedding; at the births of Scarlett, Dan and Mabel; at Evie's grim diagnosis;

at her all-clear. 'I already love it!' He was every bit as messy as the kids at crying; it wasn't a skill he'd ever refined. 'Thank you, Evie!'

She folded him in her arms and let him sob it out.

They decided to wait until the traditional three-month juncture – 'end of the first trimester!': Mike was proud of his pregnancy lore – to tell the children about the tiny Herrera waiting in the wings. (Evie liked the notion of her womb having a wings section, like the London Palladium.)

'Just, you know, in case . . .' said Evie, aware of the possible complications of giving birth at what Mike continually referred to as 'your age', as if no other human had ever reached such decrepitude. She didn't plan on thinking too hard on this topic; she would trust to luck, to the universe, to her own body, which had never, despite being sorely tested, let her down.

Practical stuff – the juggling of money, the valuing of houses, the stifled screams in pram departments – could all wait until the three-month milestone.

Impossible as it seemed, the last half-hour of the holiday had arrived. All their sunny days spent, they were legally obliged to clear off and vacate the property that had begun to feel like home.

The house was tossed, as if mildly burgled. The cat-shaped

cushion Mabel had 'packed by mistake' was replaced. A velvet stool was repositioned to cover the spot where Miles had drawn a smiley face on the wallpaper.

Paula still wore Evie's swimsuit under her dress, but Evie let it go, too busy running up, down, up the staircase, then down again, while cramming a rogue pair of Mr Men knickers into a holdall, holding together her broken toiletries bag and wondering just what Mabel *did* with the hundreds of elastic hairbands that passed through her ink-stained hands.

The solid front door stood open, impassive to the endless comings and goings. Dan dawdled through, whining, 'I'm hungry, Mum.'

'We'll stop on the way,' called Evie, stuffing cases into the boot of their car.

'We bloody won't,' muttered Mike, dragging a reluctant Patch towards the back seat.

Scarlett, with Tillie at her shoulder, asked, 'All right if I travel with Paula?'

'No kissing!' shouted Dan.

As the next in line to take flight, his dearest ambition would soon be to kiss somebody. Evie grabbed him, with a tackle that only mothers and muggers employ. She kissed his filthy head where his filthy hair parted – it smelled like Gouda – and said, 'Car, Mister! Now!'

Paula, half-in, half-out of her own car, asked if she could follow them home. 'Sure!' called Evie, fast-forwarding to the dayroom of a care-home where a wrinkled Paula wheezed from the adjacent comfy chair, 'What do I want for me dinner, Evie?'

One by one, the very big house spat out the holiday-makers.

'Bye-bye, Wellcome Manor!' shouted Mabel. 'I'll miss you!' Promptly tripping over her sandals, she had barely hit the gravel before Mike scooped her up and 'WHEEEE!'-ed her into the air, giving her no time to cry.

Checking in her bag for her front-door keys – they looked quaint, like somebody else's property – Evie called to the Ling-Little section of the convoy before finally climbing into the front seat. 'See you at home, Shen! Don't know how I'll cope in my crappy little kitchen!'

'Fibber!' Retouching her lipgloss, Shen was back in full London armour, hair puffed, bare shoulders gleaming, each finger bejewelled. 'You can't wait to get home.'

She knows me well, thought Evie, banging the car door (it had to be banged or it refused to click shut). She tugged at the seatbelt, ignoring the onslaught of daft questions from the back seat. The comforts of home were calling to her: that sweet spot on the end of the sofa, which knew her bottom so well and accommodated it without comment; scalding tea in her chipped *I* ♥ *BROADSTAIRS* mug; the feeling of just-rightness that crept through the house when the small ones were in bed, and Evie and Mike settled down with an old *Fawlty Towers*.

And yet. *I'll miss this place.* Wellcome Manor was already lost to her, hazy through the steamy windows of the travelling asylum that was their car.

As the roof of the Audi yawned open and folded itself away with orgasmic jerks and shudders, Shen said, 'I'll miss this place.'

'I'll miss the greenhouse,' said Clive.

'There'll be other greenhouses.' Shen adjusted the rear-view mirror to give her face a critical, approving once-over. 'Zane!' she barked at the boy, hanging about by the front door with his signature, attention-seeking nonchalance. She revved the engine. 'Should we consider living in the country?' she asked Clive, who was picking dried sweet potato off his watchstrap.

'I could get my PA to whistle up some sales details.'

'We'd need a pool. And some land. We could get the kids riding, Clive! So we'd need stables.' She provoked the engine again. 'Come *on*, Zane. Where's he going now?' she tutted, as the boy jogged over to Paula's car.

'What if I had nothing? What if I lost it all tomorrow?' said Clive.

'That's not going to happen,' said Shen impatiently. Then, suspiciously, 'Is it?'

'Don't worry, my petal, I'm not trying to tell you something. I'm just saying, if it did – if I had nothing – would you live in a tent with me?'

Shen gave him her full attention, ignoring Fang's grizzling and Miles's rhythmic kicking of the back of her seat. 'What,' she said, 'do you think?'

Clive held her gaze. 'I think you would,' he said, finally.

'Damned right,' said Shen.

They leaned towards each other for a slightly more smoochy kiss than they would normally share in front of the children.

'Although,' she said as she pulled away, 'it would have to be a Prada tent.' She gunned the motor once more. 'Zane!'

'Yeah, coming!' Zane was not coming, not in the least. He was loitering by Paula's car, embracing Scarlett, then Tillie, then Scarlett again, with much laughter and pushing and what Evie's mother would call 'horseplay'.

Evie wrestled her door open. 'Back in a sec.' She ignored Mike's 'You always do this' and Dan's 'I need a great big wee', to nip across the drive and take her leave, properly, of Zane.

As the girls folded themselves into Paula's back seat, Evie put her hands on his shoulders. 'You're being really sweet about the girls.'

Zane shrugged. 'They make a great couple.'

'See?' Evie was full of admiration. 'You don't have to hide your pain, Zane. Men are allowed to cry.'

'Yeah, I know that.' He inched away. 'I don't want to cry, thanks.'

'I feel a bit responsible, actually. I encouraged you.'

'Yeah, you did.' Zane's smile was angelic. 'You gave me confidence. For an old person, you were ace.'

'Why, thank you.'

'Any minute now – just watch – I'll make my move.'

'Bit late, Zane, to be honest.' Evie did a comedy waggle of the head, then hated herself for doing a comedy waggle of the head. 'That horse has bolted, love.'

'Not in my opinion. I've got it all planned. I'm gonna do it on the way home.'

'How? What are you *gonna* do?'

'While Dad's off buying petrol or having a cigar or whatever, I'm going to gaze deep into her eyes and say, "Shen, I love you."'

Evie looked at him. Hard.

'Cos you were right!' Zane was warming to his subject. 'She's never loved Dad. She's trying to make me jealous, like you said. And who cares what people think of a woman running off with her stepson. It's nothing to do with them, man. I'll quote you to the fools. *People fall for people. That's the way the world turns.*'

'Um . . . yes, I did say that, didn't I, but . . .'

'When Shen and I are living together, you're the first person we'll have round.'

'No, hang on – wait a minute.' Evie shook her head, the better to dislodge that strange and, frankly, *awful* vision. 'You *are* keen on Scarlett,' she insisted, as if telling him so would change Zane's mind. 'All the staring, the hanging about . . .'

'I was staring at Shen. Who could look at anybody else, when she's around? No offence,' he said kindly, to the old woman currently having what looked like a series of strokes in front of him. 'And I was hanging around Shen.'

'But you took the rap for the boozing. That's what a boy in love would do!'

'Is it?' Zane looked puzzled by such a boy. 'I said it was my fault cos Dad blames me whatever, so . . .' He shrugged. 'No biggie.'

'And at night you stared up at Scarlett's window . . .' Evie paused, then said in a dead voice. 'You were staring at *Shen*'s window.'

'Course!' Zane hesitated, then planted a hasty kiss on Evie's cheek before running towards Shen, who was swearing in machine-gun Chinese out of the car window.

With a pounding heart, Evie waved them off. Tomorrow's coffee at Shen's would be interesting.

'Come *on*!' Mike tooted the horn, its squawk more uncouth than ever in such stately surroundings.

Evie took in the house for the last time. The front door stood ajar. Bounding up the steps, she called merrily over her shoulder, 'Just a tick!', well aware how much both the expression and her merriment would irritate her impatient husband.

The brass door knob, round and solid and bang in the middle of the mighty black door, was worn smooth with use. Hundreds of years, hundreds of hands. And now Evie Herrera took it, and pulled it and heard the easy click of the latch.

They were locked out of 'paradise', where relationships had begun, foundered, grown.

The secret grotto, she realized, remained just that: secret.

'Goodbye, Wellcome Manor.' She backed down the steps, one hand on her tum. It was definitely rounder this morning, whether due to berserk holiday levels of ice-cream consumption or the baby, she wasn't sure. 'Thanks for everything.'

'Get a move on, you dozy mare!' yelled Mike.

'The holiday's definitely over.' Evie smiled, jogging towards the car.

'Paula drives so damned slowly.' Mike's eyes flickered to the rear-view mirror. 'As if she's part of a funeral procession.'

'At this rate we might make it home in time to leave for

our next summer holiday.' Evie turned around to inform Dan and Mabel that forty-eight men going to mow really was her limit. 'Sing something else,' she suggested.

'Something silent,' added their father.

Mike was a good driver. Methodical. Consistent. He'd insisted on keeping the wheel for the entire journey home, partly due to gallantry, partly to clear his head and try on his new reality for size.

Hopefully, by the time they'd reached London, he'd be able to think of himself as a dad of four, without cramming his knuckles into his mouth.

It'll all be OK, Mike told himself, *it really will*.

'Lorry!' said Evie.

'What?'

'Lorry. Up your bum. It's gone past now.'

'I can see lorries, woman. Lorries are big.'

Mike wished, vehemently, that Evie wasn't a backseat driver. Especially as she didn't even have the decency to do it from the back seat. *It'll all be OK*. Sometimes he didn't like to reveal just how important certain things were to him, in case the universe noticed and took them away from him.

'Caravan!' said Evie.

Along with driving, and worrying, Mike was good at making children with the woman bleating 'That caravan's changing lanes' in the seat beside him. When they got home, he would make her have a nice sit-down with her feet up, whether she liked it or not.

413

Clive's shorts felt out of place on the services forecourt, as if London's proximity made him break out in pin-stripes. 'Don't take ages!' he called after Zane, who was sprinting across the tarmac.

Tugging Prunella onto her lap, Shen let Clive expertly de-nappy Fang on the back seat. 'Pru-Pru,' she cooed to the dense, coarse-haired creature panting on her knees. 'Yes, yes, I love you too,' she said, as the little animal wriggled. The dog had gained weight in the last fortnight. 'Straight to the vet with you, for a little diet plan.' *While I'm there*, thought Shen, *I'll make an appointment to have you spayed.*

The initial operation had been cancelled, when the vet suggested that Shen let Pru have just one pedigree litter. 'I don't think motherhood is for you, Pru.' Shen rubbed noses with her pet. 'I don't want to be a grandmother yet.'

'This bloody thing . . .' Clive tussled in mortal combat with the buckles of the baby-seat. 'Why won't it . . . ?' The seat conceded defeat and he leaned on the car, spent. 'I really have enjoyed looking after Fang, darling. I feel so close to her. But . . .'

'I know,' said Shen. 'The minute we get home, we hire—'

They said it in unison. 'A new nanny.'

An ugly one, said Shen under her breath. 'Shall I find one with her own accommodation? Then we'd have Fang to ourselves in the evenings and at weekends.'

'Excellent idea.'

Leaning back against the headrest, Shen imagined the Ubers' reaction when she started hanging out with Paula at the school gates. Maybe she'd bait them a little; wear a BHS blouse.

414

Clive loomed over her, his finger to his lips. 'Miles has dropped off. Let's hope he stays that way.' Miles was a grizzler on car journeys. 'I'm just off to dispose of this.' He jiggled a rank, full plastic bag. 'But before I do, there's something I need to say.' He took a moment, then said, 'There's somebody – a woman, you don't know her, but I got close to her, Shen. For a brief moment she meant more to me than she should.' His eyes bored through Shen's sunglasses; they gave him nothing but a distorted reflection of an anxious middle-aged man.

Shen took off the glasses. Clive noticed a tiny line by the outer edge of one eye. It softened her. He liked it.

Shen said, 'You felt neglected. You're an important man with a big ego and you felt as if you deserved more. I should know; my ego's the size of a house too, and I'm better at demanding attention than giving it.' She pursed her lips before saying, 'This mysterious woman . . . she's good at making people feel loved and valued. But it went to your head. Like sunstroke. Nothing really happened.' She searched his face. 'Or did it?'

'It didn't,' said Clive. 'Cross my heart.'

'Good. Sunstroke isn't fatal. I'm glad you feel bad about it, and I'm glad you told me, because you're *mine* and don't you forget it.' She blinked. 'I need you, Clive.'

'You do,' agreed Clive. 'And what I'd do without you, I have literally no idea. Bore myself to death, possibly. I don't say it often, but I love you, Shen.'

'I know.' She let him sweat for a second. 'I love you, too.'

He kissed her – lightly, lovingly – on her cheek and withdrew, ambling towards the distant bin.

Watching him swing the nappy bag as if it was a Gucci tote, Shen considered his confession. He could have kept quiet; Clive thought he'd got clean away with his crime. He was quite a man, that husband of hers. She replaced her glasses and leaned back again.

A crackling in her ear made her jump. A cellophane-wrapped bouquet of supermarket flowers was thrust at her. 'These are for you,' said Zane. He seemed to be trembling. 'I need to say something.'

'Shoot,' said Shen.

Roofs. Chimneys. Concrete. Pavement. Gum on the pavements. Crap on the pavements. Noise. Pollution. Pigeons with fewer than the perfect number of legs. London.

The air inside the Herrera car was as thick as jam. Evie, aware that her inner thermostat would soon go haywire and stay that way for months, barely noticed. She tuned out the sirens, and Mike's gentle grumbles as he slowed for Paula, and quietly let go of something she'd been holding close.

It was only a little dream, as dreams go. Some independence, some cash, some self-respect. Something to talk about that didn't involve school or Mike or the house. The job would have been a fresh horizon, a daily adventure. Losing it was hard on Evie.

Motherhood, fourth time around, at the apparently (over-) ripe old age of forty-one was not in the small print of her life. She hadn't signed up for this. She was done with stretch marks and mood swings, and getting up in the middle of the night at the beck and call of a minuscule pink and very, very outraged person. She was done with going to the shops in a mac over her nightie, calling the Ocado man 'darling' because she'd only slept for four hours in the past week, realizing her bra was full of milk as she browsed the vegetable aisle. She was done with tiny fingers, tiny toes, doing up little buttons, holding her baby to her heart, being inside-out with love.

Sitting in this jalopy with this stressed-out man and these moany children – and, yes, even this imbecilic dog – Evie couldn't imagine anything more adventurous, more challenging, more *her* than adding to this family.

When they lost sight of Paula and started receiving panicky texts – **WHERE R U IM UP RAMP BY SAISNBURYS** – when Dan superglued his fingers to Mabel's hair, when Mike went the wrong way up a one-way street, Evie remembered that.

She remembered that *hard*.

Dear Luxury UK Getaways admin,

Please reserve Wellcome Manor for us for the same dates next year. We'll have one less adult in the party. Oh, and we'll need a cot!

Kind regards,
E. Herrera

Prologue

Marie Dunwoody loved her children, all three of them, with a ferocity beyond understanding. But every once in a while she would gladly sell them to a passing gypsy. And that Friday morning, the morning of St Ethelred's school fete, was one of those once-in-a-whiles.

'Mum,' said Iris, lavishing the last of the milk on her cereal, 'I did tell you that you need to bake something for today's cake stall, didn't I? It's got to be a . . . um . . . what was it? Oh, yeah. It's got to be a *show-stopper*.'

JULY

School Fete

Show-Stopper

Dear Iris and Rose's mum

Thank you so much for agreeing to bake the show-stopper for the school fete. Every penny made by the fete will go to the PSA and will directly benefit our pupils.

Best regards
The PSA

Their shoes squeaking on the gym's waxed floor, hordes of parents rifled bric-a-brac, lucky-dipped and bought one-eyed hunchback teddies from the craft stand.

Over at the cake stall the show-stopper was attracting attention. Of the wrong kind.

'I'm sorry, girls.' Marie took in her daughters' crestfallen faces, both so perfectly alike, with their ski-slope noses, their confetti freckles, their grave brown eyes just like their dad's. 'Next year . . .' she began, but went no further. She'd made the same speech last year: her annual promise to be the mum they deserved.

Angus – video camera, as ever, grafted to his hand – zoomed in on his mother's contribution.

'Darling, *don't*,' pleaded Marie. The world didn't need footage of her show-stopper. With minutes to spare she had had to rely on the petrol-station minimart. The realisation that just-on-their-sell-by-date French Fancies were as good as it would get had made her want to lie down among the chilled wraps and weep. She'd bought the lot, hoping to make them look . . . well, *abundant*; but, huddled bleakly on a tiered cake stand, the dozen battered fancies looked . . . well, *shop-bought*.

'It doesn't matter, Mum,' said Rose.

'Nah,' said Iris.

But they kept sneaking looks at Lucy's cake.

Lucy Gray. Mild-mannered mum of one, neighbour and nemesis. As if constructed especially to shame Marie, the woman was birdlike, a petite and neat counterpoint to Marie's more-than-adequate bosom/bottom arrangement. Her house, the largest on Caraway Close, boasted hanging baskets, gleaming windows and a perfect front lawn of neon emerald; across the way, Marie's house number hung upside down (transforming them from number nineteen to sixty-one) and the twins' bikes copulated in the porch, tripping her up each and every morning.

Lucy baked show-stoppers every other day, 'just for fun'.

Wearing a flowery tea-dress, without a speck of make-up on her wholesome face, and simpering with false modesty at the compliments raining down around her, Lucy stood proudly by her cake.

And what a cake it was!

It was a supermodel of cakes, an Alfa Romeo, a Crufts Best in Show. A multi-storey sponge high-rise, plastered with the softest buttercream and festooned with hand-made fondant roses that could deceive a bee, it came complete with its own theme tune of tinkling harps.